WINDY CITY BILLIONAIRES SERIES
BOOK ONE

YINN QUIRÓS

Content Warning

Triggers warnings include, but are not limited to: Sexual explicit content, talks about anxiety, panic attacks (on page), self-esteem issues, family issues.

Your mental health matters. Please stay safe.

"We are made of all those who have built and broken us."
—Atticus

For the girl who wishes for someone to understand her scars and love her fiercely despite them: this is for you.

Playlist

Angels Like You | Miley Cyrus
A Thousand Years | James Arthur
Adore You | Harry Styles
Be More | Stephen Sanchez
Cinema – Acoustic | Gary Go
Constellations | Jade LeMac
Curtains | Ed Sheeran
Daylight | Taylor Swift
Diamonds | Rihanna
Don't Give Up On Me | Andy Grammer
Dusk Till Dawn | ZAYN, Sia
Electric Love | BØRNS
Flaws | Bastille

Playlist

Halo | **Beyoncé**
I Can See You (Taylor's Version) | **Taylor Swift**
Iris | **The Goo Goo Dolls**
I Wanna Be Yours | **Artic Monkeys**
Let Me Hurt | **Emily Rowed**
Magical | **Ed Sheeran**
Perfect For Me | **Bradley Marshall**
Secrets | **OneRepublic**
Unconditionally | **Katy Perry**
Unmade | **Thom Yorke**
Where I Want To Be | **Forest Blakk**
Willow | **Taylor Swift**

P acing back and forth, I swear I can almost hear the big white blank canvas mocking me as I wonder what in the hell is going on with this rut I've been in for—I glance at the calendar in the corner of my room to make sure I have the timing right—four weeks!?

I gather my sweaty hair, reaching for my largest paint brush and using it to secure a messy bun. Leave it to me to use anything *but* a conventional hair tie. Once, I used straws because I had nothing else around—true story. And it didn't hold my hair very well.

Looking around, I admire every detail of my paint studio. I live in a two bedroom loft in downtown Chicago, which isn't cheap, but I got a lucky deal. Definitely meant to be. This is the smaller bedroom of the two with a floor-to-ceiling window that overlooks the busy streets and buildings. The rest of the room is sort of a mess. There are canvases all around of paintings I've done over the years. My favorite one is front and center in the room, and it's the one I look at when I'm feeling hopeless and just so, so lost. This one is the shadow of a woman in mute colors. Mostly black, with a few strokes of gray and white. Her body is not all there. It's just part of her chest, slightly to the left, with bright-red petals scattered all over the canvas. It's funny how this painting reflects exactly how I've felt my whole life.

Broken. Lost.

Which is why it's called *Scattered*. What can I say? It's fitting.

Every stroke on these canvases tells a story. That's the thing about art, you know? If people were to pay closer attention, they would all tell you something. From tragic and sad to epic and passionate stories. A painted canvas can tell you *everything* and *nothing* all at once, depending on how you look at it. I've never been good at expressing my feelings, but painting them? Well, that's a whole other story.

Standing in front of the stupid canvas that's currently on my wooden easel in the center of the room, I grab my dark-wood, oval paint palette, stained from countless painting sessions, and spread some of my oil paints. Mostly the basics—black, white, gray. I grab a medium-sized paint brush and dip it in the white then a little in the gray, since it's too dark for my liking. I don't use bright colors often, unless it's really necessary to convey an emotion or tell a certain story.

But right now, there's no reason to. I'm numb, so my paintings simply show the same.

I stroke the brush against the canvas swiftly. I have no idea what I'm going to paint, but I'm determined to figure it out as I go. I keep doing random strokes here and there, mixing more colors as I continue. There's no life to this painting, and I don't think there will be. This is how my life has been feeling lately.

Muted. Dark.

In my twenty-five years, I've never been in a rut like this.

It's kind of weird, considering I'm always surrounded by art. It shouldn't be that big of a deal. It's not like I'm a full-time artist. My mother made sure of that.

Ever since I was little, I had very little interest in extracurriculars. It was one of the things I most hated about myself. I tried many hobbies, from sports to dancing, and wasted countless hours during my childhood trying to find something—anything—that would ignite a spark in me until I found *the* one.

At the age of twelve, I fell in love with art.

And at the age of twelve, my mother broke my heart for the first time.

The memory is still fresh, like it was yesterday. Funny how the day I fell in love with art is also one of my most bitter memories. My mother never approved of my paintings, or my love for art in general. The first time I painted something I was actually proud of, it was a meadow with white, blue, and purple flowers. These were my mother's favorite colors, and I wanted to paint her something to make her feel better since my parents fought a lot. She was always under so much stress and always took it out on me. I knew she didn't mean to—or at least that's what I like to think to make myself feel better.

After I gifted her the small painted canvas and told her I wanted to quit cheerleading to pursue art, our relationship took a turn for the worse.

You will stay in cheerleading, and you will like it. Then you will go to school and choose a serious profession. Painting is a stupid hobby, and you're not even that good.

Tears fill my eyes at the memory of the moment that altered my life and self-esteem forever. That's the same moment she took the painted canvas from my hands and threw it in the trash.

I kept up with painting and drawing when I could, despite my mom making it rough, and stayed on the varsity cheerleading team like she demanded. It was always the plan, after all. My parents weren't able to afford college, so I joined a sport, became good at it, and got a athletic scholarship. And I won't lie—I was *good*. One of the top flyers on the varsity team. Talented enough that it landed me a full-ride to the University of Kentucky, where I studied business administration with a minor in history. I worked my ass off in high school, focused on all my AP classes and got enough credits toward my degree that I graduated from college at twenty years old. I took so many credits and worked myself to the bone because I didn't want to be there. I wanted to *escape*. I could have easily gotten a full-ride at NYU if my mother would have given me the opportunity. But she took away that choice from me without a second thought.

Even though I didn't pursue a career as an artist, I did find the next best thing. I'm around art all the time, and I get to discover new talent and learn the history behind such masterpieces. The canvas is my stage, the colors my actors, and the art lovers my audience. Needless to say, I'm an art geek. Once you get me talking, I will never stop.

Art has always been an escape for me, so the rut definitely isn't helping me right now. I feel so trapped in my life right now, it's affecting everything. Including the thing I'm most passionate about.

Trapped in a career that isn't my passion.

Trapped in a life I want to escape.

Trapped in the what if's.

Just... fucking trapped.

I shake my head as I stare at the half-painted canvas in front of me before grabbing it and throwing it across the room. As I'm pacing back and forth, brewing in my built up frustration, my phone pings with a text.

SOPHIA

Girl, where the hell are you?

Shit.

ME

Lost track of time, omw!

On Sundays, my best friend and I have coffee and pastries at our favorite coffee shop. I love this little place that's nestled amid tall buildings, creating a refuge for lost souls and dreamers. Walking in, I'm hit with the familiar smell of roasted coffee beans, buttery croissants, and caramelized pastries.

Sophia waves from our favorite spot—a corner table by the window with just the right amount of sunlight. Her brown hair shimmers in the sun's rays, which also highlight the mischievous glint in her eyes.

"You have that 'I've-got-gossip' glow," I remark, settling into my chair.

"Can't a girl just be happy to see you?"

I glance at her knowingly, raising my eyebrows.

She takes one look at my oil paint-stained overalls, her brows furrowing in concern. "Any luck getting out of that rut?"

"No." Frustration laces my voice, and my shoulders slump.

She grabs my hands and squeezes reassuringly. "I'm sure it'll blow over."

I roll my eyes. "So you've said the last four weeks." I wave my hand in the air dismissively. "I don't want to think about it. Let's talk about something else."

Sophia and I couldn't be more opposite. While she's loud and loves to party, I'm more mellow and prefer to go to a coffee shop, or a good museum. I guess that's why our friendship works. She's the yin to my yang and all that. The one thing we have in common is that we're both artists at heart. Her background is in journalism, but she understands my world perfectly. Instead of wielding a brush to convey stories through paintings, she uses a pen and paper to tell them. But much like me, she's forced to work on something she's not passionate about.

Though, how many people can say they are passionate about what they do for a living? I like my job, but that's only because I get to be close to what I would truly—in an ideal world—love to do for a living.

That's as close as I allow myself to get.

It's not that I'm a bad painter—I refuse to call myself an artist. It's just... rejection is scary. The thought of sharing my work outside of my creativity room makes my body shiver. What if what my mother said was true? I don't think I'm willing to take the risk. Not yet anyway.

As we share our usual rich tiramisu, Sophia asks, "Did you hear about that art heist that happened in Rome?" She works for one of the top media websites in the country, which means she is aware of what's going on constantly.

I nod, recalling the headlines about the stolen painting that was set to be auctioned later this month. It was expected to be sold for just shy of two million dollars.

Insane.

"My editor wants me to cover the story."

I gape at her. "Wow... That's amazing. I mean, are you excited?"

She shrugs. "You know I'm just working there for the meantime. And I'm sort of stuck with it, and it involves a lot of investigating, since he wants the inside scoop and all."

"He should be the one writing it, then."

She shoots me a knowing look. "You know how he is... wants to take all the credit and do none of the work."

I thin my lips. "If you need anything, let me know. You know I have some connections. Alex does, too."

She recoils at the name. "Please don't mention that man. I don't want to throw up. The tiramisu was particularly good today, and I'd hate to waste it."

I snicker at her comment, rolling my eyes. We both decided to attend the same college and that's where we met him. Alex and I were pursuing the same degree, while Sophia was pursuing English Literature. He quickly became friends with us, but then the friendship between them went belly up after a drunken college night. I've been stuck in the middle ever since.

Alex was from Chicago and decided to attend University of Kentucky to get away from the busy city, while Sophia and I were born and raised in Greenville, Kentucky. We've been inseparable since kindergarten. Just two simple small town girls who wanted to become something *extraordinary*.

I was the first to graduate, and as soon as I got that degree, I packed all my things and moved to Chicago. At the beginning, I was looking to survive. I could've done many things with a business degree, but none of them were related to art, and I hated that.

Looking back, I was definitely being stubborn, but that's something I needed to go through to get to where I am today. So I became a bartender for a while. It was easy money and it put food on the table. That's all that mattered to me at that point—survival. I had no hope.

The one hope I had died the day my mother took me away from it.

Two years later, Sophia and Alex graduated from college. Sophia moved to Chicago to pursue her writing career, and we became roommates for a while. Just two twenty-two-year-old girls in the windy city trying to make a living. She was an assistant at *Vogue Elite* at the time. I was still a bartender. Alex, on the other hand, moved to New York to open his own gallery. Sadly, that didn't work out well for him. The details are still unknown to this day because he *refuses* to talk about it. He moved back to Chicago and became a curator for one of the top galleries in the city thanks to the connections he got during his time in New York. He knew how passionate I was about art, so he taught me the ropes of being a curator. I worked endless hours to make the right connections and worked my ass off to get inside the industry.

Art is single-heartedly my whole personality, so it was easy to learn the ropes of that career. I landed a job as an assistant curator for *The Institute* and quickly climbed my way to the top. Now, I'm one of the two senior curators for them, discovering new artists and managing all the art that comes in and out of the gallery.

I shrug. "I'm still here if you need me, always."

She nods with a knowing smile then grabs her cup and takes a sip of her latte. "Now, tell me about the job offer? Are you taking it?"

I tense at the thought of it. "It wasn't an actual job offer. He said he wanted to have a meeting with me," I correct her.

She flips her hair back, rolling her eyes. "About the

possibility of you working for him. Seriously, Ari, you need to give yourself more credit."

I shrug off her comment. If there's one thing about Sophia, the woman is brutally honest. I know I *should* start giving myself more credit. It doesn't mean I can, though. Every time I have a shimmer of light, I can hear my mother in the back of my head.

Not talented enough.

Not good enough.

Simply not enough.

"I don't think it's a great idea to work for him."

"And why not?" she challenges. "The money is good. He's a huge deal in the art industry. What's not to love?"

He is what scares me the most.

With being known in the industry ever since I became a senior curator, offers pour in constantly, but I've never entertained any of them. That was until I received an email from the assistant of Damian Romano, one of the top businessmen in Chicago. According to Sophia, he's one of the top bachelors in the city as well. I have no idea why this is relevant, but she insists that it is.

From what his assistant told me, he's looking to upscale his gallery to a whole new level and they believe I'm the person for the job. The meeting's tomorrow, and I'm still trying to keep my options open. I think a change of scenery may help with how I've been feeling lately.

Or so I keep telling myself.

Everyone knows who Damian Romano is in the art industry—a self-made billionaire who worked his way to the top. He owns multiple businesses, but his main thing is art. He's a known art enthusiast who has the talent to pick up-and-coming artists, showcase them in his gallery, and help them become the next best thing.

While the change of scenery would be a welcome relief, the man is known for being difficult to work with. There are nothing but horror stories floating around about how egocentric and demanding he is. The art world is a small one, and with Damian Romano being one of the best in the business—known for his cutthroat strategies and seizing his opportunities to the max—people have things to say about him.

I give her a pointed look. "*You know why.* I'm not sure I even want it, though. I had dinner with Alex yesterday, and he insisted it wasn't a good idea."

"Alex can kiss my ass," she quips.

"Funny, I thought he already did." I grin.

Her shoulders shake with a laugh. "Oh my god, you're impossible. But in all seriousness, I think it's going to be fine. Don't believe everything people say on social media."

I hum, still unconvinced. "We'll see."

2

Damian

As I step into the gallery, Isabella greets me with a cross-armed stance and a disgruntled expression. "You're late," she points out.

"Nice deductive skills, Sherlock," I retort dryly. "One of my Zoom meetings ran long, but I'm here. Relax."

"If you weren't working since the crack of dawn and followed your calendar maybe, just maybe, you'd be on time for once," she fires back.

Isabella has been my assistant for over two years now. It was initially meant to be a temporary job, but she has somehow stuck around, even though she literally has a Computer Science degree from MIT. The woman is crazy smart, but as grumpy as they come. I appreciate her as an assistant, but, fuck, she can be aggravating.

"Walk with me." I've sparred enough times with her already that I'm ready to let this one go. I walk pretty fast, but we've done this so many times, she's already trained to keep up with me.

"Your meeting with Aria Petrov is this afternoon."

Right.

I inherited this gallery three years ago when my father passed away. He and I shared a love for art, but that was the extent of our relationship. My father had always thought I was weak and too compassionate to make it in the real world. He had underestimated me, though. I took his lessons to heart, using his disapproval as fuel for my relentless ambition. Now, I stand at the pinnacle of success, a self-made billionaire who has taken my family's humble business to a whole new level. But I'm far from done. My vision for the Romano Empire is grand, and I intend to see it through no matter the cost.

This vision includes having the best, and Aria Petrov is precisely that. While I've never met her in person, the art industry is small enough that when someone makes an impression, it sticks. I learned of her successful career as a curator and the impact she made at The Institute in such a short period of time. It's intriguing, really, and I'm more than looking forward to meeting her.

What started as a mom-and-pop gallery has become an up-and-coming sensation in the city of Chicago. Because if there's something I'm good at, it's business. My tactics are ruthless; a carefully orchestrated dance of ambition, strategy, and precision. I have built an empire from the ground up, defying every obstacle in my path, and I'm not sorry for it.

In the world of business, I have one uncompromising rule—*be the best*. It sounds cliché, that much I know, but that's how I've been able to get to where I am today. I have a reputation for outbidding, outmaneuvering, and outsmarting anyone who dares to challenge me in the art world. My adversaries see me as ruthless, and I don't dispute it. The art world is a cutthroat arena, and I am a master of the game.

As I stroll through the gallery on my way to the second-floor office, I can't resist glancing around. The gallery is a masterpiece in itself, a place where the finest art finds a home. The walls display works that hold stories, passions, and history, while the soft ambient lighting accentuates their allure.

After Isabella gives me the itinerary for the day, she exits my office, leaving me alone. I walk to my chair, but before sitting, I gaze over the city as this overwhelming sense of emptiness takes hold of me. I've got everything I could ask for—money, cars, houses—but that void inside me won't go away. I've fought my way to success, and it makes me feel absolutely *nothing*. So I keep chasing that high, keep climbing the stairs like there's no tomorrow, in hopes of burying the numbness that follows me everywhere I go. A voice always lingers inside my head—my father's.

You're a worthless, weak boy. Feelings don't matter.

You need to be a man, Damian.

I can't believe you're my son.

What a disgrace.

Scrubbing my face, I shake my head and sit, opting to work instead of wallowing about a man who doesn't deserve a second thought.

While I've heard great things about Aria Petrov, it isn't guaranteed that she's going to be a good fit. I throw myself into work, drafting questions and planning for the meeting, until I'm interrupted by a knock on the door.

Isabella enters. "She's here."

I glance at my watch. Time sure flies by when I drown myself in work to avoid any other sort of thoughts.

I nod. "Let her in."

As Isabella goes to escort our guest, I fire off an email to my marketing team in Italy. Managing multiple businesses means there's not one second to spare. There's money to be made, and I need to grab the opportunity—*always*. Art is my passion project, and ironically makes more than enough revenue, but one of my biggest businesses are my hotels. I have a few throughout famous cities like New York, Rome, and Paris. They take up most of my time, but only because I'm such a control freak.

Soft steps and the click of the door pull my attention away from my computer, and in that moment, I make the one mistake I wish I could undo—I look up. As Aria Petrov walks into the room, it feels as if she just sucked the air out of it. She dons a black long-sleeve turtleneck, complemented by white mid-rise pants that gracefully emphasize her curves. Her shiny, straight ginger hair frames her beautiful hazel eyes, and a smile graces her pouty lips, painted an inviting shade of red.

Her beauty is simply otherworldly.

Aria approaches my desk, extending her hand for a shake. "A pleasure to meet you, Mr. Romano."

I fixate on her eyes—a mix of brown and green, with a subtle hint of gold. It's as if they're pulling me in, inviting me to lose myself within them. It takes a moment to register her words, but when I do, I stand and shake her hand firmly but quickly pull back at the strange charged feeling. If Aria felt the same, she doesn't show it.

Isabella, who knows me all too well, observes the silent exchange with an all-knowing smirk before inquiring, "Anything I can get for you, Ms. Petrov?"

Aria politely declines Isabella's offer, her genuine smile warming the room, and Isabella exits, leaving us alone.

I cough, trying to hide my sudden nerves.

Why the fuck am I suddenly so nervous?

Because there's a beautiful woman in front of you that for once has left you speechless.

Fuck.

3

Aria

Sophia wasn't underestimating how handsome this man is. His emerald eyes hold me captive with a mysterious, intense gaze that pierces my soul. His skin is a deep olive color, paired with a seductive, bright smile that makes him look like a Greek god. It's ridiculous. His dark, shiny hair is styled back, not one strand out of place, and the navy blue suit fits perfectly in all the right places, embracing his broad shoulders and thick thighs. He's really tall, too, six-foot-five, if I had to guess. Even with my four-inch heels, he towers over me. I understand when people say there's something different about him. He emanates so much power and confidence as if he could destroy you by simply snapping his fingers.

He gestures toward one of the chairs in front of his desk. "Please, take a seat."

As I do, I cross my legs and drop my purse on the chair next to me. I was feeling pretty confident while putting my makeup on this morning, plastering the same old red lipstick that brings me courage when I'm uncertain about something. Now that I'm here, in front of this man that I've heard so much about, my resolve is crumbling quicker than I expected.

He sits back down and leans back in the chair, locking his gaze on me, causing goosebumps all over my arms as I internally pat myself on the back for putting a long sleeve on.

The last thing I want to show is weakness.

"I've heard great things about you, Ms. Petrov. It's not often that someone impresses me. You've achieved remarkable things. I mean, a twenty-five year old senior curator from one of the top galleries of the city, that's not something you ever see in this line of business."

The comment makes me want to crawl out of my own skin. Accepting compliments is not my forte, especially when it has to do with my job. But this has been my life ever since people learned how quickly I climbed the professional ladder, and it still makes me uncomfortable to this day.

"I enjoy what I do, and it shows through my work." The passion I have for creating art makes me really good at discovering and showcasing other people's work. Not that I'd ever admit that.

A small smile flickers across his face as he nods. "Let me get straight to the point."

Okay, then. They weren't joking when they said he was all about business.

He adjusts himself in his seat, resting his elbows on the desk and clasping his hands together. "I want you on my team, but I still need to ensure you're the right fit for the job."

Amusement takes hold of me, and a laugh slips out involuntarily. Really, the audacity of this man, speaking as if I was the one that arranged the meeting.

I arch an eyebrow. "You mean I need to make sure you're

the right fit for me." I straighten my back, sitting on the edge of the seat as I grab a strand of my perfectly straightened hair that takes hours a week to achieve and place it behind my ear. "Like you said, Mr. Romano, I'm very good at what I do, and I'm not actively seeking a change. However, when I heard that the renowned businessman Damian Romano wanted to meet with me, I was intrigued."

My heart sits at the corner of my ribcage, beating so fast, it wants to come out of my body. This isn't me. I'm not the bold type. But there's something about him that makes me want to take up on the challenge, even if I fail miserably.

His eyebrows shoot up in shock, nodding as he traces his tongue over his lips, leaving behind a shimmer of moisture. My eyes follow the movement, and linger there for a moment. Wow, even his lips are perfect. It's unfair, really.

"You've undoubtedly heard things about me," he replies, his voice laced with confidence and a hint of cockiness. "I excel in what I do, and when I want something, I take it without hesitation. No questions asked."

No surprises there. He's nothing but all smiles and cockiness, probably thinking it's endearing, a way to put people in their place. Me, on the other hand? I'm finding it quite annoying.

"So I've heard," I drawl.

He meets my eyes with determination. "I know The Institute must impose numerous rules and limitations on your work." He gives me a casual shrug. "I've been in this business long enough to understand that. I'm willing to offer you full creative control because, truth be told, I want to elevate The Romano Gallery to the next level. I want our name to resonate across the world."

I observe him intently, a faint smirk playing on my lips. Sophia always says I have the talent to read people like a wide open book, and I guess she's right, because right now I can easily gauge his intentions. He's a man that's used to people doing his bidding. It's amusing, really. But I guess you don't get to the pinnacle of success without strategizing and using people to gain an advantage.

"Your portfolio speaks for itself, Ms. Petrov," he continues. "Your exceptional eye for art and dedication to promoting emerging talents are precisely what I need to take this establishment to the next level. Am I impressing you yet?" he smirks.

"What makes you think this is what I want?" I ask with a slight tilt of my head.

"I can tell." He leans back in his chair again and crosses one leg over the other with a smug grin etched on his lips. "Call it a business instinct, if you will."

Yeah, the stories were true, alright. *Don't believe what social media says my ass.* I can't wait to tell Sophia how wrong she was.

My next question is veiled, but clear enough. "Is there any truth to the rumors people talk about?"

He thins his lips, holding back a knowing smile with a nonchalant shrug. "There's no denying I'm good at what I do. I've made tough decisions and taken bold actions in the past, but that's part of doing business with me. And that's all you need to know for now."

I nod in understanding, trying my best to conceal my curiosity. He's like a mystery painting, one I want to look at and study piece by piece. It takes a lot to be a confident person, and it takes even more to be whatever this is.

Cocky, arrogant, and smug. That's all he is.

"I am curious, though. If you're saying you're not seeking a change, then why are you here?" he asks.

Mustering the little confidence I have left, I stand and

place both hands on his desk and lean closer. His scent envelops me, strong and woody, but not overpowering. There's something so warm about it I can't quite place. There's also something so earthy and primal about it, making my insides ignite with fire.

My words are icy cold, with a hint of resolve. "I wanted to see if I was up for the challenge," I say, my voice a sultry whisper. Then, I add, "But you're just an arrogant dick, and I don't work for people like that."

With those words, I pick up my purse and walk out of his office.

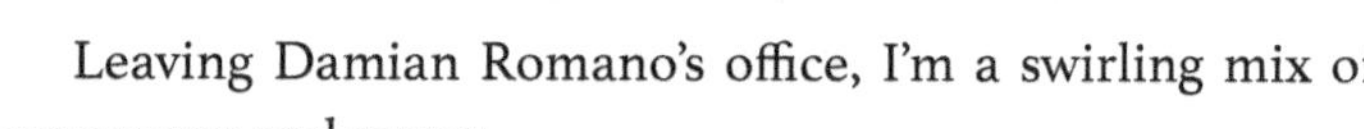

Leaving Damian Romano's office, I'm a swirling mix of annoyance and anger.

What an arrogant, smug, good-looking asshole.

The gallery doors swing open, and I step out into the bustling cityscape. The Romano Gallery is located in the heart of downtown, surrounded by towering buildings that cast shadows on the busy streets. The air is thick with the scent of street food mixed with exhaust fumes, a chaotic combination of urban life.

Seeing him in person for the first time was like time stood still. I'd seen his photos in countless magazines, but this was different. His presence was commanding, and the room seemed to revolve around him. The man is stupidly handsome, no doubt about it. Still, I have no intention of working with someone who thinks people will bend over and do his bidding as soon as he flashes one of his seductive smiles. *Fat fucking chance.*

As I'm leaving the gallery, his assistant stops me. "Are you alright?"

"Your boss is just so…" I falter for a moment, trying to find the right words.

"Cocky?" she arches a brow. "Yeah, I know."

We stare at each other for a few silent beats then erupt in laughter. And in this moment, I decide this girl is a saint, dealing with a man like that.

She shrugs. "I've grown to like him. He's often misunderstood, but to be fair, the dude always has something stuck up his ass with how serious he is all the time."

Another laugh escapes me. "I don't know about being misunderstood. I think some people are just plain assholes."

She rolls her lips to keep her laugh in check and extends her hand. "I'm Isabella, by the way."

I shake her hand. "I'm Aria."

"Yeah, I know. You're big in the industry. I think everyone knows who you are."

I shake my head. "Nah, I'm just a girl with a passion for art."

"We need that here," she replies quietly with an expectant smile.

I let out a long sigh. "I can't work for an arrogant dick, so unfortunately, that won't be happening."

As I turn to leave, a deep velvety voice from behind me interrupts, "Arrogant dick, huh? You've said that twice already."

I turn around, and there's Damian Romano, hands in his pockets, looking way too handsome for his own good.

"If the shoe fits," I reply sarcastically, forcing a fake smile.

He ignores my comment like I'm just a fly on the wall and turns to Isabella, and boy does that rub me the wrong way. "Don't think I didn't hear you agree with her."

Isabella rolls her eyes, waving her hand dismissively and

tells him about his upcoming meeting before walking back inside the gallery.

Damian approaches me, and as he gets closer, I'm hit with that stupid good-smelling cedarwood clean scent. It dizzies me for a moment, my knees buckling involuntary. I take a step back to regain my composure and maintain a significant distance between us.

With a knowing smirk, he speaks, "Listen... Let's try again, okay? Over dinner."

You've gotta be kidding me.

Tilting my chin up slightly, I shake my head firmly. "Your assistant just confirmed you're a pain in the ass to work for. *Hard* pass."

I turn to walk away, but his strong hand gently grips my upper arm. The touch is electrifying, burning me in the best way possible.

"I can confirm I'm a pain in the ass, but it's never for bad reasons," he says, his tone sincere. "I won't take no for an answer."

I stand my ground, freeing my arm from his hold, and continue to walk on the busy city sidewalk. "You can keep trying, but it's still going to be a no."

Once I'm a few blocks away from the gallery, I grab my phone from my purse and FaceTime Sophia.

When she answers, she has that post-sex look with glassy eyes and messy hair.

"Oh my God, Sophia. Were you just *fucking*!?" I half-shout in a whisper.

She grins mischievously. "Girl, no. Finished like twenty minutes ago, though."

"Okay, can you kick him out so I can meet you at your apartment? I'm in desperate need of girl talk."

"Please. You know I kicked his ass to the curb as soon as we were done." She laughs. "I'll wait for you here."

We hang up, and I head to the grocery store, picking up some good wine and cheese before meeting her at the apartment.

When she opens the door, I groan dramatically and throw myself into her arms. "Ew, you reek of sex," I tease.

She pushes me off and steps back, letting me in. "Fucking liar. I already showered."

I roll my eyes as I walk to her kitchen and grab two wine glasses and a corkscrew. I seat on the couch and place the bottle of wine, corkscrew and glasses on the coffee table, then take my heels off to get comfortable. "Today sucked."

"Was the meeting that bad?"

"He was an asshole, Sophia. So cocky with his arrogant good looks."

She raises an eyebrow while reaching for the bottle and corkscrew, opening the grape fruity goodness. "Good looks, huh?"

"He was hot, okay? Even better looking in person, but I refuse to work for him. His personality sucks."

She snickers at my comment as she serves us a hefty amount of wine in each glass then hands me one. I grab it and gulp it down, brushing my lips with the back of my hand as I hand it back to her to top it off again. Wine just takes the edge off, you know?

"Girl, slow down, it's barely dinner time," she jokes, pouring me another glass. "Was he really that much of a dick?"

I swirl the purple liquid, contemplating my words for a moment. "He was just so smug with his smirking and cockiness and his 'I'm better than you' attitude."

Sophia takes a sip of wine and lays back on the couch, chuckling. "Sounds hot."

Patting her shoulder jokingly, I say, "Your opinion doesn't count; you have questionable taste in men, remember?"

She laughs dryly. "You think you're so funny," She places both of her legs underneath her, sitting comfortably and facing me. "But seriously, the money's good. You should still take it and ignore him."

"Plus, he offered me full creative control," I confess with a tired sigh.

Her excitement spikes. "Seriously!? That's amazing! So, definitely a yes, right?"

I shake my head, slumping my shoulders. "I can't. The money and control don't make up for the fact that he's clearly difficult to work with."

Or the fact that even though he was a complete dick, I found him interesting, like a mystery I wanted to solve.

"Okay, so be a bigger person. Accept the job, be professional, and set your boundaries. He'll get the hint eventually," she points out.

I bite my lip, contemplating. He mentioned that he knows he is not easy to work with, so he is somewhat self-aware. How bad could it really be?

I glance at the clock, and it's already six. We've just been chilling on her couch, drinking some wine and watching some *Friends* reruns. It's my favorite thing to do every time my head is in overthinking mode. A good Chandler Bing joke is the best way to relax.

"I have to go. I have dinner with Alex," I say as I put my heels back on and stand from the couch.

Sophia shoots me a dry look. "Ditch him."

"You and Alex had one crazy night years ago. *Let it go.*" I blow Sophia a kiss before walking out of her apartment.

I grab an Uber and in less than ten minutes, I arrive at our favorite Italian restaurant—Lorenzo's—and find Alex sitting at our usual table.

"Sorry I'm late! I was with Sophia and lost track of time."

Alex gets up while laughing, giving me a hug. "I assumed you were with her. How is she these days?"

"Still hating your guts," I quip as I take a seat.

"Oh my, I better pay her a visit soon then." He winks. "How've you been?"

I pick up a piece of bread and lather it with the delicious garlic butter before replying, "Good. I have so much to tell you."

I proceed to tell him about the meeting, and how I turned down the job offer.

He nods and sighs. "I'm not surprised. Damian sure is a piece of work."

The way he talks about Damian has me wondering. "Wait, do you know him?"

He nods. "I worked for his father as an assistant when I turned sixteen, when the gallery was still a mom-and-pop. When his father died and Damian inherited the business, he fired me," he says with a hint of annoyance and something else I can't identify.

I frown. "How come you never told me?"

"It was a long time ago. I never thought it was important," he replies quickly, grabbing my hand and squeezing it softly. "You can't work for him, Aria. It's a bad idea."

"I don't plan to." Turning down a job where you get to

have full creative control in this industry is nuts. I'm surely losing my head, but I think I'd rather keep my sanity.

"If there's one thing I know about him, he's a persistent motherfucker, so you need to stay strong." He gives me a pointed look, his tone deadly serious.

Okay, then. Someone definitely hates Damian Romano, and out of all people, I didn't expect it to be Alex.

I will stay strong, though. I don't need him, after all. He's the one that needs me.

Damian

It's not often a person impresses me, but Aria Petrov? The exception of the fucking rule.

It has been a week since we first met, and I can't get her out of my head. Two reasons are responsible for this: first, she hasn't responded to any of my endless emails regarding my job offer, and second, the fact she had the audacity to challenge me and flat-out call me a dick makes me strangely attracted to her.

The second reason is driving me fucking nuts.

Here's my confession: I may or may not have spent the past few days trying to run into her just to have an excuse to talk to her. I meant what I said—I'm not taking no for an answer.

I've stalked her Instagram enough to figure out she has a daily routine of visiting the same coffee shop at around the same time, so I've decided to be proactive. Take matters into my own hands.

The café staff seems to know her well, because as soon as I say her name, they know who I'm talking about. I opt to pay for her usual coffee order, plus a caramel crumble muffin because the color of it reminds me of her hair. Fucking weird, I know. I find a seat far enough from the counter so she won't spot me right away and take a seat to enjoy my coffee, patiently waiting for her to walk through those doors.

The door of the coffee shop jingles, signaling someone's arrival, and when my gaze lifts and finds her, the air is sucked out of my lungs like I'd been punched right in the gut. She looks painfully beautiful with her hair in a messy bun and light makeup that highlights her soft freckles, but what catches my attention are those *damn fucking lips*. She's wearing that deep, inviting shade of red from the other day. It instantly makes me wonder how her lips would feel on top of mine. Probably warm, and soft. She wears a big smile as she orders her usual, and when she goes to pay, the cashier says something and points toward me. When she turns and realizes it's me, her hazel eyes darken with annoyance. She marches over to my table, and I hide my smirk behind my coffee cup, casually taking a sip.

Let the fun begin.

"Are you following me?" she asks, her voice a frustrated whisper-shout.

I shrug nonchalantly. "You're not answering my emails."

She lets out an exasperated breath. "Oh. My. God. You are following me! How did you even know I was going to be here?"

Popping my arm on the coffee table, I lazily rest my chin on my hand. "Instagram is a remarkable tool."

"You're *stalking* me?" She gapes at me, dumbfounded.

"Desperate times, desperate measures, beautiful," I deadpan.

Her shoulders tense as she shoots me a withering glare. I can't deny I'm enjoying seeing her flustered and annoyed by my presence. It feels like a win in my book. She rummages in her purse, takes out five dollars, and places it on my table.

I pick up the money lazily and ask, "What's this?"

"For my coffee. I don't need anything from you, except the muffin, because I'll never turn down anything caramel-flavored. Now, stop following me," she shoots back, turning to walk away.

I stand up and catch her by the arm. "Then have dinner with me."

"Mr. Romano, you've sent me over twenty emails, which I've taken the liberty to ignore. Take the hint," she retorts.

I raise an eyebrow. "I'm nothing if not persistent. I'll keep trying," I reply as I release her and swiftly drop the five dollars in her purse without her noticing.

She picks up her coffee and muffin from the counter and flips me off as she walks out of the coffee shop.

A light and amused feeling bubbles in my chest; one I can't resist. I throw my head back and burst into a genuine, hearty laugh. It echoes through the coffee shop, drawing curious glances from people around me. I don't know what's happening to me. Maybe I'm losing my mind. But all I'm sure of is that Aria, with her challenging presence, is nothing less than a mountain I want—or perhaps *need*—to conquer.

The next day, I wait for her right at the entrance of the coffee shop instead of hiding inside. Scanning the surroundings, I spot her heading my way. With earbuds in, she's nodding along to the rhythm of whatever's playing. Today, she's rocking some paint-stained overalls with a olive green sweater and white Converse. Her messy bun is held together by... chopsticks?

I frown in confusion.

Is she an artist? Those are definitely oil paint stains all over her overalls.

She still hasn't noticed my presence, so I casually walk up to her, grab one of her earbuds and place it in my ear, catching her by surprise. "You Give Love A Bad Name" by Bon Jovi plays, and a laugh escapes me.

Who knew she was a classic rock fan? Definitely doesn't look the type.

She snaps her gaze to me and she attempts to grab her earbud back. The efforts are futile, because I'm fairly taller than her. So I swiftly move, preventing her from taking it back.

"Who knew you were a Bon Jovi fan? What are you? Sixty years old?" I tease with an amused tone.

She stops the music, extending her hand for me to give her the earpiece. After a moment of resistance, I finally cave and hand it over.

"Not that it's any of your business, but yes. I am a classic rock fan," she admits.

I nod. "I can respect that."

"What are you doing here?" she asks with a bored tone.

I hold the door of the coffee shop open for her. "I told you I'm not taking no for an answer."

She rolls her eyes and mutters, "God help me."

I bite the inside of my cheek trying to contain my laugh. I've looked forward to this encounter since yesterday, because Aria's definitely unpredictable and very much unapologetically herself. You don't find people like her these days.

"Sorry, I can't help you," I say with a cocky grin.

"Did you just compare yourself to God!? Talk about a walking red flag."

"I can accept I have a few red flags, but that's half the charm, darling." I wink. "So, how about dinner?"

She keeps her eyes on me like I'm growing a third head or something similar. I've never begged so much in my life, but I have a feeling the woman before me is about to change yet another rule I've carefully perfected over the years.

"See, Mr. Romano—"

"Call me Damian."

She shoots me a quick glare with fire in her eyes. "Like I was saying, *Mr. Romano*," she emphasizes. "This cocky attitude of yours doesn't do it for me. So the answer is still no."

She walks away to go order her coffee, which I already paid for before she came in.

"We'll see!" I shout.

Without looking at me, she flips me off.

A grin escapes my lips, wondering what the hell I got myself into. This new amused feeling is addicting, and I simply can't wait to see her again and get a rise out of her. I'll wear her out eventually.

Two can play at this game, but I will always come on top.

5

Aria

For seven days straight, I've walked into my favorite coffee shop, and the first thing I spot is Damian Romano's annoyingly handsome face, wearing that wide, shit-eating grin and exuding what he probably thinks is charm but comes off as cocky.

Here's to another day, and as soon as I walk in, my eyes instinctively search for him. It's become second nature at this point. In fact, it would be strange not to see him. This time, he's seated at the back of the coffee shop with his laptop.

The man is so annoyingly persistent; he's even working from the coffee shop now. And every day, without fail, we have the exact same conversation. And every time, I lie to myself and say I don't enjoy the banter and his smiles. It's become a routine at this point, one I find myself looking forward to more than I'd care to admit.

I approach the counter to order my coffee, and the barista, wearing a wide smile, greets me.

"Aria, twice in one day? What a nice treat!"

I glance behind me, toward Damian's table, hoping he didn't hear that. He locks eyes with me, raises an eyebrow, and flashes his cocky, knowing smile.

Fucking busted.

I look away, hoping he didn't catch me blushing. I swiftly place my coffee order, and unsurprisingly, Damian has already paid for it as per usual.

I've been awake since the crack of dawn, so I headed to the coffee shop as soon as it opened. But, I can't deny I was kind of curious to see if he would show up today, hence my second visit. I have nothing to be ashamed of, after all, he's the one taking over *my* favorite coffee shop. With nothing to lose, I walk over to his table.

He appears as his usual, impeccably put-together self. My gaze lingers, and honestly, out of all the suits he's worn, this one takes the cake. It's a deep maroon color that makes his green eyes pop, paired with an off-white turtleneck sweater that accentuates his broad shoulders, and those damn pants that seemed to have been tailored by the gods, hugging his large toned legs. His dark, shiny hair is as immaculate as always; his face with a light, well-kept beard. No one has the right to be that gorgeous. It seriously infuriates me.

He glances up from his computer, and then, with a smug grin, he leisurely leans back. I pant as his lingering gaze moves up and down my body, sending a shiver down my spine.

"Fancy meeting you here. I hear it's your second visit of the day. Missing me already, darling?" He tilts his head, amusement lacing his tone.

"Do I have to change coffee shops? Because I really like this place, and I refuse to let you ruin it for me," I retort.

He scrubs his beard with a soft, hearty laugh. "Have dinner with me, and the coffee shop is all yours."

I snort a dry laugh. "Never."

"Never say never."

"Well, I'm saying never," I snap.

Our gazes lock, having a silent challenge. I tilt my chin up, raising an eyebrow. Challenging him has quickly become one of my favorite hobbies, only God knows why.

He runs his tongue across his teeth and simply smirks.

The asshole smirks.

He's been having way too much fun with our interactions. It's like a stupid game to him.

You've been enjoying them too, so don't even try to lie to yourself.

I take a moment to contemplate my options. I could keep saying no, but he's shown resilience, so I don't think he'll be stopping anytime soon. On the other hand, I could say yes, get a free dinner out of him, and turn him down anyway.

"Fine," I say, clenching my teeth.

He rises from his seat with a triumphant smile, picking up his laptop and coffee as if he has all the time in the world. Moving closer to me, he leans down and with his velvety deep voice that makes my body shiver, he whispers, "Can't wait, darling. I'll pick you up at seven. Wear something nice," Then, he walks away.

I turn around and ask, "Don't you need my address?"

He turns and walks backward, winking before replying, "Maybe you can finally reply to one of my many emails with it."

And with that, he leaves me there standing in the middle of the busy coffee shop.

Sophia walks into my apartment while I throw three bags full of clothes on my couch, sighing in frustration as I'm placing them.

"Well, hello to you too," she says while sitting on the couch, peeking inside the bags. "What's this?"

"All the outfits I could come up with on such short notice." I groan, sitting on the floor since the bags and Sophia has taken all the couch space.

I'm not a fashionista, but I do have some dresses saved in plastic bags for occasions like these. My dating life is the worst—not that this is a date, but knowing *Mr. Billionaire* he'll probably take me to a fancy-ass restaurant—so I have to dress up the part.

Excuses. Excuses.

"You look stressed," Sophia points out.

"Wow, nice deducting skills. You sure you want to be a writer? You'd make a *great* detective," I quip.

She punches me jokingly in the shoulder, and we both laugh. "Why are you so stressed?"

"*He* stresses *me* out. Being near him with the constant bickering is exhausting. And call me crazy, but I swear he enjoys pissing me off," I say in an exasperated breath.

Sophia grins mischievously. "Nah, I think he makes you nervous. You are so into him!"

"I am not." The lie just comes naturally at this point. I'm hoping if I say it enough times, I'll start believing it.

There's no denying the man is hot in the sense that I wouldn't mind if I matched with him on a dating app and had a casual hook-up type of hot. The bantering between us is entertaining, and in a masochistic way, turns me on. But on the other side of the coin, his cockiness makes him ten times more annoying. I couldn't be with someone so insufferable.

She raises an eyebrow. "Ari, we have been best friends for how long now? You know you can't lie to me like that."

I pick one of the dresses that is almost falling from the bag and throw it at her. "Whatever."

Sophia stands and places a hand on her hips. "Okay, so what are we working with here?"

When it comes to fashion, Sophia is the gifted one. I tend to dress like a quirky librarian most of the time, so I come to her when I need fashion guidance.

We go through the bags for a good fifteen minutes, until she finally finds something we can work with. A cami flared dress with shoulder knots. It's simple, yet it looks really nice with the right accessories.

As I try it on, Sophia does a circle motion with her finger for me to twirl.

"Perfect! Looks really good," she squeaks.

"And it has pockets!" I say excitedly while placing my hands in them.

"Please don't mention that during the date," Sophia replies with a dry tone.

I furrow my eyebrows. "One, this is not a date," I say while pointing one finger up. "Two," I point a second finger up, "I will always be excited about pocket dresses. Leave me be."

It's the little things in life, you know?

She bites her lip, trying to hold back her laugh.

I look at the time, and I have about one more hour to finish getting ready. If I'm going to this insufferable dinner, I might as well have fun, so I ask, "Wanna help me get ready?"

"Always," she says as we both walk to my bedroom.

So we do just that. As I do my makeup, she styles my hair.

She hums mischievously as she straightens my hair. "For not being a date, you sure are putting in a lot of effort."

"I want to look hot when I turn his offer down for the thirtieth time." I finish my makeup with my signature red lip I love so much. It makes me feel confident every time I wear it and God knows I could use some of that.

Sophia finishes with my hair and applies some oil to it. "I don't know why you insist on having your hair straight. Your curls are so beautiful."

I sigh, choosing not to reply.

When I was little, I was so proud of my curls. I always felt like a princess. Until my mom would point out how unprofessional my curls were, always making me straighten them for school and saying, *'You will thank me one day. You're not getting bullied at school thanks to me.'*

Funny how I felt I was always bullied by her at home, though.

As I kept growing, her comments got to me. I don't wear my curls unless it's in a messy bun or I don't have time to get it styled. I'm all too aware it's stupid to still care about that to this day and age. Women empowerment and all, but childhood trauma, am I right?

"Okay, you're ready, and you look like a snack."

"You talk like a 16-year-old sometimes. Has anyone told you that before?" I quip.

She rolls her eyes and replies, "Okay, well, I'm going to head out."

As she's about to leave, my phone rings. I glance at the caller ID, and it's the apartment's front desk.

I answer, "Hello?"

The voice on the other end says, "Yes, Ms. Petrov, I'm calling because you have a visitor. Can I let him up?"

I check the time; he's here ten minutes early. "No. Tell him I'll be downstairs soon."

The front desk staff sounds nervous. "Ma'am, he's insisting I let him up…"

I sigh and instruct, "Put me on speaker." Then, I address insufferable Damian, "I will be down there in a minute. Stop terrorizing the poor guy," and hang up.

Sophia raises an eyebrow. "He's here already?"

I nod. "Yeah, so wait for me. I'll walk out with you."

We exit my apartment and step into the elevator. While descending, I turn to Sophia and say, "Please behave."

"Alrighty then!" she exclaims with an exaggerated wink. Sophia has this thing where she likes to quote 90s movies and TV shows. I'm sure she just quoted *Ace Aventura* because she's made me see that movie more times that I can count.

My best friend, ladies and gentlemen. Gotta love the woman.

As we approach the lobby, there he is, leaning against a wall in a three-piece black suit. I wonder if he wears anything else besides a suit? I bet he has suit *pajamas*. Now that's a funny picture.

Sophia nudges me with a sly grin, raising both her eyebrows. His eyes lock on me, sweeping them from the top of my head to my toes before finally meeting my eyes and delivering a lazy smirk.

Sophia can't resist the opportunity to tease. "You are *definitely* hotter in person."

I shoot her a look of annoyance, whispering, "Stop feeding his ego."

Damian's velvety laugh echoes and sends a shiver down my spine. His laugh is a zip of welcome electricity; a sliver of light.

Sophia winks at me and turns to Damian and says, "Take

care of my girl," placing two fingers on her eyes and then pointing them at him, a clear *'I'm watching you'* gesture.

Damian plays along with a playful tone. "Will do."

He extends his arm, silently inviting me to interlace mine in his. "Shall we?"

I roll my eyes and walk past him, muttering, "Let's get this over with."

Damian

Aria looks absolutely stunning, her signature red lips having a way of invading my mind with impure thoughts I should definitely not be having about my potential employee. As she walks past me, her perfume invades my nostrils. It smells like some fruity shit—strawberries, maybe? Not sure, but all I know is that it's quickly becoming my favorite scent.

To avoid the hassle of driving on a busy Friday evening in Chicago, I have my driver take us to the restaurant. The drive is uneventful, and it's clear she isn't thrilled to be here. However, she's a necessary piece of my business plans, so I'll grovel if I have to. Sometimes we have to take necessary risks for a high reward. The business needs to do well.

Are you sure it's just the business? Are you sure you're not just infatuated with the woman?

No. It's strictly business. *It has to be.*

Exiting the car, she remarks, "Nice restaurant."

I've chosen one of the city's finest Italian restaurants on purpose, hoping some good food and wine will soften her up a little. I'm not above doing sneaky things and flaunting my money to get what I want.

"I know. It's my favorite," I reply with a wink.

As we enter the restaurant, the hostess promptly seats us upon recognizing me. Sometimes, the perks of being one of the city's top billionaires comes in handy.

"No wonder you're so smug," Aria whispers.

"I heard that," I say as I peruse the wine menu, stealing a glance toward her.

God, it's stupid how beautiful this woman is.

"Good," she replies, a playful glimmer dancing in her eyes.

Setting the menu aside, I drop my elbows on the table. "I'm not going to apologize for receiving special treatment, Aria. It comes with the territory, people knowing who I am. What can I say?" I shrug. I never said I wanted this attention, it was kind of a package deal. Does it have its perks? Yes. Could I live without it? Also, yes.

"The issue isn't the special treatment, Romano. It's your sense of entitlement. You're used to people doing your bidding."

"I see we've progressed from Mr. Romano; that's a step forward," I remark, dismissing her comment and returning to the wine menu.

She isn't entirely wrong about my overconfidence, but it's a facade I've learned to adapt to in the world of business. To survive, I have to play the part expected of me, and confidence is part of the package. Little do people know I have nothing but fucking insecurities coming out of my pores.

Thank you very much for that, Father.

I've learned to hide those insecurities well, bottling them up inside. The feeling of utter loss, and uselessness. It's ironic, really. I've climbed my way to the top but the voice on the back of my head that sounds like my father couldn't care less.

In a fucked up way, I'm still unworthy; too compassionate; not smart enough. I have all the money in the world, but at what cost? I'm sad; angry; lonely. I'm barely above water, almost drowning, but not there quite yet.

Will I ever be worthy of anything? Kindness; love; patience? Will I ever find someone that just fucking gets me and stays despite all of my scattered broken pieces?

These insecurities haunt me and I keep bottling them up, hoping that they don't explode one day. After all, business is a dangerous game and I can't afford to show any weaknesses.

"Brushing me off won't get you what you want," she warns, her eyes fixed on me.

"I fail to see the issue with being a confident person."

"I never said confidence. I said *entitlement*. Do you have selective hearing too?" She raises an eyebrow, her eyes flickering with an unspoken challenge.

Just as I'm about to respond, our waiter intervenes. He introduces himself, wearing a charming smile, and directing a sultry look at Aria that immediately gets under my skin, making me feel hot.

"We'll take a '70 Latour bottle for the table," I order curtly, shoving the wine menu toward him.

He turns to Aria and asks with a flirtatious smile, "And for you, love?"

Oh, this idiot is looking to die tonight, I see.

"I ordered a bottle, so you do the fucking math," I reply with a cold smile, fixing him with a hard stare.

His demeanor swiftly shifts from charming to nervous, and he nods hastily before leaving our table.

"Man, you sure are a piece of work," she mutters, irritation lacing her tone.

"Thanks." I give her a cheerful smile, knowing it will irk her further.

Seeing her fiery side has become one of my favorite parts of our recent interactions. Aria is nothing but a ball of pure fire who's not afraid of a challenge, especially when it comes to me. On the other hand, though, it makes it way easier—and fun—to annoy her.

Another waiter arrives with our wine, this time a woman, introducing herself as our new server. Aria glances at me, raising an eyebrow, and I simply shrug in response. We glance at the menu quietly for a moment, then the waiter takes our order promptly. Once the waiter leaves, I take the opportunity to get down to business.

Frankly, I'm genuinely impressed with her work and what she's done for The Institute. Having her on the team is a necessity. Does it worry me how we'll work together? Not in the slightest. I'll be the boss. She's going to be another regular employee—or so I keep telling myself.

It has to be that way. There's no other option. There's too much riding on this. Don't fuck it up by obsessing over a woman who doesn't even like you.

"I have a proposition for you," I say, taking a sip of wine.

Aria is in the middle of taking a sip as well, and her gaze shifts to me, her eyes sparkling with curiosity.

"Work for me for three months," I continue. "Let's do a trial run, and then you can decide if you want to work for me permanently or return to The Institute."

"The Institute won't just hold my job for three months, Romano," she retorts.

"They will. I have my ways," I assure her, catching her attention. "Don't worry about it," I add with a playful wink.

She stares at me for a moment, and hope bubbles inside of me. "No," she says and takes another sip of her wine.

My face remains enigmatic, but frustration is slowly building. She sure knows how to bruise a man's ego. I've sent her various offers almost daily, and she's still ignoring my emails. I've followed this woman to her favorite coffee shop, for God's sake. I'm Damian fucking Romano, a man who doesn't take no for an answer.

She will say yes. Relax. This is nothing you can't handle.

"We'll cover your living expenses," I offer.

"Pass."

"You can work part-time, same salary," I counter.

"No."

"I'll triple the original offer," I say in a last-ditch effort.

She raises an eyebrow. "Isn't that a little desperate coming from you, Mr. Billionaire?"

Oh, gee. I got a nickname now. Hilarious.

I let out a sharp laugh. "Mr. Billionaire, seriously? You couldn't come up with something better?"

She glares at me without a word.

"I'm beyond desperate at this point. I don't know what else you want from me, Aria," I admit. "Do you want me to get on my knees and beg you? Because I will."

Her face lights up with a mischievous grin. "Okay, then beg."

Wait. What?

I look at her dumbfounded.

"If you want me to work for you, you'll have to beg," she states with a knowing smirk.

I clench my fists, my knuckles white from the force. The audacity of this woman. It was a simple figure of speech. I didn't mean it. I was just trying to express how serious I am about this situation. "You're being ridiculous," I respond dryly.

She shrugs, crossing one leg, patiently waiting.

Fuck. Okay, then. I guess we're doing this.

If there's one woman in the world that can make me beg, it's probably her. With her flirtatious smile, bright hazel eyes, and long soft legs that I would just get in between them and drown—*No.* I'm not even going to finish that thought.

I get up from my chair and walk over to stand in front of her, glancing around to ensure no one is watching. I drop to one knee, feeling ridiculous, like I'm about to propose. My fingers softly graze her thigh as I grab her hand and her composure stiffens.

"This is what you wanted. Now, please work for me," I say in a pleading tone.

Her eyes sparkle with amusement as I gulp down my pride. She looks at me for a seemingly extended moment before bursting into laughter, loud and unrestrained. Confused, I watch as she struggles for breath between fits of giggles.

I eventually get back to my feet, annoyed. "Were you joking?"

She keeps laughing, unable to answer my question.

I huff an annoyed breath. "For fuck's sake."

She wipes her teary eyes with a napkin. "Oh, that was so worth it."

"Good to know my misery is your happiness. But now, pay up."

Still laughing, she extends her hand. "Okay, let's shake on it. I'm still going to need that triple salary, though."

I shake my head and laugh before shaking her hand.

Now that she's working for me, I know it's going to be anything *but* ordinary.

7

Aria

What did I get myself into?

That's my first thought as I walk into my new place of employment—The Romano Gallery. *Ugh*. The guy is so obsessed with himself that he even named it after his last name. Has a nice ring to it, very *Italian*, but still.

I take a moment to appreciate the space. The gallery has off-white painted walls so the collections can stand out. With high ceiling windows that offer natural light, giving the space a sense of elegance.

Walking all the way to the back, there's a set of stairs leading to the office space. As I climb the stairs and reach the second floor, Isabella welcomes me with a bright smile. "Good morning, Ms. Petrov."

"Please, call me Aria. I have a feeling we will become the best of friends," I say, winking as I place a coffee in front of her. "I didn't know how you take your coffee, so I brought you a vanilla latte. Hope you like it," I add with a smile.

Isabella laughs. "Vanilla latte is fine. I prefer it with extra caramel drizzle because I'm a sugar addict."

"That's exactly how I take mine!"

As I'm chit-chatting with Isabella, an annoying presence approaches my peripheral vision. Turning to see where it's coming from, Damian emerges from his office.

Figures.

My pulse spikes, and I suddenly feel ridiculously hot. The talent he has for bringing the temperature in a room to dangerous heat levels should be studied.

"No coffee for me?" he leans against his office door frame, arms crossed.

There's something about a guy leaning against a door frame that just makes me have not-so-innocent thoughts. But Damian? With his tall, brooding presence? It's something out of this world.

The man flusters me, that much I'm painfully aware of. So I decide to ignore him. Just because we work together doesn't mean I have to engage with the good-looking asshole.

Seriously, Aria. Is it really necessary to always add the good-looking part?

"I like my coffee black, one sugar. You know, for future reference, darling."

"Gee, how surprising. Your coffee order is as dry as your personality. Congratulations," I retort.

He has this professional ability to make me lose my cool around him, and I've become even better at witty comebacks. Our dynamic is odd, but it works in a strange, fucked up way.

Turning to Isabella, I say, "Listen, my best friend Sophia and I are going out next weekend. You should totally come."

Isabella's eyes gleam as she responds, "Maybe. Thanks for the invite."

I nod as my attention is drawn back to Damian and his

impeccable put together looks, which is nothing out of the ordinary. Today, he is wearing a black button-up shirt with the sleeves rolled up. He looks *good*. With his muscular arms, tanned skin that I would just love to lick and—*No. Move on. He's your boss. What the hell is the matter with you?*

I observe him up and down, unable to resist a sardonic comment. "I see we ditched the three-piece suit today."

With a mischievous glint in his eyes, he replies, "Impressive attention to detail, noticing my choice of attire."

I raise an eyebrow at Damian's response. "Didn't know you were so observant about *my* observations," I quip.

With a teasing smile playing on his lips he says, "Touché."

I give him a small smirk, then take a sip of my coffee, savoring the delicious caramelized goodness.

He continues with a smile, shrugging nonchalantly, "I don't have any meetings today. I cleared my schedule just for you, darling."

There he goes again with that stupid fucking nickname.

Damian has a smile that can bring any woman to their knees. Paired with those forest green eyes that seem to pierce your soul, any woman would be done for. I wonder how often they fall for his trap? It's extremely frustrating. The man is strikingly beautiful in a raw, uncensored way. The worst part about this is that I'm no different from those women, because he makes me feel a weird attraction I rather not entertain. How can this single man annoy me and make me attracted to him at the same time? That's some impressive talent.

I try my best to ignore the flutter spreading through my stomach. "Oh, how lucky am I to have your undivided attention for the day, Mr. Romano," I reply with sarcasm,

"Call me Damian."

"I'd rather not," I retort.

Isabella, looking flustered, mumbles, "God help me." She stands up and says, "Aria, how about I walk you to your office?"

"That'd be per—"

"No need, I'll take her," Damian interrupts, walking toward me. "Shall we?" He tilts his head in the direction of what I assume is my new office.

"Sure," I respond dryly, fully aware that it's going to be a very long day.

As Damian walks in front of me, my eyes linger, admiring his physique. The fabric of his black dress shirt hugs his broad shoulders and toned back muscles perfectly. Also—and I can't believe I'm going to say this—but he has a nice ass, too. This is outrageous.

Entering my office, it's a simple and spacious room with large windows that provide a view of Lake Michigan with an L-shaped white desk, and a gray office chair. At the center of the desk, there's a brand new tablet, box unopened, and an arrangement of wildflowers. The place is cute and simple.

Damian turns to me. "Hope you like it."

"Better than what I had at The Institute for sure," I say with a smile.

"Wow, so you *are* capable of smiling. Here I thought it was impossible," he jokes.

As I look around the office, I quip, "Only with you."

Damian pats his chest twice dramatically, rubbing his hand in circles over his heart. "And here I was, already thinking I could get used to seeing that beautiful smile more often," he says with a wink, and my cheeks heat at the compliment.

I throw a fake cough to tame down the heat on my cheeks as I walk toward the desk then slightly bend and smell the flowers. They have a slight citrus smell, mixed with rose. They smell delicious. I love wildflowers. They are so colorful and carefree. Sometimes I wish I was one. "Thanks for the flowers. They are beautiful."

"I thought of you when I saw them at the market the other day. I'm glad you like them."

I turn around, raising my eyebrows. His eyes linger on mine for a beat before he breaks eye contact and looks the other way, almost like he's... flustered.

No. It can't be.

I don't even know how to unpack what he said. The fact that he casually went to the *market* and thought of *me* when he saw some flowers makes something stir within me. No one has ever bought me flowers just because. I don't think anyone has ever bought me flowers, like *ever*.

He's just being nice. You're reading too much into it.

He's trying to make this arrangement work, that's all. Still, I don't miss the way his eyes linger when he thinks I'm not looking, or the way he calls me darling with that hearty voice of his. The man's smooth.

That man is your boss. Get it together.

"You just casually go to the market?"

"I'm a man full of surprises."

I hum. "I've noticed."

He lets out a soft chuckle as he walks to the door. "I'll let you get situated before I give you a tour of the gallery."

I lean against the desk, crossing my arms. "Honestly, you don't need to give me a tour. I can figure it out on my own. I'm a professional, after all," I retort.

He shrugs before opening the door and says, "I don't care. Meet me downstairs," as he walks out.

Accepting the fact that I won't be able to shake Damian off unless I do what he says, I decide to go along with it and head downstairs. Stepping off the last stair, I see him standing in front of a painting, seemingly lost in thought. I approach him, taking in the beautiful artwork in front of us.

The painting is simple but striking. It features earthy tones mixed with shades of gray, black, and white. There are two hands portrayed, one unmistakably belonging to a man and the other to a woman. They are on the verge of touching but not quite there as if some invisible barrier holds them back. The painting exudes a sense of longing, where both hands seem eager to connect but remain separated.

As I read the sign, I murmur the name, "Impossible Touch," and move closer to the painting. "The name is a perfect fit," I remark.

Damian closes the distance between us, his woody soft scent enveloping my senses. He nods in agreement. "Yeah, it's my favorite painting in our collection. It devotes so much..."

"Longing," I say, finishing his sentence.

He looks at me with a bright, boyish smile as he nods again. His smile makes my chest tighten and makes my stomach flutter at the sight of it.

His thoughtful expression makes him look painfully handsome, as he appreciates the simplicity of the canvas and the story it conveys. Despite Damian's ability to annoy me with his cockiness and remarks, this is the one time he looks genuinely happy by a simple—yet complex—work of art.

"Whoever your curator was before me did a great job choosing this particular painting," I say, looking at him for a moment before my eyes trace back to the painting. It's mesmerizing. I could look at it forever.

"I've carefully chosen everything that's here. I travel a lot for various reasons, so I always make it a point to visit local artists and other galleries worldwide to collect paintings." He gestures to the entire gallery. "All of this... it all tells a story. Art speaks to me, and I'm a very good listener," he rasps.

His words touch me, resonating with my own connection to art. Art speaks to me too. Not only that, but it's also my safe space. For as long as I can remember, art has helped me get through extremely difficult times. My childhood, college years, my anxiety. I don't know where I would be without it.

I nod in understanding. "Who knew you had a human side?" I tilt my head, offering a playful smile.

He fixes his gaze on me, sincerity swimming in his eyes. "This is my first and only love, Aria. Art. It's the only thing that can bring this side of me."

This sliver of information he's confessing, it's almost like an olive branch, but not only that, it tugs at my resolve to dissect the mystery of the renowned businessman Damian Romano, and what he's truly like. There are layers to this man, that much I'm sure of.

We walk the rest of the gallery as he shows me some of the special pieces he has collected over the years. The way he animatedly talks about art—how his eyes fill with pride and the way a boyish smile escapes his lips every time he tells me an important fact about the piece—makes my heart take flight. It's also the moment I realize that Damian and I have one thing in common.

Our passion for art.

Damian

It has been decided—Aria Petrov is going to be the death of me. When I offered her this position, I brought her in because she's very good at what she does. And don't get me wrong, the woman truly has a natural talent and a trained eye for this type of work. She has undoubtedly exceeded my expectations. Her ideas are innovative and I'm more confident than ever that we'll be able to scale the gallery in no time, just as I planned.

What I didn't take into consideration is this uncontrollable need to be near her all the time, and bother her until she implodes with that fierce attitude of hers I've grown to like so much. It's like moth to a flame, the way we act around each other. So unpredictable and so fucking entertaining.

I'm such a masochist.

But what can I say? I love a good challenge. Once I set my mind to something, I have to accomplish it. I don't know how, or what exactly I want from her, but the need to be *more* nags at me constantly. All I know is that needling her with my presence and getting a rise out of her has definitely become my favorite hobby. On the flip side, her presence is a constant loom, hovering over me, and affecting my way of thinking. Around her, I lose total control. My mask slips when I least expect it, and she pushes me to my fucking limit. The bickering between us hasn't let up this past month; if anything, it's escalated. It makes me fucking excited. It's like a game where the ultimate prize is unknown.

But I can't fucking wait to find out.

Today, I made the choice to wait for her in front of her favorite coffee shop, a warm cup of her favorite brew in hand. I know her order by heart now—if it's too chilly, like today, she loves her vanilla latte with extra caramel drizzle. When it's a warmer day, she always opts for an iced soy matcha with honey. With Chicago's weather being so bipolar, I noticed the trend instantly.

I notice everything she does, not in a stalker way, of course. I'm just curious about her.

If I'm being brutally honest, when I wake up, my thoughts go to her and I instantly itch to get my fix, to see that beautiful smile and big hazel eyes that change color with whatever she's wearing. I wonder what color they will be today. I hope they are that caramel light brown that blends with the light green and gold. That's my favorite of them all.

I got the bright—more like stupid— idea to come to the coffee shop, because I also miss those days where she would find me invading her favorite space, ready to banter. I've been pretty spoiled, seeing her every single day. Those stolen glances at work are simply not enough anymore. I find myself craving more of her every day. Craving the ray of sunshine she brings into my gray, dull life.

So here I stand, like some lovesick fool.

Aria turns the corner to get to the coffee shop, engrossed

in her phone—as I've come to find out it's her usual thing to do—looking incredibly beautiful. She has this endearing, quirky librarian look going on. It's really fucking cute if I say so myself. She's rocking a white long-sleeve tee with a brown cami dress, fuzzy white socks, and white Converse. Her hair is in its signature messy bun showcasing her beautiful freckles. She has little to no makeup today, except for her usual pouty red lips that would look so good around my —*Nope*. I'm not going to finish that thought. That's incredibly inappropriate.

Great, now I have a boner at nine in the morning. *Lovely*.

"Hey, Darling," I rasp.

My voice comes out shakier than I was planning because of the fucking impure thought and all. It's incredibly frustrating how good she looks all the time. I have no one but myself to blame though, since I can't seem to take my eyes off of her every time she's near me. She's like a magnetic pull, my eyes just—*accidentally*—roam her from head to toe every single time.

Her eyes find mine in suspicion as she looks me up and down. My gaze locks on hers, and I thank the heavens when I notice her eyes have a hint of that caramel brown I like so much. I could simply get lost in them. They're the first thing I think about when I wake up, and the last thing I think about before going to bed. So bright and alluring like the stars.

"Following me again, are we?" she teases.

I extend the hand holding her coffee with a tilt of my head. "Why must you always think the worst of me?"

She takes the coffee, an airy laugh escaping her lips. "I need to get one for Isabella too."

I shake my head. "Already took care of it."

She squints, dropping her gaze to my hands where I'm holding my coffee. "So where is it?"

"Dropped it off at the office and came back to wait for you," I say honestly.

"Why?"

Her question throws me for a loop. "Why what?"

"Why did you come back here?"

The lie slips easily off my lips. "Well, to give you the coffee, of course. Didn't want you to spend money on a drink I already got you. You know?" My voice comes out a little strained at the end, and I'm hoping it doesn't give my bullshit excuse away.

Her eyes lock on mine, and God, her fucking eyes are so beautiful. They're a welcome reprieve of the racing thoughts that go through my mind every second of the day.

She takes a hefty sip and groans in satisfaction. "How do you know my order?"

"I asked Isabella." The lies keep rolling off my tongue like second nature. I'm so infatuated with this woman that I know everything I could possibly have learned without crossing stalking territory.

Tilting her head toward the sidewalk with a smile, she replies, "Shall we? These paintings are not going to discover themselves."

We start walking quietly toward the gallery, and while I typically take my car everywhere, I wouldn't change this for the world. Any moment I get to spend with her outside of work is a blessing in disguise. I should be setting that professional boundary, but it's been blurring more and more every day, and I'm not sure where I stand anymore.

"What did you think about the potential collection I sent you?" she asks, taking me out of my trance.

"It was too abstract for me."

She nods, swirling her cup of coffee as she ponders. "I actually agree for once."

I stop dead in my tracks, eyebrows shooting up in surprise. "I'm sorry. Did you just *agree* with me?" Closing the distance between us, I place the back of my hand on her forehead, checking her temperature. "You don't have a fever, but Hell must be freezing over as we speak."

She swats my hand away with a glare. "Have I ever told you how annoying you are?"

A smile plays on my lips. "No. But I'm sure you're about to enlighten me."

"Well, for the record, you are," she replies with a hint of amusement, crossing her arms.

Something unknown possesses me, and I find myself extending my hand, grabbing one of her hair strands, and placing it behind her ear. Her cheeks flush at my movement, her freckles looking adorably cute with the soft scarlet color all over her face.

"Noted," is all I reply with a wink and continue walking. "But in all seriousness, I think I like the theme we've been sticking with. Impressionism is the way to go."

It has been a transition ever since we started working together. We're honestly still transitioning because our styles are so different, so we've had to come up with a middle ground. Aria is amazing at what she does and has the patience of a saint. I'm as picky as they come and she's willing to work with me and has been helping me make this a reality, but also pushing those boundaries and making me expand to other styles.

She catches up to me, and bites her lip. The move is so ironically sexy, I almost bump into someone since I'm paying absolutely no attention to what's happening in front of me. All my attention goes to her, *always* her.

"If you're serious about wanting your gallery to resonate in the industry and make an impact, you need to open your mind, Damian. A mix of different styles. Be different for once."

Arriving at the gallery, I open the door for her and nod, considering her words. "I guess you do have a point." I sigh.

She stops in her tracks and turns around. "I'm sorry, did you just *agree with me*?" she asks sarcastically. She goes to check my temperature, amusement dancing in her eyes and I indulge her, just for the hell of it. Her soft hand touches my forehead, and the touch is simple, and light, but it burns all the same, with a charged electricity that seems to happen between us every time we are near each other. Her touch affects me in every way possible, but it's addicting nonetheless.

"You don't have a fever either." She hums. "Isn't that weird?"

"Oh yes, *so* weird," I reply with an amused tone.

She rolls her eyes as she takes her hand away from my forehead, then quickly goes upstairs to have her morning gossip with Isabella. They're getting friendly quickly, which I appreciate because I've known Isabella for a while now, and I've never seen her with any friends. I have a soft spot for Isabella, not that I'd ever let her know. I prefer to stay as the annoying asshole boss, but I'm extremely glad she's finding some people to hang with.

As I walk upstairs, I overhear Aria ask, "Are you going out with us tonight? You didn't go last time, so you owe me!"

Isabella nods, which makes Aria jump excitedly like a kid. "It's going to be great! You'll love Sophia. Just beware, she's a little unhinged." She giggles.

I lean on Isabella's desk, casually sipping my coffee. "I can confirm she *is* unhinged."

She hits my forearm as she gapes at me in disbelief. "Don't you dare speak about my best friend like that."

I raise my hands in surrender with a chuckle. "You're the one who mentioned it; I'm just confirming. Where are you guys going?"

Aria side-eyes me and smirks. "Wouldn't you like to know?"

Okay, then. Consider me officially fucking curious.

I laugh, opting not to spar with her, wanting the nice moment we had during our walk to last. Leaving the girls to their gossip, I walk toward my office to get some very much-needed work done. As I close the door slowly, I overhear Aria saying they're going to a new club downtown.

A club? Where preppy stuck-up guys go to pick up women because they have nothing better to do and are so terrible they don't know where else to pick up women?

Over my dead fucking body.

I shake my head, trying to escape the uncomfortable, stupid feeling. Why do I care? She's a grown ass woman, one who can make her own decisions. As I sit down, I try to ignore the sense of dread in the pit of my stomach. The idea of her going to a club, where men are going to be dancing with her, touching her hips, and getting too close for my comfort has my blood boiling. It suddenly gets too fucking hot in my office, and as I take off this suffocating tie to get some relief, an idea pops in my head.

I have to come up with an excuse to keep Aria here late. That's reasonable, right? I'm her boss. I can ask her to stay and to complete a task or something. I pace around the office, trying to come up with a reason. Anything that'll prevent her from going.

Finally, I find the perfect and truthful–*ish* excuse. We're missing one more piece for our collection, and there's an auction happening soon in New York that's extremely important and securing tickets to attend is a must. With this in mind, I stride to her office and knock before entering.

She looks up from her computer, her eyes flashing with a hint of irritation. I've noticed she despises interruptions, considering they disrupt her workflow or whatever the hell she calls it.

"The New York auction... I'm having trouble finding tickets." I get straight to the point.

She frowns. "*The* Damian Romano is having trouble finding tickets?"

Shit. I should've come up with a better excuse.

"Yes," I answer dryly.

She drops her pen on the desk and massages her temple, letting out a sign. "Well, I'll try to find something."

Not good enough. It's time to pull my annoying boss card. "This needs to be resolved today."

She shakes her head. "I have way too many meetings as it is."

"Then, you're going to have to stay later than normal," I counter.

"I have plans."

With a bored tone, I say, "Cancel them."

She gapes at me in disbelief.

"Petrov..." I warn.

Her eyes light with fire and annoyance. A small laugh escapes my lips and this causes her back to stiffen, her eyes shooting daggers at me now.

"Romano," she snaps, standing up from her desk and stalking toward me. "The auction isn't until next month. We have time."

I thin my lips, staying silent. She has a point, but I don't fucking care. If this is what will keep her away from a club,

I'll be an asshole. It's for her safety. I'm just a normal human being concerned for another *normal* human being. If anything, I'm being a good person, a *saint* for that.

You can keep telling yourself those lame excuses. Doesn't mean it's true.

"I don't need reasons to want things when I want them," I point out as I close the distance between us, amusement in my tone, despite the irritation in her eyes. "Get. It. Done."

She offers a humorless laugh, then gives a sarcastic bow. "Anything else I can do for you, *boss*?"

I fix my cufflinks and reply, "No."

"Okay." She strides past me, a drift of her fruity perfume invading my senses. She smells like strawberries and a hint of sweet vanilla. It's intoxicating, and something I could quickly become addicted to. She opens the door of her office, and says, "Can you please get out now, so I can get to my endless list of things I have to do? Including something I know you're more than capable of doing."

As I slide my hand into my pocket, I exit her office. I turn around to utter another word, and she murmurs something along the lines of *asshole* and *raging dick* before she shuts the door in my face.

I shake my head with a laugh, deciding to leave her be and go to my office. I don't fucking care what she thinks, I will go to any length to get what I want. She had to find out sooner than later. The sense of relief floods over me like a savory triumph.

I can't shake the possessiveness when it comes to her. It's like a caveman feeling that sneaks up on me, grabbing on hard and throwing all rational thoughts through a window.

Like I said, she's going to be the *death* of me.

I glance at the clock, and it's almost nine o'clock in the evening. *Huh.* Time sure flies when I have an endless amount of work.

Since Aria started working here, I've made it a habit to stay until she leaves, whether or not I've finished my work. Leaving her alone in the gallery doesn't sit right with me.

Lost in thought, I'm interrupted when she storms into my office, dropping some paperwork on my desk.

"I got you two tickets. So you can go and take whatever woman is dumb enough to go with you," she says in an annoyed, dry tone.

I'm surprised at how quickly she managed to secure the tickets. Even though I used this as an excuse, I truly was having difficulty finding tickets—okay, that's a lie. All I needed was to make one single call, but you know, it's a good thing I didn't try. This was the perfect excuse.

"How did you get these so quickly?"

"I have my ways."

I nod, then make a decision. "You're going with me. I can use your eyes on this collection."

And if I'm being honest, I would love nothing more than to spend time outside of the gallery with her, even if it's slightly work-related.

I'm officially losing my fucking mind here.

"I can't. I have too much to do here."

"This is not up for discussion, Aria. Now go home; it's late."

She checks her watch and protests, "It's barely nine. I'm going out."

I maintain my composure and casually ask, "Where?"

She raises an eyebrow. "Who are you? My keeper or something?"

Fuck.

"Just making conversation," I reply nonchalantly.

"Right. Because you're such a conversationalist. They should hire you to do a speech class with how much you talk," she replies sarcastically.

I glare at her. "Do you sit down every day and write down jokes at my expense?"

"*Yup.* I keep a diary and all." she throws me a playful wink. "Well, gotta go. Party awaits." she wiggles her fingers in a goodbye gesture and exits my office.

I release an exasperated sigh and lean back in my chair, rubbing my temples. This woman pushes me to boundaries I didn't realize existed, and she's oblivious to it. Grabbing my belongings, I head out, deciding to text the one person who might have the information I need.

ME

> You know of any club openings happening tonight?

ENZO

> Always.

ME

> Picking you up in twenty, so get ready. We're going.

ENZO

> Who are you and what did you do with my cugino?

ME

> You think you're so hilarious. I mean it, be ready.

Not sure what possesses me to make this rash, stupid decision. I'm not the type of guy that goes out, much less *clubbing*. I'm Damian-fucking-Romano, for God's sake, if you see me out, it's always about business. When it comes to her though, all my logical senses get dulled. I make decisions that are not entirely in my control, just what my stupid heart decides to do at the spur of the moment. The idea of her being in a club, getting touched by strangers makes my heart beat out of my fucking chest with how angry it makes me feel. It's an uncomfortable and unfamiliar feeling I don't understand, but this doesn't mean I won't act on it—damn all the consequences.

So I guess I'm going to a fucking club tonight.

Music is blasting throughout my apartment as Sophia and I get ready for the club when the doorbell rings.

"That's probably Isabella! I gave her guest access!" I shout at Sophia as I walk to open the door.

"Making another margarita. Got it!" she says, running from the room to the kitchen.

Opening the door, I hug Isa and let her in. Me and Isabella haven't been friends for a long time, but I've noticed that she can be a bit shy at times, so tonight I'm determined to bring her out of her shell, and anyone around Sophia tends to do just that.

Sophia comes to the door with three margaritas in hand, shoving one into Isabella's hands and says, "Hi. So lovely to meet you! Here! Start drinking. You have some catching up to do."

"Okay," Isabella says, unsure.

I laugh. "Sophia, be a little less intense. *Jeez.*"

"Let's get ready," Sophia says, then looks Isabella up and

down. "Girl, we're putting some more makeup on you. I swear, with that beautiful face, you'll look like a model."

We keep drinking and start putting makeup on, Sophia going a little too heavy with Isabella's eyeshadow, claiming that her eyes are the size of a Bratz doll and she needs to take advantage of it. Honestly, my favorite part when I do go out is getting ready, not the actual going out part. But Sophia will literally drag me by the hair if I change my mind. And honestly? I'm in serious need of letting loose for once.

Working with Damian is stressful as it is, but that's not even the problem—I can easily handle him, even when he thinks he's getting a rise out of me, I just play into his games. Okay, that's half a lie. Sometimes he does get the best of me and gets under my skin, but it's kind of our thing now. One I look forward to more than I'd ever care to admit. The problem is the feelings he stirs when I'm near him. That man sure has a talent for making me have not-work-appropriate thoughts of things I would die for him to do to me.

Going out, meeting a nice handsome stranger, and dancing with my friends is the cure for these stupid feelings —wrong wording—let's call it desire, that sounds way better. I would love nothing more than to give into the temptation. Take a bite of the forbidden apple, savor the taste well. But that absolutely cannot happen. He has to remain as my very annoying boss. And I have to keep reminding myself everyday, if that's what it takes.

I opt for a red sleeveless mini dress that accentuates my curves, paired with chunky white heels. With my hair down, embracing its natural curls, and lips adorned with my signature red color, I stare at my reflection, attempting to hype myself up. My natural hair makes me uncomfortable, but today I'm determined to break out of my comfort zone.

Confidence is my goal, even with my mother's voice echoing in the back of my head.

Your hair is a mess, Aria, fix it.

You look like a bird's nest.

No boy is ever going to ask you to the dance if you keep wearing your hair like that.

Why did you have to get your father's hair?

I shake my head, trying to get the useless thoughts out of my head and instead, chase the burning sensation down my throat with a shot of tequila. For one single night, I want to forget about my problems. Forget about the fact I'll never become an artist. Don't get me wrong—it's not that I don't like my job—but it's not what I really want to do. I'd love nothing more than to release my endless collections and actually do something I'm passionate about. Maybe even have my own studio where I can teach kids how to paint. Explore new things. Learn new ways to express my art.

A humorless laugh escapes me, one I chase with another shot of tequila. Me? Become an artist? *Please.* I can barely show Sophia my paintings before feeling embarrassed. My mother made sure to shame me enough times, I started believing no one would appreciate what inspires me. What makes me happy.

"Okay, girls, are we ready?" Sophia asks. "Let's take a selfie in the mirror before we leave." Sophia grabs her phone and has us pose in front of the mirror.

This is nice. This is exactly what I needed.

I muster the realest smile I can for the picture, swallowing my feelings down. I'm tired of feeling sorry for myself. Tired of wondering. For once, I want to take charge of what I truly want.

But I'm not ready. And I don't think I ever will be.

"Pass me that picture. I want to post it on Instagram," I mention as we're walking out of the apartment.

Sophia nods, immersed in her phone, probably already editing the picture to have it publish-ready. Sophia is very into appearances. Working around the world of journalism, you kind of have to be. People keep a close eye on you when your job is to do the same to others. Vicious cycle and all.

As we're walking to the car, I ask, "Hey, how's the article about the art heist going?"

Sophia shrugs. "I've found a few contacts from Rome, tried to do some interviews, but nothing crazy. Since the investigation is still taking place, they are being very cryptic about it."

"It was a very expensive, rare painting. I'm surprised you were even able to find people to interview."

"I spammed their emails, called nonstop. You know, the norm."

I shake my head with a laugh as we get inside the Uber. While I know this is not what she wants to do with her life, she's still an extremely good journalist, so I don't doubt she'll be able to make this story shine.

Sophia sends me the picture, and I post it with a simple 'night out with my girls' quote. I barely use Instagram, so as I'm going through the notifications, I notice Damian followed me.

I frown.

Damian doesn't follow anyone except for his business accounts. *Weird*. It was probably a mistake.

When we arrive at the club, it's extremely packed, which is expected since it's opening night. Leave it up to Sophia to flirt with the bouncer, letting us in right away as people look at us like they want to skin us alive.

"How did you even do that?" Isabella asks Sophia, gaping at her, impressed.

Sophia flips her hair dramatically. "I have my ways."

I roll my eyes. "Sophia is a shameless flirt. Men go head over heels for her."

"I can't believe you're single," Isabella says.

"I have terrible taste in men," she replies, as I say at the same time, "She has terrible taste in men." We look at each other and throw our heads back with a laugh.

"But regardless, I prefer to be single. I have more freedom, ya know? Let the playboys get played by me." Sophia shoots us an exaggerated wink.

I know my best friend pretty well, and even though she does enjoy the one-night stands, she is also a hopeless romantic. I know it must get lonely. She just doesn't voice it.

Entering the place, it's total chaos, packed with so many people, it's a bit of a challenge to move without bumping into someone. The club has two floors, and it's lit up with rainbow neon lights that are blinking all over. Downstairs, there are two bars on opposite sides, and in the middle, a dance floor with a bunch of small tables scattered around. Upstairs, it's like a big circle around the dance floor, making that VIP section pretty spacious.

We arrive at the bar closest to the VIP stairs entrance to get some tequila shots. I'm sure Sophia has this calculated, hoping to meet some random guy from VIP and snag us a spot. I welcome the liquid courage for fun, especially if I'm going to be dancing with anyone.

"1, 2, 3, shot, shot, shot!" Sophia yells while Isabella and I take a shot at the same time.

Isabella grimaces, then decides to chase it with a soda. Me? I embrace the burning feeling. It's half of the fun. Helps me forget about a certain set of emerald green eyes and killer smile. Feeling all light and a bit buzzed, Sophia grabs both Isabella and me, dragging us to the dance floor. Suddenly, my favorite jam, "Who's That Chick?" by David Guetta and Rihanna pulses through the club, and it's like an instant energy boost. I let the music guide me, swaying my hips to the beat. Isabella joins me, and we're both dancing, jumping, and laughing, totally feeling the buzz.

Sophia is cornered by a guy quickly—as per usual—and a couple of songs later, she returns to us. "Jack has a VIP table and two other friends," she yells over the music, wiggling her eyebrows.

I look over her shoulder who I assume is Jack, and he's your typical preppy guy. I can only imagine what the other two guys look like.

"Absolutely not." I shake my head.

Sophia ignores my complaint and drags us both with her to the stairs. We enter the VIP section, and the area is filled with sizable tables and a less crowded bar. The guy Sophia met leads us to a table where two of his friends are chatting and drinking. One of them, with his tanned skin, dark blond hair, and a lazy smile, catches my attention. He notices and responds with a flirtatious smile.

Guess I'm dancing with a stranger tonight, nice.

Exactly what I need to get the *he-shall-not-be-named* guy off my mind.

Sophia notices the lingering eye contact and decides to play matchmaker. "Didn't you say you were a little tired from all the dancing? Sit right here. We'll be at the bar with the guys." She winks at me, then grabs Isa's hand, while the other two guys follow after them.

I laugh. "Sorry. My best friend loves to play matchmaker sometimes. I don't have to sit here, I'm fine," I say, starting to walk to the bar.

The handsome stranger briefly grabs my hand to stop me, and when I don't feel the same charge of electricity I get every time Damian touches me, the disappointment hits me out of nowhere.

He drops it, grabbing his beer back and leaning back on his seat. "That's fine. I don't mind her playing matchmaker. You're beautiful." He winks. "Do you want to dance?"

I hesitate for a moment, before replying, "Sure. I'm Aria, by the way," as we walk downstairs to the dance floor.

"I'm Theo." He smiles at me, and another wave of disappointment hits me when his smile doesn't hit the same as Damian's.

Why can't I stop thinking about him? I'm so pathetic.

"Beautiful name for a beautiful redhead," he says, grabbing one of my curls with his finger and playing with it.

His game is a bit lame, but he has good looks so I don't mind. It's not like I'm looking for the future father of my children at a club. Just some innocent dancing and flirting will do.

Hitting the dance floor, the beats of "Woman" by Doja Cat kick in. Theo snags me by the hips, our bodies colliding in rhythm. Closing my eyes, I let the music take over, enjoying the dance with this stranger. Turning my back to him, we sway closer, feeling the vibe in sync, bodies moving together. His hands wander over my stomach, and while I'm cool with some dancing closeness, one of his hands decides to venture south. I quickly grab it, trying to keep things in check. While I agreed to dance with him, I didn't sign up to get groped in the middle of a club. Despite my attempt to signal some boundaries, he doesn't take the hint and keeps traveling his hand until it's close to my inner thigh.

"I need to find my friends. They're probably wondering

where I am," I say, using it as an excuse to put some distance between us.

Despite that, he turns me around, grabbing my hips and pulling me back into the dance, his hands freely roaming, this time reaching for my ass.

"Please, let me go," I plead, my voice shaky.

"Come on. We're just dancing," he dismissively replies, licking his lips while leering at my chest. My attempts to break free become useless, making me increasingly uncomfortable.

"Let me go," I assert, pushing him with all my strength, causing him to stumble.

He retaliates by grabbing my wrist. "You fucking bitch. You're the one who looked my way first. Why are you acting so innocent now?" he retorts, tightening his grip.

"You're hurting me! Let go!" I yell back, desperate to break free from his death grip.

Out of nowhere, someone grabs my hips from behind, gently pulling me backward and stepping in between me and the guy.

"She told you to let her go."

The touch is strangely familiar, igniting a burning and thrilling sensation I've experienced before. The unmistakable scent of cedarwood invades my space. My breath catches as the clean aroma intoxicates me, leaving me slightly dizzy. The lingering sensation on my hips, where his hands were moments ago, still burns in the best way possible.

"Yeah? And who the fuck are you?" Theo questions, pushing him.

"I'm the guy who's going to break your teeth if you don't get the *fuck* out of my face."

"Mind your business, dude. I'm just here trying to get

some pussy. She was asking for—" Theo can't finish the sentence because the man delivers a solid punch. Theo crumples to the floor, crying out, with his nose bleeding profusely.

In the dimly lit club, with only the pulsating beat of music and neon lights flickering, the man stands tall, with broad shoulders and dark hair. While it's hard to recognize the face once he turns around, I don't need to. Because I can recognize that silhouette anywhere.

It's Damian's.

10

Damian

T his place is loud, and I'm officially fucking annoyed.

Right after I punch the guy, the bouncers come our way, trying to understand the situation. Once they recognize me and realize I was the one who punched the creep, they pick up the guy and kick him out of the club without a second thought.

I sigh, turning around to see Aria standing there, her face drained of color, eyes bulging in surprise.

"Outside, *now*," I growl, pointing to the door. She doesn't say anything, doesn't even acknowledge me, and simply walks outside.

I've never lost my shit like that. I have a reputation to maintain, and being a knight in shining armor is definitely *not* one of them. This is probably going to bite me in the fucking ass, and I can't even pretend to care.

I take off my jacket and place it on her shoulders. I'm way taller than her, so my jacket hugs her whole body, almost like she's using it as a dress. A primal unfamiliar sensation comes over me as I decide to cover her. It's not chilly tonight, but I would gouge anyone's eyes out who dares glance at her for one more moment. She has this mini dress that marks her curves, leaving nothing to the imagination. She looks like a goddamn dream.

Focus. Now's not the time to be salivating over her.

"Are you okay?" I ask, cradling her face.

She meets my stare with a soft nod, her eyes brimming with tears threatening to spill over at any moment. With a sniff, she whispers, "Thank you." Her voice trembles slightly, and her body shakes from the adrenaline.

I arrived at the club about two hours ago with my cousin, Enzo, and his best friend Matteo. Once we arrived, Enzo went to pick his flavor of the night as usual, and Matteo stayed next to me, waiting for the girls to come in. He doesn't have to tell me what I know. The only reason he came with us is because I told him Isabella was coming as well. Their history is more than a complicated entanglement, so I didn't even dare to question why he stayed next to me, just as vigilant, eagerly waiting for the girls to arrive.

I stayed in the VIP area, keeping an eye on the door and the floor for any signs of Aria. An hour later, she walked in with the girls in tow. It took me a minute to recognize her, because tonight, she has curly hair. I felt like someone punched me right in the gut, something that has been happening lately every time she enters a room. Really, I don't understand how she manages to take my breath away every single time. I've seen her countless of times, with messy hair, straight, braids—but her curls take the fucking cake. She looks so fucking beautiful. I wonder why she never wears her hair like that. It suits her, alongside her fiery personality and otherworldly looks.

I wanted to go to her right away and stake my claim like a senseless caveman, but I held back. The last thing I wanted was for her to think I was stalking her. I don't even understand—not fully, anyways—why I decided to show up. My gaze remained on her, scrutinizing every move with intent. Not long after they arrived, a preppy stuck-up guy was leading them upstairs, so I positioned myself in the corner of the VIP bar, hiding from her like a coward. I didn't want to leave anything up to chance and make her believe I was there for her. I managed to convince myself I was there because I felt like going out. Or at least that's what I told Enzo as he grilled me with questions during our drive. The girls walked to a table where some guys were sitting. My blood instantly boiled, and the place had started to feel so much more crowded at the sight of her smiling at another man.

The same fucking smile I love to see every minute of every damn day.

I gulped my bourbon to calm down the aggressive sensation and not go to her. God knows I held back, gripping the glass so hard I ended up breaking it.

They were clearly flirting, more him than her, but nonetheless—*fucking flirting.* As they were walking downstairs to the dance floor, I witnessed how he turned around and grabbed one of her curls and swirled it around his finger. My first instinct was to grab a fucking knife and cut his finger off for him daring to touch her hair like that.

My fucking hair.

I shake my head as the thought creeps in, because this is insane. She's not mine to claim, never will be.

As they started dancing, the place suddenly felt smaller, and smaller. Sweat trickled down my back, my knuckles white from grabbing the table as hard as humanly possible. My body was raging—*screaming*—at me to go to her and take her away. I kept my eyes on her the entire time, following her every move, every breath, every sway of her hips. I quickly noticed when she started to feel uncomfortable. And, *fuck.* I hated the way he touched her without her consent, and the way he started groping her.

I never believed when people say they see red when extremely angry. I've always been a cautious man. It's the way I do business, because losing your cool is not an option —people would eat you alive if you showed any sign of emotion or weakness. I finally understand the saying, though. My legs took on a life of their own, quickly storming to them. My arms too, pushing people out of the way, yelling at them to move the fuck away from me. My heart pounding —*hard*—and chest tightening with anger like never before. I gave the guy the opportunity to walk away from a situation, because I'm a gentleman before anything. That's how my mother raised me, but the way he talked about her snapped something inside of me and my instinct was to punch him. I would've killed him if they would have let me get away with it.

Zero fucking regrets. I'd do it a million times over.

I extend my hand for her to grab. "Come on, I'll take you home."

She shakes her head, taking a step back. "Isa and Sophia are still inside with that guy's friends. I need to go get them."

"It's already taken care of. Now, let's go. This is not up for discussion," I say sternly.

She hesitates, her eyes traveling from my hand to my eyes.

"Do you trust me?" I ask softly. Desperately hoping she does. It would kill me otherwise.

She bites her lip with a nod.

"I promise you're friends are safe," I rasp.

I texted Matteo as we were walking out of the club,

ordering him to look after the girls. He quickly agreed, and I'm sure it had everything to do with Isabella and nothing to do with him wanting to be chivalrous.

She takes my hand hesitatingly and without putting up a fight, which fucking breaks something inside of me because her fiery personality is nowhere to be found. She's shaken up, and I wish I could do something more to make her feel better. An Aria without her witty comebacks and banter is not one I could live with. Guiding her to the valet, they bring my car out and I quickly open the passenger door and wait for her to get in.

Without a word, I get in the car and start driving. I'm still trying to shake off the anger coming out of my pores, because this is the last thing she needs. I don't blame her, at all. She was trying to have some fun, and it fucking sucks some creep ruined it. I should have stopped her from going to the dance floor with him, if I had let my instincts take over, she would have been safe.

She leans back on the headrest, looking outside at the city lights.

"Are you okay?" I know it's a stupid question, but I ask it anyway. Not hearing her sweet voice is killing me.

"Yeah. I mean, I probably deserved it. I said yes to dance with him anyway." She lets out a humorless laugh.

The raging feeling to go back and punch, kick, and break the guy's teeth for making her feel like she is to blame for the situation comes rushing back like a beast clawing its way out of its cage.

I shake my head. "No, Darling. Just because you said yes to a dance doesn't mean you signed up to get groped."

"Why were you there?" she asks in a whisper, changing the topic.

"What do you mean?" I deflect.

"You, at the club. That is not your scene, at all." Her eyes meet mine with suspicion.

I shrug. "I was there with my cousin and his best friend." *Technically, not a lie.*

"Uh-huh," she says, unconvinced. "Well, thank you for saving me or whatever. Very chivalrous of you."

I raise an eyebrow. "Chivalrous, huh? That's an upgrade from arrogant dick," I retort.

"Don't get used to it," she quips back.

And my girl is finally back with her funny banters, making me instantly relaxed.

'My girl' sure has a nice ring to it.

"Are you hungry?" I don't want to just drop her off and be on my way. I want to make sure she's okay, and feels safe. And a selfish part of me wants to make this night last as long as possible.

"Considering I've only had endless margaritas and tequila shots without food because Sophia wanted us to get drunk... Yes. I'm starving."

"Sophia sounds like a real piece of work." I shake my head with a laugh. That sounds something my cousin, Enzo, would totally do, too.

"Yes. But I love her nevertheless." She lets out an airy laugh.

We keep driving in silence the rest of the way until we arrive at a Mexican food truck near the gallery I often enjoy. I park and quickly get out of the car to open the passenger door. The air smells like carne asada and cilantro, the food truck busy with activity.

We order our food, and they quickly call our names. There aren't any seats, and we don't want to sit inside the car, so we opt for the sidewalk. I go to my car and bring out another jacket and place it on the sidewalk so she doesn't have to sit on the concrete, wanting her to be comfortable.

We eat without saying much, just watching some kids run around the parking lot as we eat our tacos.

As she's taking a bite, I ask, "Are you ever going to follow me back on Instagram?"

She pauses mid-bite and looks at me, surprise lacing her face. "So, you did follow me on Instagram. I thought it was a mistake."

I take a sip of my pineapple soda with a frown. "Why would you think that?"

"Because you only follow your business accounts."

I hum, opting for not replying. It's true. I'm not a huge social media person, and I barely follow anyone, because if I'm being honest, I couldn't give a rat's ass about what people are up to. But Aria isn't like *other* people to me.

And here's to hoping she never finds out.

"Well?" She arches a brow.

I bite my taco and chew thoroughly, taking my time to respond. "No comment." I'm not about to tell her she's become my business somehow. Much less confess she's been invading my every thought.

She rolls her eyes, but doesn't press the issue. "Never thought you were a food truck kind of guy."

I act offended. "What is that supposed to mean? I can enjoy some good street food."

She places her container next to her and raises her hands in defeat. "You know what I mean. You're always so put together, in suits, eating at expensive restaurants."

"I enjoy the simple things. Don't always believe what you see on social media." My thoughts are raging at me, wanting nothing more than to tell her the truth.

Don't believe what you see for a second. It's all a mask. It's not real. This is the real me. You make me want to be myself around you and it's fucking confusing.

She looks at me, nodding. "Right..."

She keeps eating in silence as I try my best to not stare and admire the sight of her. My stomach fills with a thousand butterflies, ones I can't keep at bay. Only she could make me feel such nervousness and a tingling sensation all over my body. She's more relaxed now, and I love how she can still be so beautiful by simply sitting on a sidewalk eating tacos.

A bit of sauce lingers on the side of her mouth, and without a second thought, I gently wipe it away with my thumb. She pauses for a moment, our gazes locking with the movement.

My surroundings dull, blocking any distractions and noises. I can only see *her*—beautiful curly, auburn hair, red lips, and those big hazel eyes that invite me to get lost in them. Her eyes are like an autumn forest, a kaleidoscope of green and brown, with a hint of gold. Every time she looks at me, I'm the luckiest man in the world. There's only one thought floating through my head right now, looming in the back, nudging me to do it.

To find out what her lips taste like. To kiss her until we need to catch our breath. Until our lips get swollen from owning each other's mouth.

I wonder if she tastes sweet. Like strawberries, or maybe caramel.

Fuck, what I would do for one single kiss.

What the hell am I thinking? This is the last thing I need. I *can't* do this. We *can't* do this.

The thought is enough to bring me back to a crashing reality. I stand abruptly and blurt, "Are you done? I'll take you home." My tone comes out more gruff than I intended, but this relationship needs to remain professional. The line keeps blurring, but I can't cross it, and I'll keep drawing it until it's engraved in my brain.

She stands up, surprise lacing her face at my tone. "Uh, yeah. I'm done."

Nodding, I walk to the car without waiting for her. She quickly falls a step behind, and we get in.

The rest of the car ride is cold and uncomfortable. She just gives me directions to her home, and I drive in silence. As time ticks, her demeanor changes. She's pissed. *Good.* I need her to put distance between us, because I don't think I'm strong enough to do it by myself. The last thing we need is to get involved with each other. There's too much riding for me to risk it. The gallery. My empire. The promise I made to myself all those years ago to become someone my father never expected me to be. My mask needs to go back in its place and treat her like I would any other. I need to keep my distance and gain back the control I've so carefully crafted my whole life.

Arriving at her place, she mutters a quick thanks, takes off my jacket, leaves it on the passenger seat, and walks away without saying goodbye.

I don't leave until I see her pass the lobby and enter the elevators, ensuring she's safe. Leaning back against the headrest, I let out a deep sigh. I can't think straight when I'm near her. I just punched a guy because of her. I tell myself it's because I wanted her to be safe, and to some extent, it's true. But deep down, I come to the realization that I do know what this unfamiliar, raging, primal sensation is.

Jealousy.

11

Aria

Looking at the painted canvas in front of me, I let out a satisfactory sigh.

Finally.

After being uninspired for so long and beating myself up about it every chance I got, I finally had the chance to play around with my paints and brushes all weekend. Granted, I've barely had time to think about this since the gallery has been taking all my time and space. Not that I mind; after all, it keeps my mind busy. Keeps at bay those dark thoughts that seem to loom over me constantly.

The sense of feeling trapped, unworthy, just an overall mess. Then, feeling bad and ungrateful about how I'm feeling, because despite everything, I have a good career. So what if I'm not a professional artist? I still get to be around art. That should count for something.

The endless cycle fucking continues.

After arriving home Friday night, my emotions were in high gear—so angry and confused. Frustrated at Damian; at the situation. All I wanted to do was blow off some steam. So I did—the only way I knew how.

My blissful weekend is coming to an end now as I give the painting the finishing touches. This one portrays a man and a woman in mute tones—white, black, and different shades of gray. The man has his hands behind the woman's neck, their bodies pushed together, leaving little to no space while their lips hover so close they're practically kissing. It portrays so much longing; desire; *temptation*.

It expresses exactly how I feel after that passing moment between us—tempted. I know he wanted to kiss me. The air crackled with wild electricity. You could cut the tension with a knife. For a moment, it felt like it was just us, and there was only one thing I wanted: his lips on mine. I wonder if the kiss would have been gentle, his lips tentatively hovering over mine. But knowing Damian, and his strong personality... it would have been possessive and fierce. He looks like the kind of man who likes to take charge, and I would have happily complied. I would have let him thread his fingers through my hair and deepen the kiss. I would have let him kiss me until my lungs demanded air, and even then, I doubt I would have stopped.

The idea of kissing him feels so right, yet so fucking wrong. It's impossible to get him out of my head. Every time I close my eyes, all I see is his silhouette at the club after saving me. His gentle touch around my face, making sure I was alright. His green eyes piercing mine, giving me that involuntary tingling sensation all over my body.

I clean the sweat off my forehead with my forearm as I take one last look at the painting. My cheeks hurt from how much I'm smiling. The root of this painting comes from feelings I can't understand yet. Feelings I want nothing more than to push down and forget about, but it doesn't stop me from being proud of myself.

I like my job, but today, dread consumes me. It's been two days since my weird encounter with Damian at the club, and all I want to do is hide seven feet under the earth and never come out. There's one question that's been stuck in my head ever since.

Why was he there?

The little I know about him, going out is not his scene at all. He's all about business, making money, and ultimately, getting a rise out of me every chance he gets.

Arriving at the gallery, the place is bustling with activity, which is strange considering we aren't open to the public yet. After much back and forth, we decided to host an opening gala once we complete the gallery collection. We're still missing one piece, but hopefully, we'll be able to get one at the New York auction.

Taking the steps to the second floor, I walk to Isabella's desk, finding it empty. There are lots of people—mostly men, dressed in all black—going in and out. I frown in confusion and knock on Damian's office door.

I hear multiple male voices from that side of the door, angry whispers going back and forth.

"Come in," Damian says from the other side of the door.

Entering, the first thing I notice are Damian's baggy eyes, messy hair, and his button-up shirt sleeves rolled up. He looks like a wreck, probably didn't get a lick of sleep.

"You're dismissed," Damian says, pointing his fingers at two guys. One looks remarkably similar to Damian, just slightly shorter and bulkier, and the other guy is blond, with deep blue eyes. They both nod and leave.

"What the hell is going on?"

He lets out a long sigh. "Someone broke into the gallery Friday night, right after I dropped you off."

Taking a closer look at him, he's wearing the same outfit from the night of the club.

"Have you been here all weekend? Why didn't you call me? I could have helped." My voice laces with concern.

He looks up, his face void of emotion. "With what, exactly? There was nothing for you to do. I have it under control."

"Go home, Damian. I got the rest."

He shakes his head as he goes through a few documents. "I'm almost done here anyway. By the way, they stole the main piece."

My blood runs cold at his words. We've carefully chosen every single item in the collection. We've been working on it diligently since I started. That painting is extremely important; it sets the theme for the rest of the gallery. This is the worst case scenario possible. All the work we've poured, going down the drain.

"We have the auction next month. Maybe we can find something there," I offer.

He rubs his eyes, letting out a frustrating sigh. "That doesn't work. Statement pieces are hard to come by. The auction doesn't guarantee we'll find any. We need connections, anything. I have a couple of people who owe me favors. I'll see who I can call—"

I interrupt. "No. I got it. I'll make some calls and see what I can do."

He hesitates for a moment before nodding.

I try not to take it personally. After all, I know who I'm working with. He's a control freak. It's surprising we've gotten this far. Though, I can't deny it stings a little because I've done nothing but prove myself these past months.

I do my best to muster a smile as I walk out of his office. Before leaving, I look back and say, "Please go home and get some rest."

I don't know why, but concern floods over my body, almost like instinct. Yeah, I'm pissed off they broke into the gallery and stole from us. I'm also a little pissed about him not calling me, asking for my help. But mostly? I'm concerned about him. I know how deeply he cares for this gallery. He has poured his heart and soul into this project. We all have.

Settling into my office, I fire off some emails and make calls to a few connections I have made over the years, desperately seeking anyone willing to do business with us. I debate whether to call Alex. I know he has a couple of connections, but there's one little problem—I haven't exactly told him I started working for Damian. It's not like I owe him anything, but he's a close friend, and he made his feelings extremely clear when we last spoke.

Biting my lip, I muster the courage and call him. Keeping my reasons for wanting to meet vague, we agree to meet at our usual spot. I arrive about thirty minutes before him, trying to go over my notes and hoping for the best that he'll be willing to help me. Alex arrives, walking toward our table, so I get up and receive him with a warm hug as always, then sit back down.

"You sounded worried over the phone, everything okay?" he asks, settling into his chair.

"Listen, I'll get straight to the point. Someone broke into the gallery Friday night and stole our main-themed piece. I'm in desperate need of a replacement, and we're also missing another statement piece. We can't wait until the auction. I need to speak to someone like... yesterday," I stress.

"Someone stole from The Institute?" He tilts his head in confusion.

I sigh, contemplating my next step.

Might as well get this over with.

"No. They stole from The Romano Gallery."

He frowns. "*And*? Why do you care what happens to that gallery?"

"I work for The Romano gallery now." I bite my lip.

"What!?" he whisper-shouts.

"The offer was great, and honestly—"

He smacks the table, startling me. "Of course it was fucking great. Damian will trick anyone into anything. I can't believe you let him buy you like that!"

I tilt my head, gaping at him.

Buy me? Who the hell does he think he is?

I grit my teeth. "First of all, I did *not* let him buy me. Or have you forgotten the name I've made for myself?"

He huffs. "Yeah, thanks to me!" he shouts, his face draining of color as he comes to the realization of the stupidity that came out of his mouth.

I shake my head in disbelief as I get up and grab my purse. "Wow, Alex. That was low, even for you."

As I'm walking away, he gets up and grabs me by the forearm and drops my purse in the process, all my stuff scattering all over the place.

I groan in frustration as I scrunch down, picking up my things. He leans down and helps me, putting my things back in my purse as he hands it back.

"Ari, I'm sorry. I wasn't thinking. You caught me off guard."

I stand with a huff and push his chest with one finger. "No, go ahead. Tell me how you really feel. Seriously, Alex,

I'm grateful for everything you've done for me, but all you did was teach me the ropes. *I did the rest.*"

"I know. I'm sorry," he pleads. "Please, let me make it up to you. You know I would do anything for you."

I know he would, which is why what he said hurts even more. I'm not stupid. I know Alex has had a crush on me for years, which is ridiculous considering he literally slept with my best friend, but who am I to judge? It doesn't change anything, because I've never seen him as more than a friend. A really good friend. The comment stings, because what if he's right? What if the only reason I became such a famous curator is all because of him?

The logical part of me tells me the idea is ridiculous. I was the one who found my own internships and connected with the right people. Not only that, but Damian fucking Romano hired *me*. The pickiest man alive was so impressed with my work he decided to take a chance on *me*. But then, there's that insecure little twelve-year-old girl that has doubted every step I've taken. Every choice I've made tells me that; yeah, he's probably right. And it fucking hurts. My heart squeezes knowing that for better or for worse, my mother will always be right. The insecurities will cripple me when I least expect them and burst wide open.

I let out a defeating sigh. "Forget it, Alex." Storming out of the restaurant, I'm fuming. My stomach is churning from hunger pains, and my mind's going a millions miles per hour. How fucking dare he? I'm insecure as it is when it comes to accepting any type of help and the one time I do, it bites me in the ass years later. That's just my luck, I guess.

I arrive at the gallery and make my way upstairs, and enter Damian's office without knocking. He's sitting at his desk, with his arms crossed on top of it as he rests his head.

Of course, he rather sleep in his office chair than to listen to me. It's like talking to a wall sometimes.

I let out a small fake cough and he startles, then looks up and rasps, "Hey."

"Hey," I say softly. "I thought I told you to go home."

He laughs as he scrubs his eyes. "Good thing I'm the boss and I don't have to listen to you." His voice is gruff with sleep, it makes my pulse spike.

I roll my eyes. "I came in to tell you that I—" My phone pings.

I look at it and it's an email from Alex.

Fucking great. Wonder what the hell he wants now.

From: Alex Brown

To: Aria Petrov

Subject: Rome Meeting Details

I was able to get in contact with one of my contacts from Rome, and they agreed to meet with you. Only catch is, both you and Damian Romano have to be at the meeting. Two days from today. I know it's last minute, but take this opportunity. I know they only said yes because it's Damian.

I'm sorry for what happened. I hope this can make up for it. If you need anything else, let me know.

—Alex

I smile faintly. He's trying to get in my good graces after his big fuckup. It's going to take more than that to make me feel better, and even though that insecure part of me screams to not take this opportunity, I still do. Because this job is too important to let my insecurities filter through.

"Aria?" Damian says, pulling me out of my trance.

"I figured out our issue. A curator from Rome can meet us in two days. We will have to leave tonight to hopefully make it in time and actually be rested for the meeting."

He stands, grabs his phone, and starts texting. "Got it. I can have the jet ready in a few hours. Be ready at seven. I'll pick you up."

I bite my lip nervously as I nod.

A two-day trip with my boss, what can *possibly* go wrong?

Damian

I pick up Aria at seven o'clock sharp, just as promised. I'm still exhausted from the past three sleepless days, so I decide to have my personal driver take us to the airport.

It's only Monday, and this week has already been shaping up to be the shittiest week. I still can't believe someone stole from under my nose. All I know is that whoever did this is going to pay for it painfully. I will fucking make sure of it.

On top of it, I haven't stopped thinking about my *almost* kiss with Aria. Which is funny considering all I did was work nonstop all weekend, and somehow, I still found the time to think about her. And now, the *cherry on top*—a two-day trip with her. I'm equally parts concerned and excited to be alone with Aria. I've been wanting to get alone time to sort through these annoying feelings I can't seem to place. I'm an art enthusiast; of course. So I'll treat this situation the same way I study a piece of art. Scrutinize it. Understand it. Find the meaning behind it. Find out why this woman, with her fiery personality and all, has filtered her way through my thoughts; becoming the center of my attention. I want to understand why I can't seem to stay the fuck away from my employee.

It irritates me to no end; the inability to keep my emotions in check around her. My mind just takes all rational decisions out of the picture and makes my heart take over.

Fuck. This is going to be a long trip.

But it's okay. I just have to remind myself this is just another challenge I need to conquer. And *I love challenges.* And the last think I'll do is let emotions get in the way.

Yet, that's all you've been doing.

I can and will control myself.

Can you really, though?

The car ride has been silent, and tension has been building up between us since this morning when she walked in through all the chaos. It's not that I don't trust her. I do—really—I trust her more than I do most people, but there wasn't any point of ruining her weekend. There wasn't anything she could have done to get the painting back.

She did make this meeting possible, though.

Honestly, I've been kicking my ass for not calling her. She... well; I've come to learn she wears her emotions on her sleeves. She was clearly hurt that I didn't ask for her help, and the knowledge makes me feel like shit.

Ha. Hilarious. Here I thought you weren't capable of emotions.

The ruthless businessman isn't. But this man she brings out of me like it's her calling? This one does. The emotions I've kept buried over the years just slips and pulls my mask away. Doesn't matter how hard I try to hold on, they just... fight back. For her. For what it could be.

I welcome the silence between us, because what I've

been doing this whole time is stealing glances here and there, admiring her from afar. She's wearing a basic hoodie, leggings, and white sneakers. Knowing this girl, she always opts for comfort. Her face has no makeup, making her natural gold freckles shine on their own. There's something about her natural looks that makes her more attractive, more... *her.*

I wonder how her skin would feel beneath my touch, how it would feel to explore every inch of her, or how her pouty red lips would feel on mine. The power she holds over me is maddening, and she doesn't even know it.

"I can't believe you're wearing a whole suit for a red-eye flight," she remarks, pulling me from my thoughts.

I smirk. "I'm Damian Romano. I have to be ready at all times."

She rolls her eyes, making me relish in the familiar push and pull of our dynamic that leaves me feeling a slight thrill and frustration.

Heading to Italy makes me nervous. When my father passed away and I inherited the business, my mother decided to stay permanently in Italy by herself, wanting to be close to what my dad loved. Though Italian by birth, I was raised in Chicago, where my father pursued his version of the American dream.

My conversations with my mother are frequent, and I support her financially out of gratitude for how she raised me. But every time I see her in person, she loves bringing up my father. She has always had a guilty conscience over my strained relationship with him, even though there's literally nothing she could have done. It wasn't her fault. My father was an asshole, and I always got the short end of the stick. It's as simple as that.

Snapping back to reality, I ask, "When's the meeting?"

"In two days," she mutters while deep in thought, looking at her phone and typing.

I snap my fingers in front of her face, drawing her gaze to mine. "What are you doing that's so important?"

She looks at me with a hint of irritation that always seems to appear when she's upset with me.

My favorite kind of look.

"I'm writing some notes for the meeting. This has to go well. We have no other option."

"Forget about that," I counter. "We can work on it tomorrow over lunch. You work too much," I say as an excuse, when in reality, all I want is her attention.

She raises an eyebrow. "Look who's talking, the guy wearing a suit because he 'has to be always ready'"

I laugh, running my tongue over my teeth, trying to contain a witty comeback. The bickering between us is a game that only fuels the intensity of my attraction toward her. Call me a masochist if you will, but I fucking love how she challenges me. I can't deny I would love nothing but to shut her mouth with my cock, or have her scream my name as I fuck her into oblivion.

So much for controlling yourself, Damian. Fucking seriously. Where the fuck did that thought come from?

We arrive at the airport, and my team swiftly grants her clearance as we make our way to my jet.

She glances around, visibly impressed. "Nice jet, *boss*," she playfully taunts.

I chuckle, shaking my head but choosing not to respond. It took me five years to invest in my own private plane. Even though I make billions of dollars a year with the various companies I own and invest in, it's hard to spend money. Sometimes it feels as if I don't deserve it, even though I worked my fucking ass to get to where I am. Deep down, in the back of my head, I'm still like that worthless little boy my father despised so much. The one that's too compassionate to make it into the real world.

She walks around, surveying the spacious interior of the jet before settling on a corner to claim as her own.

"Not there, that's my seat," I state firmly.

She shoots me a look, a mix of challenge and incredulity in her hazel eyes.

I raise an eyebrow, my amusement at her audacity growing. I let out a fake cough and casually slip one hand into my pants pocket, a sly smile playing on my lips. I meet her gaze with an air of seriousness that only heightens the tension between us, and she continues to hold my gaze, her defiance clear. As always, she decides to take the high road, because this is what we do and sits on the plush leather with a smug smile on her face.

With calculated intent, I slowly approach her, taking my time to place my bag neatly under one of the seats. Then, in one swift motion, I place my hands on her hips and I lift her as if she weighs no more than a feather.

She gasps. "Damian, put me down right now! Are you insane!?"

I scrunch down to place her in the seat next to mine. My eyes find hers, and she looks away as her cheeks redden, making her freckles pop. There is little to no space between us, and as she's getting herself comfortable in the seat, her gaze meets mine as she licks her bottom lip. My eyes involuntarily travel to them, and I lick my own without thinking. Her fucking lips are calling my name, begging for me to take them, and I have little resolve left in me to keep my distance. My eyes travel farther down, noticing her chest rising and falling, her breathing becoming choppier. She wants me to kiss her. I know it. The air crackles with that familiar electric intensity. If I move just a few more inches closer, I could close the gap between us and grab her by the nape of her neck and give myself a delicious taste.

Somehow, I manage to snap back to reality, and I stand abruptly. She looks the other way without a word, admiring everything about the space, refusing to look back at me. Taking a seat next to her and pulling out my phone, I start typing away emails.

She grabs her bag and goes to stand, but I grab her arm and stop her. "What are you doing?"

She looks back at me confused. "I'm moving to another seat so I can be out of your space."

I shake my head and pat the seat next to mine. "Sit. I just wanted my regular seat, that's all."

I'm particular about these things. I always sit in the same seat. It's the little things I'm always a control freak about. It's a hard habit to break.

Her eyes flicker with that fiery resolve I love. "No, thank you. There's enough space for me to sit somewhere else."

"Do you want me to grab you like a sack of potatoes and drop you on this seat? Was once not enough?"

Her back stiffens. "You wouldn't dare."

Raising an eyebrow, I go to stand but she quickly places a hand on my shoulder to stop me, then sits down next to me with a huff. "I can't believe you were going to do it again."

"I'll never reject a dare."

"Yes, I can see that now."

I smirk and get back to my phone. The tension in the cabin is palpable, and I savor the electrifying atmosphere between us, knowing this trip to Italy is going to be *anything* but ordinary.

13

Aria

After the longest ten hours of my life, we're finally in Rome. I mostly slept on the plane because I was so exhausted and the last thing I wanted to do was to deal with Damian's shenanigans. When Damian woke me up, my head was resting on his shoulder, and boy did that made me wake up in a flash and take some very much-needed distance from him.

I've been to Rome a few times, and I love it here. The city is rich in its architecture, history, and culture. I still remember the first time I came here, because it instantly felt like home. This place brings the inspiration I crave and my fingers already itch to paint even though I'm exhausted.

The flight was interesting, to say the least. Damian's presence is so damn consuming, it gives me little to no space to breathe. That's just him, though. He could bring every-one's attention by simply existing. It's like his aura commands it, and people are more than happy to oblige.

My skin burns, still remembering his fingertips on my hips when he effortlessly lifted me from his seat. The sensa-tion still lingers, unwilling to let go. My breath hitches at the reminder of that quick passing moment, which, call me crazy, but I'm so fucking sure he was about to kiss me. The worst part is, I would've let him own me at that moment. Let his lips devour mine and finally give into the temptation, and let his hands roam every inch of my body, leaving a trace of that addicting burning sensation on every place he touches.

Great, now I'm flustered.

Arriving at the hotel, all I want is a cold shower and a comfortable bed. The jet lag is hitting me hard right now, and more than anything, I need some solitary time.

Approaching the front desk, there's a tall, blonde woman ogling Damian up and down. Pushing her cleavage together as she offers him the most flirtatious smile.

"Hello, Mr. Romano," she purrs, her tone flirtatious. "I hope your flight went well. The rooms are ready," she says as she hands him the keys.

The way she ogles him makes me feel queasy, and an unexpected pang of jealousy.

He remains unfazed at the obvious intentions of the blonde with—what I'm sure are—fake tits.

A ping of insecurity hits me unexpectedly as I look down. Mine are, well, extremely small in comparison to hers. My mother always made fun of the way they looked, always said I needed to eat more protein if I wanted them to grow. Who even came up with that myth?

The woman clears her throat, but he remains engrossed in his phone, not even sparing her a glance. A laugh escapes me at his indifference, a reaction that doesn't escape her notice. She turns her attention to me, scanning my basic, travel-worn attire. I knew the flight would be long and comfort will always be the priority. I wished I would have worn something nicer, though, because my insecurities are filtering through as every second passes.

With a fake smile, she shoots back, "If you're looking to book a room, we're booked months in advance, and we're probably out of your budget anyway."

This fucking bitch.

I lock eyes with her and let out a disbelieving laugh. Before I can respond, Damian intervenes.

He looks up from his phone, his voice firm. "She's with me."

The woman blushes and mumbles an apology. Damian doesn't address her as she's apologizing, instead, he signals for one of the bellhops, who promptly arrives to take our bags.

As we're following the bellhops to our rooms, he turns around unexpectedly and tells the woman, "Oh, and by the way, you're fired."

What the fuck? I shoot him a confused look. Why is he firing someone? Seriously, who even gave him that authority?

Her demeanor changes, and she simply nods and scurries away.

"Why did you just fire a woman at a random hotel?"

"That's a stupid question. You're smarter than that," he snaps.

His tone makes me take a step back for a moment. This is just like Friday night all over again. We have a moment and he completely shuts down and acts cold; distant and like a total asshole.

I frown at his comment, though, trying to put the pieces together. Then, it hits me.

"Wait. *You* own this hotel? How many businesses do you own?"

"Too many to count," he drawls.

His confession takes me by surprise. Sure, I know he's a self-made billionaire, who worked his way up to the empire he has today. Known for always putting his work first, never seen with a woman, even though they all fall head over heels for him. Also well-known in the artistry world. From the research I did, Damian is known for owning multiple businesses, but his niche has always been art. So that's what I focused on, getting to know Damian Romano the gallery owner and art enthusiast, not the billionaire. I should've probably done more research on what he does, but it never seemed relevant. I was never interested to know how he got his success, I just wanted to know if the rumors in the art industry were true. And so far, people have exaggerated. He's not ruthless, not in my eyes. He's just really passionate about what he does. He demands perfection, as every other respectable and successful person in the art industry would do. I don't think I'll ever understand the vendetta people have against him. He could be less of an asshole, sure, but I guess you don't get to the top by being nice.

As the bellhop leads us to our rooms, I'm counting the minutes to get away from him. Being in close proximity with him brings up stupid ideas and emotions I rather not entertain.

Arriving at the suite, that sweet idea of being alone goes smoking up in the air in an instant. The suite is nothing short of luxurious, but instead of separate rooms, it consists of two elegantly appointed bedrooms, a spacious living room, a fully equipped kitchen, and a breathtaking view of Rome's architectural richness.

A lump forms at the pit of my stomach as I take in the place. The suite is big, and both rooms are on opposite sides, but the shared living area is sure to make our interactions inevitable.

Nervous energy floods through my body.

This is not what I had in mind *at all*. Will I be able to maintain my distance from him for the duration of the trip? How can I when we're practically roommates? Will I be able to resist the magnetic pull that seems to draw us closer every time we're near each other? This is a stupid idea, which surprises me because he's a calculated man, and this is a *huge* miscalculation.

He's playing with me. That's gotta be it. This is what he does—haunts me; throws little nibbles here and there to see how I'm going to react. He loves getting under my skin and thinks I don't notice.

I notice everything.

"Why can't I have a room on another floor or something?" I ask nonchalantly. "I thought we were going to have separate rooms."

He stares at me, his expression enigmatic. It infuriates me, the way he can conceal his emotions and his thoughts. It's like staring at a blank canvas, not one single idea in sight. I imagine this is how he's able to be so successful. His enemies aren't able to read one single thought that goes through this man's head. But I know better than that now, this is how he protects himself. How he stays in a safe bubble, keeping people at arm's length.

"The woman at the front desk was right. We were sold out months in advance. However, this suite is always available for me when I travel here."

There goes my fucking plan to keep my distance from him for the remainder of the trip. I just need to pull my shit together and get through it. No big deal. How difficult can it be?

Might as well wave goodbye to my sanity and self-control.

14

Damian

I have a confession: I may or may not have arranged for us to share a suite together. I could have easily made separate rooms happen. While I want to keep my distance from her, because of my irrational decision making and all, I still went ahead and did the exact opposite.

I shouldn't be surprised by now that I made yet another idiotic decision—but yet, here we are. Questioning my every step.

In my sick mind, I figured if we share a suite, she won't get any bright ideas to bring anyone here. Even though I know this trip is strictly business, the possibility drives me insane, and I prefer to live in fucking peace. I'm not above scaring any potential dates she brings here, even though the logical part of me knows she won't. Though, nothing is stopping her from going someplace else, but she wouldn't be that unsafe... or so I'm hoping. I'm going to assume the best because I can't afford to think otherwise. The last thing I want to do is make any other rash decisions.

This is fucking ridiculous. I barely recognize myself anymore. Business is my thing; never allowing personal matters to interfere. With her though, it's as if my carefully constructed walls are starting to crumble. I want her close, near enough to sense her presence, but far enough to maintain the illusion of professionalism. That sounds so goddamn backwards, but I have *zero* fucks left to give.

I'm officially losing my mind.

After we arrived at the suite, I didn't see much of her for the rest of the day. She's avoiding me, and I can't lie, it stings a little. For the better part of the day, I'm engrossed in work, catching up on emails and rescheduling in-person meetings that were disrupted by this trip. I even reached out to my mother to arrange dinner. Anything to keep my time occupied and away from Aria, because two can play at this game. If she's avoiding me, that's fine by me. It's not like I was expecting a magical time or anything.

Why does it bother me so much that she's fucking avoiding me?

As it nears seven o'clock, my stomach grumbles, and I realize I haven't eaten since we boarded the plane. My usual sense of organization has been shaken by her presence, leaving me scattered. Leaving the confines of my room to grab something quick to eat, my phone demands my attention as always, so I'm absorbed in it as I enter the kitchen area. It isn't until I glance up that I see Aria standing in front of the open fridge, lost in thought. She has her hair pulled up into a messy bun, and an oversized sweatshirt that sparks a tinge of jealousy in me; clearly, it's men's clothing—from an ex, probably. The thought of that pisses me the fuck off. Even knowing that, she manages to look beautiful. The kind of beauty that stings. I make a mental note to make that sweatshirt disappear and hopefully replace it with one of my own, because I rather she looked beautiful in *my* clothes.

Yes, Damian, because that's extremely appropriate to do. Normal boss and employee relationship.

Maybe if I say it enough times, I can convince myself it's okay and perfectly normal.

"Hey," I rasp.

She jumps at the sound of my voice. "Jesus, you scared me," she says with a nervous chuckle, her voice soft. "I'm starving but don't know what I'm in the mood for. I was thinking cereal, or maybe a—"

"Aria," I interrupt.

"Yes?"

I bite the inside of my cheek, trying to hide my laugh. "You're rambling, Darling."

"Sorry. I tend to ramble when I'm exhausted," she confesses, amusement dancing in her eyes. "I'll get out of your way." She turns to walk away, heading for her room.

We've barely seen each other since we arrived this morning, and while I know spending time with her; talking with her; and being in close quarters is a stupid idea, it doesn't mean I want it any less. She brings this sort of relaxation when I'm near her, like I don't have to be Damian the businessman around her. I can just be me. The thought should be jarring—and in a way, it still is—but I *could* indulge in it once in a while.

"I'm hungry too," I say. "I'll make us something."

She looks at me like I've grown three more heads. "No, that's okay. I can eat tomorrow. I'm beat anyway."

"Aria..." I hesitate for a moment before I decide to be more assertive. "Sit. *Now.*"

With a dramatic roll of her eyes, she lets out a sigh but obediently takes a seat at the kitchen island.

Good girl.

I meet her gaze briefly before turning my back to start on the food. She remains quiet, the air charged with that same familiar tension that hangs between us whenever we're close. We remain quiet for the most part, both of us probably a little too exhausted to keep up with the banter.

As I'm finishing the plating, Aria walks up to the fridge and takes two bottles of water, then sits back down as I place one of the finished plates in front of her.

"A grilled cheese and tomato soup?" she arches a brow. "Consider me impressed."

I nod and take a bite myself, savoring the simple, yet delicious, flavor. "I love grilled cheese," I admit before taking a sip of water.

She picks up the grilled cheese and dips it in the soup, and with an appreciative groan, she takes a generous bite. "Not sure why, but this is the best grilled cheese and tomato soup I've eaten." She closes her eyes, savoring the taste.

Bowing sarcastically, I say, "You're welcome."

There's something about her that I admire. She has a way of making the simplest things appear like a ray of sunshine. Who knew someone could look so beautiful eating something so simple? I'm engrossed in her beauty, the way her eyes roll every time she takes a bite and the way her lips hover over the spoon.

Fucking beautiful.

My eyes linger to the point that she notices.

She wipes her mouth with her thumb. "Do I have something on my face?"

She doesn't, but I nod anyway as I get close to her and run my thumb across her perfect lips, and a zip of electricity runs from my thumb to my cock. I shake my head and scoot backward, feeling startled by the spark. Her back stiffens, and her cheeks change to a light scarlet color, leaving a trace of red that emphasizes her beautiful freckles.

After our meal, she loads the dishwasher as I focus on cleaning the rest of the kitchen. Once she's finished, she starts the dishwasher and perches herself on the kitchen counter, swinging her legs back and forth. "Who knew you were such a good cook?" she teases.

I stand in front of her, rolling my eyes playfully. "You're hilarious. It was just grilled cheese and canned soup," I reply, my tone dry.

She chuckles. "I can barely make eggs."

"I can teach you." My words come out before I have a moment to think.

Why am I looking for more ways to spend time with her? Seriously, *what is wrong with me?*

She perks up. "Really? You have time?"

Her eyes gleam with excitement, and that simple look tugs at my heart; grabbing hard and refusing to let go. How could I say no to her? She has no idea I'd do anything to see that smile more often.

I pick up a hand towel and dry my hands as I shrug. "Anything for you, Darling."

She blushes and mumbles something along the lines of *God* and *killing me*.

"Thank you for offering. I'll take you up on it. Also, thanks for the food. It was really, *really* good."

"So you said after groaning with pleasure," I say with a laugh.

"What can I say? I'm a sucker for good bread and cheese."

As we chat and laugh, our proximity changes. She's given me space to get closer, and I've moved into her space without even realizing it. The shift is gradual, but when we finally become aware of how close we are, a charged silence falls between us. I look down and I notice how her thighs are slightly open, giving me the space to get in between her legs, which apparently my subconscious took the offer of.

Closing my eyes, I exhale to calm my breathing. A beat passes and I open my eyes, my gaze locking between her legs—*again*—and noticing her lacy underwear.

Her deep, red, lacy underwear.

God fucking dammit, I curse internally.

My cock seems to like the sight of the flimsy lace, because it automatically comes to life at the most untimely moment. Our eyes lock, and I don't miss the way her chest heaves, or the glassy look in her irises that are showing the temptation and the wanting. The attraction we feel is undeniable, and it's eating me alive like fire under my skin. It's impossible to extinguish. Every nerve in my body tingles with a rapid growing need that's quickly leaving my rational mind out of the equation. I want—need—to kiss the fuck out of her. I want to crash our lips to the point of no return. I want to drown myself in her pouty lips, her soft skin, her curves. *Fuck*, this is painful.

"Aria," I murmur, my hand reaching the back of her neck and closing in the little gap that's left between us. My gaze drops to her parted lips, and I hover my own over them. The feel of them makes me swallow back a groan. I'm holding by the smallest fucking thread right now, holding on for dear life to not do what my body is screaming at me, begging for me to do. "Please, tell me to stop." My voice is laced with desperation, because I can't hold on any longer. She's the one who has to put a stop to this. I'm... I'm just not strong enough anymore.

Her delicate fingers thread through my hair. "Don't you dare stop," she breathlessly replies.

My control snaps at the sound of her sweet, needy voice. As our lips are about to fully—*finally*—meet, the hum from the loading dishwasher snaps me back to the crashing reality, shattering the moment. She startles and pushes me away as she hops off the counter.

"Uhm, well…" she begins, attempting to regain her composure. "I'm exhausted, so I'm going to bed. We have so much to do tomorrow, and we should probably catch some sleep, and—" She pauses and meets my eyes with a flustered look, realizing she's rambling again.

Trying to gain my composure, I ask, "Tomorrow, work lunch to go over the meeting notes?"

She nods quickly without another word, then walks to her room and closes the door and locks her door with the softest *click*.

The lock of her door mocks me for royally fucking up, once again. And just like that, the intensity of the moment dissipates, leaving me standing alone in the kitchen with the need to go after her. But I know better—that is the last thing I should do. Even if all the bones of my body scream at me to go after her, I won't.

I can't.

I wake up exhausted in a tangle of sheets and thoughts. I barely slept last night, my mind replaying over and over again another almost kiss between us.

The reality of the situation is that I'm here with him for business. *Strictly* business. I remind myself of that as I sit up in bed and push my hair away from my face, letting out a frustrated groan.

I force myself out of bed and head to the bathroom to freshen up and start getting ready for my lunch meeting with Damian. The last thing I want to do is see him, because if memory serves right, the man shuts down every time we have a moment. These games are getting old really fucking fast, and I don't think I can handle another cold version of him. Fuck this. And fuck him for shutting down every time, too.

Yeah, like you're any better.

Well, at least I'm not an asshole about it.

As I'm getting dressed and reviewing my notes, I can't shake the restlessness that has settled within me.

I need to get laid.

That's it. I need a distraction to keep my mind off Damian and the stupid games we've been playing. He's had more than enough opportunities to make a move, but if there's one thing I know about him, he's a calculated man, and whatever this is between us, it's the opposite of that.

I've been single for a while, and maybe it's time to indulge in a one-night stand. It's not something I've done often, but maybe it's exactly what I need to forget him. With that decision in mind, I reopen the dating app on my phone and begin browsing through potential matches.

Is this really the best way to forget about him? About the attraction I feel for my boss? There's only one way to find out, I suppose.

After spending time swiping left and right, I'm able to match with a guy who is also in the city for a work trip. After talking for an hour or two, we set up a dinner date later today.

Perfect. My plan is already working.

As the clock ticks toward 11:00 AM, I can't escape the looming dread of our lunch meeting. I know I have to face Damian, and my nerves are working overtime. I slip into a sleek turtleneck long-sleeve shirt, paired with high-waisted pants cinched at the waist by a thick, shiny black belt. It's a bit chilly today, so I opt for an oversized blazer to keep me warm and complete the ensemble with my usual black Louboutin heels.

Arriving at the hotel's restaurant to meet Damian as we had planned, I scan the room, quickly spotting him. He looks striking in his simple, yet well-put-together, outfit. He's wearing a knitted black tee, and a gold necklace hangs against his chest. His light beige pants hug his perfectly toned legs, and a gold watch adorns his wrist, pairing extremely well with his deep olive skin.

My stupid heart skips a beat at the sight of him. He looks really good—*too* good.

Approaching the table, our eyes meet and a flush of embarrassment reaches my cheeks. I've been admiring him for longer than I intended. Still, I'm determined to maintain my composure.

Taking my seat, I offer a simple apology, "Sorry I'm late."

"You're ten minutes late, and I have places to be," he snaps.

The man who was so close to kissing me in the kitchen seems so distant now, and whilst it's fucking disappointing, I'm not surprised by his attitude at all. This is what he does. He shuts down completely, and builds his walls right back up. We take one step forward, then two steps back. The dance is getting tiresome and annoying. I honestly thought we were past this, but I should've known better than to think this was going to be easy.

Before I can reply with what is sure to be a sarcastic response, a man approaches us with a confident stride, his presence commanding attention. He extends his hand toward Damian, greeting him with a hearty handshake and a friendly smile. "Hey, didn't know you were coming. I would've set up a meeting if I knew."

Damian returns the handshake, offering a nod of acknowledgment. "Last-minute work trip, you know how it is."

He's the same guy who was in Damian's office the other day. The one that Damian shares some physical similarities with. The only difference between them is his deeper tan and whiskey eyes.

"And who do we have here?" His gaze shifts to me as he raises a curious eyebrow.

Damian introduces me with a casual tone, "This is Aria

Petrov, the curator of the gallery. Aria, meet Lorenzo Mancini, my cousin."

I extend my hand, meeting Lorenzo's firm grip with my own. As we exchange pleasantries, a thought occurs to me as I glance at the restaurant's name. "Do you own Lorenzo's in Chicago?" I ask curiously.

Lorenzo's nod is accompanied by a charming smile. "I own a couple around the world. And please, call me Enzo," he says with a friendly wink.

Out of the corner of my eye, I notice a subtle change in Damian's demeanor. His shoulders tense slightly, his expression growing unreadable. Without missing a beat, Lorenzo observes Damian's reaction, his smirk hinting at an unspoken understanding as he excuses himself.

"I'll leave you two to it. Enjoy your meal. It was nice to meet you, love," he says, offering a knowing nod before walking away.

The meeting is long and fucking dreadful. Damian's critiques are harsher than usual, picking apart my ideas and pointing out flaws I hadn't anticipated. It feels like he's going out of his way to challenge me.

I bite my lip, trying to contain any witty comebacks and maintain my composure. If he wants to be a dick about it, fine. If this is how he wants to draw the line, that's fine too. I'm not stooping to his level. There's no denying that a lingering sense of unease has settled over our meeting, making it hard to concentrate. It's as if the electrifying chemistry we share is now sparking in a different, more volatile direction. Finally, we manage to wrap up the meeting, and he doesn't waste a moment before rising from his seat.

"We're done here. I have to go," he says curtly, getting up from his chair and walking away.

I quickly stand and grab my purse, following after him, and somehow manage to catch up to him in these uncomfortable heels. "Is this how it's going to be from now on?"

He refuses to look at me, and keeps walking. "I don't know what you're talking about."

"*Ha.* Honestly, Damian, you're a lot of things, but I never thought being a coward was one of them."

He stops dead in his tracks, snapping his cold green eyes to mine. Honestly, out of all the looks he's had, this one is the most intimidating. There's not an ounce of feelings, or spark for that matter, behind them. "Forgive me for trying to keep a professional boundary," he replies coldly.

"We're way past that and you know it," I retort.

He looks sideways and lets out a tired sigh, scrubbing his face with his left hand. "I don't know what you want from me."

My shoulders stiffen at his resigned tone. My heart drops in the pit of my stomach. That's the thing, I don't *know* what I want from him, but it's definitely not this.

Letting out a shaky breath, I whisper, "Nothing. Absolutely nothing," and then walk away from him.

16

Damian

I've spent the whole afternoon holed up in my room, drowning myself in work to occupy my mind and maintain my distance from Aria. Now more than ever, I regret my decision to share a suite with her. It was a stupid idea, and now I'm paying the consequences. Staying away from her seems the safest route for now to keep the tension that has been brewing between us at bay.

My inner self screams at me to let go of the reins, and stop trying to restrain myself. I'm hanging by a thread that's growing more precarious every moment I spend looking at those beautiful eyes, or those plush lips that demand my attention, or every bantering moment that happens between us.

Fuck.

I'm already in an irritable mood as it is as I'm getting ready to have dinner with my mother. I love that woman to death, however, her consistent references to my father have always been a sore point for me. We have a complicated relationship, to say the least, and today I'm in no mood for her to go down memory lane and try to revive those distant and very few good memories we had as a family. It sucked being an only child. It's not like I had any siblings to relate to or play with and overall be a normal child. The closest thing I had was Enzo.

Arriving at the restaurant, I stride to our usual table and find my mother, looking as elegant as ever. When she looks up, her face lights up with joy at the sight of me. Rising from her table, she envelops me in one of her warm hugs.

"È così bello vederti tesoro," *It's so good to see you, honey,* she says, her smile radiant. "Sei molto bello." *You look so handsome.* Her touch is tender as she gently pinches one of my cheeks.

Returning her warm smile, I take my seat and reply, "Grazie, Mamma. Tu sei magnifica come sempre." *Thank you, Mother. You look beautiful as always.*

While my mother speaks English well, she enjoys speaking her native language more often than not, and I always enjoy brushing up on my Italian for good practice. Our waiter arrives and we order our usual wine and appetizers. We talk about my job and her recent travels.

"You're doing wonderful things with the gallery, honey. Your dad would be proud."

I let out an incredulous laugh. "Yeah, right."

Her eyes soften as she grabs my hand and caresses it with her thumb. "I know that your dad was... how do I say this?" she ponders.

"A complete and total asshole?"

She glares at me. "Attento al tuo linguaggio, Damian." *Watch your language.*

I bite the inside of my cheek, doing my best to contain my tongue. I love my mother, and the last thing I want to do is fight with her. It's exhausting having these useless conversations over, and over again. He's not here anymore, so it doesn't matter. The damage has been done, and I have the broken pieces of my heart to prove it.

"He regretted everything, you know. He told me so on his deathbed," she whispers.

I let out an exasperated sigh. "Drop it, *Mamma*."

When my father's health started declining, they moved to Italy, so he could spend the last few months he had left in his homeland; close to everything that he knew well. I was angry and resentful at everything he'd done to me and our relationship was so damaged that I never came to visit. The worst part of it all though—what eats me alive—is I don't regret it one bit. I would never tell my mother, of course, her heart would be broken if she ever found out. Even though, deep down, she knows I gave up caring a very, *very* long time ago.

She finally drops the topic and the atmosphere goes back to being warm and inviting. Everything's going smoothly as we eat and catch up on our lives. My gaze shifts toward the entrance, and time stands still as I watch Aria walk into the restaurant, grasping all of my attention like a shiny, bright diamond. She's wearing a short, emerald green satin dress that emphasizes her beautiful curves. A small heart gold necklace adorns her neck, complementing her soft pale skin. And those heels, the same ones that she had on this afternoon during our meeting. Her hair cascades in shiny waves, her freckles hidden beneath her full face of makeup, and that fucking red lipstick that's been haunting my dreams and thoughts since the day I met her.

My stomach flutters at the sight of her and my heartbeat quickens as I keep admiring her. My gaze drops to her waist, and my stomach flips and threatens to throw back up the few glasses of wine and appetizers I've had as I watch how a preppy-looking guy wraps his hand around her waist, guiding her to a table. I do my best to ignore what they're doing, trying to focus on what my mother is talking about, but my blood is pumping with anger and jealousy knowing she's on a fucking date.

What did I expect? I've had more than enough opportunities to make my move and didn't. These are simply the consequences of my own actions, but fuck, does it bother me.

I can't believe she's on a fucking date.

Gripping the sides of the table, my knuckles turn white as my vision blurs. My mother keeps talking, but the ping in my ears from the anger doesn't allow me to hear one single thing. My mother follows my line of sight to where Aria and her *preppy fucking date* are sitting. What's that about, anyway? Who in their right mind wants a guy that looks like *that*? He looks like his name's Chad. What kind of name is fucking Chad, anyway?

Fuck, I'm angry.

"You know her?"

I hesitate. "Uh, yeah. She's the one I was telling you about. The curator from my gallery."

She hums knowingly. "She's pretty. Like, princess-type of pretty. You have good taste."

I frown. "What's that supposed to mean? She's just my employee."

She scoffs. "You forget I raised you. I know you better than anyone. You like her."

"I do not," I challenge.

Just as I say that, Aria laughs at one of Chad's—yes, his name is Chad in my head now—jokes. Her airy, soft laugh rings through my ears, and the place starts to feel small and hot. What's so funny about his stupid jokes, anyway? He doesn't deserve her laughs. *No one does.* She's too worthy.

My mother glances at me smugly as I take my glass of wine and gulp it in one swing, trying my best to act like nothing bothers me.

It's not my business who she dates. It's not my business who she dates. It's not my business who she dates.

I'm hoping if I repeat it enough times, it will fucking stick.

My mother picks up her purse. "You've already paid the bill and I'm tired, so I'll get out of your hair."

I grunt with a nod, not taking my eyes off Aria and her stupid date.

She grabs my hand and squeezes it. "I'll just say this one thing, honey. If you want the girl, go get her before it's too late. You are kind; selfless; and have the biggest heart I know, and I don't say this because I'm your *Mamma*. Open yourself to love. You deserve it."

I give her a soft nod, trying to take her words in. *I don't know about deserving love. Much less from the kindest and most wonderful woman I've met in my life.*

As my mother leaves, I serve myself one last glass of wine and drink it in one gulp, savoring the burst of dark cherry flavor, hoping the alcohol will settle my nerves.

Why is it so hot in here?

I need to walk out of this restaurant before I do something I regret. As I'm getting up, my legs take on a life of their own and I stride to the bathroom which passes right in front of their table. Doing my best to not stare, I feel her eyes on the back of my neck, burning me. Pacing back and forth in front of the bathroom door, I clench my hair with a fist as I let out an exasperated groan. The jealousy is eating me alive right now. We almost kissed yesterday and today she's on a fucking date? *Unbelievable.*

I pat my chest a few times then make a few circular

motions, trying to ease this achy feeling. But it's not helping. *Nothing* is helping.

Only one thing will.

Making a split-second decision, I make my way to their table before I talk myself out of it. It's time I take the opportunity and make it mine before it's too late.

I *want* her. *Need* her. She has to be *mine*, and *only* mine.

Sitting down next to her, I throw my arm possessively over her shoulder. My gaze falls on the guy, a smug, condescending laugh escaping my lips. He's your typical preppy blond guy who peaked in high school and never moved on from those glory days. It's unbelievable this is who she's having dinner with.

"Thank you for keeping her company while I was at work, Chad."

"What the hell are you doing?" she hisses.

Ignoring her question, I turn my attention to *Chad*, who is still trying to make sense of the situation.

"My name is Hunter, not Chad."

Another laugh escapes me. I don't know which name is worse.

I shrug. "It doesn't really matter what your name is, *Chad*. I hope you've enjoyed your time with my girl," I say, my tone firm and controlled. "But you can leave now."

She stomps on my foot with her heel hard enough that I bite the inside of my cheek to stop myself from wincing.

She grits her teeth and shoots me a withering glare. "We're *not* together. You don't have to listen to him."

The man frowns. "Who the hell are you, man? Leave us alone."

Pft. This man has a death sentence.

With a warning tone in my voice and a death glare, I say,

"You really should go now. We don't want to cause a scene in the middle of this very busy restaurant, do we?"

"Whatever," he murmurs with a roll of his eyes. "This isn't worth it."

As soon as he leaves, she rises from her seat with her purse in hand and marches out of the restaurant with a fury that burns in her eyes.

I let out an exasperated groan and follow after her. "Aria, wait!"

She quickens her pace. How is she walking so fast with those heels? Seriously.

I take three long strides, quickly catching up, given the height difference between us and grip her arm gently. "Aria, I'm trying to talk to you. Look at me."

She turns to me, her eyes aflame with anger. "Damian, what the *fuck* was that? Seriously, why on earth did you do that?" Her voice is sharp as she shouts at me, frustration evident in her every word.

I stand in front of her, letting the sounds of cars honking and walking people around us fill the silence, offering no immediate response. What can I say? That I'm jealous? Damn right I am. The reality of this situation is that I want her to be mine and it's fucking frustrating. There's this constant feeling that's been eating me alive since she walked into my life. A feeling I don't understand. A feeling that refuses to *let. Me. Go.*

She crosses her arms, her frustration growing as every second passes.

My temper flares, and I lean in closer, my voice low and seething. "Watching you with another man drives me insane."

Her back straightens. "You don't get to decide who I see, Damian. That's insane," she replies in a dry tone.

I *know* my actions are insane. But that's the thing, when I'm near her, rationality abandons me, and all that's left is this uncontrollable torrent of emotions.

A humorless laugh escapes me. "I'm well fucking aware of that, but I can't think straight when I'm near you. You invade all of my thoughts every waking moment. Your presence is everywhere. It's *suffocating*." I gulp. There's no turning back now, I'm knee-deep in this already. It's now or never. "I want you, and that's the fucking truth," I whisper.

She takes a step back, her face shocked by my confession. Her anger softens into something else, something more complex. "This isn't how it works. You can't just lay claim to me."

"Funny, because it seems like I just did," I deadpan. I sound like an asshole, but I'm done tiptoeing around the situation. The attraction is there, *both* ways.

She laughs, a sound laced with frustration and disbelief. With exasperation, she raises her hands in the air. "I can't do this with you, Damian. One moment, you're cold and distant. Then, you're close to me, almost kissing me!" She's practically shouting, her chest raising and falling in irritation. "You're infuriating! I don't understand what you want from—"

I don't let her finish the sentence because I know *exactly* what I want. Closing the distance between us, I firmly grasp the nape of her neck, and lock our lips in a fierce, deep-seated kiss. I kiss her like she is my only source of air, and I am running out of time because that's exactly how I feel every time I'm around her.

She's my weakness; my lifeline; my anchor, all in one.

Her initial shock melts away as she responds to my kiss with equal intensity. Our anger, our confusion, and our desires all merge in this passionate livid moment, like liquid fucking fire. The intensity of our connection grows with each passing second. With every kiss; every lick; every ragged breath. Her lips are warm and soft beneath mine, and the taste of her is *intoxicating*. Her sweet, light scent is dizzying and addicting in a way I didn't think possible.

She wraps her arms around my neck, pulling me closer, as though she's just as starved as I am. The world around us fades, and all that matters is the taste of her, the feel of her, the way her touch makes me feel, and the electricity that unravels between us.

My tongue clashes with hers, and I let out an appreciative groan that she swallows with her lips. This feels right. Good. *Meant* to be. *Made* for me. Our kiss is a divine revelation, one I can't get enough of. It's opening my eyes to the possibility of what we can be.

My hands travel from the nape of her neck, tracing her back all the way down to her ass, where I grip and bring her closer to me. There is zero space between us as we keep kissing, licking, and nipping and she's still not close enough. I want more, more, *more*. My lips feel numb, but I refuse to stop, because the sensation is euphoric, too much and not enough, all at once.

17

Aria

The feeling of his lips on top of mine is better than I could have imagined. It's taunting, passionate; *exciting*. His cologne envelops me, with its smoky wood tones, pushing me to the brink of insanity. As my body melts into his, a wave of dread hits me like a cold tide, and I push him away, our ragged breaths filling the charged silence.

What did I just do?

Anxiety takes over me as I start pacing back and forth. He's my boss, and I've grown to like this job. Granted, I've only been working with him for a few months, but I love the work we're doing at the gallery. I love the fact that I have full creative control. Why did I let him kiss me? Better yet... Why did *he* kiss me? He isn't known for relationships, quite the opposite, actually. Gossip columns and the news always speculate when Damian will bring a woman into his life. Why is he doing this? To have a one-night stand?

This is insane. I'm not sleeping with my fucking boss. *I can't.*

Yeah, but that feeling between your legs says otherwise.

Should I just get it over with? A one-time thing to get this growing need out of the way? No. That's totally insane.

Or is it?

Okay, Aria. Pull yourself together. You're spiraling.

Having a breakdown in front of him isn't an option. I'm better than that.

In a rush, I hail a passing cab, its approach signaled by the growing headlights. He looks at me, confusion on his face evident as his eyes flash with concern and *hurt*, and God, that look kills me. I don't want to hurt him, but I can't do this. One of us is going to end up hurt. That's the only possible outcome. Opening the cab's door without a second thought and getting in, I firmly shut the door. He runs to the door and starts pounding the window, calling my name.

I can't do this. I can't even look him in the eyes. I'm so ashamed.

My chest tightens, as a feeling I know all too well floods through me.

The clammy hands. Sweating profusely as I shiver from the cold I know doesn't exist at this moment. Every sound around me is starting to fade, and my breathing is getting shorter by the second.

Yup. I'm having a panic attack.

This is just great. The *last* thing I need.

Getting non-stop panic attacks throughout my whole childhood while my parents fought, or as my mother would tell me everything was my fault is something I can instantly recognize. I hate this crawly feeling around my chest, like a monster trying to take me away.

It's not real, Aria. Snap out of it.

Focusing on what's happening around me helps cease the panic attacks most of the time, so I just need to focus.

Focus. Focus. Focus.

Almost all the noise has faded away, but I can faintly hear Damian's screaming at the cab driver in a foreign language. Italian, maybe?

The door of the car opens and he sits next to me. His hands reach my face, but I can't feel them. I'm too far gone, but at the same time, all too aware of how far gone I am and it's making the anxiety worse.

Desperately scanning my surroundings in the tiny cab, I try to find anything to anchor me. As if guided by some cosmic force, my eyes lock onto him. His mesmerizing shade of emerald green draws me in, offering a moment of relief from the storm that's brewing inside my head. The corners of his eyes deepen with worry and understanding, and somehow, that helps me feel better. *Seen.*

With every intentional breath, I force myself to focus on his eyes, finding tranquility in his gaze.

"You're okay," he whispers, kissing my forehead before placing my head on his chest. "You're okay."

I nod, holding back tears as I come to the realization that Damian's presence has become the anchor I didn't know I needed.

We arrived at the hotel a few hours ago, and without saying a word I walked into my room and crashed. It's three A.M. now, and my stomach grumbles, demanding the food I didn't get to eat. Putting on a pair of cotton shorts and tying the mess of my hair in a bun, I walk out of my room to get something quick to eat and a steaming cup of tea to go back to bed.

I stop dead in my tracks when I find Damian sitting at

the island with a mug in front of him. He's lost in thought, not even acknowledging my presence.

"Trouble sleeping?" I whisper.

He startles slightly, his gaze lifting and meeting mine. "Something like that."

Nodding, I stride to the kitchen and grab a mug and a bag of chamomile tea. His eyes follow my every movement, the intensity of his gaze making my body burn. The kitchen is filled with tension, the sound of me opening the tea bag filling the charged silence.

"There's hot water left in the tea kettle."

I nod. "Thanks."

Walking to the tea kettle, my heartbeat quickens as the tension keeps brewing between us. A knowing silence.

I wonder who will break first.

My hunger is no longer present, so I only pour the hot water into the mug and drizzle in a little raw honey. I love the taste of it, so pure and sweet, but not in a sugary way.

Grabbing the hot mug, I embrace the warm feeling in the palms of my hands as I take a sip and lean against the kitchen counter, staying as far away as possible from him. He's like a magnetic pull. My hand itches to brush his hair in between my fingertips, and caress his strong jawline and his shoulders. After the panic attack, it's probably the last thing I should be focusing on, yet here we are.

The silence is so deafening that I'm at my breaking point. The need to be honest and open up is nagging. He deserves to know it wasn't his fault. Anxiety comes at you at the most unexpected times, when your feelings are in high gear and your body is on high alert.

I sigh, breaking the silence. "What you witnessed was a panic attack."

He looks at me expectantly, and I take that cue to continue, to lay it all out there. Be honest with someone for a change.

"I've gotten them since I was a kid. Well, I got them so often that it was like a normal routine. Now, though, they are few and far between, usually triggered when I'm feeling too much at once."

He nods in understanding, his eyes filling with worry, maybe pity.

"Please don't," my voice trembles, "don't look at me like that." My throat closes up, the words refusing to come out now. That look right here is why I don't open up. I don't need anyone's pity. Anxiety is a very real thing and people need to stop tiptoeing around it.

He stands from his chair, striding toward me until he's right in front of me, hovering with his tall build. "Like what? Like I care? Because I do. I care about you very much."

I look to the side, refusing to meet his warm green gaze. "Like you pity me." My voice is small now, the words barely coming out. My cheeks flush from embarrassment.

I know we have developed some sort of friendship—if you can even call it that— and attraction, but he's also my boss. And I've never been this vulnerable in front of people, not even my best friend.

He grabs my chin and lifts my face, gently forcing me to look at him. His eyes are filled with a sense of understanding; a knowing look.

I, too, understand you.

I, too, am you.

"I do *not* pity you, Darling." He gulps, his eyes pleading. "If anything, I relate to you," he whispers with a hint of hurt and shame.

My heart shatters at his vulnerable tone. My first

thought is, *Who broke you?* My second thought comes right after, one that alarms me and shocks me through my very core.

How can I help? Because I, too, need help. So much help, and I want it to be you.

Only *you.*

Damian

I've been tossing and turning in my bed since last night. Opted for some tea that I thought would help, but after having that conversation with Aria in the kitchen, I was left even more wired and ended up getting no sleep whatsoever.

Seeing this side of her, so vulnerable and hurt, broke something in me. But more than that, it made me relate to her. My brain is working overtime, millions of questions left unanswered.

Who broke her?

How can I help her?

How can I help her if I can't even help myself?

That's the question that has me pondering the most. I've barely managed to pick up my own broken pieces, how can I pick someone else's? The feelings I've developed for her just went to a whole new level, knowing that she needs someone. I want to be that someone and be there for whatever she needs. I want to be the one to make her dark days sunny. How can I, though? When I'm the darkest day of them all.

This territory is unknown to me. All I've focused on is in

my business and building my empire. Going against every memory I have with my father.

You'll never become someone, he'd said. But here I am, a self-made billionaire.

You're too weak. You wear your heart on your sleeve, he'd said. But here I am, with my perfectly crafted mask, showing the world how strong I am.

But it's all a damn lie.

My mask is a lie.

I'm broken; empty; lonely.

To see her like me, it opened up old wounds I've been avoiding. Wounds I didn't—*don't*—want to face.

I haven't even stopped to think about the kiss and what the hell this means for us. What if she regrets kissing me? It's not like we spoke about it. Her panic attack was more than a sign, though. It's clear she's having mixed feelings about it.

Maybe she doesn't regret it after all. Maybe it's all in your head.

I want to talk to her about this. God knows I do, but where do I even begin?

Do I want her to be mine? *Yes.*

Why am I hesitating, though? The reasons I refuse to accept are there, front and center.

Because I'm terrified of being rejected. Terrified I'll hurt her because I don't know how to care about myself. How can I expect to care for someone else?

You already care.

You care more than you allow yourself to admit.

My brain is scrambled, my thoughts all over the place, and I can't pinpoint a plan of action. Which scares the fuck out of me, because I'm a calculated man. Hell, I've calculated every move since I created my empire. In life, if you don't get your shit together, it's going to keep throwing you a million things at once until you drown. And right now, I'm fucking drowning with the uncertainty.

Today's the meeting, so I have no other option but to push every thought away. Otherwise, I'll fuck everything up and the gallery can't afford it.

With everything that has been going on, the break-in is the last thing on my mind, but I know we need to get to the bottom of it, which is why I'm arriving at the restaurant now before the meeting so I can speak with my cousin.

I spot Enzo at the bar with a stack of paperwork. The man is a gambling and partying addict, but he's also a workaholic like me.

"You know you have an office for a reason, right?"

Enzo looks up, offering a mischievous grin. "You know I love being on the floor, making sure the staff is doing okay."

"More like to flirt with your staff. Seriously, Enzo, you're a walking liability."

"You worry about yourself, *cugino*." *Cousin.*

Adjusting my cufflinks, I get right to business. "Did Matteo find out who hacked my security system?"

He sighs before taking a sip of his whiskey. "No, not yet. But he said he's close."

I lean in, my tone sharp and serious. "Tell him if he needs motivation, I don't mind breaking a few of his teeth."

He waves his hand dismissively. "Noted. You're not as scary as you think you are, by the way."

All I do is glare at him. *Dick.*

He looks around, and I see the amusement in his eyes as he asks, "Where's the redhead?"

"Why the fuck do you care?" I've been on edge since yesterday and the last thing I want to do is entertain Enzo. He loves playing games, like a fucking child.

He smirks, knowing he got a rise out of me. "Okay, then. Sore subject, got it," he says as he gets up from his seat. "Consider it dropped, for now." He gives me a pointed look as he picks up his paperwork and walks away.

Great. Looking forward to the million questions he'll throw at me next time I see him.

I'm sitting at the bar with my usual bourbon that I'm convinced I shouldn't be drinking due to my lack of sleep, but it's the only thing that can offer a moment of relief. The hair on the back of my neck rises in response to that knowing strawberry sweet scent I've grown to obsess over. Turning around, my gaze locks with Aria's, but she quickly looks away, her face blushing in a savory pretty scarlet color.

She's so radiant it hurts.

She's wearing a pencil skirt that goes all the way down to her knees, paired with black tights and a white long-sleeve blouse. Her hair is straight, and her face is full of makeup. My eyes drop momentarily to her plump lips, and they look so inviting that all I want to do is grab her by the waist, place her on top of this bar, and kiss her until our lips grow numb.

I grip the empty bourbon glass, my knuckles going white, trying to control my emotions. The bartender places another drink in front of me, which I quickly take and drink it in one gulp, welcoming the burning feeling.

"You're here early," I say nonchalantly, trying my best to keep my composure. Only one person manages to make me nervous, and it's the one standing in front of me with all her curves and bright smile.

"Yeah, I wanted to drink a glass of wine before the meeting to calm my nerves," she says as she takes a seat next to me.

"You really think you should be drinking alcohol after yesterday?"

She crosses her legs, leaning back in her seat. "Please, if anything, alcohol will calm my nerves for this meeting."

With a raised eyebrow, I give her a pointed, knowing look. "Yeah, well. I just want to make sure you're safe."

She examines me with an inquisitive expression, as if she's trying to solve a puzzle. "You're really nice when you want to be, huh?"

Only for you, it's what I want to say.

But I offer a casual shrug instead and reply, "I don't know what you're talking about."

She sets her hand on my arm, giving it a tender squeeze while she whispers, "I'm serious. Thank you for yesterday." She sighs. "I typically go through my... *issues* alone. It was nice to know someone cared for a change."

She lets go of my arm, leaving it with an empty, achy feeling. Her touch felt nice—addicting—and I want more of it. So much more.

Her words are like a splash of cold water, making my body all too aware. Why would she think no one cares about her? Why does that statement bother me so much? I want to unravel all her layers and discover what lies behind those fiery eyes. To find out what—*or who*—broke her.

She drinks her glass of wine as we talk about the meeting and how we're going to counteroffer, depending on the issues we come across. The way she talks about art makes it even more exciting. I always thought we were polar opposites, that the only thing we shared in common was our love for art, but with everything that happened in the last twenty-four hours, there is so much more than I thought. I wonder when she fell in love with it and why. Regardless of how it happened, it brought her to me and I can't help but feel thankful.

The meeting transpired quickly, but not the way we

exactly hoped. They only agreed to sell us one painting, when in reality we need two. We're going to have to go to the New York auction after all, which, to be honest, is a perfect excuse to travel again with her.

She pushes the restaurant door open and sighs in frustration. "I'm sorry. I can't believe my plan didn't work."

"You got us one painting. I'm not too worried. We have the auction coming up soon"

She quickly shakes her head. "I already told you I can't go. I'm planning the gala, remember?"

"We can't have any gala if we don't find the last statement piece, now, can we?" I question.

She looks up at the sky and murmurs something along the lines of *God help* me and *I can't do this again.*

Flashing a grin, I reply playfully, "Aw, come on. Is traveling with me so bad that you can't do this again?"

Tilting her head, she crosses her arms. "Considering what happened yesterday, I don't think it's the best course of action."

My heart skips a beat as the cruel realization sinks in.

So she does regret it after all.

I opt not to say anything, because really, what can I say? I'm sure as fuck not sorry it happened, and I refuse to lie. It fucking stings to know she regrets it, especially because the kiss felt like it was meant to be. I felt like she responded to it, but maybe she just got wrapped in the heat of the moment. Maybe I did, too.

Then, why can't you stop thinking about it?

19

Aria

We're finally back home, and the first thing I did when I landed was call an emergency girls' night with Sophia and Isabella. My girls came through—not that I had any doubt—so now we're at my apartment, wearing some comfortable pajamas as we sip on some mojitos Sophia has been making all night.

I'm feeling the buzz, so I decide to get it over with. "Damian and I kissed," I whisper between their fits of giggles about a horrible date fiasco Sophia had last week.

Isabella shrieks at my confession as Sophia hums proudly, like she almost knew it was going to happen.

"What the hell were you thinking?" Isabella whisper-shouts.

I jump from my seat, ready to defend myself. "He kissed me! I was on a date minding my own business. He interrupted us with this out of nowhere possessive caveman vibe and scared my date off. We got into a fight and as I was in the middle of shouting at him, he… he just grabbed me and kissed *me*!"

Isabella groans in disbelief as I down the rest of my

mojito in one gulp, getting ready for the questions they're going to fire my way.

Sophia straightens in her seat. "Okay, okay. The real question here is, how was the kiss?"

Isabella groans. "Don't answer that."

Sophia hits Isabella's arm with her elbow. "Shut up!"

I sigh as I close my eyes and sit back down, remembering the kiss. That kiss was... desperate, addicting—*euphoric*. And every bit demanding. I can still feel the way his tongue met mine, and the way he nipped my bottom lip with animalistic need. I can still hear the groan that rumbled deep within his chest, like he was relieved. Like he'd been ready and looking forward to it. The reminder still haunts me, sending a shiver down my spine and making my belly tighten with a throbbing need.

"It was good, like... *really* good. But it was a mistake. I know it can't happen again, but I can't lie that I wouldn't be too upset if it were to like... happen... again," I say as I bite my lip because I know what I'm saying sounds crazy.

"Did anything else happen?" Sophia asks, raising her eyebrows.

The better question is what *didn't* happen? Between the panic attack and the brief moment we had in the kitchen, where he, for the first time ever, brought his walls down enough and confessed how he relates to me. I want to keep that moment close to my chest, so I'm not even going to mention it.

I shake my head. "Just a kiss. I stopped it, freaked out, and left." Technically, not a lie. I *was* trying to leave.

"You should bone him." Sophia shrugs.

"Absolutely not," me and Isabella say at the same time.

Isabella grabs my hand and squeezes it. "It's up to you,

honestly. I just... I know him. He's a complicated man to say the least. I don't want you to get hurt."

"I mean, as long as you and Damian are clear on what you guys want, it can be a purely physical relationship. No harm, no foul," Sophia points out.

True. What's the harm?

Your heart is in harm's way. You know you can't handle this.

I am so tired of overthinking though. For once, I want to jump into the unknown and see where it takes me.

I love Sundays. Well, most of the time. Except when Sophia cancels our brunch because of work. She said she was still working on the article about the Rome heist, trying to contact the lead investigator on the case. The hype around this heist has yet to die down, with people wondering who was crazy enough to steal such an important piece. If they catch whoever did it, they are in for some *serious* trouble.

I tried to drag Isabella out, but she was a no-go. Decided to stay in and do whatever the hell she likes to do. That girl is too closed off, you can never get a read on her.

I really like this friendship we've been developing, all three of us. Sophia is the wild one, I'm the calm one, and Isabella is the grumpiest of us all. We make quite a trio.

Since I have no plans whatsoever, I will take advantage of the solitary moment and work on my painting. I've been feeling inspired lately, so it's best I keep going before I get into another rut. I did a quick run to the craft store, getting some necessary things like pencils, painting, notebooks, and a few small canvases. I tend to draw sometimes, but not as often as I paint. There's something so liberating about getting my hands dirty with paint, and the way my body always hums with excitement when I create a new piece.

I enter the lobby of my apartment building and I'm hit with the clean cedarwood scent that has become so familiar and sends a shiver down my spine every time I'm near it. As I look up, I see Damian standing there, in all his six-foot-five glory with a lazy smile and casual T-shirt and—are those *jeans*? The world must be ending. I also notice the grocery bags he's holding, leaving me officially confused.

"Uhm, hi?" I say more as a question than a greeting.

"Hey, Darling," he replies with that melting, beautiful smile of his.

Okay, this is definitely not Damian. We should be bickering by now, like we always do.

"What are you doing here?"

He lifts the grocery bags slightly. "I bought groceries, I'm teaching you how to cook. Remember?"

I nod, vaguely remembering. But I thought that was a joke and by the look of the groceries and the casual wear, I think he meant it.

"Damian, look—"

He interrupts me, "Aria. I'm just here to cook with you, that's all."

Why am I not convinced then? I don't think us spending more time together after what happened is the best idea, especially because we kind of swept it under the rug. We left too much hanging in the air. Is this really what we should be doing?

"I already have plans."

He looks at my bag from the craft store and raises an eyebrow. "Do you paint?"

"No," I lie.

It's not something I like to share with people. Only a few

know, like Sophia, or—regretfully—my mother. It's something personal. And the last thing I would do is tell the grand Damian Romano I paint. That would be ridiculous.

"Hmmm. So what plans do you have?"

I come up blank, so I just blink at him, hoping my brain catches up and comes out with an excuse.

He laughs, shaking his head as he starts walking to the elevators. "That's what I thought."

Shit. I guess we're cooking or whatever.

20

Damian

My fingers itch with the need to touch Aria as we stand next to each other in the elevator. There's only one thought in my head, and it's front and center—I want to kiss her. *Again*. And badly.

Did I use the cooking class as an excuse to spend time with her outside of work? Maybe. I did say I was going to teach her, and I'm a man of my word.

Do I have other motives? I guess I'll find out.

It pissed me off we had a *one* five second conversation at Lorenzo's and moved on like nothing happened. Because something *did* happen. We both felt it. I'm not being delusional.

I'm a man of actions, not words. So I'll have to show her that I'm here for her; even if the uncertainty is eating me alive. At the end of the day, the need to care for her and be with her outweighs everything else.

As we walk into her apartment, she runs to one of her rooms, which I take as an opportunity to look around. This is exactly how I expected her apartment to look. Full of colors and paintings hanging all around, which makes sense. She's a curator, so I'm sure she loves collecting things for herself. Taking a closer look, a particular painting catches my attention.

This painting shows a woman underwater. You can't really see her face, but you know it's a woman because of her body shape and the fact that she's only wearing under-wear. She's not exactly drowning, but the colors, which are mostly muted tones, express some sort of... overwhelm. Her hands hang like she is letting go and giving up on trying to come out of the water, but she's not scared. She's just... done.

I know the feeling all too well.

It's a beautiful fucking piece, not something I've seen in a while. I look around the painting trying to see the initials, but I don't find any.

Weird.

She walks out of the mysterious room, locks it and we stride into the open kitchen.

"Okay, what did you bring?" she asks.

I place the groceries on her counter, then take the items out of the bag.

She grabs one of the boxes. "Pasta, really? I can make that. Give me more credit than that." She rolls her eyes.

I tsk as I take out the other ingredients. "We're making a vodka sauce from scratch, tastes a million times better, and it's easy to make."

Aria's eyes brim with excitement. "Hell yes, I fucking love vodka sauce. I usually buy canned ones, though. Pretty good."

Oh my. "I miei antenati si saranno rivoltando nelle tombe mentre noi parliamo."

She tilts her head, confused. "I have no idea what you just said."

I let out a soft laugh before translating, "My ancestors are rolling in their graves as we speak."

"Oh, right," she laughs. "Because you're Italian. *Duh*. I knew that."

"Sì." *Yes.*

"Since I know a bit of Spanish, and I think the languages are similar, I'm going to assume you said yes. It's a shame I don't know the language, because I enjoy going to Italy very much."

"Well, yeah. The artistry world in Italy is one of the best, even though people debate whether it's actually the UK."

She shakes her head. "I agree with you. The culture and how preserved things are in Italy is unmatched."

"Yeah, plus, you know, Italians, we're as sexy as they come," I joke with a playful wink.

She picks up the box of pasta and throws it at me as she murmurs something along the lines of *jerk* and *you wish*.

I laugh, gathering all the ingredients and taking out an apron from one of the bags and putting it on.

She starts laughing, or more like wheezing, really. "You brought an *apron?*" She snorts in between giggles, making me laugh now. "Okay, Martha Stewart. I see you."

The joke's on her, because I brought something for her as well. As I take out said item with a grin plastered all over my face, I walk toward her.

She takes a few steps back. "No! I am *not* putting that on."

My shoulders shake as I laugh. "You have to. It's the rules."

"Who says!?" she shrieks.

"I do." I keep laughing as I plaster the chef hat on top of her head.

She takes out her phone to take a look. "I look ridiculous."

I clear my throat as I pick up the pasta box that fell on the floor. "You could never. You look beautiful."

Placing the box on the counter, I steal a glance at her. Her shoulders are stiff and her cheeks are colored with that pretty soft scarlet all over. I swiftly grab her phone and before she has a moment to react I snap a picture of her. She gasps in disbelief as she tries to reach for it, but I am way taller than her, so it's easy to keep it out of her reach. I send the picture to myself for keepsake, then give her the phone back.

"You better delete that picture!" she demands, pointing one finger at me.

"*Nope.* Now, enough complaining, let's cook," I say as I pat her chef hat.

She puffs, but brings out the pots and pans I ask her for, and we get started on the sauce right away. She's a lousy learner, so I'm definitely bringing something more challenging next time just to mess with her.

Next time? Not sure what is wrong with me, but spending time with her outside of work is turning out to be nice and a change of pace. A smile escapes me as she drops some tomato paste in the pan and watches it like a hawk, so it turns out the right color as I instructed when I made the sauce on my own so she could take her own notes and ask any questions. It's her turn this time around, and she keeps insisting that she can do it without any guidance. She scrunches her nose in a cute way every time she's confused, then shrugs and continues to dump the ingredients.

"Pretty sure that was a little too much salt," I point out.

"I like salty things."

I laugh. "You can never accept when you're wrong, can you?"

She flips me off as she keeps throwing the ingredients and scrunching her face. It's fucking hilarious.

My heart quickens at the sight of her, so beautiful and carefree. Dare I say she looks *happy,* and knowing I was able to get a smile out of her and help her have fun makes me really fucking happy, too. I haven't felt this relaxed in, well, ever. This is a moment I want to burn into my memory, preserve it like a precious piece of gold. No amount of money or success can compare to this simple moment.

When we're finally done, we exchange plates as we sit down to eat. By looking at the plate, it looks promising, but I'm ninety-nine percent sure she put in way too much salt, so I'm a little nervous.

She takes a huge bite out of hers and lets out an appreciative groan. "Damn you, Damian Romano. With your good looks and amazing cooking." She closes her eyes as she takes another huge bite.

"Good looks, huh?" I taunt.

She puffs. "Sue me, Romano. You know you're good looking. You're literally cataloged as one of the top bachelors in Chicago."

I thin my lips, trying to not laugh. Only if she knew that even though I'm considered one of the top in the windy city —in both business and looks—I have insecurities that I'm afraid to admit out loud. Being a self-made billionaire is a blessing and a curse, all at the same time. Yes, I'm grateful I was able to make a name for myself and live the life everyone dreams of but very few get. On the other side of the coin, though... it's lonely. You can't tell what's real or fake. Which people genuinely want to get to know me and become a part of my life? And which people are simply following me for the name, fame, and money? I put on this tough exterior because I don't want people to take advantage of me, but also, being an asshole has taken me to new levels. The line has blurred over the years, and I don't know where I stand anymore.

"It's your turn to try. Chop, chop." She claps excitedly.

I shake my head with a laugh as I grab the fork, taking a generous bite. I try to contain my cough as I start chewing. I push through, though, because her eyes are brimming with excitement, waiting to hear my opinion.

Yup. This is way too fucking salty.

But the way she looks at me, grinning ear to ear, her eyes dancing around nervously and moving her hands excitedly, I will eat anything she makes. I'll make anything look fucking edible if it means seeing her this happy.

As I finish chewing and swallowing my food, I drink some water, then say, "Definitely passed. It's good."

"Really?" she asks excitedly as she grabs her own fork. "Let me try!"

Before she can get to my plate, I move it quickly, taking a few huge bites back to back, not letting her.

She gasps. "That's so rude! I wanted to try it!"

Just trying to be a gentleman and protect your health.

I shrug as I take the last bite. I cough, trying not to choke with all the food I have in my mouth.

"Next time," I say with a full mouth, trying not to twitch my eye with how salty it is.

Yeah, next time I have to make sure she doesn't use half the bag of salt. I'll die of hypertension if all her foods are this salty.

At least you'd die as a happy man.

She gets up and hits me in the shoulder as she grabs the plates. I plaster a grin on my face, noticing that she didn't complain about the next time, and fuck if that doesn't give me the tiniest bit of hope. I don't care if I'm reading too much into it. I can work with this.

She walks to the sink and turns on the water, putting gloves on to do the dishes.

I take the gloves from her and put them on. "I'll wash, you dry, okay?"

"Do you even know how to wash dishes?" she jokes, raising an eyebrow.

I flick her forehead softly. "You think you're so funny? Heads up, you're not."

"I'm a hoot, don't you forget it." She flips her hair dramatically.

I shake my head, doing my best to contain my laugh. Our dynamic is, well... weird, but it works. The constant bickering is what we know best, and it's how we get along. But something has shifted between us, and call me crazy, but I can tell she feels it, too. Yeah, we still joke, but it's charged with something different. Lighter. *Flirtier.*

As we work in silence, our hands touch a couple of times as I hand her the new dishes to dry. And even though I have gloves on, it doesn't stop the zing of electricity that runs from the top of my fingers all the way to my toes every time we touch.

And fuck, is it addicting.

"Hey, can I ask you for a favor?" she asks, pulling me out of my thoughts.

"Sure, what's up?"

She fidgets her fingers, trying to come up with the question. "Can you like, not mention anything to Isabella about the panic attack I had during the work trip?"

I look at those beautiful hazel eyes that right now are filled with worry. The sting in my chest hurts at the sight of her. She looks terrified, and I hate that. I want nothing but to make her feel safe around me.

Taking off the gloves and putting them on the counter, I place my hand on her warm cheek. "Of course. You didn't have to ask me. I wasn't planning to. Your secret is safe with me."

Her head rests on my palm as she closes her eyes and sighs. "Thank you." She gulps. "Your secret is safe with me, too, you know?" she whispers.

With my thumb, I caress her soft skin as I watch her intently. There are so many things I want to say to her right now.

I know. I trust you with my life.

You're the quiet in my loud.

In the storm of my life, you're the serenity that anchors me.

Instead, I nod.

The air fills with a thick tension. She's being vulnerable with me, again. It makes me feel good; accomplished. I've got the feeling she hates being open in front of people, so the fact she's doing it with me gives me another sliver of hope.

Her eyes open softly and she looks up, locking her gaze on me. And *fuck*, I could get lost in those deep hazel eyes—scratch that—I already do. And her lips, that for the first time don't have her usual inviting red, but I dare say they've never looked more enticing than this moment in their natural soft, plush pink color.

Her eyes, though, are my kryptonite. "You're eyes are so fucking beautiful, darling. Did you know that? I could get lost in them forever," I confess through a rasp.

Her glassy eyes snap to mine in shock at my confession. She starts roaming her gaze all over my face. I do the same, because honestly, I don't tire of it. Her hand lifts up softly, her delicate fingers interlacing with my hair. While I usually have my hair brushed, not a strand out of place, today I opted for a natural look, letting my lazy curls roam free and do their thing.

"Never seen your hair like this. I like it," she compliments.

I brush my thumb over her lips and whisper, "And I've never seen your lips without their usual red. They're lovely." I smile lazily.

I could compliment every inch of her. Every freckle; every strand of hair; every curve. She's perfect. I wish nothing but for time to stay still, to have the opportunity to stay here in this moment forever. She, with her fiery self, somehow infiltrated my life and has become the light that deep down I wished for, but never thought I could find.

ow do you walk into your place of employment and act like everything's normal?

After spending all day with Damian yesterday cooking, laughing, and having the best time, I'm left in the middle of a stir of emotions I don't understand. I got to see another side of him for once—a normal, sweet, and really fun guy. His emerald eyes which are typically beautiful, but dull, were so full of light and life, and I wish I get to see that life in him every day from now on.

I haven't even told the girls what happened yesterday, and I don't think I want to. Selfishly, I want this moment for myself and to keep it safe in a bubble.

Finally giving up, I walk into the gallery, do my best acting, and pretend my Sunday was just a normal, reset day. Nothing groundbreaking happened.

Except something did happen, and you haven't stopped thinking about it.

Walking up the stairs, Isabella welcomes me and darts her arms and hands, wanting me to give her the usual cup of coffee I bring her every day. I place the cup in her hands, and she quickly chugs half of it in one sitting.

"Tired?"

She nods. "I stayed up late reading. My eyes still hurt, and I was in serious need of another cup of coffee." She stares at the drink carrier with two cups. "I see you're tired too."

"Oh no, the other one is not for me. It's for..." I blush lightly.

"For...?" Isabella prompts.

"Damian."

She brings her hand to my forehead. "Do you have a fever? Who are you and what did you do with my friend?"

I push her hand away and roll my eyes. "You're ridiculous."

Isabella squints in suspicion. "Since when are you guys friends?"

"I'm just trying to move on from, you know..." Technically, not a lie. I am trying to move past *something*. We're definitely not in boss and employee territory now. It's more. Maybe friends.

Pft. Yeah, right. *Friends*.

"Say less." She looks at the computer. "He doesn't have any meetings right now, so you can go in."

I nod as I walk to his office door and knock, opening the door. He's engrossed in some paperwork, not noticing my presence. Every step I take and the closer I get, the quicker my heart beats. He has his usual suit, dark gray this time, with a black turtleneck sweater since it's getting chillier in Chicago, but what fucking gets me is his hair. He doesn't have it with his usual put together style. Instead, he's letting those lazy curls hang, just like he did yesterday.

He looks up and lets out one of his lazy smiles that

makes my knees tremble every time, leaning back in his chair. "Morning, Darling."

I take one of the cups out of the drink carrier and place it in front of him.

"Good morning," I manage to get out, hoping he doesn't notice my shaky voice.

He looks at the coffee cup, then looks up at me. "What's this for?"

"A thank you coffee for yesterday. Can't believe I'm going to say this, but I actually had a nice time."

He nods his head in agreement. "Glad to be of service."

I hum in agreement, slowly walking backward to leave his office. Weird thing is, I *don't* want to leave. Somehow, I crave his company. I want to do it again. Stay in that bubble.

The idea is totally crazy. It'd be inappropriate to have that type of relationship and be hanging out outside of work so often. But we've crossed the line so long ago; it's nonexistent at this point.

He picks up his coffee and takes a sip, then licks his lips. The movement is so annoyingly sexy, I'm pretty sure I'm staring like a fucking idiot. "Anything else?"

"We're still missing one statement piece. Have any leads?" I say quickly, trying to act nonchalant.

"We're going to the New York Auction next weekend, remember?"

"Right!" I snap my fingers. Even though I am *well* aware I have to go on another trip with him. "Okay then, I'm gonna go get some work done," I continue, waving awkwardly.

"Alright," he says.

"Alright," I repeat.

He flashes his killer bright smile and tilts his head. "Anything on your mind, Darling?"

What is it with this nickname that makes me blush every time? *Ugh.*

"Just making some mental lists for today, that's all. Anyway, if you need anything let me know," I say as I quickly walk out and shut the door before I embarrass myself any further.

Isabella shoots me a curious glance. "And what is wrong with you?"

"Nothing. I'm going to work," I murmur as I walk quickly to my office and lock the door.

What the hell is wrong with me?

I couldn't even think of my usual quick remarks that I like to throw every time we talk. It's like something between us shifted yesterday, and I can't pinpoint what it is.

You know damn well what it is.

Letting out a frustrated groan, I hit my head against the door. The feeling of uncertainty sucks. I'm walking with blinded eyes, but the excitement to get to the finish line clouds my judgment, even though I have no idea what to expect once I get there. That damn kiss changed everything between us, and I don't know how much longer I can keep on pretending nothing happened. He's doing a fucking great job at it.

Spending time with him yesterday was also a terrible idea. That side of Damian, so human and kind, is making me feel all kinds of things right now.

My phone rings, taking me out of my thoughts. Without looking at the caller ID, I pick it up.

"Hello?" the voice I can recognize from anywhere says.

"Mom?"

I haven't heard from her in over four years. Why is she calling? Something must have happened.

Soon after I graduated high school and went to college,

my parents got divorced—which I expected, and if anything, I'm upset it didn't happen sooner—and we just kind of all drifted apart. I moved to Chicago, and I haven't looked back ever since. My parents were so unhappy with each other they made me miserable in the process. Their marriage never worked, and somehow, I always was at the receiving end of their marital problems. As I kept growing up, it got more exhausting, damaging our relationship more. Especially me and my mother's.

"How are you, Aria?"

"Good," I say curtly. "How are you?"

"Same old, same old. I'm calling because I'm visiting Chicago soon, and I want to see you."

I hesitate. "You know, Mom, my schedule is really busy. I don't know if I'll have time."

"Busy doing what? For the love of God, you aren't a doctor or a lawyer. You just work at a museum. I'll be arriving next weekend. We can have dinner."

I inhale and exhale, trying to even my breathing. This is something I picked up when I went to therapy during my college years. Being on the varsity cheerleading team, having to keep up good grades so I wouldn't lose my scholarship, and taking extra credits to graduate early really did a number on me, to the point that therapy was a requirement.

That comment right there is one of the many reasons why I cut ties. I can't play pretend with her, not anymore. I got really good at masking my emotions while under her roof, because otherwise, she would have made it impossible for me.

I grit my teeth. "I'm actually out of town next weekend. So I'll catch you next time."

"I'm staying for a couple of days. We can have dinner or something once you're back."

I let out a resigned sigh. "Fine. Just send me the details. I gotta go." I hang up, not wanting to listen to her voice anymore.

Closing my eyes, I try to calm down the beat of my heart that's lodged in my throat. The walls start to close in, so I open the door quickly trying to situate myself. I run toward the stairs and take them two at a time, running to the gallery doors and pushing them open. The windy city breeze welcomes me, my cheeks feeling the sharp chilly day. It brings some relief to my overheating body. But it's still not enough, so I take my coat off, welcoming more of that wind, hoping to feel lighter.

The feeling doesn't come.

The signs of a panic attack start settling in. My hands get clammy, my body shivering even though I'm sweating profusely. The sound of the busy city street starts to fade as the sound of my own hard and fast beating heart takes over. My vision is blurry with tears, as I start hyperventilating. My cheeks suddenly warm at the touch of two hands that caress them, brushing away the nonstop tears.

Someone's talking to me, I think. It's hard to hear over my fast beating heart. I close my eyes, trying to center myself.

It's a male's voice. A familiar deep, demanding voice.

"Aria, breathe for me, *Tesoro*. Come on, I know you can hear me."

Tesoro.

That brings me back. Little by little, my vision clears, and I'm met with those deep emerald green eyes I've grown to obsess over. I focus on them as my breathing calms down, the sound of the busy city coming back.

"That's my girl," he says, gripping my cheeks gently. "I thought I lost you there for a moment. Are you okay?"

I blush, loving the sound of—*my girl*—coming out of his mouth. My heart flutters, because for the first time in my life, someone has been able to help me stop my panic attack symptoms before they got too far. With his commanding presence and gentle touch, he saved me from the dark parts of myself. And it's a relief, because if I had to choose someone to take me out of the shadows; to bring me into the light—I want it to be him. *Always him.*

22

Damian

I fucking hate coming to Vortex.

One of the most exclusive private clubs of Chicago —scratch that—the world. An invite-only exclusive club, where all the top businessmen from around the world come to enjoy the endless amenities or complete multimillion-dollar business transactions. The inside of the club is exactly as expected—fucking tacky. Apparently, the appeal of this place is that they have kept it identical to when it was founded.

The ceiling is full of chandelier lights, and the main room has leather seats with tables scattered all over the place, and a bar at the corner of the room where they only keep top-shelf alcohol. The building has four floors, the top being an immense library that includes all the classics; plus all the books the founding members have written. The third floor is a casino, while the second floor is a full spa and gym, as well as a basketball court and boxing ring. The first floor is the entrance, typically where people hang out at the bar, or sit around the tables to talk. Walking in, I look around until I spot Enzo and Matteo sitting at the back of the room, playing chess.

I always feel so out of place here. It makes my skin crawl. Being a self-made billionaire puts you in that odd spot where people who come from old money don't want anything to do with you, and the other half is focused on themselves, trying to keep up with their self-made appearances. The only reason I got a membership is because I needed the connections when I was creating my company. It was out of pure necessity. The guys like meeting here once a month, whether it is to just sit down and play chess or talk business. Enzo kind of has to come here more often than not, since he's on the board. One of the founding members was our great-great-grandfather, so the vice presidency title has been passed down through generations. The only reason I escaped the responsibility is because we're cousins from my mother's side. The position is only passed through the sons of the Mancini family, more specifically, the oldest of the bunch. He didn't have that much of an option because he's an only child, so this means he's gonna have to get cracking and make a child before our uncles go after the position. It comes with power and connections anyone would kill to have. Though, I don't think he cares that much. He kind of got stuck with the socialite responsibilities by default.

I walk toward them, taking a seat next to my cousin and leaning back into the comfortable plush leather, crossing my legs.

"Checkmate," Matteo says with a grin as he moves his bishop, cornering Enzo's king.

Enzo slaps the table and murmurs, "Bullshit."

"You've always sucked at chess, *cugino*," I taunt, gaining a glare from Enzo as he flips me off.

To be honest, no one can beat Matteo. Even I can admit that, and I'm really good at chess. The man is a fucking genius. Too smart for his own good. One of these days he's going to get himself in some serious shit, because he's one reckless motherfucker, too.

Enzo smirks, his eyes haunting with amusement as he asks, "How's that *cute* employee of yours?"

This little fucker.

I glare at him without giving a response. And he just laughs as his eyes flicker with mischief, knowing damn well what he's doing.

"It's alright, Enzo. At least you can beat me in poker." Matteo grins.

He points a finger at Matteo. "Yeah, because I don't let you fucking card count. If I did, you would win and you know it."

Matteo shrugs as he leans back on the couch with his arms behind his head, closing his eyes and humming.

"Why in such a good mood, Carter?" I ask.

"Well, if you must know, Romano—"

I snap my hand up, interrupting him. "You know what? I actually don't care. Let's get this shit on the road. I have places to be."

More like I can't get back to work fast enough to see a particular redhead. I haven't been able to get Aria out of my head since I helped her through her panic attack.

I wonder how often she gets them.

I researched how to help someone through one, and thankfully, the tips worked. Something strange possessed me and before I knew it, I was knees-deep in research. I wonder what triggered it. From what I found, it said that if you ask too many questions too fast, another one can be triggered and I wasn't willing to risk her safety like that.

Also, it's really none of my fucking business—even though, deep down, for some unknown reason, I want to very much make it my business.

"I have one of the guys that broke into the gallery in custody," Matteo says.

I raise an eyebrow, intrigued. "Okay, tell me more."

"I have my guys trying to break him, but he's a tough fucker." Matteo shakes his head in disbelief.

"Do we know who hired him? Or why he targeted me for that matter?"

Matteo taps his temple with his index finger twice. "We found a foreign bank account under one of his aliases that has two million dollars in it. And it has one single transaction, dated around the time it happened."

"Damn, Damian, who the hell did you piss off that they were willing to pay two million dollars to break into your gallery?" Enzo asks, laughing.

That's the thing—I have no fucking idea who would do this. And that's what irritates me the most. Who the fuck is targeting me? Where do I even start looking? I have the feeling this person is right under my nose, but they are covering their tracks well.

Matteo nods, agreeing with Enzo. "That's what I'm trying to find out. It doesn't make sense." He shakes his head. "How much was the painting they stole worth again?"

"Only thirty grand," I confirm and murmur, "I wonder why they paid him so much."

"I don't think this was a solo job. He has to be sharing the money with other people. But I haven't been able to find anyone else," Matteo points out.

I close my eyes, massaging my temples, trying not to lose my shit.

Matteo grips my shoulder and squeezes it. "Don't worry

too much about it. We'll get to the bottom of it," he says confidently.

I thin my lips, contemplating my actions. I'm so fucking close to saying fuck it, get involved, and punch the answers out of him myself. But this is why I pay people to do things for me. Being thirty-five, I've learned a thing or two in business, one of them is to always have people around you, because you can't do it all.

"How about a game of chess now, Romano?" Matteo asks.

"No fucking way. It bores me to play with you."

He snorts at my comment. "Only because you always lose."

I flick his forehead, causing him to hiss. Enzo laughs, so I flick him, too.

"What the hell was that for?"

"For asking questions you shouldn't be asking," I say dryly.

He places his palm on top of his mouth, trying to hide his smirk as he says, "*Right*. I forget Red is a touchy subject."

Through gritted teeth, I reply, "She has a name, and it's not Red, idiota." *Idiot.*

"Who are we talking about?" Matteo asks curiously.

"You remember when we went to the club? He wasn't there to have fun. He was there to follow a certain *employee* of his," Enzo taunts, trying to get a rise out of me. "I'm surprised you like them young, *cugino*. Consider me proud."

"She's twenty-five years old, not fucking nineteen. Stop making me look like a fucking creep," I snap.

There are worst things than a ten-year age gap between two consenting adults.

Why are you so upset? It's not like she's with you.

"Aha, so you *do* like her," he retorts smugly.

"Like you even care that I wasn't there to have fun. You disappeared the second we got there," I say deflecting, trying to steer the conversation away.

Enzo shrugs. "Well, yeah. I go to clubs to hook up, not to go babysit a grown woman. You do know she can make her own decisions, right?"

I wave my hand dismissively. "You don't get it."

And he truly doesn't. Enzo is nothing but a player, getting high off playing games whether is with women or actual gambling. He has never taken anything seriously once in his life, and I don't think he ever will.

"I get it. Love makes you a fool," he jokes.

"*Love?*" I say in an incredulous tone. "Please, Enzo, give me more credit than that."

Do I think about her all the time? *Yes.*

Do I want to spend all my waking moments with her? *Also, yes.*

Does the possibility of her being with someone else drive me to the brink of insanity? *Abso-fucking-lutely.*

But I am *not* in love with Aria Petrov.

Or so I keep telling myself.

23

Aria

"Carry on Wayward Son" by Kansas blasts through my apartment as I pack for New York since we're leaving in a matter of hours. My room is a mess and I don't even know where I'm standing. Frustrated, I throw myself in bed to rest, except, I'm so uncomfortable because I have a pile of clothes and shoes in the bed after trying to come up with some decent outfits. It took forever, but I'm pleasantly surprised with my choices.

Why am I so nervous?

Uhm, jeez, I don't know. Maybe because your boss kissed you and you're kind of hoping it happens again?

I groan, murmuring some insults to myself. I'm fucking ridiculous. He's not kissing me again, not after what happened. Having a panic attack after someone kisses you is a clear sign to not try it again. But the thing is... I want the *exact* opposite. To feel his strong hands roaming my body as he trails kisses from my lips, to my collarbone, my abdomen.

I shake my head, trying to get the image out of my head. Closing my eyes for a moment, I let the music drift me away as I rest my eyes. Suddenly, someone jumps on top of me, startling me.

"Sophia Evans! You scared the fuck out of me! How did you even get in here?" I yell over the music.

She dangles my spare keys in front of me. "You gave me these, remember?" she yells back.

I glare at her as I stand from my bed to turn off the music. "Yes, for emergencies. Not for this!"

"I knocked on the door, but the music was so loud you couldn't hear me," she replies with a *duh* tone.

"What are you doing here anyway?"

"I brought you the dress you asked me for," she says, walking back to the living room.

I follow her. "Thank God. I honestly forgot."

"You seem distracted lately. Are you okay?" she asks, concern lacing her tone.

I'm far from good. I'm drowning in the uncertainty of the situation with Damian, my mother is coming next week, and I want to crawl out of my skin just thinking about it. The last thing I want is Sophia to worry about me, though. It's better this way.

Always pushing people away. It's what I do best.

I wave my dismissively. "Of course, I'm good."

She hums with an *I don't believe you but I'll drop it for now* tone, and walks back to my bedroom, snooping in my suit-case. "Need any help with outfits?"

My shoulders sag with relief. "I think I'm good, actually."

For the first time ever, I planned my outfits carefully. The only thing I was missing was the dress for the auction, but Sophia came to the rescue as always. My insides brim with excitement as I think about the trip. Outside of being near Damian, which I'm equally parts nervous and looking forward to, I love New York. The gastronomy and the museums are my favorite parts of the city, of course. We're staying longer than a few days since he has some business there, so I already have an itinerary planned out. Let's hope he doesn't get any ideas to put me to work, because he already gave me the okay to take a couple of days off, and I'm taking all the advantage.

"How's the article going?" I ask Sophia as I fold the dress neatly and place it in my open suitcase.

Sophia slumps her shoulders, sitting on the bed. "Please let's not talk about it. It's been driving me insane. Max has been drilling me to get it done, but the sources I find keep falling through. Everyone is being extremely cryptic about it." She grabs her ponytail and starts playing with it. "Which, I mean, makes total sense. This heist was a big deal, you know? Honestly, this article shouldn't be a thing, but hey, I'm just following orders."

Humming in understanding, I sit next to her. "Yeah, I get it. Maybe he'll drop it soon."

"Maybe." She waves her hand dismissively. "What about you? Are you planning to do any more kissing?" She wiggles her eyebrows, making kissing noises.

Grabbing my pillow, I throw it at her, blushing. "Shut up."

After Sophia leaves, I'm brushing my hair, putting it in a messy bun when I hear a knock on the door. I put my brush away in my travel bag as I take one last look in the mirror, then walk to the front door and open it.

"I made it to the visitors' list, huh?" Damian asks with a playful smirk, leaning against the door frame.

I roll my eyes. "Shut up and come in. I'm almost ready."

I try to act my normal self as he walks in, enveloping the room with his usual clean cedarwood scent that I've grown to obsess over. Walking to the kitchen, I ask, "Do you want anything?"

My loft is open floor, so the kitchen and living room are next to each other. I've hung some of my art all around to keep the place looking nice and alive. The living room has an L-shaped soft white sofa and a corner loveseat next to the floor-to-ceiling windows that I typically use to drink my tea and read.

He follows me to the kitchen and sits in one of the island chairs. "Nah, I'm good, thanks."

I go to the refrigerator, welcoming the cold breeze on my cheeks. I don't really need anything, but he has this talent for making me feel flustered when he's near. And today is no exception. He has on gray sweatpants that leave *nothing* to the imagination, and a black hoodie. His curls are loose, and I'm not trying to read too much into it, but the fact that he's been wearing his hair like that since I told him how much I like it makes my stomach turn with butterflies, like a stupid high school girl.

We decided to do a late flight, since we don't really have anything pressing waiting for us at New York since the auction isn't until Sunday night, and it's only Friday.

I grab a bottle of water and sit next to him. "I thought you had to be ready at all times," I joke as I look at him up and down.

He lets out a small laugh with a shrug. "We're arriving at midnight. And it's not like we're going to a hotel or anything. Really, who's gonna see me? I can enjoy comfort even once in a while."

I take a big gulp of water, trying to avoid looking at how

his sweatpants hug his strong legs and form the silhouette of his shaft. Seriously, gray sweatpants should be illegal to own. Might as well be fucking naked. "If we aren't staying at a hotel, then where are we staying?"

"I have a condo near Central Park," he says, getting up.

Why does the fact that we're staying at his place make me feel some type of way? It feels... personal. The Damian I know wouldn't do something like this. But he's been different lately, showing another side of him that, well, I enjoy.

"Where are your bags?" he asks, getting me out of my trance.

"In my room, let me go get them."

He nods as I walk away, bringing my suitcase and work travel bag with me. He holds his hand out, offering to take my stuff. I nod as I give him my things, our hands touching for a brief moment. Without thinking, I take two steps back as the warmth of one simple touch electrifies me from the tip of my fingers to the rest of my body in a millisecond. Shivers travel down my spine, making me stiff.

Maybe staying with him at his condo is not such a great idea. I'll just get a hotel instead. That's the logical thing to do.

So why am I hesitating to tell him that?

You know damn well why you're hesitating.

I want nothing more than to spend more time with him, and try and discover where these feelings are coming from. So maybe, just maybe... being in such close quarters again is actually not a bad idea.

Make up your damn mind, woman.

We walk out of my apartment, and as I lock my door, I'm spiraling inside. It's frustrating, not knowing why this is happening to me. But I'm nothing but determined to figure out the need to be near him, get to know him, and unravel those layers he has. I want all of him, I just don't know where to begin.

Damian

I have no business in New York except for the auction. So why exactly did I tell her we're staying a week? I don't fucking know. She was so excited talking about how much she enjoyed New York, the words just sort of came out. I may or may not want to spend as much time as possible with her outside of work, and this seemed like the perfect excuse. I'll just tag along on whatever she's doing, and come up with excuses later. That seemed like a fool-proof idea to me at the time, but right now, I'm not too fucking sure.

Arriving at the jet, Aria takes a seat on the opposite side of mine.

"Not daring to take my seat this time around?" I taunt.

She glares at me. "No. Because last time you acted like a deranged animal about it."

"Sit next to me, come on." I pat the seat next to mine.

"No, thanks."

I raise a challenging eyebrow at her. She does the exact same, letting her firecracker self make an appearance. Getting up slowly, I make my intentions obvious. She holds my gaze, unfazed, giving me a silent challenge. Little does she know, I love challenges. Especially when they come from her. As I get closer, she bulges her eyes as she realizes I'm not backing down.

"Okay, okay!" She palms my chest, stopping me from grabbing her. "I'll move. Jesus. You were seriously going to do it again, weren't you?"

I sit down, shrugging. "You should have waited to find out."

"You're deranged," she murmurs.

I smirk triumphantly. "What's the plan for when we get to the city?"

Her face brightens as she starts telling me all about her plans and the spots she wants to visit. It's hard to concentrate on what she's saying, and I find myself getting lost in her eyes that brim with excitement every time she mentions a certain spot she really wants to visit.

"Are you doing all of this by yourself?" I ask.

"I mean, yeah," she laughs. "I don't know anyone in the city."

I hum without saying a word.

The flight is short, but we arrive a little past midnight, and I'm officially beat. Aria fell asleep quickly after we took off, and now I've been trying to wake her for the past ten minutes, and damn, the girl sleeps like a rock.

"Darling," I whisper. "We're here. Let's go."

I don't know when or why I started calling her darling. It felt fitting. I can think of a million other nicknames that suit her, too.

Sunshine.

My sunshine.

She brings light to my cloudy; dark days. Just like when the sun comes out after a particularly rainy day.

She's snoring really softly, and a smile escapes me at the cute sound that's coming out of her. She moves a little, but makes no effort to open her eyes. Deciding she's probably not going to get up unless I shake her, I opt to swiftly grab her and get her out of the plane myself. Her head is pressed against my chest, and my heart wants to come out at the proximity of us. I walk out of the jet, then gently place her in the car, making sure she's comfortable, then I get in so they can drive us to the condo.

The rest of the car ride is silent, except for her soft snores and mumbles here and there.

She talks in her sleep, and I'm definitely going to taunt her for it once she wakes up.

As we're arriving, she opens her eyes softly and yawns. She straightens, looking around confused.

"Wow, you're awake. Thought you were incapable," I taunt.

"How did I get here?" she says through a tired yawn.

"I spent ten minutes trying to wake you up, but you sleep like a rock. So I just lifted you in my arms and took you to the car."

She hides her face with her palms with a groan. "Oh my God, that's so embarrassing. I'm sorry. I was exhausted."

"I can tell," I say with a laugh.

We get out of the car and I grab our bags as she looks up, staring at the building. "Damn, this is a tall building," she points out.

"You live in Chicago, and you're surprised to see a tall building?" I ask dryly.

"Whatever." She rolls her eyes.

We walk up the entrance, where the bellman grabs our bags and goes into the elevator with us as he places in the key and marks the ninety-eighth floor.

"We're staying on the ninety-eighth floor!?" she whispers-shouts.

"Again, Darling, are you even from Chicago?"

"I'm not, actually. But I've been living there only four years, right after college."

Well, that's interesting. Also makes me realize I don't know much about her. Not as much as I would like, anyway. I want to know her likes, and dislikes, what makes her laugh, and what makes her sad. I want to get to know... *her*. *All of her*. Her faults and all. I'll make it my life's mission until I know every piece of her, not just the surface-level stuff.

As the elevator doors open to the living room of my condo, the bellman places our bags at the entrance and promptly leaves.

This condo was one of my biggest purchases when I started making money. At the time, I was spending more time in New York than anywhere else, so it made sense. It's a two-bedroom condo with floor-to-ceiling windows that looks over Central Park and the rest of the busy city lights. It's mostly decorated in muted colors—black and gray, with a hint of white. I have a few of the early pieces I started collecting around the apartment that gives the place a more scaled and elegant look.

I grab her bags and tilt my head in the direction of the rooms. "Let me take you to your room."

The guest bedroom is right across from mine, but the room still has privacy with its own walk-in closet and bathroom. She walks into the room, taking her shoes off and sitting on the bed as she undoes her messy bun, letting her curls fall in beautiful waves.

"Oh my God. I could stay here forever," she says with a

satisfying groan as she lays on the bed and spreads her arms, enjoying the comfort.

"It better be comfortable. That mattress costs twenty-five thousand dollars."

She sits up quickly, gasping. "Damian, that's outrageous! Are you insane?"

"Not insane. Just had a really expensive interior designer." I shrug.

She shakes her head with a laugh, getting up and walking around the room, admiring every detail. "Okay, wow. This closet is insane." She laughs in awe, going into the walk-in closet and admiring it.

I follow after her as I laugh with her and nod in agreement. "Yeah, I'm not even sure why I got this place. I don't really have people often. Just my mother, and that's rare. She doesn't like traveling."

"She lives in Italy, right? That's who you were having dinner with that night at the restaurant?"

I raise an eyebrow. "I didn't realize you noticed I was there."

"I always notice when you're in a room," she says in a matter-of-fact tone.

"Why?" I ask, surprise lacing my tone. My heart quickens, a million thoughts running through my head.

Does she think about me, too?

She has this way of pulling me like a magnet when she's in a room.

Do I make her feel the same?

"You have a very commanding presence. It's like when you're in a room people just gravitate toward you. Must be your million-dollar suit," she teases with a soft laugh.

A feeling of disappointment floods through me. I don't know what I'd hoped for, but it wasn't that.

I act offended. "Okay, I may have a twenty-thousand-dollar mattress, but the most I've spent on a suit is like twelve grand, so you're incorrect."

She giggles, murmuring, "Whatever."

She keeps looking around, and I follow her aimlessly. Her presence is commanding, too. I wonder if she knows the effect she has on people—on *me*. My whole body gravitates toward her when she's near. I always know, automatically, when she's in a room. With her bright smile and golden freckles that can captivate anyone, and her red curly hair that cascades in such rocky waves and takes my breath away, every single damn time. With those fiery hazel eyes I can get lost in for countless hours, and I wouldn't even mind, because as long as I'm near her, nothing else matters. Having her by my side makes me feel like everything will be alright. She's become such an important part of my life. Not sure when it happened, or how. It just did.

It's scary trusting people, because that has never gotten me anywhere. We are made of all those who have built and broken us, and I'm so fucking broken. I never thought someone could filter their way back in and make me *feel* so many emotions all at once. It's a euphoric feeling I don't want to let go of.

"I shouldn't have slept on the plane, now I'm wired and hungry," she whines.

"Lucky for you, we're in the city that never sleeps. What are you in the mood for?" I ask, walking to the kitchen and opening the drawer where I keep the takeout menus.

She follows after me, humming. "I would kill for some dumplings right now. Know of any good spots?"

"I've never had dumplings before, actually."

She takes a step back, her hand flying to her chest in surprise. "Yeah, no. We have to rectify that."

I take out all the Chinese and Japanese menus I can find and hand them to her. "Here you go."

She giggles excitedly as she sits down at the island, spreading out the menus in front of her.

My body hums with the need to get closer and touch her unruly beautiful curls, maybe even trace her freckles with my fingertips.

Is this what obsession feels like?

She looks at all the options, and I keep a safe distance between us because if I get any closer, my body will probably get a mind of its own and do things that can scare her off.

She looks up, locking her gaze with mine. "What are you doing over there?" She pats the seat next to her. "Let's choose together. Maybe some flavors sound interesting to you. Let's have a feast."

I ponder for a moment, then I give myself an inner pep talk.

I'm not some horny teenager. I can keep my hands to myself.

Without saying anything, I sit next to her. As she explains what a dumpling is, and how many options or different ways we can eat them, I find myself nodding along, but not really listening, because all I can notice is the way her eyes gleam excitedly when she mentions a type of dumplings she prefers, and the way she scrunches her nose when she mentions the ones she hates. The way she takes a strand of her hair and plays with it as she keeps talking. We agree on ordering from different places, not repeating any flavors, and ordering all the types.

As we wait for the food, we sit on the couch and watch *The Greatest Showman*, a musical she suggests. I'm not even paying attention to the movie, because my view is so much better. She sings along to every single song and quotes the script before the actors even talk, as if she has seen it hundreds of times.

This, right here, is something I could get used to. Come home every day and watch whatever musical or silly movies she wants to watch. Order takeout. Teach her how to cook every Sunday. Live a happy, normal life.

I quickly shut those thoughts down, because really, who am I to think I deserve something like this? To have a partner to love and spend the rest of my life with?

What makes me think I deserve her?

The food arrives little by little, and we definitely underestimated how much we ordered. We have a total of twenty bags, from twenty different Chinese restaurants, and some Japanese ones as well. We opt to sit on the floor of the living room and open all the bags, but she does it in a very specific and organized way, so we can know which places we liked and didn't.

"This way, next time you come to New York, you can order from your favorite spot," she says excitedly as she keeps organizing the takeout containers.

Only if you come with me, too.

The comment is at the tip of my tongue. Because I hope next time she's here, too. She makes everything more fun; better; vivid with color.

We start with her favorite type of dumplings: steamed. Then, we start doing mix and match, so I can explore my horizons, she claims. And we quickly find out that I'm more of a pork kind of guy, not so much chicken or shrimp.

"This one tastes so gingery." She makes a *blech* face as she takes a napkin and spits it out.

"I like it. I think I like ginger." I shrug, savoring the sharp, citrusy taste.

"Don't get me wrong. I like ginger. I just don't want it to

be the center of attention. Ginger is more like a palette cleanser, like when you eat sushi. You know?"

I nod in understanding. "Alright, What do you rate it?"

She taps her cheek twice with her index finger, pondering. "A three, just because I appreciate how fresh it tastes, so I gotta at least give them that. How 'bout you?"

"A four."

She rolls her eyes and groans, dropping her chopsticks on one of the open containers.

I furrow. "What?"

"This is the twelfth dumpling we've tried, and you keep giving them the same rating," she replies with an exasperated breath.

"None of them have been impressive yet."

"Are you kidding!?" she shrieks as she finds dumpling number six and grabs the paper bag and shoves it in front of my face. "Are you telling me you didn't like Mrs. Yeng's pork dumplings!? They had so much soup and all the flavors just burst in your mouth."

"Will it make you happy if I give Mrs. Yeng a higher rating?" I ask, holding back a laugh.

"It definitely wouldn't hurt. I thought she deserved better." She puffs, dropping the bag back where it belongs and crossing her arms. I almost believe she's genuinely offended.

"I'll give it a six, then," I relent.

She squints at me for a moment, before nodding firmly. "Okay, that'll do for now."

I can't possibly eat anymore, but we started this game of rating every dumpling we try, and also, I like the idea of spending time with her, talking about every random thing as we stuff ourselves.

By the fourteenth dumpling, she is ready to call it quits, but somehow, she pulls through.

She huffs. "I don't think I can move. Matter of fact, I'll sleep right here." We're both sitting on the floor, our heads resting on the couch as we both look up, trying to get over the food coma.

"I can't believe I let you talk me into eating twenty dumplings." I laugh, struggling to breathe with how stuffed I am.

She hits me on the arm playfully. "You repeated some of them! You ate like thirty."

"Some of them were very good."

She sits up excitedly. "Ah ha! So you accept that not all of them were the same rating."

I let out a sigh. "I guess not."

"And? Go ahead, say it."

I roll my eyes and confess, "Mrs. Yeng's was definitely a ten."

She gets up and starts doing a triumph dance that looks both hilarious and terrifying. "I knew it! Man, you make things so complicated," she says, sitting back down.

I sit up, locking my gaze on hers. "How so?"

"Like, if you really liked some dumplings more than others, why did you give them all the same rating?" she asks with a confused frown, like she couldn't fathom the thought of giving the same rating to something so simple.

I've quickly come to realize this woman doesn't play when it comes to dumplings. It's kind of endearing. "Because what if the next one is better than the previous?" I ask.

"That's so... pessimistic."

"I like to say I'm realistic," I counter.

"No. Because being realistic would mean you can accept

that there can be multiple good things, not only one," she counters back.

I shrug, resting my head back on the couch seat, looking at her. "I've learned to keep my expectations at a minimum, keep hopes at bay."

She places her arm on the couch and rests her chin on the palm of her hand. Her eyes study me intently, like I'm some sort of scientific object she needs to discover and understand. "You are a mystery, Damian Romano," she murmurs.

"That's half the charm," I say barely above whisper with a playful wink.

The truth of the matter is, I always had to keep my expectations at a minimum. The majority of my life I expected so much from people—my father, to be more specific—that I eventually learned to let things go. Until it became part of my routine, and even when it comes to the most mundane things—like dumplings—I've kept the same rule. Because when you stop expecting things from people, you start building your own expectations for what you want, and work harder for it. It's a motto I've lived by, and I don't plan to stop anytime soon.

I guess this is the difference between us. She's a dreamer, I can tell. She sees the best in people, even when she shouldn't. I wonder why. But if I think about it, this is probably why I'm so attracted to her. Because she sees the world so differently. Like life is an adventure, and that it's okay to expect better from people.

That it's okay to have hope, too.

She yawns as she gets up. "I'm heading to bed. I have a long day tomorrow."

I nod, yawning. "Good night."

She nods back and walks to her room. She stops and

turns around, her fingers fidgeting nervously. "Listen, I know you must have a million things to do tomorrow, but if you want to come with me, you can. I'm just going to do some touristic things I like doing every time I'm in New York. I'm also going to The Met, thought you'd be interested." She smiles at me, shyly.

My heart quickens at the thought of spending all day with her. This is what I wanted. So why am I hesitating? If I do this, there's no coming back. I can control myself to an extent, and spending the whole day with her is certainly risky.

The hesitation must have shown in my eyes because she suddenly stiffens.

Before I can reply, she says, "Forget I said anything. You're probably busy anyway."

"No, no," I interrupt her quickly, anxiety crawling at me at the thought of me missing this amazing opportunity to spend more time with her. "I was just thinking if I had anything pressing for tomorrow. But I don't. So, yeah. That sounds nice."

Her shoulders drop with relief. "Okay. See you tomorrow then."

I let out a huge breath as she leaves, letting my shoulders relax as I close my eyes.

Maybe it is okay to have hope, after all.

25

Aria

I slept like a baby. I don't know if it was the twenty plus dumplings I had last night, or how easygoing the night was with Damian by my side, as we laughed and talked about the most random things.

This is definitely not good for my heart, but yet, here we are.

After that food coma, I had the great idea to invite him to spend the whole Saturday with me. I cringe just thinking about it, because it definitely feels like a date and the worst part is that he has no idea. Maybe he was just being nice, tagging along, making sure I wasn't by myself.

Or maybe he wants to spend time with you, and you need to stop overthinking so much.

It's chilly today, same as it usually is in Chicago, so I opt to wear black leather pants with a black long sleeve shirt and a brown puffer jacket with my usual white Converse. I wake up extremely early to deal with my nest—aka, my hair —and straighten it, feeling a thousand times better now that it looks put together. I've considered a perm, but every time I'm about to make the appointment, something just makes me stop. It's like, if I go through with it, my mother wins somehow. And I'm too petty for that.

I walk out of the room to find Damian waiting for me in the living room, looking so well put together as always. That man has the kind of beauty that is raw, and anything but ordinary. He's wearing a white turtleneck sweater, with black pants, boots, and a trench coat. Today, he has his lazy curls again, and the sight of him just does something to me. That man can rock his curls, always. But again, this is Damian who we're talking about, he looks good no matter the look he has going on.

"Ready?" he asks, getting up from the couch.

I nod.

"Lead the way. What do you want to do first?" He asks.

"Are you hungry? I was thinking we can go to this tiny, cutesy coffee shop that's near here. They have the best caramel iced latte, and they use nugget ice, which is the best type," I say excitedly.

"Darling, it's like thirty degrees outside," he says, baffled. "Also, nugget ice? Ice is ice. It all tastes the same."

That nickname makes my knees buckle. It's the way he says it with his deep hearty voice. The way he says it like he actually means it.

"So? I will not pass up the opportunity for their iced caramel latte. I rarely visit New York. Now, come on." I urge with my hand. "Also, no. It doesn't taste the same. Nugget ice is the best. You're gonna have to trust me on that."

He shakes his head and laughs. "Okay, come on. Let's go."

We take the elevator and walk outside, where the driver from last night welcomes us.

I shake my head. "We're not taking the car."

He frowns. "What?"

"We're walking. Everything's near, plus, if we're going far, we can take the subway."

We look at each other for what seems the longest minute of my life, then he throws his head back, exposing his neck as he lets out his velvety, deep, sexy—okay, *enough*—laugh.

"What's so funny?" I ask, confused.

He stops laughing abruptly. "Wait, you're serious?"

"Yes, come on!"

"Okay, let's compromise. We can walk, but if the places we're going are far, we'll take the car. I am *not* getting in the subway."

"Okay, princess," I murmur.

He raises an eyebrow. "Did you just call me *princess*?"

"Yup." I shrug with a knowing grin. "You're acting like we're going to die if we walk. Nothing's going to happen."

"It's New York. Something's always happening, Aria," he answers with a dry, bored tone.

I start walking toward the coffee shop. "Up to you if you want to follow me. I'll keep going," I yell without looking back.

He lets out a defeated sigh and quickly catches up to me. He is so stupidly tall, it shouldn't be allowed. And let's not even talk about his body, which was definitely tailored by God himself.

Can you maybe stop thinking about the way he looks, or how handsome he is for one fucking minute?

Ah, only if that were possible.

I'm surprised he's not dating anyone. I don't think I've ever seen or heard anything about his love life. Then, I remember my first day at work, when he told me that his one and only love is art, and it always will be.

My heart is doing this thing where it tugs deep in my chest. Because my stupid, idiotic feelings are ten steps ahead of the rest of my body and jump to conclusions, creating false hopes. The thing is, it's not like I can pinpoint when this started. He has been more present, and he's been sneaking into my heart slowly, but surely. The lines between professionalism and something more are blurring from my end. Is it a bad thing I hope the lines are blurring for him, too?

We arrive at the coffee shop, and it's surprisingly empty. We quickly order our coffees and pastries, and Damian pays for everything before I even have the chance to get my wallet out. Once we receive our order, we decide to sit at a table by a window that overlooks Central Park.

He's looking out the window as he opens a straw and places it in my cup, then opens another one for himself. It's the little things he does that fill my stomach with a colony of butterflies.

"I can't believe I let you talk me into ordering an iced caramel latte." He shakes his head in disbelief.

I let out a triumphant laugh. "You'll thank me in a second."

He rolls his eyes as he takes a sip of the latte, not making one single expression, so I have no idea whether he likes it or not. He drank about halfway, so I'm assuming he does. Setting the cup down, he takes his bagel and eats it like he has all the time in the world. As I watch him, all I can think of is how he can make something as simple as eating a bagel hot. Like, seriously? He needs to tone it down. I don't understand how he doesn't have women jumping up on him like cats.

I prompt him to say something. "Okay, the suspense is killing me. Did you like it?"

He shrugs. "It's alright."

I groan. "You're lying, but that's fine. I'll let it go."

We eat the rest of our breakfast as we go over the plan for the day. I love doing it all, going to The Metropolitan Museum, Rockefeller, you name it. Luckily, since we're officially in winter, the ice rink at Rockefeller is open and it's definitely my top activity to do.

"So, what's on the agenda for today?"

"Oh, you know, the usual. Ice skating, drinking hot chocolates with extra marshmallows, The Met."

His eyebrows furrow, confused. "Did you just say *ice skating*?"

"Of course. You can't come to New York close to the holidays and not ice skate."

"Aria, I am a thirty-five-year-old man. What makes you think I'm going to ice skate?" he drawls.

I point a finger at him, shaking my head. "You signed up for this. Don't be backing out on me now."

"Well, I signed up to spend time with you. I certainly didn't count on these *adventures*," he counters, raising an eyebrow.

My heart flips knowing he agreed to go with me simply because he wanted us to spend time *together*. And damn it... the butterflies in my stomach fly all over, making me feel queasy in the best way possible. My cheeks heat, and I'm grateful I overdid my blush today, because otherwise he would be able to notice. This is so confusing, we kissed *once*, then I decided to move on from it, act like nothing happened—which he happily ran with—and now this. Do I want to keep pretending nothing happened? Or do I actually want to make a move? It's not like Damian will make a move again.

"Just say you don't know how to skate. There's no shame in that," I taunt.

"Well..." He grimaces.

"You've never been? Not even when you were a kid?"

He shakes his head, then casually shrugs. "My father was too busy hating my guts and running a struggling business to care."

Whoa.

The confession catches me by surprise, because he's a very closed, reserved person. All I can do is nod in understanding, because I don't want to scare him off by trying to have an open heart-to-heart session in the middle of a coffee shop, because knowing him, he's going to shut down. But I can't deny it, I'm dying to unravel all of his secrets and find out what drives him to be the way that he is.

"I'll teach you. I'm pretty good." I wink.

"Great, can't wait for that," he replies sarcastically.

Okay, if someone would have told me I was going to spend my day teaching Damian Romano aka grumpy ass how to ice skate, I would have laughed and said, '*Yeah, no. You're crazy.*'

We rented the skates for two sessions back to back, because I knew the first one was going to be a mess, and I was right. The man has two left feet, and doesn't know how to move correctly.

I sit down on the bench to take my skates off, and as I'm untying them I let out a groan. "Oh my God, I forgot how much this hurts."

He sits next to me and laughs as he starts untying them and putting his shoes back on. "I can't feel my feet anymore."

"You better feel them soon, because we have to skate again in half an hour. What should we do while we wait?"

As he's tying his shoes, he replies, "Stay here. I'm going to go get us some of that famous hot chocolate you've been talking about."

"I can go, too. Just give me a sec," I say as I start putting my shoes on.

He places his hand on mine, stopping me. The touch is brief, but just as electrifying as it has always been. "Your feet must be killing you. I got it, Darling. Just rest."

In other instances, I would keep insisting, but my feet hurt so much that I just nod and let him go by himself.

He comes back quickly with the sweet, hot cocoas—mine with extra marshmallows—and the gesture is small, but sweet nonetheless. I love how he remembers these small stupid details I tell him like it's no big deal.

As we drink them, we start talking about things we've never done, or places we've never visited.

"I've never snowboarded before," I say.

"I actually have. Me, Lorenzo, and Matteo go almost every year to Colorado."

I hum. "Colorado. Sounds pretty."

"You've never been?"

I shake my head. "I lived in Kentucky my whole life, studied there, and then moved to Chicago. I just started traveling recently."

"I can probably talk Lorenzo and Matteo into inviting you girls to the trip next year. Well, at least you and Sophia. I doubt Isabella will want to be where Matteo is."

"Rough history?" I ask, curious. Me and Isabella have never talked about her past, except the fact that she graduated top of her class at MIT.

"You could say that," he responds vaguely.

The second skating session starts and we start right away before it starts getting any busier.

I skate backward as I instruct him. "Don't forget to bend your knees, otherwise you will fall on your ass, and you're going to hate your life tomorrow."

"I can't believe I'm doing this. The things I do to spend time with you, seriously," he murmurs with a soft, hearty laugh that makes my skin prickle with goosebumps.

My cheeks blush at the confession, and my mind wanders off to God knows where after hearing that, and I bump into the railing, causing me to fall forward, almost hitting my head.

Damian stops with the railing, then tries to scrunch down to the best of his ability. "You okay?"

I groan as I get up. "Yeah, I'm okay."

"Don't forget to bend your knees," he says, mimicking me.

I flip him off as we both start laughing.

We continue skating for one more hour, laughing my ass off every time he falls and refuses my help trying to get up, which results in us standing in the same place for five minutes as he figures it out. By the end of the session, he's finally getting it, and we actually end up having a lot of fun.

We laugh *a lot*. Fun and simple, like it always is when he starts to bring his walls down little by little. Seeing his shoulders relax and that gorgeous smile has quickly become my undoing. Little by little, Damian has found his way into my heart, and I can't even say I was blindsided, because deep down, my heart always knew.

And the knowledge scares me.

CHAPTER 26 DAMIAN

As I was taking my skates off and returning them to the rental stand, Aria went to one of the food stalls and got the biggest cream cheese pretzel she could find, and to top it off, she made me eat half of it. I'm not even mad. That shit was fucking delicious.

I don't think I've ever had this much fun, in like, well, ever. Sure, I go on vacations once a year, and I go out with Lorenzo and Matteo from time to time, but this is different. She has this way of making me feel light and relaxed, naturally sharing her positive energy, making the people around her just be... better.

And I'm a simple man who wants to follow her wherever she goes.

She makes me want to become a better person. It's as simple as that. With her, I can do the impossible.

To actually, truly, be happy for once.

Never in a million years did I think that was a possibility. It's not that I'm unhappy with my life, but I've always been content, but unfulfilled. Always looking for the next best thing, trying to fill that dread and emptiness that rests deep inside of me.

Except when I'm with her.

All I want to do is make these moments last forever, put us in a bubble, and just... *be.*

She groans, limping. "I don't know why we skated before going to the museum. I'm beat."

My body feels super sore too, but I refuse to make this day shorter. I want to spend as much time with her as possible before we go back to our normal professional relationship.

Yeah, like you can ever go back to that.

"Well, too bad. You promised The Met. I haven't been in years." When I was able to afford any sort of traveling, this was the first place I came to. My first stop was The Metropolitan Museum, where such fine art as "Autumn Rhythm" by Jackson Pollock and "Self Portrait With Straw Hat" by Vincent van Gogh reside. It had been my dream since I was a little kid to go, but my father was struggling as it is with his gallery, so we couldn't afford it.

"Which painting are you most excited to see?" I ask.

"Mmm," she ponders. "Probably Bridge Over A Pond Of Water Lilies by Claude Monet. I love his work. It's so... peaceful. I could stare at it for hours if they let me."

We arrive at the museum and since it's a Saturday, it's definitely busier than normal, but we enter quickly and go to our favorite spots. We see the different collections from Asian to Egyptian art, and much more. We decide to leave the European paintings for last since that's mostly what we came for.

As we're roaming the European Paintings section, I'm barely paying attention to my surroundings. I'm mostly looking at Aria, because even though there is nothing but rich history in this place, all I can focus on is *her*. The way her eyes beam with excitement when she sees one of her favorite collections, to the way she scrunches her eyebrows as she studies a new painting, trying to discover the secret and history behind it. She likes to come up with her own theories and damn this girl is good, proving once more why she's one of the top curators in the industry.

"Okay, this one," she points as she reads the title, "*Cypress in Moonlight.*"

I nod, trying to regain my focus on the painting instead of the beautiful woman standing next to me.

"I can tell you off the bat, the style, in particular, is very similar to Vincent van Gogh with the way the cypress and both potted plants are dominating this scene, even though there's so much going on in the background, your eyes just go directly to that cypress."

I nod in understanding, taking in the painting, trying my best to focus on the background, but my eyes keep moving to the cypress automatically.

"I bet you didn't even notice the two shadows in the back," she points out.

I gaze over the painting, trying my best to ignore the cypress and potted plants, noticing a shallow street next to the buildings, where there are indeed two shadows walking. "Such attention to detail," I say in awe.

"Indeed," she whispers.

We look at a few more statement pieces before we realize it's already closing time. Being surrounded by art is a quick way to lose track of time, getting so involved in the rich history and the story each piece tells. It's truly amazing.

As we exit the museum, we're hit with the cold wind of the night. It's a little past nine in the evening, and the city is bustling with activity as always.

"Are you hungry?" I ask.

"I'm starving, but I'm so tired. I say we order takeout."

"As long as it's not dumplings, I don't think I can eat those for a while." I shudder with a grimace. Those dumplings were delicious, but I had too many at once.

She rubs her hands together, seeking some warmth as a laugh escapes her lips. "*Ha.* Liar. You know you loved them."

"True," I confess.

My driver arrives and I open the door for Aria. Thankfully, she's so exhausted she doesn't protest, which I appreciate because my body is so sore from ice skating, and I don't think I can walk anymore. The drive is short, and we go back to the condo as we go over the eating options, deciding to go simple and order some pizza.

Nodding toward her room as I pick up the takeout pamphlet, I say, "I'll make the order, you can go take a shower."

"Oh, thank you. Because I'm so cold, I can't wait to feel some hot water against my skin," she says through a giggle, walking to her room and shutting the door.

I bite my lip trying to contain back a groan, because now I have an image in my head of Aria's soft skin with droplets of water glistening all over.

And I'm officially losing my mind again. Get it fucking together.

Shaking my head and trying my best to get that image out of my head, I opt to call the restaurant instead. I have no idea what type of toppings she likes, so I order a few different combinations.

As I wait for the food to arrive, I sit down and open my laptop to take a quick look at my emails, trying to get ahead for the upcoming week and putting out any fires that need my attention. I've been so distracted with Aria, I've barely paid attention to my phone, much less my email. I have hundreds of unread emails—not surprising— with random requests and meeting reminders. As I glance at them, I notice an encrypted email.

From: Unknown

To: Damian Romano

Subject: None

You need to fire Aria Petrov. There will be consequences if you don't.

What the fuck?

My phone rings, and Matteo's name shows up on the screen. I don't hesitate to pick it up.

"I just saw the email," Matteo says from the other line.

I thin my lips as I close my eyes, trying to keep myself together and not let the rage that's slowly simmering take over.

"I'm already tracing the email, relax," Matteo continues, somehow sensing my rage brewing.

"Do you think this is related to the break-in?"

"I don't doubt it. Who the hell did you piss off?" Matteo asks with a hint of amusement in his voice that ticks me off.

"How much time do you have?" I retort, gritting my teeth. I'm a fucking billionaire in a cut-throat business. I have enemies coming out of my fucking ears.

"I will keep you posted," Matteo says before hanging up.

Who the fuck is doing this? But more importantly, why? Is it another gallery that maybe wants her on their team? I don't think she has gotten any other offers, but even if she did, she wouldn't take one.

Or would she?

No. No way.

As I'm brewing in my thoughts, my email pins with another encrypted email notification.

From: Unknown

To: Damian Romano

Subject: None

You have a 24 hours to meet my demand, otherwise, you can sit and watch the consequences of your own stupid actions.

As I'm reading the email, Aria comes out of her bedroom. My back stiffens and I snap the laptop shut with a little more force than necessary.

"You okay?" Aria asks as she approaches me.

I look back at her. "Uh, yeah. Why?"

She holds my gaze for a moment as she dries her hair with a towel, then shrugs and sits next to me. She can't find out what's happening. She's going to want to get involved and I have this gut strange feeling I can't pinpoint, but all I know is, I want her as far as possible from this situation.

Before she can drill me with more questions, the food arrives and we sit down and open all the boxes. I definitely ordered way too much, but better be safe than sorry.

"You're so extra. A bacon pizza would have been fine," she grabs a slice and takes a bite, "but thank you."

"What if you preferred pepperoni? Or veggies? I didn't want to risk it," I shrug, picking a piece of my own and biting into the cheesy, bready savoriness.

She swallows her bite before replying, "I hate pepperoni."

"Wow." My eyebrows shot up in surprise. "I think you may be the only person in the world that hates pepperoni."

She shrugs. "It's disgusting. Don't ask me why, because there's no rhyme or reason for my hate for it. I hate the taste, and it's so greasy."

"Bacon is greasy, too," I point out.

"Yeah, but at least it tastes good," she counters with a playful smile, then takes another bite.

I shake my head with a laugh. That's her, alright. No rhyme or reason for the things she likes. We keep eating and talking about art, our college years, and anything random we can think of.

"Do you have any siblings?" I ask.

She shakes her head. "Only child, fortunately. I don't think any other normal child could have survived my mother," she says with a laugh that doesn't reach her eyes, and that tugs at my heart in an unsatisfactory way.

She's so unapologetically herself, no matter what. It's my favorite quality about her, but I can't help but wonder if it's because of all she's endured. I can relate, in a sense. I believe what breaks you makes you stronger. You can either face your problems or run away from them.

I chose the latter, deciding to take my father's struggling business and turn it into the empire it is becoming today. But at the same time, I refuse to look back and forgive everything I went through with him, because even though he's not here, he doesn't deserve my forgiveness. Fuck that. I don't want to be the bigger person, even if it's the right thing to do.

You don't always have to do the right thing, not if it means sacrificing your sanity.

"Do you have any siblings?"

I shake my head. "The closest thing I have to a brother is

Enzo. He lived in Italy until his late teenage years, but used to visit Chicago every summer, and we would spend our time together," I say, reminiscing the few good memories I have.

Her eyes soften as she grabs my hand and squeezes it in a tender, loving way. The feeling is electric, and I never want to let go.

"Boy, do I feel sorry for you if Enzo is the closest thing you had. He seems unreliable," she jokes.

"Surprisingly, he has been the only constant in my life," I confess.

Despite Enzo living a hard life, training since he was a literal child on how to think and behave like a businessman, preparing to take over the Mancini name, he taught me everything I know. Helped me build my business plans, invested his time and energy, but most importantly— *believed* in me. It's difficult to accept how the tables have turned, how somehow, for some reason, he has lost his way in life. He's not the man he used to be. That's for sure.

We finish eating, and she insists on making hot chocolates, even though I'm so stuffed and don't think I can ingest anything else, I accept it. Because it just means I have a few more minutes with her. As we both sit on the couch, facing each other, and she's talking about her first days working for The Institute, a moment of honesty takes over me for a chance.

Without thinking, I say, "Can I confess something?"

She looks at me expectantly and nods.

"I don't want this day to end," I whisper.

She doesn't falter, nor does her body language change in surprise. She grabs my mug and places it on the table next to hers. Taking my hand and interlacing our fingers, she whispers, "Me neither." She looks down, avoiding my gaze.

My heart quickens at her words. Here I thought the feeling wasn't mutual, that she was just being kind, wanting to make sure I didn't spend my Saturday alone. Because that sums up Aria Petrov.

Fierce. Selfless. Kind.

Our bodies shift closer, and I tuck one of her hair strands behind her ear. She looks up, with her bright hazel eyes, and I get lost in them once again.

All I can do is admire her. Her beauty is fucking *overwhelming.*

Both of my hands find the base of her jawline, and as she melts to my touch, I whisper, "Penso di essermi innamorata di te." *I think I'm falling in love with you.*

"What does that mean?" she asks softly.

"That you're beautiful," the lie rolls off my tongue easily, because I'm not ready to tell her the truth. Not yet, anyway.

Before she can respond, I close the little distance we have left with a soft, yearning kiss. I've been wanting to do this ever since we last kissed, and fuck, it feels good to feel her lips on mine. She kisses me back with the same softness and need, reciprocating my feelings. While the first kiss was fierce, and desperate, this one is the exact opposite. It's like time is staying still, and we have nothing else to do but to explore each other's mouths. The kiss is consuming; intoxicating. I could die a happy man right now. There's no other place I would rather be.

Her lips part, and I let out an appreciative groan as my tongue clashes with hers. She tastes *so fucking sweet.* I've never considered myself a sweets kind of man, but for her? I could indulge in it for the rest of my life. My teeth find her bottom lip, and I bite it softly. A low, soft moan escapes her lips as I bite the soft flesh. She wraps her arms around my shoulders, fisting my hair and bringing us closer, and God, it's driving me insane. I could happily get lost in her touch, her delicious taste and her dizzying scent and never come back.

My weakness; my lifeline; my anchor.

Mine. Mine. Fucking mine.

27

Aria

As I fist his hair to bring us closer, he groans as our tongues clash once again, licking and exploring. If I were standing up right now, I'm sure my knees would have buckled. One of his hands roams my curves, arriving on my waist, and grips it softly, breaking us apart from the kiss.

"Darling," he rasps through a ragged breath.

That damn nickname.

"Yes?" I breathe out.

"Can I confess something else?"

I nod as I bite my lip, trying to contain a smile.

"I've wanted nothing more than to kiss you again since last time," he says through a sultry, promising whisper.

"Me too," I confess.

His eyes lock with mine, a million questions clouding his gaze. "Do you want me to stop?"

And I know why he's asking, because last time it didn't end all too well for me. But this time it's different, because I want nothing more than to get lost in him. In his touch. To be *consumed* by him. Be *burned* by him.

"Don't you dare stop, and I mean it this time," I reply breathlessly.

He lets out a throaty laugh that makes my insides melt and kisses me with such passion, it envelops me and puts me in a haze. His hand travels underneath my shirt and starts traveling upwards, cupping the bottom of my breast with his warm, exploratory touch. It leaves a burning sensation throughout my whole body as his hands continue to claim me, like he's a starved man that has been wanting nothing but to worship my body.

He kisses my neck softly, nudging my shirt, silently seeking permission to take it off. I bring my hands up in an invitation, which he quickly accepts, grabbing the fabric and getting rid of it. His gaze travels slowly from my eyes, to my lips and all the way down to my breasts. His eyes are filled with such admiration and lust, it makes me feel nothing but worshiped; desired; and wanted.

No one has made me feel so much with one simple look.

"You're fucking killing me," he says through an appreciative groan.

I blush and look away, suddenly feeling ashamed.

He cups my cheek, gently forcing me to look at him. "Look at me, *Tesoro*."

I meet his green irises, and they rake over my body appreciatively as they grow two shakes darker. The look alone makes my clit throb.

"Semplicemente bellissima."

"What does that mean?"

He caresses my bottom lip with his thumb, and huskily whispers, "Simply beautiful."

My chest tightens at the compliment. His eyes are filled with a sincerity that makes me believe him.

I am beautiful. I am worthy. I am more.

This time, I close the distance and kiss him fervently. The way our lips dace together becomes more frantic by the second as his hands roam my body, worshiping every inch with his burning; electrifying touch.

His kisses travel down my neck, chest, and abdomen until he arrives at my waist. He looks up, his eyes seeking permission. I nod quickly as I close my eyes, my chest heaving at the warm touch of his hands as he takes off my shorts.

An appreciative growl escapes his lips when he realizes I have no underwear on, revealing how wet and ready I am for him. The sensation is too much. I crave more of his touch—more of *him*—in every sense of the word. He kisses my inner thigh, his lips roaming close to my center; teasing and biting softly.

"Damian, please," I beg through a heaved breath.

I don't even know what I'm begging for at this point. I'm so pent up with need, I could come by the way his hand caresses my legs and the way he's kissing my inner thighs.

He flattens his tongue against my center and licks in one fell swoop, so torturously slow, I roll my eyes in plea- sure as I gasp for air. His tongue is hot, and slick, I instantly crave more. The way he devours me, and the way his mouth kisses me like it was made for him. Like *I* was made for him, it's all too good and too much at the same time.

"*Fuck*," he groans. "You taste so fucking sweet, baby."

"Damian," I moan, his sultry words making me even wetter and filling me with a need I didn't think was possible. And here I thought the man couldn't be more perfect.

He starts licking and teasing, giving me enough friction to build me up, but not enough to take me over the painful edge. I move with the rhythm of his tongue, riding his face, wanting nothing more than to chase the sweet, needed relief.

He stops and I let out a whimper, missing his mouth already. He brushes a finger along my center, coating it with my arousal before slipping it inside of me. As his finger slides in and out of me at a taunting speed, his thumb starts moving in soft circles around my swollen clit.

"Oh, *fuck*. I need more, Damian. Please, give me more." My heart is lodged in my throat and my clit throbs painfully against his thumb every time he brushes it.

"Tell me what you want, Darling," he whispers as his lips hover over my inner thigh.

I mumble something inaudible, because I can't seem to form coherent sentences as his hands roam all over me and as his warm breath prickles my skin.

"I can't hear you," he taunts as he abruptly stops touching me. "If you want something, you're going to have to tell me."

I open my eyes as I lock my gaze with his, and the fucker has a playful smirk in his face.

Oh, this man is good.

I lick my lips and exhale breathlessly. I can't believe he's going to make me say it. "I want you to make me come, please," I whisper shakily.

His eyes fill with eager hunger, placing both of my legs on top of his shoulders as he shifts between them. "You're such a good girl," he praises. "And your wish is my command, Darling."

This time, he slips two fingers inside of me as his mouth closes around my clit with a hard, delicious suck. The pressure shoots up my spine, rapidly building my orgasm. I squirm beneath him, feeling overwhelmed by the sensation of his fingers and tongue in my pussy. His digits slide in and out of me more rapidly, the sound of my arousal filling the room. In any other instance, I would feel ashamed, but it makes the moment so much more depraved, it just makes me wetter instead. His tongue remains steady on my clit, making deliberate circles. Giving me the right amount of friction I desperately need. The orgasm sneaks up on me, my vision blurring as a million fireworks explode inside my body. I moan his name over and over again as I squirm beneath him, trying to get off of his hold, but his iron grip doesn't let me. Looking down at him, his eyes, the ones that are filled with such desire and lust lock with mine as he licks every bit of my climax, not letting one single drop escape. And he looks so primal, and dirty, just drinking every ounce of me, I feel like I could come all over again just by looking at him.

It takes me a moment to come down from the high, the satisfaction. Once I do, he stands and extends his arm to me. I grab it and get up from the couch, still feeling dizzy. He scrunches down with my shorts in his hands, then softly taps my left leg so I can lift it, then my right, putting my shorts back on.

He takes my discarded shirt and stands in his full height, then lifts my arms and puts it on. Once I'm dressed, he places his hand at the nape of my neck, closing the space with a soft kiss. I can taste myself on his lips, and that makes my legs clench involuntarily.

Brushing a hair strand out of my face, he whispers, "Good night," then turns around and starts to walk away, leaving me in a swirl of uncertainty and confusion.

I grab him by his forearm to stop him. "Wait. Where are you going? What about you?"

I'm trying my best to mask my hurt. That's it? Just a

casual hookup—if you can even call it that—and he's going to walk away?

He shakes his head. "It's fine."

I take a step back. Okay, now I'm officially offended. "It's *fine*? That's all you have to say to me?"

Just as I thought we were making progress. Just as I thought he was finally letting his walls all the way down, he builds them right back up.

A humorless laugh escapes him. "Trust me, you don't want to hear what I really have to say, Aria."

"Try me," I challenge.

He grazes his teeth with his tongue, weighing his words. The tension is building rapidly. Electricity flickers all over us; *between* us.

Oh, God. Maybe I'm not ready to hear what he has to say at all.

He stalks over me, closing the distance between us. "It's no secret I want you." He gulps, his eyes locking with mine. Oh, those beautiful haunting green eyes that are filled with so much uncertainty; with an unspoken emotion. My heart tightens, and I turn breathless with the intensity of them.

"But I don't just want half of you," he says with a hint of hurt in his voice. "I want your good days; your bad days, and every day in between. I want *all of you*. I can't bring myself to meet you halfway."

His confession shocks me, leaving me speechless. I'm frozen, standing still as my mind runs a million miles per second. I've never been *wanted*, not like this. All of my relationships have been mediocre at best. Along the way, I convinced myself that's all I deserved. I didn't accept more, because, how could I? Not even my parents can love me properly, and they're supposed to, for God's sake. What makes me think I deserve anything more?

He closes the little distance left between us, hovering his lips over mine, ever so closely.

With a strained, pained whisper, he says, "If we do this, I'm determined to be your last. You and I, Aria, we're endgame. Are you ready for that?"

All I want to do is scream—*Yes! That's all I want! All of you!*

So why am I hesitating?

The realization crashes over me like an icy wave.

I don't feel worthy of this. This wonderful man before me, that's bearing his heart out to me, I'm not worthy of it—of *him*. I'm not worthy of an epic love that consumes every bone of my body. I'm not worthy of *anything*.

He nods knowingly, letting go of me. Leaving a cold distance between us that makes my stomach tighten. The silence is deafening, and my throat starts closing in as my eyes fill with involuntary tears. There's so much I want to say, yet I can't find the right words. I don't even know where to start.

He turns around and starts to walk away as my heart screams at me, loud and clear.

Stop him! Stop this! Go after him!

His fingers curl around the door handle, ready to turn it, but he pauses, his voice breaking the silence. "I'll be here when you're ready. I always will be."

With that, he turns the handle and steps into his room, shutting the door behind him, leaving me and my racing thoughts all alone.

I'm exhausted. I got little to no sleep after everything

that transpired last night. Damian's words were an endless loop in my head.

I want your good days; your bad days, and every day in between. I want all of you. I can't bring myself to meet you halfway.

You and I, Aria, we're endgame. Are you ready for that?

Are you ready for that?

Are. You. Ready. For. That.

I want to be ready, God, do I want to. But how do I even begin to open myself, to let someone come into my life and love me, when I can't even love myself?

Maybe if I'm just honest and lay it all out there, we can figure it out. It's no secret he has his issues, too. Maybe this is what we need. Learn from each other. Rely on each other. Maybe, for once, I don't have to go through the storm alone.

If I had to choose someone to share my dark days with, it'd be him. No doubt.

Looking at the clock, it's almost noon. I definitely over-slept, but I didn't really get to fall asleep until about three AM, and even then, I was still waking up every hour.

The auction is tonight, and I'm really looking forward to it. One painting. That's it. That's all we need to complete the collection, throw the gala, and let the new story of The Romano Gallery commence.

These past few months have been amazing. Having full creative control not only helped me professionally, but it also inspired me to start painting again. I met Isabella, who is now one of my closest friends. And... *him*. He's the best thing that has come out of this.

I groan as I get out of the most comfortable bed I've ever been on. Deciding to get my day started, I take a shower, and wash my hair to make sure I can get it clean and ready to style it for tonight. I don't have to start getting ready yet, since the auction starts at seven, so I put on a comfortable yoga set and my oversized sweater to go out and get some coffee and a late breakfast.

I stride into the kitchen and spot Damian sitting on the bar stools, drinking a cup of coffee and having what seems like a very intense conversation over the phone. He looks over his shoulder and shoots me one of his killer smiles, and quickly hangs up the phone without saying goodbye to whoever he was speaking with.

I reach the counter where there's a spread of pastries, eggs, and fruit. My stomach grumbles as if on cue, and my mouth is already savoring the sweet taste of croissants.

"I got breakfast from that coffee shop you like. I also got you an iced caramel latte, which is in the fridge. Ordered it without ice, so it wouldn't melt."

I nod, walking to the fridge to get the caffeine I very much need.

"I also got you a cup of ice, since I know you like theirs. It's in the freezer," he continues.

My cheeks blush at the simple fact that he remembered such an insignificant thing like the type of ice I like. But that's Damian for you.

Always thoughtful.

I grab the cup of ice from the freezer, open the lid, and pour the sweet caffeinated drink over the ice. Silence falls over the kitchen, the hair from the back of my neck prickles as his gaze focuses on my every movement as he bounces his legs and fidgets with his phone. Dare I say, he looks almost... nervous.

It's actually kind of cute.

"Thanks for the coffee," I say with a smile, then take a sip of the caramelized goodness.

He nods without saying anything.

My gaze lingers for a moment, before I grab a plate and grab a pastry with fruit. My mind is running with so many thoughts. Last night, I had more time to reflect and I practiced a handful of scenarios, but the reality is so much different. There's so much I want to say, and this is as good a time as any, but I second-guess myself every step of the way, like I always do. Afraid of messing up. Afraid of saying the wrong thing.

Before I can speak up, he walks up to me. "Aria, listen, about yesterday."

I gulp, dropping the plate next to the pastries and turning around. "Damian—"

"No, please. Listen," he interrupts.

I thin my lips, shaking my head. "No. Let me speak first."

His eyes are pleading, expectantly. He thinks he did something wrong. It's written all over his face. Little does he know, he gave me the courage to face my fears. Gave me the courage to reflect that I, too, feel so much for him.

I let out a shaky exhale, trying my best to calm my nerves, and lock my eyes on his. Somehow, amidst everything, I've started to find peace in his forest-green eyes. When I get lost in them, I know everything will be alright.

I've never been open to anybody, but with him, it feels *right; safe; meant to be.*

"I'm a complicated person, to say the least. I think you've seen enough to confirm that."

He shakes his head, grabbing my hand and giving it a gentle, caring squeeze. "You're not complicated at all. Trust me on that."

He says it with such conviction, I almost believe him. But I'm a complete mess. My whole life, I've done things to make other people happy. It's not lost on me the mistakes I've made in my life.

I've convinced myself I'm a shit of an artist and refuse to pursue what my heart truly desires simply because I'm afraid of rejection. Afraid of looking ridiculous. Afraid of embarrassment. Doesn't matter that I managed to place those boundaries four years ago with my mother by disappearing off of the face of the earth, because she came back, and as soon as she did, I let her walk all over me with one single phone call.

All my life, I've worked my hardest to be someone I'm not. Look a certain way. Dress a certain way. Those boundaries I placed are a lie, because she's always in the back of my head, like an inner voice telling me how worthless I am. The worst part is, I believe it. What's even worse? I don't know how to stop believing *it*.

I inhale deeply, trying to hold back the tears that want to escape. "Believe me, you're wrong."

"You're just fighting your demons the best way you can, *Tesoro*. Believe me, I know that." He hangs his head in defeat with a sigh. "I've been fighting my demons, too. Every fucking day."

His voice is one of conviction. Of a man that has been through Hell and back, a man who is so, so tired. *A man I can relate to.*

"I want to open up to you, I do. But only if you're willing to do it too, Aria. I meant what I said yesterday. I can't do things halfway," he shakes his head, "Not with you."

"I want to. I do. But I don't know how," I confess with a strained whisper.

He closes the distance between us, bringing me in for a hug. His scent envelops me, making me feel at ease. *He smells like belonging. Like home.*

He kisses the top of my head as the tears fall down my

cheeks. It's too late to stop them. This man, right here, can bring so many emotions out of me without feeling judged.

"Open up to me, Darling. I promise to catch you if you fall, always. Just let me be there for you."

There's no doubt in my mind that he will, in fact, always be there for me. I can trust him. I *will* trust him.

"I believe you." I sigh. "I just need time. It's," I gulp, trying to find the right word, "hard."

He brushes his knuckles against my cheek with a tender touch as he nods. "I'll be here when you're ready. Because you're worth it."

The rest of the afternoon goes by quickly. I decide to stay in and study the potential pieces that are being auctioned today. I promised myself I wasn't going to work, but this has to go perfectly. This is when my perfectionist personality comes into play, becoming a double-edged sword. There are some interesting pieces being sold today, but there are still other pieces that remain a mystery. They typically like to create some hype within the community so more people attend.

My hair's in a sleek updo, allowing my pearl white love heart earrings to shine, adding a gold bracelet with a heart charm on my wrist that pairs well with the earrings. The dress that Sophia let me borrow is a simple one-shoulder long-sleeve made of black satin with a side slit that's a little risqué. Since I'm taller than Sophia, the slit is settled higher than it normally would, but I'm trying not to think about it too much. I just need to remind myself: *I am beautiful.*

I pair the dress with my usual black Louboutins' and red lip that more often than not, makes me gain confidence.

Putting some perfume on, I glance at my phone to make sure I'm not running late.

I take one last look in the mirror with a sigh. It's hard not to be self-conscious. This dress is tighter than I remembered, and I had to opt out of wearing underwear because the lines were showing. So I'm most definitely out of my comfort zone right now. The only thing I have going for me today is that I took the extra time to get my hair done. There's not a strand out of place, especially my ungodly curls. Otherwise, I'd have more than enough reasons to go through a whole spiral over my looks. Being a woman sucks. The way I look consumes my every waking moment. It runs my life. It determines my mood, the way I don't love myself. *Everything.*

Thank you very much for that, Mother.

I close my eyes, taking a deep breath. Trying my best to remember to be kind to myself. All I hear is my mother's voice in the back of my head, making up things she most definitely would say if she were here.

That dress is too tight. Have you been gaining weight?

At least your hair looks nice. It would look better with a perm, though.

Shaking my head, I practice one round of breathing, trying to calm my anxiety. Knowing I need to see her in just a few days is definitely fucking with my head.

Walking out of the room, my breath hitches involuntarily as I spot Damian. My knees buckle at the sight of him, because God, this man's beauty is so raw and overwhelming.

He's in an all-black tux, his vest is of black satin material, same as my dress. His pocket has a gold lapel chain with a king's crown, the stones are blood red, the same color as my usual lipstick. His hair is slicked back, and his face is freshly shaven, giving him a clean elegant look.

We walk out of the condo and before we get in the car, he flashes me a boyish smile that makes my heartbeat quicken, tightening my chest. He extends his hand and closes the distance between us once I grab it. He places his other hand on my hip as his nose lingers on the side of my neck, taking a soft inhale that suddenly makes me feel extremely hot in the middle of the New York winter.

My hand travels to his gold lapel chain, my fingertips tracing the red stones. "I like it. It's very you," I taunt.

He smirks, locking his gaze on mine. "I chose it because the stones reminded me of you."

My face laces with surprise at his confession.

He places a soft kiss close to my lips, then whispers, "You look so damn beautiful, *Tesoro*."

He opens the door, and before I get in I turn around and ask, "I've been meaning to ask, what does *Tesoro* mean?"

He smirks, licking his lip before replying, "Treasure."

Oh, I'm so, so fucking screwed.

Damian

I can't take my eyes off of her. I'm pretty sure I look like a creep right now, but I couldn't care less. Here I thought the possibility of her looking more beautiful was impossible, but she proves me wrong once again.

"You're staring," she whispers with a giggle.

"You really do look beautiful."

"Yes," she rolls her eyes playfully, "I gathered that from the other six times you've told me during this ten minute car ride."

"What can I say? I don't want you to forget."

She places her head on my shoulder with a laugh. "Right."

I almost said fuck it when she came out, because all I wanted to do was stay home so I could tear that fucking dress off and worship her the way she deserves.

My cock stiffens at the thought of me between her legs, exploring every inch of her body, and making her come until we're both delirious and exhausted.

God, this is fucking killing me.

As we get out of the car, the entrance is bustling with

activity. There are paparazzi all around since this is one of the most prestigious auctions in the world. All well-known artists, gallery owners, and even celebrities attend every year.

Aria's looking around, taking it all in. She stops dead in her tracks and grabs my arm as she keeps looking around nervously, which is understandable, since it's her first time coming here. I place my hand around her waist and press my fingers reassuringly. She looks at me and takes a deep breath with a nod as we both start walking to the entrance.

"Wait, is that Damian Romano?" a woman whispers.

"Seems so. Who is he with?" another woman whispers back.

I roll my eyes as we keep walking to the carpet to get our photo taken. For business owners like me, it's important we come here to make connections, but also, the auction lineup they have is usually quite impressive, and I always make it a point to leave with a piece or two. Most people treat this like a party, where they come to drink and gossip as they desperately try to get into the elite's inner circles. It's sickening, really.

Approaching the carpet, she tries to wiggle herself out of my touch, whispering, "I'll be inside."

I grip her waist. "Where do you think you're going?"

"What do you mean? They can't take pictures of us. That won't be good for your reputation," she replies back with a confused frown etched on her face.

I raise an eyebrow. "My reputation, huh?" I laugh, kissing the top of her head and whispering, "*Tesoro*, I couldn't give zero fucks about my reputation. Now smile."

She shakes her head, her shoulders shaking with laughter as she places her arm on my back and looks at the cameras with a bright smile.

That damn smile. I'd give anything to see that plastered on her face always.

While everyone is trying to get my attention, as paparazzi are shouting at me to look their way, all I can do is look at her. With her bright smile and natural charisma, and the way her cheeks blush from the compliments they're shouting at her.

So fucking beautiful.

I don't care what the rest of the world is doing, because I just want to stay here forever in this exact moment. Those big bright hazel eyes find mine, and her eyes sparkle with so much happiness, it makes my chest tight with emotion. I simply grin back at her like an idiot.

Once they finish taking our pictures, *Fathom Vanity*, the magazine company owned by *Fathom Group*, who is in charge of the auction, is having one of their reporters interview some people, and while I typically steer away from that side of things, the reporter is running, trying to catch up with us. I can't deny it makes me feel a little bad, so I give her the benefit of the doubt.

"Mr. Romano! I'm Rachel Zae, reporter for Fathom Vanity magazine. Can I have a moment of your time?" the woman asks, panting.

I nod curtly, glancing at my watch. "Only have a few minutes, so make them count."

"I hear you've almost completed your gallery collection. Is that why you're here tonight? Anything you can tell us on how that endeavor is going?"

"Certainly." I nod curtly. "Without giving much away, all I can say is that I'm really looking forward to re-opening The Romano Gallery and showing you what we've been working with," I look at Aria. "I had the wonderful opportunity to hire this beautiful woman, Aria Petrov, one of the top curators in the industry. She's really been taking over the creative control of the gallery, and has been doing some wonderful work."

Aria smiles shyly and nods without saying anything.

Rachel, the reporter, opens her eyes wide. "Wow. That's... surprising. What do you have to say to the people that usually find working with you extremely difficult? What made you change your mind and let," she looks at Aria from head to toe, "her take creative control?"

I let out a humorless laugh. The look she gave Aria doesn't escape me, and she's about to be fucking sorry for it. "She has a name. It's Aria Petrov, by the way, in case you've forgotten. And I have nothing to say to that. She's extremely good at what she does." I grab Aria's hand and interlace our fingers as I look at her with a warm smile. "And I trust her." I look back at the reporter and nod curtly. "No more comments. Thank you."

Aria leans toward me. "Thank you for that."

I shake my head. "I didn't do it just for you. I truly believe you're good at what you do, Darling. Please don't let people think otherwise."

And that's the truth. I won't allow people to doubt her ability, and I will make sure that's known. My promise to her was real, too. I'm here for her, always. I will defend her with tooth and nail. This doesn't change the fact that I hired her because I knew what she could bring to the table was nothing short of amazing.

She pats my chest jokingly with a playful wink. "Come on, Romano. Give me more credit than that. I know I'm good."

"Good. You best remember that, always."

The auction is being held on the second floor of Fathom Group's two-story gallery, while the first floor is where people socialize. I typically come alone, because the last thing I want to give people is ammo to talk about my personal life and start their gossip. That's all people love to do in this industry, and it bores me. I'm nothing but glad that she's here with me though. She's the calm in my storm, and the serenity she brings me is something I've grown to love.

"Wow, this place is *nice*," she whispers.

"That's Fathom Group for you."

The place is nothing short of extravagant. With high-ceiling walls, and a spiral staircase in the middle that takes you to the second floor. Typically, there's nothing but art all around, but today, there are high tables scattered with candles causing a low light setting, giving it a sense of elegance.

As we're walking, a few people stop me to introduce themselves, and while they're talking nonstop, Aria is nodding and smiling along, while I have nothing but a scowl on my face. I have no interest in these people and what they have to say. All I want is to be left alone with Aria, and go to our little bubble where all I see and listen to is her.

She hits me softly with her elbow. "Would it kill you to be nice?" she whispers.

I roll my eyes. "This is how I am during these activities. They bore me."

She chuckles, looking at me knowingly. "God, you're such a snob."

I shrug. It's not that I'm a snob. It's that I know these people see me as less by the simple fact that I don't come from old money. I worked my ass off to get to where I am, and with this being such a small community, they always hate the outsiders. It's a bunch of hypocrites who want to play nice with me when they see me once or twice a year. I'd rather not entertain them.

"Oh my God, is that Henry Anderson?" Aria whispers to me excitedly.

"How do you even know who Henry Anderson is?" I raise an eyebrow.

"Sophia's a hockey fan, and obsessed with that man. God, she would die if she knew he was here. He's definitely more handsome in person."

A tinge of jealousy floods through me at her comment, but that's Henry Anderson for you. At the ripe age of eighteen, he was drafted by the NHL, making him one of the youngest players to join the roster. The Canadian is known for being a trouble maker, getting traded from team to team when the organizations don't know what to do with the amount of issues he causes. He recently got traded to the Chicago Strikers, so let's see how long he'll last. The man is known for being a menace in and out of the ice, too. He's also a notorious playboy, with a different woman in every city he plays at. With the amount of money he makes, it's not surprising.

As I'm about to reply to her comment, Henry walks our way as he extends his hand to me.

"Hey, man. Long time no see," he says as we shake hands and pat each other in the back.

I nod. "Yeah, man. I haven't had time to go to any games."

"Because you're a workaholic. It wouldn't kill you to go out once in a while. Matter of fact, we should hang out once we go back to—" He stops mid sentence, his eyes finding Aria's.

I already don't like where this is going.

"Who do we have here?" he asks with a flirtatious smile.

"Henry Anderson, nice to meet you, beautiful." He winks, extending his hand to Aria.

While Aria reaches out, I place my hand on her waist and grip a little too possessively.

"Aria Petrov. So nice to meet you. My best friend is a huge fan of yours," she replies with a smile.

Henry looks at my hand placement and smirks knowingly. He may be a playboy, but his Canadian roots make him too respectful. He knows she's off limits. That doesn't mean the man doesn't like to push people's buttons, though.

He smiles. "If she's as beautiful as you, I definitely need an introduction."

"Aria, if you love Sophia, please don't do that," I deadpan.

She snorts with laughter.

Henry takes a step back, acting offended. "Oh, come on, Damian. You hurt me. I'm a gentleman," he remarks jokingly.

"Sorry, Anderson, but I love her too much. I could never do that to her," she says with a playful wink.

Aria excuses herself to go to the restroom as Anderson and I go to the open bar, grab a few drinks, and keep talking about his contract with the Strikers, my latest business adventure, and just overall catching up. We used to hang out a lot, but our schedules are so hectic, I see him maybe once a year in events like these. Taking a glance at my watch, I notice Aria hasn't come back and it's been a good fifteen minutes since she left. Shaking Anderson's hand and saying goodbye, I start looking around for her, dread settling in the pit of my stomach.

29

Aria

Coming out of the bathroom, someone gets in my way and grabs my forearm, completely stopping me.

"Aria?"

I turn around, recognizing the voice instantly.

Alex and I haven't spoken since our last fight. He sent a couple of follow up emails to find out how the meeting went, but I never replied. I'm still pissed, to be honest. Never in a million years would I have thought that one of my closest friends thought I was a charity case. Did he help me at the beginning of my career? Absolutely. But *I* did the rest.

"Alex, hey," I say with a curt nod.

"How are—"

I interrupt. "I better get back, the auction is starting soon. Good to see you," I say.

Alex grabs my arm gently. "Don't go, please. Let's talk."

We don't fight often, honestly. I think during our college years we fought maybe once, so this is gray territory for both of us. I relax my shoulders and nod, following him to a corner of the room.

"How've you been?" he asks.

"Good," I reply dryly.

He lets out a frustrated groan as he scrubs his face with one hand. "Aria, come on. This has been going on for long enough. Don't you think so?"

"No, Alex. I don't think so," I retort. "After all, you thought I was your charity case this whole time."

Alex looks at me suspiciously. "Is this about Damian? Have you guys talked about me? He got in your fucking head, didn't he?" he asks a little too loud for my liking.

I look around, noticing people around us looking at us as they whisper to each other.

"Would you please lower your voice?" I snap.

Alex claps his hands together, laughing humorlessly. "I knew it. I told you working for Damian was a fucking bad idea. But you just never listen, do you?" he shouts.

"Not that I owe you any explanations, but Damian is not even aware that I know you. Now if you excuse me, I have to get back," I say, turning around and refusing to be a part of this ridiculous conversation.

Before I can get any farther, Alex grabs my arm roughly. "We're not done here."

Before I can reply, I hear Damian behind me. "So help me God, Alex. If you don't get your fucking hands off her right this second."

Alex looks over my shoulder and huffs. "Oh, for fuck's sake. Get out of here, Romano. This doesn't concern you."

Damian walks closer to us, his presence making me tremble. He gulps his glass of bourbon in one swig, placing the empty glass on a nearby table as his demeanor changes completely in a terrifying, worrisome way. His usual green eyes are dark now, his presence a thick mist of fury and anger.

He grabs Alex's hand, taking it off of my forearm. "I won't repeat myself twice," he says through gritted teeth as he grips his hand hard, causing Alex to groan from pain. "Now, now, don't go causing a scene," Damian sneers. "What would people say, *golden boy*? Aren't you scared of what people are going to think of you, as always?"

Alex gulps, his gaze snapping to mine. "You're not going to do anything about this?"

"You will *not* speak to her, or breathe the same air as her for that matter. Do you understand me? Or do you need my fist to meet your face to make it clear enough?" Damian says in a conspiratorial, lethal whisper that shakes me through my core.

Alex's green eyes grow two shades darker, as he shakes his head. "You will regret this, Aria. Mark my words," he says with narrowed eyes, storming away.

Damian places his hands on my face, caressing it softly. "Are you okay?"

"I'm pissed." I sigh. "But I'm okay."

"I think we should go."

"No, absolutely not." I shake my head.

"Are you sure, Darling?" he asks softly.

I nod. "I'm sure."

He nods, backing out with an extended arm. "Shall we, then?" He smiles.

I smile back, interlacing my arm with his as we walk toward the stairs.

As we sit at the auction, nothing catches our attention. We want to make sure the last piece ties the collection together. If it weren't for that break-in, we would have been done and already open for business.

As they keep showing the pieces, he whispers, "This collection is worse than I thought."

I nod. "And this is very different from what I was expecting. It seems like the hype they decided to do around this was a bunch of bullshit," I whisper back.

He places a hand on top of his mouth, trying to contain his laughter.

"This upcoming painting is guaranteed to be exciting for everyone here," the auctioneer begins saying, "for all romantic folks out there, I present you *Impossible Touch*."

My eyebrows knit together as I hear the name.

Must be a coincidence.

As they are exposing the painting, my face drains of color.

"Let's start the bidding at thirty thousand dollars. Do I hear thirty?"

No. That's impossible.

Someone raises their paddle and yells thirty.

"I hear thirty. Thirty going once," the auctioneer says.

Someone else raises their paddle and yells thirty-one.

"I hear thirty-one. Thirty-one going once," the auctioneer continues.

Another person raises their paddle as it becomes a tug of war.

Before my two very own eyes is the very first painting I admired on my first day of work. Where Damian told me his first and only love was art.

The painting that was stolen from us.

Everything is moving too fast, my brain is barely catching up to what's happening.

"Damian," I say through a gasp, turning to look at him, but find his seat empty instead.

Looking around nervously, I can't find him anywhere.

What the fuck is going on?

It must be fake. It's impossible that the *Fathom Group* got their hands on that painting. There has to be a reasonable explanation for this.

I get up from my seat to walk out of the auction madness, barely registering what's happening around me, the voice from the auctioneer is far away as anxiety takes hold of me. As I'm walking out of the room, I hear someone yell fifty-three thousand dollars. There's a full-on tug-of-war over the painting.

Our painting.

Running to the first floor, I find Damian having a very heated discussion with an older gentleman. Getting in earshot of them, I recognize the gentleman as Charles Fathom, current CEO of *Fathom Group*.

"Romano, you need to calm down. There must be an explanation for this," Charles says with his hand in the air, trying to calm Damian down.

Damian pushes his chest with one finger. "You will be hearing from my fucking lawyers," he says, then storms out of the building.

"Damian, wait!" I yell after him.

He turns around, his eyes softening. "I'm sorry I disappeared. It's just... I am so fucking pissed right now, Aria."

His eyes have a hint of fury, but it subsided significantly as soon as he spotted me. His hands are trembling, from the anger, I suppose. I'm shaken up too, my anxiety looming in the back of my head trying to take a hold over me. But no. It's my turn to be here for him. Just like he's been for me.

Most importantly, I want to support him in whatever he needs.

My voice laces with hope. "Do we know for a fact that's our painting? Maybe it's a fake."

"I asked Charles where they got the painting, and he was nothing but vague. Refused to provide the code number for it," he says, typing on his phone rapidly. "I have my lawyers on it, though," he continues.

I close the distance between us and place one of my hands on his face, forcing him to meet my eyes. "Are *you* okay, though?"

He sighs, taking a moment before replying, "Now that you're here? Absolutely. It will be fine. Nothing we can't handle. We should probably go, though."

I nod. "Of course. Let's go."

As we're on our way back to the condo, I have a million questions. This makes no sense. If that is our painting, did they steal it? But even if they did, they wouldn't be stupid enough to auction it to the public.

Nothing makes fucking sense to me, and looking at Damian, he looks as confused and lost as me.

30

Damian

I've been in a meeting with my lawyers and Matteo since I got back from the auction. It's late, and I'm barely registering what they're saying. Anger still simmers throughout my body, and I just want this to be over.

First Alex, now this. *Fuck.*

Also, how does Aria even know Alex? I have a million questions racing through my head right now, and I'm on the verge of snapping.

"We can't simply hack into their system, Carter. This is not how it works," Liam Hawkins, my lawyer, says.

"You guys move at the pace of a snail. I can find out in no time if that's in fact our painting," Matteo counters.

"That's *illegal*," Liam says exasperated.

I snap and hit the table. "Oh, for fuck's sake!"

Everyone quiets down, all eyes looking at me expectantly.

I glance at Matteo. "Carter, we can't fucking do that, especially because I am very much looking forward to suing the fuck out of them." Shifting my gaze to Liam, I say,

"Hawkins, I don't know what to tell you, man, but you need to light a fire under your team's ass because this needs to be done as of *yesterday*."

"We're doing everything we can—"

"I don't want excuses. I want actions. You're dismissed."

Liam nods as he gets up and walks out.

"Damian, you know I'm right," Matteo begins.

"Not now, Carter. I'm seriously pissed off and exhausted. Find out what you can," I lock my gaze on him, "*legally*."

"You're no fun," he murmurs as he stands. "I'll see what I can find. Now if you excuse me, I'm going back to Chicago. Real dick move making me travel all the way here. Have you ever heard of video chatting?"

"This was too important, and it needed to be in person, you know that. And I would have traveled back, but Aria's with me. I didn't want to wreck her plans."

"You could have left her alone. She's a big girl," he replies smugly.

I glare at him and dismiss him with my hand.

"I see." Matteo raises his eyebrow. "Who knew you were the possessive type?" he jokes.

"Get the fuck out. I mean it, Carter."

He salutes mockingly with a laugh and walks out of the office, leaving me to brew in my own thoughts.

The car ride back to the condo was silent. I was firing off emails left and right, trying to gather everyone to strategize —which went horribly, I don't know what I was thinking— and Aria was seemingly lost in her thoughts. Once we arrived, she went straight to her room and I went straight into my home office and got down to business.

I've had problems with people before. It's part of the business, you know? But this is too far. *Too fucking far.*

And, God, to top it all off, Alex fucking Brown. He's like a leech that refuses to die. I can't resolve what's happening with the painting, but what I can do is find out who he is in Aria's life, and what the hell happened today between them.

As I walk out of the home office, she's on the couch with a blanket and comfy PJs watching what seems to be another musical movie. She is devoid of makeup, but still has her hair updo, and she looks fucking beautiful. I love the way her freckles pop when she doesn't have any makeup on.

Her eyes find mine with a soft smile. "Hey. Did you get anywhere?"

I sigh, sitting next to her. "Not really. But hopefully soon."

She hums in understanding. "What are we going to do? Are we taking the painting back?"

I nod. "I mean, if it turns out to be ours, we'll take it back, but I don't think we should use it for the gala."

She ponders for a moment, fidgeting with her blanket. "I agree. It would create too much unnecessary drama. I'll look into a new artist."

I kiss her forehead in gratitude. This woman just gets me, and always wants to help. It feels good to know I have someone I can trust. "That would be great. Thanks, Darling."

"No problem," she says before going back to watching her movie.

I muster all the courage I have and ask, "How do you know Alex?"

No point in beating around the bush.

She takes the TV remote and stops the movie as she tells me the story about how they met in college, and how he taught her the ins and outs of the business and much more.

"We are close friends. Well, we were. Until we had lunch a few months ago..." She glances at me. "On the day the paintings got stolen, actually. We needed the help, and Alex had the connections we needed, but I hadn't told him I was working for you and when I did he did *not* handle it well at all." She sighs. "It escalated quickly. He basically called me a charity case and now here we are."

"Alex and I go way back. It's not a good story, and I'm going to go out on a limb and say he's already told you his side."

She nods without saying anything.

"Figures," I say humorlessly.

She grabs my hand. "He didn't say much, really. Only that he worked for your father and when he passed, you inherited the business and fired him."

I nod. "Did he tell you why, though?"

She shakes her head.

"My father and I didn't have the best relationship. He treated Alex more like his son than he ever treated me. Not that I minded, anyway. When my father passed, I truly believed he was going to leave the business to Alex. But he didn't. Alex didn't handle that well and started this stupid vendetta against me." I shake my head, trying to simmer down the anger that's boiling within me at the reminder.

I continue, "He started making connections in the industry, trying to get ahead of me. He made a competition between us in his head and couldn't get over the fact that I inherited the business and that I started making decisions he hated, decisions that were helping the gallery move forward."

Her brows furrow. "If you would have told me this before, I would have told you that it doesn't sound like him, at all. But now, I'm not so sure."

"The thing is, he started making the wrong connections. Dangerous ones. I truly tried to make it work between us, but he was out to destroy the business. I had to make a decision for the good of *my* company, so I fired him." I shrug.

She nods, but her face remains enigmatic. "Thank you for telling me."

My leg starts bouncing, and before I lose the courage, I ask, "Do you believe me?"

I sound so fucking vulnerable I want to kick myself in the ass.

For once in my life, there's a sliver of hope that she'll believe me, because I have no reason to lie to her. Knowing Alex, he's probably been trying to get in her head, but I hope that she's smarter than that.

I know she's smarter than that.

"Damian, of course," she says softly, placing her hand on my bouncing leg, making me stop. "Why wouldn't I?"

"He's been your friend for years, Aria," I mutter.

She shakes her head. "I don't think the person he was portraying was the real one. The Alex I encountered today was completely different. I have no reason to believe a person like that."

I let out a sigh of relief, my shoulders relaxing.

She squeezes my hand. "You must be beat. You should go to bed."

"I'm too wired to go to bed. I'm gonna go take a shower and come back. Maybe we can order takeout?"

"God, *yes*, I'm starving." She laughs.

I nod, getting up and walking to my room, and getting in the shower quickly. The stream of hot water drips on my shoulders, the warmth giving me some relief after all the tension from today. Closing my eyes and resting my forehead against the cold tiles, I let out a sigh of relief, grateful that she believed me. The last thing I want is for our relationship to become strained, especially over someone like Alex.

Aria has become such an important person in my very gray life. I don't ever want to let go. It may sound selfish of me, but I'll gladly be labeled as as such if it means I get to keep her in my life forever. The light she has brought into my life is one that has taught me that having hope is more of a possibility with each passing day.

Hope that I can become something more; be happy for once. Become someone worthy of love.

Getting out of the shower and getting dressed, I open my laptop to check my emails as I do every night before completely disconnecting. The first email is yet another encrypted one, from the same blocked sender.

From: Unknown

To: Damian Romano

Subject: None

You were warned. Now, sit and watch.

I snap the laptop shut, a groan of frustration escaping me. Who the fuck does this person think I am? I'm not a puppy to control, especially not from a person who refuses to face me head-on. Picking up my phone, I turn it off and simply disconnect. I know Carter is already on top of it, so I'm going to let it go and get back to my little bubble with Aria and enjoy the moment.

With everything that has been going on, Damian and I decided to cut the trip short and head back to Chicago as soon as possible. We've both been so busy that we haven't even had a chance to talk about *us*. I'm not even sure if there is an us to talk about. After the heart-to-heart we shared in the kitchen, everything is just kind of hanging in the air. Which is definitely not helpful for my anxiety.

He's been working nonstop on the stolen painting issue since everything blew over. *Fathom Group* agreed to a meeting with him and his lawyers to come up with a resolution. It turns out the painting was, in fact, the real one. They claim they got it on a market trade in Europe from a small brand-new company, but when we tried to find more information, we found out the company had dissolved a few days after the painting was sold. Needless to say, *Fathom Group* did zero research when they did this trade and I'm sure more than a couple people lost their jobs over it.

We're back to square one with no idea who stole the painting or why, much less why they sold it to one of the biggest companies in the industry, and how the hell they managed to pull that off. After careful consideration, we took the painting back—since it's rightfully ours and all—but ultimately decided not to use it for the collection. Damian's legal counsel has tried to keep the story under wraps, and deal with it as quietly and diligently as possible, but that doesn't deter the media from talking about it. Too much press, and too much unnecessary drama that we don't need for the opening of the gallery.

And we're unfortunately still one painting down.

Damian had to fly out for the meeting right after we landed, so today, it's me and Isabella working at the gallery.

After getting our usual coffee order, I arrive at the gallery earlier than usual to try to get a head start on that one piece we're missing. As I look for the keys of the gallery in my purse, I can't seem to find them.

Weird. Maybe I left them at home.

Typically, Isabella comes in really early in the morning to set up for the day so I rarely open up the gallery, but I probably left them at home after cleaning my purse or something.

"Hey! You're here early," Isabella says, catching up with me at the gallery entrance.

"Yeah, I want to get this painting fiasco done. If not, we're going to have to postpone the gala, and that'd be embarrassing." I laugh.

She rolls her eyes. "These rich art wannabes will be fine if it gets postponed, I promise."

I bite my lip trying to contain back my laugh. The little I know about Isabella, she comes from old money, her family is ridiculously rich, but she is so down to earth it's actually impressive.

"How was New York? Was Damian a pain in the ass?"

I stutter, "I–I mean, we–I–he." I laugh nervously. "He was perfectly nice. We had a nice time, except for the whole stolen painting drama."

She looks at me suspiciously. "What are you not telling me?"

"Nothing," I answer quickly.

"Aria..."

"We kissed again, okay? And we may or may not be *exploring* things."

I am totally not mentioning the mind-blowing orgasm he gave me, because—and I mean this with all the love in the world—Isabella tends to give some lengthy sermons about boundaries, and whatnot. She's just a grumpy righteous woman. Gotta love her for that. But sometimes a girl doesn't want to hear it, you know?

"That is such a bad idea, Aria! A recipe for disaster." She shakes her head.

"Maybe not, Isa. I like him a lot. Plus, we had a nice time in New York. It was so much fun, like we were in our little bubble."

"Okay, I get that. But real life is not a little bubble. He's your *boss*. Also known for not doing relationships at all. The man is like a robot."

I let out a sigh as I take the keys from her hand and work on opening the doors. "You're worried about me, I get it. But I'll be fine."

"You've become one of my closest friends. I just want to make sure you won't get hurt in the process. I tend to be overprotective sometimes, I'm sorry," she says, squeezing my forearm.

As we're walking into the gallery, I bring her in for a sideway hug. "I know, and I appreciate it. I promise I'm fine."

We head to the second floor and get straight to work.

From the last conversation I had with Damian, we needed to find a new artist as soon as possible, to give them the opportunity they need to enter the industry on the right foot. I spend most of my day on social media searching for any artist who may be trending, and while the ones I find are talented, they're not what I'm looking for. It might sound quirky, but there's something magical about stumbling upon new artists. When I connect with someone's art, there's this unique feeling that clicks for me. A feeling I absolutely can't explain.

The feeling is not there, and it's frustrating. Basing my choice over a feeling should probably be, well, not appropriate, but this is what has gotten me places and it's the way I've been able to make a name for myself.

Feeling defeated, I check the time. Time has flown by and I didn't even get to eat today.

As if on cue, my stomach grumbles.

I walk out of my office to find Isabella and invite her for dinner. "Isa?" I yell.

No response. She's probably in the gallery basement again. I swear one of these days she'll disappear for real, and I'm just going to think she was down there the whole time.

As I'm firing off an email from my phone to one of the gala vendors, I yell again, hoping she'll hear me this time. "I am dying for some burgers and fries. Wanna go have dinner with me? Eat our weight in chili fries?"

"That sounds good."

I'm startled by the deep voice that comes from the stairs entrance. Looking up, I see Damian standing there, looking as handsome as ever, with his boyish smile, his green eyes sparkling with amusement.

My heart quickens, as it always does every time he's

near. It's been a few days since I last saw him, but I swear it felt like forever. And if I'm being honest, I missed him.

"You're here," I say.

He laughs with a nod. "I'm here."

"I thought you weren't arriving until next weekend."

He shrugged. "Honestly? I came back early because I missed you."

His confession makes me blush. God, this man is smooth. He knows how to stroke a girl's ego.

"You said something about burgers and fries?" he asks.

I stutter, "I—yes. Burgers. Fries. Me. Starving."

Being in front of Damian has completely short-circuited my brain, and forming coherent sentences is definitely not at the top of my priority list.

He closes the distance between us and drops a kiss on top of my head, making my stomach fill with a million butterflies. "I know the perfect place for us to go, *Tesoro*. I sent Isa home, so we'll close up and go, okay?"

As we park in front of the building, I look at the bright pink and yellow sign that flashes *Fred's Diner*.

"A diner!? Who knew you were so down to earth, Romano," I joke.

"*Please*. They have the best chili fries in the city, no doubt."

As we enter, the interior reveals a 1950s-themed diner with the typical red and white booths, a classic jukebox in the corner currently playing "Sweet Home Alabama" by Lynyrd Skynyrd, and an open kitchen where the sounds of sizzling food fill the air. One of the few memories I have with my Nana is going to her favorite diner. When Gramps died, she was lonely, so our weekly dates to the diner were our way of bonding, talking about him, how he bravely fought the war, and how they met. The nostalgic ambiance brings a smile to my face as my mind fills with all those happy, loving memories.

There's a sign that says, *Please wait to be seated*, but Damian opts to ignore it. He grabs my hand and leads us to a booth.

Arriving at the booth, an elderly woman with gray hair and a bright smile walks toward us. "Damie, how many times do I have to tell you to wait upfront until we seat you?" she asks in a gentle, sweet voice, gently grabbing Damian's cheeks.

Wait.

Damie?

"You know I'm not a stickler for the rules," he replies while laughing.

I've officially entered the twilight zone somehow, where there's an alternate Damian Romano I didn't know about.

She looks at me, her eyes filled with wisdom as if she had lived many lives. My heart tugs at me hard. She reminds me so much of Nana.

"And who is this lovely lady? Damie, it's rude to not introduce us," she scolds.

He rolls his eyes and says, "This is my girlfriend, Aria. Aria, this is Louise; she's the owner of the diner."

My eyes snap to his, feeling like a deer caught in the headlights.

His girlfriend? I guess that solves the whole 'what are we' question.

I extend my hand to Louise, but instead, she brings me in for a hug. "Nice to meet you, sweetie." She lets go and adds, "God bless your heart, dating this Grinch. You're doing charity work here."

"You think you're so funny," he says dryly.

I don't know what's happening, but I've never seen him joke so much. And who is this woman who even has a nickname for him?

Maybe a relative?

I vaguely remember reading somewhere that the only living relative he has is his mother, so it can't be that.

Louise hugs him sideways, patting his forearm in a caring way. "I'll let you kids get settled. I'll bring over the menus in a moment."

"No need. We will both take a double bacon cheeseburger with chili cheese fries and a cookies and cream milkshake."

She pats his chest twice. "Let her order for herself. What if she wants something else? You're ridiculous," Louise says before turning to me. "I'll bring you a menu, 'kay?"

"You don't need to. That actually sounds really good," I reply.

We sit down as he reaches for the coffee pot that's on our table and a mug. "Want some coffee?" he asks.

I gape at him. So he's just going to move on like nothing happened and not explain himself? I don't think so. "Who are you, and what did you do with Damian Romano?"

"What are you talking about?" he asks dismissively, serving himself a cup of coffee.

"I don't know, *Damie*, you tell me," I tease.

He grabs a packet of sugar and empties it into his mug, then picks up a spoon and stirs the coffee. "I have been coming here since I was little. Lou and Fred have been like parental figures besides my mom."

I don't miss the way he only mentions his mom. One of

these days we're going to have to sit down and have a long talk. There's something in him I recognize. Something I relate to so much. "Fred?" I ask, curious.

He sighs, rubbing the back of his neck. "He died last year. Lou has been running the place with her daughter."

His tone is laced with a hint of sadness that he tries to disguise with a fake cough. I simply nod in understanding. He seems to really like this place, and my heart tugs, because he's sharing it with me. I've never seen him so at peace, and it is a welcoming change. I want to get to know Damian, the real one. The mask he usually wears for the world is far from his true self, and I'm determined to unmask every layer of him.

I don't want to push the topic further, so I quickly change the subject, going back to our joking banter. "Ordering food for me, what a gentleman," I say in a teasing tone.

With a playful wink, he replies, "You said you wanted a burger and fries, and I'm here to deliver. Whatever my girl wants, that's what she'll get."

My stomach flips, and it feels like a thousand butterflies are scattered all over it, making me blush and just... feel so many things at once.

My girl.

"So, I'm your girlfriend? When did we establish that?" I ask, arching a brow and crossing my arms.

He hides his smirk behind his cup of coffee, taking a sip. "I told you I'm all in, and that means you're mine. Problem?" He raises his eyebrow in a silent challenge.

This side of him makes me melt into a puddle. The man who isn't afraid to take what he wants. Not that I mind being claimed by him, anyway. Damian makes me feel worshiped and wanted. He's kind, thoughtful, and loving. I couldn't have asked for anyone better.

The food arrives quickly, and we are served a delicious and enormous double bacon cheeseburger with a side of chili cheese fries that smell amazing, along with a cold and creamy milkshake. If there's one thing about me, I'm not ashamed to eat on a date. What can I say? I'm a foodie, and I'm unapologetic about it.

The fries have a perfect golden color and the chili smells incredibly well-seasoned with plenty of beans—my favorite kind.

As I savor the chili fries, a groan escapes my lips. "Oh. My. God." I roll my eyes. "You were right. These are the best."

"I don't know why you doubted me; I'm always right," he quips.

"*Damie*, so humble," I mock.

He cringes. "Please don't call me that."

"But why not, *Damie*? It's such a cute nickname," I continue to tease.

He gives me an eye roll while flashing one of his boyish smiles that can melt any woman.

As we eat, we talk about anything and everything, trying to get to know each other.

"What made you continue with your dad's business?" I'd always been curious. From the magazines I'd read, the gallery had grown from a tiny mom-and-pop shop that his dad owned.

He swallows his food and then takes a moment to answer, pondering; almost hesitating. "I don't know. It's complicated and a very long story I don't want to bore you with," he finally says. "What about you, though? What made you want to become a curator?" he asks, steering the conversation away from his own history.

Sensitive subject. Noted.

It's hard to explain why I love art without confessing how much I love to paint. How can I explain that the only reason I became a curator was because I was so desperate to keep a connection with art? It was all I could think about doing that wouldn't be as risky as becoming an artist. I've come to love and enjoy this side of the industry. It's the type of job that you'd have to be passionate about to succeed, and in a way, I am passionate about discovering new art.

Just not as passionate as creating my own, though.

"I've always loved art. I enjoy discovering new artists and learning the stories behind every painting. I like to teach people what I've learned because every painting tells a story —of love; temptation; sadness; and anger. To be surrounded by it every day is wonderful. I love it."

He nods in understanding, giving me his full attention. We look at each other for what feels like a long, intimate moment. A silent acknowledgment of what's happening between us.

Louise walks up to our table, asking, "Can I get you two lovebirds anything else?"

"Just the check, Lou, thanks," he says.

She shakes her head. "No. It's on the house, so don't even try. I will always be thankful for all you've done for me. For Fred. All of us." She grabs his cheeks in a tender, loving way. "Thank you for coming, as always." Her gaze finds mine. "And I hope I get to see you more often. He's never brought a girl here, you know." She winks, then walks away.

That makes my insides melt. And deep down makes me feel straight up special. Like I'm worthy to be a part of his life.

We get up from the booth as he places a few hundred bills on the table. My eyes bulge in surprise and I bite my lip, trying to contain my smile. That's Damian for you, he'll be hell bent on doing whatever he wants out of kindness. He grabs my hand and interlaces our fingers as we're walking out of the restaurant.

Something is eating at me, so I ask, "What did she mean by that she will always be thankful to you?"

While he opens the passenger door for me, he says, "Fred died of cancer. I covered his chemotherapy since their business wasn't doing too well."

My eyes find his in surprise. "Wow, that's amazing, Damian. Really."

He shrugs. "It wasn't a big deal."

I've come to understand he has a good heart that's often misunderstood. Helping someone without expecting anything else in return? Helping a struggling family? That's the kind of man Damian Romano really is.

A primal sensation to feel his lips on mine comes over me. He's significantly taller than me, so I tip-toe, grabbing the nape of his neck and kissing him softly. A kiss that conveys all the emotions words can't possibly articulate. This is a man that has wanted nothing but to be loved, and I can tell, that is the one thing he's never gotten. A broken soul can recognize another, after all. And Damian? He's been trying to pick up the broken pieces of his life, overcompensating with the money, the cars, the success. In the same way, I overcompensate in my work, looking for anything that can fulfill that damn void.

As I retreat to my seat in the car, the realization washes over me—I'm falling in love with this complex man, and it terrifies me to my very core.

32

Damian

First thing I did when I landed was go straight to the gallery in hopes of seeing Aria. I fucking missed her. Being without her these past few days was strange, and my body was itching all over with the need to see her bright smile and sunny personality.

My body hums with excitement and relief that I got to share a favorite childhood memory of mine. I've never shared that my favorite place out of all places is a '50s-themed diner, but it felt right. And she loved it, which made me feel instantly at ease.

Parking in front of the apartment building, she asks, "Do you want to come in and watch a movie or something?"

"Can't get enough of me?" I ask with a teasing tone.

I'm fucking glad she asked, because all I've been wanting to do is spend more time with her.

I'm obsessed with this woman.

She shrugs. "You're not the worst company, believe it or not."

"I agree. I'm a fucking treat."

She pats my arm jokingly. "Cocky much?"

I shrug. "Something like that."

***

We're on her couch watching a silly rom-com Christmas movie that she somehow convinced me to watch, even though it's not even Christmas. She claims that since we're close to the holidays, it counts. I'm not going to argue with her logic. I'm happy with whatever she wants as long as I get to spend more time with her.

"So, he was her first high school boyfriend, and they both randomly reunite in a town that looks like the North Pole?" I quip, dripping with sarcasm.

I've never understood why women go crazy for these movies.

"Yes. Isn't it great?" she replies, returning from the kitchen with a bowl of caramel popcorn, "Want some?" she offers.

I shake my head, still feeling stuffed. "I don't know how you can eat anything else. I'm still full."

She shrugs, settling down beside me, dangling a piece of popcorn in front of my mouth, forcing me to try it. With an eye roll, and feeling defeated, I take the bite. An appreciative groan escapes me, grabbing a handful of the caramelized goodness. This shit tastes *delicious*.

She raises an eyebrow, teasing me. "I thought you were full."

"I don't know what you put in here, but it's addicting."

She laughs as she grabs another piece of popcorn and eats it, humming in satisfaction. "I made caramel from scratch with the girls the other night. Well, it was Isabella, really. She's really good at that kind of stuff. It's good, isn't it?"

"Oh, yeah. Isabella is a great baker. I had to ban her from bringing more baked goods to work because I was gaining weight."

She gapes at me. "So you're the reason why she never brings me treats?"

I pat my belly. "This body doesn't take care of itself. I gotta watch these abs."

"Oh my God," she huffs. "You're impossible."

With a laugh, I bring her closer to me and kiss the top of her head, inhaling her addicting scent. "Have I ever told you you smell like strawberries?"

She looks up at me. "It's the perfume Sophia got me a few years ago, custom-made. She always says I look like a strawberry, so I should smell like one, too."

"Can't argue with that logic."

She shakes her head with a laugh, grabbing the blanket that's folded next to her, covering us up with it. With my arm across the back of the couch, she rests her head on my chest. My heart flutters, just enjoying ourselves in a very domestic, normal kind of way. A normal I've never experienced. One I would love to experience again, as long as it is with her.

We continue watching the movie, sharing popcorn, and enjoying each other's company. I struggle to pay attention to the movie, all too aware of our proximity. Only she could make me feel this nervous, like a teenager on his first date.

The movie ends, and she turns to me with enthusiasm. "That was good, right?" she asks.

"Nah, not really," I lie.

The movie wasn't amazing, but it wasn't terrible either. Once I got past the whole town looking like Santa's personal factory, it was actually kind of nice.

"You're totally lying." she teases.

"Me? *Pft*. Never," I say innocently.

Glancing at her, my body fills with the familiar warmth I get every time I'm near her. This emotion is one I've never experienced, one I'm unfamiliar with. But it's nice, nonetheless. There's also this primal feeling that I'd do anything to always make her smile. Protect her fiercely. If anyone hurts her, let's just say I'd better get myself a good criminal attorney because I wouldn't be above murdering anyone who dares harm her.

She slipped through the cracks of my heart, and once I noticed, it was simply too late. Doesn't matter how high up those walls were, she tumbled them down one by one.

I'm so fucking glad it happened.

I pull her onto my lap and settle her between my legs, facing me. She wraps her legs around my waist, and her arms around my shoulders.

Brushing her hair gently, I whisper, "I had a nice time today."

She nods, her expression a mix of emotions. "Me too. It was nice to see this side of you."

Her words are a welcome reprieve, making me feel at ease. I don't usually show this side to anyone, but with her, it feels right; *easy*. I want nothing more but to prove that I can be more than the cold, distant man she first met. She's a breath of fresh air in my life, one I don't want to let go of, ever. I'll keep sharing all of my sides, the good; the bad; the ugly. I'll do anything—and I mean *anything*—to keep her with me.

I hold her chin and give her a gentle kiss. Her lips taste like sweet caramel with the mix of buttery popcorn, and it's fucking addicting, knowing it comes from her. It's enhanced;

somehow. I want to remember this forever, the way she feels, the way she tastes. She kisses me back with a soft whimper, and my fingers thread through her hair as I bring her closer to me and deepen the kiss. We melt into each other's bodies as our tongues continue to explore our mouths, and I graze her bottom lip with my teeth, a raw need overtaking every nerve in my body as our breathing grows ragged.

I swiftly turn her around and lay her down on the couch, and she wraps her legs around my waist tighter, bringing us closer. My cock stiffens by the proximity of us, and a moan escapes her mouth when she feels my hardness against her center, one I greedily swallow as I continue to kiss her like she's my only source of air.

She finds the hem of my sweater and stops the kiss abruptly to take it off, then her lips meet mine again with such force and need as her delicate fingers trace the ridges of my abdomen. The touch is addiction and so fucking electrifying, I shudder. I'm quick to take off her sweater, too, revealing her lacy black bra. Her peaked nipples peek through the lace, begging for attention.

My hand meets her cheek and I caress it softly. "You are the most beautiful woman I've ever seen, Darling."

She lets out a soft whimper at my words, her face blushing with a beautiful scarlet color.

I lower my mouth to her chest as I remove her bra, revealing her pink, perfect nipples. My mouth eagerly takes one, sucking and teasing, tracing the perfect round shape. I swirl my tongue around it and suck once, winning me a throaty moan from her pouty lips.

Her moan is like fucking music to my ears.

Cupping and squeezing her other breast, I let out a low

appreciative growl at the feeling. My hand fits perfectly, like she's fucking made for me. Like we're two pieces of art coming together, becoming one. As I keep teasing her, my hand travels south, sliding her skirt and tights off. I press my thumb against her clit slightly and feel how wet and ready she is for me, even though there's a piece of fabric between us. Knowing how needy and desperate she is for me drives me fucking wild.

I tsk. "Look at you. All wet and needy for me already." My lips travel downward, and I take my time exploring her soft skin, tracing every inch of her body with slow, torturous kisses. "You're just desperate for it, aren't you?" I rasp against her lower abdomen before dropping another kiss.

"Yes," she moans breathlessly. Her lips part and glassy eyes filled with need meet mine. With a triumphant smile, I continue to taunt her with my kisses until I reach her thighs.

She squirms beneath me, trying to direct me where she needs my mouth the most.

I let out a throaty, dark chuckle. "Patience, baby." I start to lick, kiss and softly nip her inner thighs. I'm having too much fun taunting her, knowing she's ready for me to take care of her. I want to take my damn time, because I've been dying for this moment. My cock protests against the zipper of my jeans painfully. I'm so fucking ready for her, too. "I'll be fucking you so deep and so hard that neither of us will remember our names. Promise."

Another moan escapes her lips at my words. My girl likes it when I talk dirty to her, and she's in for a treat because I got a lot to say.

My hands travel along her legs, caressing and enjoying the feel of them. I could explore her forever, and never tire. I'm not exaggerating when I say she's perfect. There's no place I would rather be than here, with her.

Her chest heaves, breathing unevenly. "Damian," she pleads, "I need more, *please.*"

I look up, admiring her flushed face. "You want me to eat your pussy until you're a dripping mess? Is that what you want, *Tesoro*?"

She squeezes her thighs, nodding rapidly as her head falls back on the couch. I'm so ready to worship her the right fucking way. All I want is to drown in her and die a happy man.

I stop kissing her inner thigh. "Look at me, and tell me what you want."

She looks at me with glassy eyes. "Yes, Damian. That's exactly what I need," she says through a soft moan.

My name on her lips followed by that moan becomes my undoing. With a satisfying growl, I tear her underwear and open her legs wide. Her pussy is so pink and wet, my cock all but screams at me to let him out. But this is all about her now. I take so much pleasure knowing she'll be screaming my name in a matter of minutes.

"You look so good open for me. Ready for me to taste this pretty cunt of yours," I growl, getting comfortable between her legs and wrapping them around my shoulders. My mouth latches on her throbbing clit and I suck it eagerly, enjoying how she writhes beneath me. Her nectar drives me wild, like I'm a starved man, and the only thing that can satisfy this hunger is *her*. As I keep licking and sucking, I slip a finger inside of her, which grants me a moan.

"Oh, God. Please don't stop," she cries out as I slowly add a second finger.

Her moans are a sweet symphony to my ears, and I don't know how much longer I can hold on with those throaty delicious sounds.

"Look at you. Begging like a good girl. So fucking pretty,"

I say with a smirk, then lick her center once again, coating my tongue with her delicious arousal.

My fingers slide in and out on a steady rhythm as I keep licking and sucking her clit, wanting nothing more than to see her unravel before me. Looking up, the sight of her brings a satisfaction nothing else can. Her messy hair, flushed face, and peaked nipples make her look irresistible. She's a work of fucking art. My muse, and I'm a starved artist, eager to explore her.

I'm a successful man, with many businesses, money, you name it. I can have any materialistic thing I want. But she's all I fucking want. *All of her.*

I curl my fingers and seek her sensitive spot. She tenses for a moment before surrendering herself to the pleasure, her hips moving in rhythm with my touch.

"Right there. *Please*," she begs, her eyes rolling back, her legs shaking slightly.

She looks like a goddess, and I'm more than willing to worship her. I'd do anything for her.

My movements remain steady as her pussy grips my digits. The room is filled with the sound of her moans and her wetness, and there' something so euphoric about it, it's making me painfully hard.

"Be a good girl and keep riding my fingers, don't you dare stop." I suck her clit one last time, placing enough pressure that makes her moan and squirm beneath me. I lock her legs in place, not letting her move as I keep sucking eagerly as her climax takes over. I drink every ounce of her like she's a heady cocktail I never want to stop sipping. She's still riding her wave, moaning my name like a prayer and softly riding my face.

Once she comes down from her post-orgasm haze, my gaze locks with hers as I bring the fingers that were inside of her to my mouth and lick them clean, not wanting to waste that sweet nectar of hers.

I let out a groan as I savor her. "Deliziosa." *Delicious.*

I stand and drop a soft kiss to her lips. My eyes find hers once again, silently seeking permission.

"What are you standing there for?" she purrs, licking her lips. "*Fuck* me."

Those words instantly switch something primal in me. I swiftly grab her and place her legs around my waist and I walk us to her bedroom. Placing her on the bed, I pepper her neck with kisses as my hands caress her thighs, her calves. I'm addicted to her body. To the feel of her skin. I can't stop, even if I tried.

Her lips find mine and she kisses me with such fervor, I get lost in the taste of her. The smell of her. We don't break apart, not even for one second. It's like we're each other's lifeline, and we're afraid we'll run out of air if we stop kissing each other.

Her hands roam my chest and abdomen until she arrives at my waist, eagerly unzipping my jeans. Before throwing my jeans and boxers on the floor, I take out my wallet and retrieve a condom, rolling it on quickly. My body thrums with excitement and expectation. I'm more than fucking ready to be inside of her, to see her unravel beneath me.

She lays on her back, her eyes gleaming as she admires every inch of my naked form.

"Enjoying the view?" I ask with a smirk.

"Mhm," she nods, "and wondering how I'm going to fit you inside of me."

I climb on top of her and grab her hair in a fist to expos her neck and lick it intently. She tastes like sweet poison, and I'm more than happy to drink from her. Her body shivers with goosebumps as my warm tongue travels from her neck to the nip of her ear.

"Don't worry about that, *Tesoro*. Enjoy the moment," I whisper in her ear, nipping it softly.

I get on my knees and open her legs wide. The head of my cock meets her entrance, and I slowly start to slide inside of her. My gaze lowers to that spot between us, and satisfaction floods through my veins as I watch—no, *admire* —how her pussy grips me tight. I stifle the moan that wants to escape me by biting the inside of my cheek. I'm trying so hard to be a gentleman right now, giving her the chance to adjust to my size, but the feel of her warm tight cunt is dizzying, and I don't know how much longer I can hold on to my sanity.

She gasps and closes her eyes as I slide one more inch inside of her.

I place my hand on the back of her neck and squeeze it gently. "Aria, look at me. Look at me as I slide my cock inside of you. Watch how fucking wild you drive me, *Tesoro*. I want you to see how good we look together," I say gruffly. Desperate to see her eyes.

She obeys without protest, and locks her gaze on mine as she wraps her arms around my shoulders, bringing our bodies closer and causing me to slide inside of her more than I was planning to.

"I can't hold on any longer. I need to feel all of you, Damian. *Now*," she begs.

The little sanity I had left *snaps* and I fill her to the tilt. The way she grips my cock is an exhilarating sensation, a perfect tight fit. I pick up the pace, as her nails dig into my back, causing a delicious form of pain.

"What a good fucking girl, taking my cock so well," I

growl in her ear then give it a soft bite. "*Fuck*, you feel amazing," I moan.

Oh, the things I could do to this woman. The things I could say. I'd give the world to her, no questions asked. Our bodies move together in a symphony of need and desire. She wraps her legs around me, drawing us even closer as our moans and the rhythmic sounds of our bodies fill the room. It's an out-of-body experience. I'm in a trance, enveloped in the way she looks, the way she feels, and the way she smells. I worship her body with my mouth, with my cock. I make her fucking mine with every thrust. My balls tighten as we keep moving at a faster pace. Our movements become sloppy and needy, demanding release.

I lift both of her legs and place them on top of my shoulders, the position allowing me to dive even deeper. So deep, I never thought it was possible to feel her even more, but I do. As I hit her sensitive spot, her pussy tightens around my cock, and I eagerly keep thrusting, wanting nothing more than to bring her another moment of sweet release.

Grabbing her face as she moans my name, I force her to look into my eyes. "Be a good fucking girl and come for me, *now*, Aria. *Do it.*" My voice hits a deep octave with a low growl. I can't hold on any longer, and she needs to let go before I do.

She bites her lip, trying to stifle a moan as her pussy starts milking my cock, her orgasm unraveling as I thrust once more. She's riding the wave of her release, and my body shivers, my head spinning as I'm coming with her. The sensation is overwhelming, and so, so good. As our high subsides, I gently slip out of her and kiss her forehead before laying her on my chest. I take off the condom and throw it in the small trash can next to the bed.

We both lay there, trying to calm our breathing. Looking

at the ceiling, my mind races with so many thoughts and emotions I've never experienced in my life. With her, I've found something I didn't know I was missing. When I said I was all in, I meant it, with my whole fucking heart. The feeling is both exhilarating and terrifying. I'm not a hopeful man, much less a dreamer, but there's something I know for certain: I'm prepared to do whatever it takes to keep her by my side, *forever*.

33

Aria

The sun rays come through my window early in the morning, waking me up. I sit up and stretch my arms with a big yawn.

I'm exhausted.

We had more than enough rounds last night, and I'm feeling the consequences today.

The left side of the bed feels cold to the touch, disappointment flooding through me.

Did he leave?

After we took a shower together—that ended in the most amazing shower sex— and we got in bed, I fell asleep as soon as my head hit the pillow. Last thing I remember is him kissing the top of my head and hugging me as he whispered good night.

I stand and walk to my closet and grab my favorite oversized sweater. It's the only thing I kept of my ex because the thing is so damn comfortable, I refuse to throw it away. Looking over my drawer, I notice our clothes neatly folded.

So he actually didn't leave, and he's a clean freak.

Walking out of the bedroom, I call out, "Damian?"

"I'm in here," he says from the other room.

My studio.

No. No. No. Did I forget to lock it up last night?

I was so wrapped up in him, in the heat of the moment, I must have forgotten. I typically lock the room when I have people come over. When it comes to my art, I'm so sensitive about it—mostly ashamed—if I'm being honest. Which is why even though I have some of my pieces hanging all over the loft, I make it a point to not sign my name. It's not something I wish to share with the world, not anymore. It feels like a strange fever dream at this point.

My body trembles as I walk into the studio and find him in the middle of the room, in his boxer briefs, his eyes dancing in awe from one painting to another. Most of my favorite pieces are hanging in this room, since I like admiring them and using them as inspiration. Thin, white blankets stained with paint are scattered all over the hardwood floors to avoid any stains. White canvases of all sizes are all over the place, and a floor standing easel in the middle of the room with an unfinished painting.

He looks over his shoulder, and my stomach feels queasy as his gaze locks with mine. His eyes are filled with awe; and pride. It makes me feel so vulnerable and exposed, I want to crawl out of my skin.

"This is amazing, Darling. Did you paint all of these?"

I look away, embarrassed. "Yes. It's just a hobby. Can you get out of the room, please?" I sigh.

"A *hobby*?" He shakes his head, amazed. "You're a full-on artist, Aria. Why didn't you tell me?"

My hand takes a life of its own and starts scratching my neck, and my arms. My skin is itchy all over, like a sudden rash taking over. "I'm not an artist, *trust* me." I let out a humorless laugh, shaking my head. My voice trembles as I ask, "Can you please get out of the room now?"

His brows furrow in confusion as we both walk out of the room. "I'm sorry. I was on my way to the kitchen to get some water and saw the door open, a painting caught my eye and I just got lost in it. In your art. Your beautiful art, may I add."

I nod, locking the room. "I'm just very weird when it comes to my art, okay?"

He squeezes my arm in reassurance. "Wanna talk about it?"

"I'd rather not."

"Aria..." There's a warning in his tone. "When are you going to open up to me? I'm here for you."

"It's not like you open up to me either," I retort.

He flinches at my comment and nods. "It's not easy for me."

"*Ha*. And you think it's easy for me? I don't want you to look at me differently, Damian." I gulp. "You mean too much to me now."

And that's the truth. He's too important to me and my life is too complicated. My insecurities are too many to count.

He brings me in for a hug, kissing my forehead. "I told you, I'm here to catch you if you fall. Always. But we can talk about it when you're ready. And you're absolutely right, I need to open up too. I will."

I don't think I will ever be ready to dump years of childhood trauma on anyone. I feel safe around him, sure, but that doesn't mean I'm ready to clue him into something so personal. Not even Sophia knows the extent of it, and she's my best friend.

But this is the man you are falling in love with. When are you going to open up? Let him in before you lose him.

It's just so hard. How do you share something you were reprimanded for doing since you were little? My brain is not wired to do that. I tried working on that issue in therapy during college, but it meant I had to face so many years of childhood trauma. So I stopped showing up and started hoping for the best. I've never truly given it a fair chance, but I need to figure out a way to do it. *Soon.*

"Are you hungry? I was going to make some breakfast."

I nod. "I'm starving. Let's make it together."

He hums in approval. "How does French toast sound?"

"Easy enough to make." I shrug.

He's making the French toast and bacon as I cut up strawberries and bananas into small pieces.

"You should give me something else to do. At this rate, I won't learn anything." I pout.

He shakes his head with a laugh. "Not after the vodka sauce incident."

I frown. "What are you talking about?"

He looks at me, regret clouding his gaze. "It was so salty. Why do you think I didn't let you eat any and pretty much swallowed it in one go? You were so excited and proud of it. I couldn't break your heart like that."

I set the knife down and look at him. My stomach flutters like never before at his confession. The act is so silly, but it's the little things he does that make me feel special.

Tip-toeing in front of him, I place my hand on his jaw and bring him closer for a quick kiss. He melts at my touch and deepens the kiss, enveloping me in his masculine clean cedarwood scent like a warm blanket.

As we break apart, I wave my hand at the kitchen counter where all the ingredients are spread. "I like this look on you. Very domestic," I joke.

He smirks. "I'll show you *domestic*," he says as he swiftly picks me up like I weigh no more than a feather and drops me on the kitchen counter. He quickly reaches for my sweater and takes it off, then sears me with a fierce kiss.

"I hate this fucking sweater," he says in between kisses.

"Why?"

He gives me a knowing look. "Because I know this is a man's. So, you know what? From now on you can only wear *mine*."

With calculated intent, he walks to the trash can and throws it in, then grabs the leftover from the whisked eggs we used to make the French toast and throws them on top of the sweater, completely ruining it.

"Who would have thought you were a jealous, petty man?" I declare with a teasing *tsk*.

He walks back to me, and I wrap my legs around his waist to keep him closer. I've never been a fan of physical touch. Well, how can you really be a fan of something that you never learned? My family wasn't known for their loving personality. But with Damian, it's a constant craving. A need to be touched by him, be close to him.

His hands travel up and down my outer thighs, caressing them softly, leaving a trace of goosebumps. He hums, amusement lacing his tone. "What can I say? You just make me that crazy."

Before I can respond with a witty comeback, he kisses me fervently. This man hasn't done anything, and I'm already wet and ready for him. His hand travels south and with his index and middle finger, he brushes my center, picking up some of my arousal, causing me to moan.

He brings his finger to my mouth. "Suck," he orders.

I eagerly do, and there's something so hot and possessive that thrums inside of me knowing I'm tasting myself on his fingers. Damian's eyes darken with a primal lust, his gaze following my every movement, like the way I roll my eyes in pleasure, and the way I lick my lips with contentment. My core clenches at the sight of him.

"I need you inside of me. *Now*." Without a second thought, I take his boxer briefs off, and grab his cock, sliding my hand with a soft, feathery touch back and forth.

A throaty grunt comes out of his lips at my touch. He centers himself to push inside of me, but he stops abruptly and murmurs, "Shit."

"What happened?"

He hangs his head in defeat. "We don't have condoms."

I rest my head on his shoulder and groan, but then remember when Sophia bought me a huge box of condoms for my birthday as a joke, and I put them in what I label my messy drawer.

"Bedroom drawer, top left. There's a box of condoms."

He nods and goes to the room to retrieve the condoms and comes back. "Were you anticipating lots and lots of sexual encounters in the future?" he asks, raising an eyebrow and pointing at the huge box of condoms.

"Sophia gave them to me for my birthday. Said I needed to," I use air quotation marks, "let loose."

He nods knowingly with a laugh. Already knowing how Sophia is. "Say less."

"Now shut up and fuck me, yeah?"

He closes the distance, grabbing me by the neck and squeezing it softly. "Feeling like a brat, are we?"

"Maybe just a bit," I say, licking my lips and placing my hand on top of his, squeezing a little tighter.

Damian makes me act so differently, so bold. I would let this man do anything to me, because I know I'll always be safe around him.

With an appreciative groan, he rolls on the condom quickly and fills me to the tilt, my eyes rolling at the delicious sensation. His cock is a perfect fit, and I embrace the fullness of it. Enjoying every single inch.

He starts moving with a punishing, teasing pace that drives me to the brink of insanity. My nails find his shoulder blades, gripping with force to keep from moaning his name and begging him to fuck me harder.

"I know you want to scream my name, Darling, so let's hear it. I want to hear every sound that comes out of you as I fuck this tight pussy of yours." He hisses as he starts picking up the pace. It's like he knows what I need and exactly when I need it.

"Yes, Damian." I nod breathlessly, moaning his name over and over, giving in to the need. I can't think clearly when he fucks me like this, much less come up with any witty comebacks, because all I can focus on is the feeling of his throbbing cock inside of me, and all the delicious sensations that come with it.

That wins me a grunt of approval, then he suddenly slides out of me, takes me off the counter, and spins me around, bending me over. Without giving me a moment to catch up, he slides right back inside of me in one swift motion, leaving me breathless and gasping for air.

"Is this okay?" he asks breathlessly without moving an inch, ever the gentleman, always making sure I'm okay.

"*Yes,*" I moan. "More than okay."

He starts to move slowly, and I desperately meet him

halfway, thrust after thrust. He loves to taunt me, that much I've learned. His cock is filling me in ways I didn't think possible, but the movement is not enough, so I start moving faster, *desperate* to feel more.

"I wish you could see right now how good your pussy is taking my cock from behind," he says through a deep growl. "So wet." *Thrust.* "Tight." *Thrust.* "And fucking perfect." *Thrust.*

I have no response to his dirty words, the only thing that comes out of my lips are moans after moans, but I can feel how the heat at the bottom of my belly is brewing, and how my pussy clenches around him every time he talks to me like that.

Damian fists my hair, and the feel of his strong hand and the tug makes me clench again. Who knew I liked being treated like this? I sure didn't. He brings me closer to him, pressing my back against his muscled chest.

His mouth is pressed against the side of my neck, the warm breath making my skin prickle with goosebumps. "You're such a good little slut, letting me fuck you like this in your kitchen."

"That mouth of yours, Damian. I fucking swear it's going to be the death of me," I say in between moans.

A dark chuckle escapes his lips. "Yes, Darling. I know you love it when I talk to you like the slut you are. Your pussy clenches and tries to milk my cock every time I do."

As if on cue, my pussy clenches, making me feel his cock even more.

"Oh, *fuck*," Damian moans in between grunts as he starts to pick up the pace and finally gives me what I so desperately want.

He's fucking me relentlessly. There's nothing sweet or cute about this moment. I'm being thoroughly fucked right now, and I love every second of it. Because I know, when the heat of the moment passes, he'll go back to being the sweet guy he's always been.

I meet every punishing thrust of his, our groans and slapping skin filling up the room. His moans are so throaty and primal, I could come just by listening to them. His cock starts to hit that delicious spot, and my orgasm builds more rapidly than I anticipated.

"I'm coming," I say through a whimper.

With his unoccupied hand, he reaches my clit and starts touching the sensitive flesh in circles. "That's it," he hisses in my ear. "Come for me, Darling. Milk my fucking cock and make a mess. And don't stop moaning my name until you're done coming."

I nod and close my eyes, enjoying the tingling sensation that's overtaking my body as I moan his name over, and over, and over again. As my body tenses, Damian pinches my clit softly and that... sends me over the edge. My orgasm erupts, and my legs shake as I let out a moaned cry, doing my best to ride the wave. He lets go of my hair as he thrusts a few more times, his body tensing as he follows his own release. Once we both come down our high, our bodies start to relax and he kisses the side of my head as he slips out of me.

Damian discards the condom, then takes a hot towel, gets on his knees, and cleans me, the sight of him making my heart quiver. It's the simple things that have made me fall in love with him. After he's done, he goes to my bedroom and comes back with his sweater, lifting my hands and putting it on me.

"There you go. You look so much better now."

I tip-toe and give him a peck. "I sure do."

He hums in agreement, giving me another kiss. "Okay, let's eat."

We both clean the kitchen after finishing our breakfast, laughing as we exchange embarrassing college stories.

I glance at the kitchen clock. "I can't believe we lost track of time. We're so late for work!"

"Thankfully, you're sleeping with the boss." He wiggles his eyebrows.

I hit him on the shoulder. "Not funny."

He laughs. "Too soon?"

"Way too soon," I confirm with a laugh.

"I told Isabella we're taking the day. I don't know about you, but I could use the break."

I slump my shoulders. "Me too, but I can't. The gala is next week and we're still missing a piece."

He walks to me and hugs me from behind, kissing my neck softly. "It'll be fine. We will figure it out. Let's just take the day, okay?"

Nodding, my phone pings with a calendar notification. My face drains of color, and my body tenses beneath Damian's touch as I hover over the notification.

Reminder: Lunch with Mom at Lorenzo's.

Fuck.

"Everything okay?"

"Yeah, uhm, I forgot I had a lunch date with my mom today," I say, plastering a fake smile.

I've been so busy I honestly forgot to cancel. What am I going to do?

"I can get out of your hair if you want."

I bite my lip, feeling my anxiety crippling in. My chest

tightens at the thought of seeing her after four years. My mother is good at acting like a martyr when I won't give her attention, and it always makes me feel like complete shit. If I cancel, she'll just make me feel guilty and I'll end up feeling even worse.

So, just go have lunch. It'll only be like two hours. You can do two hours.

I don't think I can, not alone. I close my eyes, counting backwards.

5, 4, 3, 2, 1.

He stands in front of me now, squeezing my shoulders softly. "Aria, look at me."

I open my eyes, a sense of calm washing over me as he pierces me with his deep green gaze, worry crossing his face.

"I have an idea. How about I go to lunch with you?" he asks softly.

That's insane. Meeting my mother is a sure way for him to run the opposite way.

I shake my head. "Absolutely not."

"You're clearly having issues with this. I want to be there." He caresses my jaw with his knuckles softly with a faint smile.

"We've barely started dating. I'm not introducing you to my mother."

"Why not?"

She's insane—that's what I really want to say. I open my mouth to say something, anything, but I come up empty.

He grabs my hand, interlacing our fingers. "It'll be fine. I told you, I'm all in, *Tesoro*."

I can't lie... the offer is tempting. He can act as a buffer and maybe my mother will get her shit together and keep the condescending comments to herself.

"Okay, deal."

What can possibly go wrong, anyway?

34

Damian

We're on our way to Lorenzo's, and the tension radiating from her keeps growing as we approach the restaurant. Her demeanor changed as soon as she told me about this lunch. She's quieter, fidgeting her fingers, and biting her nails. I don't think I've ever seen her this distraught, and my chest clenches as this primal sense of protection finds a way inside of me. Wanting nothing more than to hold her and shield her from what's bothering her, I have no idea what I'm walking into, but I'm prepared. I'm not above fighting tooth and nail over her, including her mother. Anyone who comes after her is fair game in my world.

The driver stops in front of the restaurant, and I'm praying to the heavens that Enzo doesn't show up at his restaurant today, because the last thing I want to do is deal with his annoying ass. Getting out of the car, I extend my hand, letting her grab it as she's exiting.

Stopping in front of the restaurant's door, I turn to her, grabbing her shoulders and giving them a gentle squeeze. "Are you okay?"

She rolls her eyes. "For the tenth time, yes. I'm fine."

Her eyes say otherwise, though. The way her gaze clouds, her eyes turning a darker, dull color is telling me something completely different. I don't want to add more pressure than she's under right now, but it'd be nice to have a grasp on what the fuck is happening. She's afraid, that little I can tell. She probably believes I won't support her, that I'll run away. If only she knew there's nothing she could do that would make me walk away from her. I'm on her side, and always will be.

I let out a resigned sigh. "If I see you're getting too uncomfortable, we're leaving, okay?"

"So protective," she jokes.

My shoulders relax a little at her witty comeback. At least she's joking, I'll take that. Bringing her in for a hug, I kiss the top of her head and inhale her sweet strawberry scent, whispering, "Oh, you have no idea."

Walking in, she lets the host know the name of the reservation. The hostess nods and walks us to the table where a woman with black, long hair is sitting, giving us her back.

"Hi, Mom." Her voice trembles slightly.

Even the tone of her voice is different. It's more careful, almost afraid. She's not the firecracker I know and have grown to love.

The woman looks up, and I'm met with the same set of eyes as Aria's. Well, the same color, anyway. They don't hold the same fire as Aria's eyes do. They're dull. She gets up from her chair, giving Aria a glance over. "What have I told you about your hair?"

What the fuck?

She winces like the words physically slapped her somehow. "I didn't have time to straighten it, sorry."

What in the actual fuck is going on here?

Aria's mom puffs. "I swear to God, Aria. At this point, I'll never be a grandma if you don't start taking care of yourself. How are you going to attract any male prospects looking like that?"

My blood pressure spikes as I hear the words come out of her mouth. The woman is so self-centered that she hasn't even noticed I'm standing right next to her daughter. And what the fuck is that comment about? Aria's fucking stunning. Her hair is my favorite quality. It reminds me of fire and essence, and all the things that are good in life.

I lick the top of my teeth and fake cough to announce my presence. "Hi, Ms. Petrov. I'm Damian Romano. Aria's *boyfriend.*" I extend my hand, a fake smile plastered all over my face. The type of smile I throw to slimy businessmen who try to pull one over on me and think I have no idea.

Aria looks at me, surprise lacing her face as she mouths *'What the hell are you doing?'*

I shoot her an *'Act cool'* look.

Aria's mom studies me from top to bottom, her eyes glinting with curiosity. She takes my hand, shaking it. "Please, call me Eleanor."

We walk around the table as I bring out a chair for Aria, letting her sit next to her mother.

"Wow, a gentleman. How lucky," she comments condescendingly.

Sitting next to Aria, I grab her hand underneath the table and squeeze it in reassurance.

"How was the drive?" Aria asks.

"Exhausting." She rolls her eyes. "So, Damian, what do you do?"

"Mom," Aria warns.

She looks at Aria innocently. "What? Can't I be concerned? I'm your mother after all."

My eyes want to roll hard listening to this woman speak. As a businessman myself, I've learned to read people over the years and uncover their intentions with one look. And her intentions don't come from the right place, that much I can tell. I'll be a gentleman though, because the last thing I want to do is make Aria more uncomfortable. I will fake a smile if that's what will make her feel better.

"I own multiple businesses, hotels, and restaurants," I wave my hand around, dismissively, "I actually co-own this restaurant with my cousin. But I mostly work in the art industry. I have a gallery."

"A gallery?" she sneers. "Can't imagine an art gallery bringing you that much income."

Oh, this woman is insufferable.

I shrug. "It brings me enough. It's how I became a billionaire after all." I smile coldly.

She nods, her eyes gleaming with interest. "Wow, that's surprising. Probably with your family's help, huh?"

"Mom, stop," Aria says.

"My father's dead and my mother has always been a homemaker," I deadpan.

Two can play at this game.

"Oh." Her demeanor changes, clearing her throat, embarrassed. "Sorry to hear that."

Before I can respond, the waiter comes to our table and takes our drink and food orders at the same time per my request, because the last thing I want is to delay this insufferable lunch any longer.

The food arrives quickly and while they're talking about her hometown, and what random jobs she's been doing for a living to survive, talking about her new—and unemployed —boyfriend, I mostly remain quiet, watching how their dynamic works. Eleanor just sneers, comments, and critiques about anything she can think of, or acts a martyr the whole time. Talking about how the world has wronged her, complaining most of the time while Aria puts on a brave face and doesn't falter, trying her best to change the topic toward a more positive subject. I'm this close to giving this woman a piece of my mind, but Aria doesn't seem uncomfortable, so I've been holding back.

"So, how did you two meet?"

Aria shifts in her seat. "At work."

She frowns. "The Institute?"

Aria shakes her head. "I quit a while ago. I'm a curator for Damian's gallery, actually."

"So he's your *boss*?" Her tone is condescending, dripping with disgust. "How old are you?" she asks me.

The question makes my left eye twitch. I won't lie... I haven't considered the age gap between us. Ten years may be a huge gap for a lot of people, but we're both consenting adults.

"You don't have to answer that," Aria says to me, glaring at her mother.

"I consider her my partner more than anything. She has a really good eye and has been taking creative control over the gallery," I manage to say in a cool tone. "As far as my age goes, I'm thirty-five. Not sure how it matters in this conversation, though, considering your daughter and I are both consenting adults."

She waves her hand dismissively. "Age is very much important. I don't want my daughter to be taken advantage of."

"That's rich coming from you," Aria says barely above a whisper, and I bite the inside of my cheek trying to hold my laugh back.

It seems that her mother didn't hear her, because she

continues by saying, "I've always told her art is a waste of time. Well, I guess there's exceptions, you being one of them." She looks at Aria. "And honey, you have a business degree. Put it to good use."

The realization comes at me like a strong wave. Now I understand why she was so uncomfortable this morning when I was in her studio, admiring her art. How she quickly dismissed it as a hobby and nothing else, when in my years of experience there are a few artists I can say are actually talented. She's amazing, and I don't say it because I've developed feelings for her. This woman has created so much insecurity in Aria, that she can't see her worth. I wish she could see herself through my eyes. I admire her talents, how strong she is, and beautiful, and witty. This woman, the one that calls herself a *mother,* has no filter, and no regard for her own daughter. Aria had told me on the way to the restaurant she hadn't seen her in about four years, and now is crystal clear why.

"I am putting it to good use, in my own way. Just drop it, Mom, okay?" Aria says, her voice trembling slightly.

Eleanor sighs. "Fine. I actually wanted to ask you something," she says, batting her eyelashes.

Aria's shoulders tense as she nods, letting her mom continue.

"Me and John are trying to buy a house, since you know, your father left me with *nothing.* But our credits aren't that good, so we need a co-borrower. That's actually why I'm here, to ask you if you'd be willing to help us out? Put the loan in your name too. Please?"

"Mom, I—"

I interrupt, "Oh, you've got to be *fucking* kidding me right now."

Eleanor places a hand on her chest, gaping at me. "Excuse me?"

I grab the corners of the table, my knuckles going white with how hard I'm gripping it. I've been trying to hold back, but I am at my wit's end. *Fuck* this. *Fuck* her.

"Let me get this straight," I say through gritted teeth. "You haven't seen your daughter in over four years, and the first thing you do when you see her is critique her hair. Her beautiful, wonderful hair, may I add? Then, throughout the whole lunch, you just ask your condescending questions and sneer comments as she sits there taking your *shit*." I stand from my chair, placing both of my hands on the table and leaning forward. "And now you're asking if she can do you a *solid* and put her credit on the line for *you*?"

The whole restaurant is looking at us and I couldn't give zero fucks at this point.

She gasps. "I don't know who you think you are—"

"*No.* I don't know who *you* think you are barging into Aria's life, not caring about her passions, her likes, or the great job she has been doing at the gallery. So you can go ahead and *fuck off*," I sneer.

Aria's looking back and forth, nervously. She gets up, placing a hand on my chest. "Damian, let's just go."

My blood is pumping all the way to my ears. I'm seeing red, and my heart wants to come out of my fucking chest. How dare this woman treat her like this! A woman that's supposed to protect her, cheer for her, be there for her?

But again, a lot of undeserving people become parents.

Like my father. Like this woman before me.

I point a finger at her. "Listen to me and listen to me very carefully, if you contact Aria ever again, you will answer to me. Forget you ever had a daughter, because you don't fucking deserve her."

I look at Aria, and my heart fucking breaks. Her eyes are so dark, dull, filled with a sadness I can't take away. There's not much I can do, but I will sure as hell protect her from this woman. I don't need her to tell me what's so clearly obvious. This has been going on for long enough, and it's time someone steps in for her and takes care of her for once.

"Let's go, Darling."

She nods, picking up her coat and purse. As we're walking out of the restaurant, Eleanor is hot on our heels, following us.

Once we're outside, she yells, "Aria, you're seriously going to allow this?"

Aria stops dead in her tracks and turns around, her eyebrows furrowing and lips parting slightly in disbelief. "You know what? *Yes!*" she yells back. "I *am* going to allow this. Because I am sick of you and the way you've made me feel my whole life." She shakes her head, her voice breaking. "I refuse to take this anymore. I'm an adult now. I'm not a twelve-year-old kid looking for her mother's approval anymore. Leave me the hell alone." She lets out a shaky exhale. "Do not contact me ever again," she says, her voice slightly above a whisper.

Her words are masked with such deep hurt, a hurt that makes my chest rumble, my body growls at me to make it better. To take her pain away.

Opening the door of the car, I let Aria get in first. Looking over my shoulder, I glare at Eleanor. Her face's red from embarrassment and anger.

Good. I hope she feels like shit.

Getting in the car and shutting the door, I quickly bring Aria in for a hug. As soon as her face rests on my chest, she lets out a pained sob. It's a sob that holds so much emotion, and pain she's held over the course of her life that has been dragging her down. And I just... hold her. I hold her as she lets years of bottled-up frustration, sadness, and anger. All I can do is fucking hold her as my heart hurts for her. Screams for her. If I could take her pain away and make it my own, I'd do it in a heartbeat.

I furrow my brows as I bring a hand to my face and wipe away a... a fucking tear. The love I have for this woman is so powerful, that her pain has become my own. I gulp, my throat hurting from all the pent up emotions I'm holding back. "I'm sorry for putting you in this situation. But I don't regret it one bit."

She pushes away from me, and looks at me with red puffy eyes. "Wait, why are you crying?"

I sniff, letting out a humorless laugh. "If you hurt, I hurt, *Tesoro*. You're such a wonderful woman. You deserve the whole world, and I'm sorry. I'm sorry I didn't see you before. I'm sorry I didn't understand what you were going through. I had to stand up for you. That was the only way to make up for it."

She grabs my cheek, shaking her head. "You have nothing to make up for. You being here for me is more than enough. *Thank you* for standing up for me. God knows, otherwise, I'd never have done it."

My heart tugs at the sight of her with her red stuffy nose and puffy eyes. I want to make her feel better. *God*. It's hard to swallow, because my throat feels like it's closing up again. I close my eyes and breathe for a moment, trying to center myself. Everything happened so quickly and I was so upset and high off adrenaline, I hadn't had a chance to take a step back and realize what the hell was happening. All I fucking know is that Aria was being hurt, and I couldn't stand that.

The realization hits me like a strong wave, crashing against the walls of my heart and enveloping me in the cold realization. I would *burn* the world for her. *Kill* for her. If it meant she'd be safe and happy. If it meant I could get to see that beautiful smile, and those bright eyes that are like a breath of fresh air in my life.

Because she's my safe space.

The light at the end of a tunnel.

My hope.

The love of my fucking life.

eing with someone who cares about me and puts me as a priority in their life is a strange, unique feeling. One I can't explain. Is this what being wanted and cared for feels like?

After the lunch we had with my mother, which was a disaster—and that's putting it mildly—we decided to definitely take the rest of the day off and stay inside.

I've never cried so hard in my life, and I've never thought I would feel so much lighter after making such a life-changing decision. The thing about loving someone so narcissistic is that you don't know how to cut them off, or how to make them stop taking from you and pulling the fire in you away. I don't think I would have ever allowed myself to completely cut my mother off forever if it weren't for Damian. Even though we hadn't communicated in years, the door was always open. But now? It's finally completely shut.

My head rests on his chest as we lay in bed, just staring at the ceiling in silence. The sound of his even heartbeat fills my ears, our breathing syncing.

My head snaps up, looking at him as I break the silence. "You really meant it, didn't you?"

His gaze meets mine, knowingly. I don't need to clarify what I'm asking. He knows damn well what that question represents.

"Yes, *Tesoro*. I meant it. Every word."

That he would be there for me, always. That he'll catch me if I fall. There's no doubt anymore, because today, he proved himself. He knew I was falling; drowning, and he kept his promise. Stood up for me and gave me enough courage for me to actually stand up for myself, too.

My mouth dries, the emotions clogging my throat. There are many things I want to say.

He shakes his head. "Don't."

My voice trembles. "I-I don't know how I'll ever repay you."

He grabs my hand, placing a soft kiss and interlacing our fingers. "I have you, and that's all I need. And if anything, I should be thanking you. Allowing me to see this part of your life made me realize some things of my own."

I sit up and lean my head against the headboard, looking at him. "What do you mean?"

"Seeing your mother act like this, it did something to me. God, I've never been so angry. But it also made me realize that I need to open up to you." He sighs, sitting up and mirroring my pose. "Because even though the circumstances fucking suck, you and I are more similar than you think."

I thin my lips with a soft nod. Somehow, this confession doesn't phase me. To me, it's no secret the mask Damian places for the world. It's never fooled me.

"My father and I never had a good relationship, and that broke me. It broke me so fucking much." His voice trembles at his confession. "Imagine me, an 11-year-old kid who had no idea why his father despised him, belittled him. Then, the hurt turned into hatred the older I became, because I realized he simply didn't like me for who I was. He hated the kindness he saw in me. Saw me as weak. When he died, I didn't feel sad. I felt anger; resentment." He closes his eyes and gulps, trying to hold back the tears that are threatening to spill over.

My hand finds his jaw, caressing it. "Don't hold anything back, Damian. Please. I'm here."

He inhales sharply, nodding. "All the stories you've seen and heard about me, it's not me. Today, when I saw how different you acted around your mother, it made me realize that version of me is the one I created for my father. I was so determined to prove him wrong, I became someone I'm fucking not. Even though he isn't even here to witness it."

His confession breaks my heart. This man before me, right now, isn't Damian the *adult*. It's Damian the *kid*, the one that has been so lost; sad; angry. The one that wanted to make his father so proud, that he ended up becoming someone he's not proud of. And I understand so much about what he means, because that's the thing about being around someone that makes you feel like the best parts of yourself are the worst. You become weak and useless around them; sometimes, to the point you don't even recognize yourself anymore.

I squeeze his hand reassuringly with a nod, wanting him to continue. To let it all out.

His tears stream down his cheeks now, one by one, his voice barely above a whisper. "Don't get me wrong... making it my life's mission to demonstrate I'm not weak, that I could make it in life is what allowed me to, well... make *it*. But at what cost? I've been alone my whole life. I don't know what it feels like to be loved; to be cared for, all because of someone who is not even here anymore, and that I'm pretty sure wouldn't have cared if he were. I lost myself along the way for nothing."

My tears are the ones falling down my face now. My heart hurts for him, for his past self. Anger boils within me knowing he's been alone all this time, battling his own demons. A sense of protectiveness overtakes me, because I'm the one that wants to show him those things. Love him. Take care of him. Make him see he's not alone in this world. That he can rely on someone and let me catch him if he falls for once.

Wiping my tears, I sit up on the bed and grab his face and kiss him with all the longing and the need I can muster. He wraps his hands around my waist and brings me into a hug. And he hugs, *hard*. He hugs like I'm his anchor and he wants nothing more than to get out from underneath the water, to stop drowning. And I'd gladly be that. His anchor; his lifeline—because he's mine, too.

Breaking up the kiss, he places a soft kiss on my neck, whispering, "Thank you. For listening, for—"

"Don't. You don't have to thank me. I'm here, Damian. *Always*."

The gala is happening this weekend. I'm a nervous wreck and have been on work mode pretty much nonstop. We never found the last statement piece, and I've been trying to not beat myself up about it, but the anxiety has been slowly creeping in and I'm finding it more difficult everyday. The feeling of failure is one that nags at me the most. It's one that has been looming around me pretty much my whole life. Damian, on the other hand, isn't too concerned—which is so strange— and it's another thing I'm trying my best to ignore. I'm still trying, even though realistically speaking, I can't find and secure one in time. But, I'm nothing if not persistent.

"I think I have a lead," I say as my way of greeting, entering his office.

He frowns. "What are you talking about?"

"The painting, *duh*," I say in an '*obviously*' tone.

"Oh, I meant to tell you I figured it out. We have it. It will be here on the day of."

I raise my eyebrow. "I'm sorry, what? No," I shake my head as I point a finger up, "one, I need to see it and approve it," I point another finger up, "two, we can't simply do it the day of. We need to register it, set it up."

He waves at me dismissively. "I said I got it handled."

"Damian, I've worked extremely hard on this collection. I'm not letting you put in a random painting without my approval," I say in an exasperated breath.

He raises an eyebrow. "Hate to do this to you, Darling, but I'm pulling the boss card. The painting gets here on Saturday, and I will personally make sure it gets set up correctly, okay?"

Un-fucking-believable.

"You're an asshole," I murmur.

He lays back on his seat, his chin resting on his fingers, amusement dancing in his eyes. "What did you just say?"

I cross my arms and lift my chin, challenging him. "You heard me."

He gets up from his seat slowly with a predatory fiery look on his face, making my legs clench.

I love it when he looks at me like that.

He places his hand at the base of my neck as his lips brush mine slightly. "You'll pay for that later," he whispers.

"Don't threaten me with a good time."

"*Brat*," he says, trying to contain his laugh.

I pat his shoulder, jokingly. "*Asshole*."

He laughs, closing our small gap with a kiss. I place my arms over his shoulders, relaxing in his touch as he envelops me in his addicting scent. His other hand grabs my waist and pulls me closer as he intensifies the kiss.

Isabella knocks as she's coming in. "You guys are so gross and sickening."

We separate and look at her as we both laugh.

"Sorry your love life is drier than the desert, Isa," he jokes.

"Oh, *boo-hoo*, poor Isabella," she mimics. "I'm *fine*."

I let out a giggle. The thing is, Isabella is absolutely okay with the way she lives her life. She claims men suck, has no interest in them, and is happy with her books and Marley, her dog.

"There's someone on the line for you," she continues.

He looks at his watch. "Oh, right," he looks at me, "don't leave without me."

"I have a girls' night with Sophia and Isa. But tomorrow?" I ask.

He gives me a peck as he nods. "Fine." He glares at Isabella. "You guys better stay in."

"No, Damian. We're going clubbing and we are letting Aria leave with the first hot guy we see."

He raises an eyebrow in challenge. "Yeah? Careful, or I'll send Carter to look after you guys."

Isabella sneers at the sound of Carter's name. "Don't mention that fuck-face."

Damian snickers at her comment and kicks us out of the office to take his call.

I don't know Matteo Carter well. All I know is that he's Damian's head of security, and I believe he had told me in passing that Isabella and Matteo went to MIT together. I've never asked her the story behind it, and he seems to be a sore subject.

Isa hits me in the stomach with her elbow. "You are so smitten."

"I am not." I blush.

I absolutely am.

"You owe me ten bucks, Isabella, pay up," Sophia says, extending her hand.

"I do not," Isabella counters.

I stare at them, confused, as I sip on the homemade margarita and pet Marley, who's currently in my lap sleeping. "What the hell are you guys talking about?"

"We bet whether you and Damian were going to get together or not." Sophia shrugs nonchalantly as she sips her drink.

"You bet that they were going to fall in love," Isabella corrects.

Sophia looks at her, incredulous. "And you don't think they are? Didn't you hear how he defended her honor with her mom? If that's not a confession of his love, I don't know what is."

Isabella looks at me expectantly. "Well... are you?"

Am I in love with Damian Romano? I haven't thought about it.

Lies. Filthy, filthy lies.

"We're exploring things," I tread carefully. "We haven't said anything like that to each other."

Sophia groans. "Ari, that man is so in love with you. I could tell the day I met him. I can read people well, you know?"

The irony is that Sophia is actually good at judging people, except the people she dates. She does the exact opposite; it's actually hilarious.

"He does look at you like you're the only person in the room," Isabella confirms.

Sophia extends her hand again. "Aha! So you accept it, pay up."

Isabella groans as she gets up from her sofa and looks for her wallet, taking a crisp ten dollar bill out and handing it to Sophia.

"Thank you very much," Sophia chirps.

"I can't believe you guys bet on that behind my back."

Sophia grabs my hand and squeezes it. "I will say this in the best way possible, because you're my best friend and I love you, but you aren't the easiest. If I would have said that, all you would have done is try to prove me wrong, even though you know I'm nothing but right."

I rest my head on the sofa, looking up at the ceiling. I close my eyes and the first thing I picture is him. His smile. His addicting kisses. Wanting nothing more than to get lost in him.

Damian is kind; thoughtful; selfless. He cares for me like no other man has. My heart quickens at the thought of what this means. He's all I think about. Hell, if I hadn't made plans with the girls I would be in his apartment, or him in mine. The thought of loving him is not scary. No. It's the exact opposite. He grounds me, and makes me want to be my best self.

36

Damian

Walking into the coffee shop, the staff waves and smiles at me. This is Aria's favorite spot, but it honestly ended up becoming mine too. I order my coffee and sit down as I'm engrossed on my phone looking at my emails, because the work never stops. Especially with the gala happening so soon.

An annoying, persistent presence stands before me, so I look up and find the last person I thought I would find here.

Alex.

"What do you want?" I snap.

Alex, with his smug, dick face casually sits down, unbuttoning his suit. He drops his elbows on the table, interlocking his fingers. "Tell me something," he starts.

Oh, here the fuck we go.

"You think Aria will buy your story forever?" he asks.

I stare at him with a bored expression. "I don't know what the hell you're talking about."

"Oh, but I think you know," he says casually.

I really, really don't.

"Stop projecting and leave me the hell alone, Alex.

You're just upset because Aria finally got to see you for the person you really are."

He licks his lips, his eyes glinting with amusement. "Threatened much?"

I roll my eyes at his useless and baseless comment. Alex has always been insecure, and has always wanted to prove he could compete against me. So, the delusional man that he is, he created this fake competition in his head.

Locking my phone, I place it on top of the table and lean back in my chair as I tilt my head. "Of what, Alex? You're a nobody. A guy so desperate to become someone that you have fucked your reputation along the way. How you kept Aria in the dark about your sketchy associates, I have no idea. But get this through your thick head," I tap the side of my head twice, "you and I will always be at different levels."

"Someone sure thinks highly of himself," he sneers.

I thin my lips, trying to contain my laugh. His entitlement is too funny, too entertaining.

"I hold nothing against you, Alex. I get it. But, please, leave me and Aria the hell alone and mind your fucking business."

He glares at me. "I bet you're fucking her."

"That's none of your concern."

He laughs. "Enjoying my sloppy seconds?"

Fuck being the bigger man.

Without a second thought, I get up and punch him right in the nose. Alex groans in agony as he falls on the floor, his nose bleeding profusely.

I scrunch down and grab him by his dress shirt. "You listen to me, and listen to me clearly. You will not reach out to Aria, talk to her or even *think* about her," I say through gritted teeth. "Because I will fucking kill you if you do." I let go of his shirt as he falls back on the floor with a *thud.*

Looking up, the whole coffee shop is staring at us, eyes wide. As I walk to the exit, I make a stop at the cash register and drop five dollars on the tip jar before walking out.

"You did what?" Aria gapes at me.

"He did it to himself. Talking about you like that." I shrug, crossing my arms and leaning against the bathroom door frame, meeting her gaze through the mirror.

"You didn't have to come down to his level. He's an immature little shit, and a liar at that." She puffs. "I can't believe he implied we slept together. I've never seen him that way and he knows that, since college, may I add. But thank you for defending my honor, very chivalrous of you."

I grunt. "I've been wanting to punch him forever. It felt good."

She laughs as she gets closer to the mirror, putting her signature red color on her plump lips.

"Do we really have to go to this thing?" I groan.

She glares at me over her shoulder. "Considering it's your cousin's birthday and he invited us, yes. We really have to go. Come on, it'll be fun."

I don't know about fun, because Enzo's idea of fun is to get shit-faced while clubbing. And he's turning thirty-five, by the way. Hard to believe when he still goes partying like he's in his early twenties.

I close the distance between us and wrap my arms around her. "Most I can do is an hour, especially because all I want to do is come back home and fuck you in this pretty little dress and those fuck me heels."

She laughs. "Fuck me heels? What the hell does that mean?"

"It means I want to fuck you completely naked, right in front of this mirror while you only wear those sexy heels, *Tesoro*." I wink, then drop a kiss to her neck and inhale her sweet addictive scent.

She looks stunning with a V-neck short black dress that hugs all her curves and makes her breasts look perky and perfect. As soon as she opened the door to let me in, my cock stiffened. She paired them with a pair of suede black heels that give her a few more inches, but she's still significantly shorter than me.

It's hot. She's hot. And I'm fucking obsessed.

She turns around as she places her arms on my shoulders with a playful tsk. "Maybe you'll get lucky tonight."

I raise an eyebrow. "Maybe?"

She shrugs. "Depends on how you behave."

I laugh as I kiss her, then bite her bottom lip playfully. "You will be coming on my cock tonight. There's no doubt about that."

She hums as she walks out of the bathroom, swaying her hips, leaving me mesmerized, like always.

37

Aria

I love Sunday brunches with Sophia, and now they're even better with Isabella joining us. We've been chatting, gossiping. You know, girl things.

"I had the best sex of my life yesterday," Sophia blurts out.

"I'm going to need something stronger than this if we're going to talk about your sex life," Isabella deadpans.

I giggle at her comment. Sophia's life is far from boring, and I'm so used to it already that it's legitimately funny when people react to her shenanigans.

"I told you guys I wanted to go have mimosas!" Sophia pouts.

"It's nine in the morning. I'm not looking forward to a hangover because with you it's all or nothing." I glare at her.

She waves dismissively. "Can I talk now?"

"Yes, do tell us, Sophia. Who's the mystery man?" Isabella asks, intrigued.

"That's the worst part. I have no idea! We danced, then we started making out and it just kind of snowballed from there." She grimaces. "We had sex in a cleaning closet," she quickly adds, hiding her face with both of her hands in embarrassment.

Sophia Evans, ladies and gentlemen. God, I love her, but the woman is insane.

"Wait, you were at the club yesterday? I was at the club with Damian for his cousin's birthday. How come I didn't see you? Actually, how come you didn't invite me?" I eye her suspiciously.

"I was with my sister," she gives me a knowing look, "and how come you didn't invite *me*?" she counters.

Blah. No wonder she didn't tell me. I hate her sister, but for good reason. She's horrible to Sophia and takes advantage of her. Overall, a terrible human being. I know better than to bring it up, because it's a sore subject for Sophia. But she knows me well, because putting us together in one room is a recipe for disaster.

I laugh. "Damian's cousin is a lot. You'd hate him, trust me. Be thankful I didn't invite you."

"So you didn't even get his number?" Isabella questions.

I wave a hand dismissively as I lay back in my chair. "She doesn't like to repeat."

She groans as she breaks a piece of her cheese Danish and eats it. "This repeat would have been worth it. The dude gave me like three major orgasms in a matter of minutes. I was so dizzy and exhausted, I left the club right after. I didn't even think about getting his number."

Surprise laces my features. It's not everyday Sophia says something like that. She's a player, after all.

"Well, if it's meant to be, I'm sure you'll see him again," Isabella says hopefully.

I stuffed myself with so much coffee and pastries that I'm full and jittery at the same time—worst combination ever. I'm definitely going to have a lazy Sunday. Maybe watch some movies as I wait for Damian to come home.

Without him, the apartment feels so empty, but when he's here? It becomes *our* home. He stays with me more than he stays at his place, so it definitely feels like ours.

As I step into my apartment's main lobby, I spot Alex sitting in the waiting area. I haven't spoken to him since everything went down at the auction, and honestly? Good fucking riddance. I was finally able to realize Alex is not who he says he is. I'm not certain he was ever being truthful. Our friendship was based on a lie. It's as simple as that.

Alex strides toward me. "We need to talk."

His left eye is swollen, and a laugh almost escapes me as I say, "Nice shiner. Looking for another one? I can call Damian again if you want your eyes to match."

He gets closer. "I fucking mean it. We need to talk."

I give myself some space from him, shaking my head. "We certainly don't. Go home, Alex."

He grips my arm tightly. "You're seriously going to throw away our friendship over Damian fucking Romano of all people?"

I laugh with a hint of disbelief as I pull my arm out of his grasp. "You don't get it, do you?" A heavy sigh escapes me as I contemplate how to phrase my next words. "You're not a good person. Or a good friend for that matter. It took you a total of five seconds to discredit my work, say that I owe it all to you, and—"

He interjects, "Well, it's true."

Oh, this is unbelievable.

Every time I think he's hit rock bottom, he finds a way to dig even deeper and create an entirely new level of disbelief.

Making my way to the elevator, I jab the fob on the elevator screen and select my floor, tapping my foot impatiently as the elevator doors toy with my patience.

"Aria," Alex groans. "Come on."

Turning sharply, I snap, "Leave us alone. I mean it. Go about your life, because I'm done with you."

He shoots me a knowing look. "You're in for regrets, Aria. Remember this moment well." With that, he strides out of the building, leaving me seething.

Damian

"Where's your phone, Romano? I've been fucking calling you for days," Matteo quips, strolling into my office.

I recline in my chair, casually gesturing. "Why, yes, Carter, come on in. Sit down. Can I get you something to drink while you interrupt me?" I say with a sarcastic tone.

With a dismissive gesture, he unbuttons his suit and takes a seat in one of the guest chairs in front of the floor-to-ceiling windows that overlooks Lake Michigan and drops a manila folder onto the coffee table.

"If you would have answered your phone, I wouldn't have to come all the way here. You're a pain in the ass, did you know that?"

I shrug. "I lost it a couple of days ago; haven't had the chance to go pick up a new one."

And truth be told, not having a phone for the last couple of days has been peaceful, and the idea of going to the store to pick up a new one isn't exactly appealing. I've been able to focus on the gallery since the gala is happening tomorrow, and spending every waking moment with Aria. Haven't even slept at my place for God knows how long. If anyone needs me, they can email. If it's an emergency, they know where I work.

"I thought you might be interested in this." He taps the manila folder twice.

I furrow my brow as I rise, heading toward the folder.

Before I can grab it, Carter intercepts. "I don't want you bulldozing when you see this. I've got everything in check, but it's my job to fill you in on this."

My gaze narrows at him as I reach out with a grabbing motion, and he sighs, handing over the folder.

My eyes bulge in shock as I go through the contents of the folder. There are pictures of me and Aria at the coffee shop during the time I was trying to convince her to work for me. Us, in New York, skating and at the museum, capturing every moment. But what gets my attention are all the pictures of Aria by herself. Walking around the city, arriving at her apartment. There are *hundreds* of pictures.

"What the *fuck* is this, Carter?"

"You've had a shadow tailing you for months now. To be frank, I've been aware of it for some time, but we opted to keep you out of the loop while we collected more intel."

I shake my head. "I don't care about me. Why are they following Aria?"

My heart thrashes against my chest and my hands shake just thinking about her being in any potential danger. This has gone too far. One thing is to fuck with me, I can take it. But her? *Off-fucking-limits.*

He casually shrugs. "I don't know much, yet. But I've got someone watching her back to keep her safe. We caught the two guys tailing both of you, but they're tight-lipped. Found another foreign account with one transaction. Same as last time."

"I swear to fucking God, Carter, I don't know why I pay you."

He points a finger at me in warning. "I'm doing my best, Romano. I don't know who the hell you pissed off, but it's definitely not a solo job. Now, what's your plan for the email threats?"

I've received a handful more threats here and there, giving me yet another chance to fire Aria. That's simply not fucking happening. I don't know what the hell this person gets out of this, but I'm not bending my wrist for anyone. "I'm not firing her."

He puffs. "Even if your whole empire is on the line?"

"Please, these people don't scare me one bit."

Matteo locks his gaze on me, expectantly, probably jumping to his own conclusions. "I'll be damned." He laughs.

"What?"

"You love her, don't you?"

"I don't know what you're talking about," I say nonchalantly, fixing my cufflinks.

He smirks. "I can't wait to tell Enzo this. He will have a parade with this information."

I point to the folder. "Was this all? If so, get out. I have work to do."

Matteo gets up and shrugs as he walks to the door. Before opening it, he looks at me over his shoulder.

"What now?" I glare at him.

"It's good to see you in love. You look happy," he opens the door, "don't fuck it up," he finishes as a way of goodbye.

I knock on Aria's office door as I open it softly. "You ready?"

She looks up from her computer with her bright smile that tugs my heart every damn time. "Hey, yeah. One second."

We've both been working ourselves ragged for this gala, and we're more than ready for it to be over. I know she's still stressed because she wasn't able to find the last statement piece, even though I told her I'd take care of it. But that's Aria for you; dedicated to the very end.

She picks up her purse, getting up from her desk. "Okay, I'm ready."

"You hungry?" I ask.

"Starving," she groans.

"Good. We're cooking today."

"You mean you're cooking today, because you never let me do anything?" She pouts as we're walking out of her office.

"I cherish my health, *Tesoro*. You over season too much." I laugh, grabbing her by the waist and placing a kiss on her forehead.

She rolls her eyes as she murmurs, "Jerk."

"I still don't have my phone. I'm picking it up tomorrow. You have the app to set up the alarm, right?"

She nods. "But I don't have the keys. I lost them. I looked around my apartment and I couldn't find them. Maybe they are at Sophia's. I still haven't asked."

"That's fine. I got them," I say as I take them out and close the doors.

Once the alarm and doors are set, my driver is waiting for us upfront, so we get in quickly to go to her apartment. I love staying at her place. Mine is so dark and lonely, while hers is so homey and welcoming, and she hasn't kicked me out, so that's a plus. Because it has become my favorite thing every night after I get off work to go to her house and be with her.

As we walk into her apartment, I ask, "Are you nervous for tomorrow?"

She shakes her head. "I'm relieved. I can't believe I let you talk me into doing a whole gala. I'm not doing this ever again."

"I honestly don't want to do this again ever, but it'll be good for the gallery. I'm really proud of you. You've worked your ass off for this collection, and it's really good," I say hoarsely, my heart swelling with pride.

Her cheeks blush as she looks away, avoiding my gaze, taking a strand out of her hair and placing it behind her ear. "Thanks, I guess," she whispers.

I grab her soft face with my hands. "*Tesoro*, look at me."

She looks up, her eyes gleaming with emotions I can't pinpoint. Shyness? Pride? Relief?

I give her a soft, quick kiss. "Who knew you were so shy?"

She pushes me jokingly. "Shut up. Let's cook. I'm starving."

We fall into comfortable silence as I prepare the vegetables and seasonings and she makes dessert, just enjoying each other's company.

I have a million things to stress about. The gala. The stolen painting. The threats.

But when I'm with her, I forget everything. I'm not Damian Romano, the ruthless businessman, or the serious mystery guy no one can seem to crack open. There's no facade, no mask. I'm... *me*. The guy I lost so many years ago; the guy before the money. Before my father's death.

She makes me want to be the best version of myself, and

I don't know how to ever repay her. Looking over my shoulder, I notice Aria has her concentration face on. Eyebrows furrowing, the tip of her tongue slightly out on top of her bottom lip as she carefully mixes the dry and wet ingredients, making sure she doesn't over-mix them. My heart screams at me to grab her in my arms and tell her how I'm feeling.

I take a big gulp as I go back to prepping our food. I don't know how to express my feelings, because honestly, I was never taught. I learned how to keep my emotions in check and how to avoid caring for people, but Aria? She knocked down my walls, one by one. With her fiery personality and quirks that I've grown to simply fucking love.

One day. One day, I'll be ready to say those three words.

"Come here, try this," I say as I take a spoon of the pasta sauce and blow it softly so it doesn't burn her.

She walks to me and opens her mouth as I feed her with the spoon.

She opens her eyes excitedly and nods. "It's good. The kitchen suits you, *Damie*."

"Don't call me that," I deadpan.

She bats her eyes jokingly. "Yes, sir."

"That's more like it." I wink.

She shakes her head with a laugh, getting back to her baking. I could get used to this. Come home every night, cook together. Come into a house that's *ours* with Aria's personality all over. Hang all her wonderful paintings, family pictures.

She's my present, and my future. I see no one else, but her. Like a glowing star that infiltrated my heart, *brightening* my life. *Breathing* life into me.

We finish eating dinner as we talk about our day, me

completely omitting the whole pictures and threats situation, because the last thing I want to do is worry her.

"Okay, time to try the dessert. Come on!" she says, standing up and grabbing a small plate where she places a few sea salt chocolate chip cookies. She places the plate in front of me and looks at me expectantly. "If it sucks, tell me, okay? Don't lie to me."

I nod as I take a bite, letting out a groan of satisfaction. The sea salt is perfectly contrasting with the semi-dark chocolates, and the cookie is crunchy on the outside but chewy on the inside. *Fucking perfection.*

"Darling, these are the best cookies I've eaten in my life," I say as I stand from my chair and grab her by the waist, placing a kiss on the top of her head.

"Yeah?" She hugs me by the waist, her eyes meeting mine with gleaming pride.

"Yeah." I nod as I grab the nape of her neck and kiss her softly.

She melts to my touch, as always. It's my favorite thing of hers, always melting into me, like she knows I've got her.

Because I do. And always will.

"But I think you taste sweeter, though. There's no better dessert than you," I say in between kisses.

She laughs on my lips. "*Smooth.*"

I laugh before deepening the kiss. Her hands travel all over my chest, arms, and my back. Her touch alone makes my cock hard as a rock. I move my hands down to her thighs and swiftly pick her up and wrap her legs around my waist as I guide us to the bedroom.

I place her on the bed, and she starts unbuttoning my shirt while I grip her waist, trying to contain the little control I have left. She takes off my shirt and quickly takes hers off, revealing a pale blue lacy bra.

I let out an appreciative groan as my hands travel to her breasts and trace her nipples with my thumb.

She roams my abdomen with her soft, delicate fingertips, making me shiver and leaving a burning electric sensation behind. I get on my knees and leave a trace of kisses on her legs as I remove her flimsy skirt, revealing her matching soaked pale blue underwear.

"Did you wear this for me?" I rasp.

She bites her lip. "Maybe."

My kisses start traveling upward slowly, taunting. I take my time kissing, touching, and appreciating every inch of her. "You're so fucking beautiful," I whisper as I kiss her inner thigh, removing the lacy, flimsy underwear.

Her chest heaves as she throws her head back, letting out a soft moan as my mouth gets closer to her core.

"Fuck, *Tesoro*, you're *soaked*." My tongue licks her slit fully, then I slide a finger into her, slowly.

"*Damian*," she moans.

As I feast on her; licking, sucking, nibbling her throbbing clit and one of my fingers slides in and out of her, touching the spot that drives her crazy, my other hand explores the rest of her body. Her legs; her hips; her perfect breasts. She rides my face and fingers, seeking more friction, and I more than happily comply.

I slide my finger out of her, causing a frustrated whimper out of her. I laugh huskily as I wrap both of her legs around my shoulders and simply ravish her. My mouth exploring every inch of her soaked cunt, my tongue pumping in and out of her, mouth-fucking her. Her wetness coats my whole face, making a delicious fucking mess.

"Damian, I need more, please," she begs.

She doesn't need to explain, because anything she asks

for? I'll provide. There's nothing she can ask for that I won't do. I would go to the ends of the world and back to please her. With my mouth, I take her throbbing clit and suck as I slide two of my digits back inside of her and start fingering her at a punishing, fast pace. The sounds of her moans and her soaked pussy fill the room.

"Come for me, Darling. I want to taste you, *now*," I order, then start circling her clit with my tongue.

This drives her wild and over the edge, quickly becoming undone. Her pussy clenches my fingers as she screams my name, riding them as she comes down from her ecstasy.

Aria's eyes are glassy, her face content. Her knees meet the bed as she reaches for my dress pants and boxers, swiftly taking them off, revealing my throbbing cock. She licks her top lip eagerly, clenching her thighs as she enjoys the sight of it.

"Open your mouth," I demand with a rasp as my thumb brushes her sensitive clit

She looks up to me, eyes eager as she opens her mouth. I place my thumb in her mouth as I whisper, "Suck. Taste yourself."

Like the good girl she is, she listens. Sucking my thumb eagerly, tasting her own wetness, rolling her eyes in satisfaction as she lets out a soft moan.

"You like tasting yourself, baby? You taste so fucking sweet, don't you?" I ask, fisting her hair softly and locking our gaze.

She nods, letting go of my thumb with a loud *pop*.

"Use your words, Darling."

"Yes," she moans.

I reach the back of her bra, unclasping it and letting the

flimsy fabric fall on the bed, revealing her perfectly peaked nipples. Playing and pinching them causes a throaty moan from her.

"You look so beautiful moaning, enjoying yourself," I whisper in her ear.

"I bet I would look even better sucking your cock," she says breathlessly.

That simple comment makes me snap, and I let go of the little control I had left. "On your knees, now," I say, stroking my cock twice, precum leaking out of it.

She gets on her knees and wastes no time, licking the precum eagerly before sliding my throbbing cock in her wet, warm mouth.

"Merda," I hiss. *Fuck*. A throaty moan escapes my lips.

The sensation is too much. Her soft hands cup my balls and massage them as she bops her head, my cock sliding in and out of her mouth and swirling her tongue in circles when she's near the head.

I grab her head and start pumping in and out of her at a soft, punishing pace.

"You love it, don't you, me filling your mouth?" I growl as I keep the taunting, slow pace.

She hums and nods eagerly, moaning as she grabs my ass to push my cock all the way in her mouth and choke on it.

"*Merda*, that feels good. Don't fucking stop," I grunt.

She picks up the pace, and I meet her halfway, mouth-fucking her. Her moans are getting consumed by my cock inside of her mouth and I fucking love it. Her watery eyes lock with mine, and I get so lost in those beautiful eyes of hers that are filled with so much lust and pleasure. She looks so confident; so sure of herself, taking pleasure in this.

I slide my cock out of her mouth and get on the bed, grabbing her by the waist and sitting her on top of me.

"No more of that. I need to fuck you. I want to be inside of you when I come," I say, lifting her waist slightly, my cock meeting her entrance. "Shit, wait. We need a condom."

As I'm trying to stand, she stops me. "I'm on the pill, and I haven't been with anyone since my last testing, which was clear."

My cock twitches with excitement at the prospect of being inside of her completely bare. To embrace myself in her warmth. "I'm clear too, and I've also never done it without a condom," I wrap her legs around my waist. "Are you sure about this?"

She nods with a soft smirk and locks her gaze on me as she pushes herself into me in one fell swoop and gasps, my cock completely filling her.

"Fuck, Damian, I'm so fucking full," She moans as she starts grinding, moving slowly back and forth.

My hands roam over her soft legs until I find her hips and stop her for a moment, closing my eyes. "You feel so good, fuck. Wait, I need a moment," I say, trying to catch my breath.

If I don't take a moment, I'll come too soon. I want to get lost in her body, her delicious moans, and I want to enjoy every second of it.

She whimpers, grabbing one of my hands and placing it on her breast, and starts moving again, slowly.

Squeezing her breast, I start moving with her.

Looking down as I pump in and out of her, I groan, "You take my cock so well, Darling."

"And you feel too good," she says through a breathy moan.

The room fills with the sounds of our moans as we both

start picking up the pace, our bodies moving together in synchrony. I bring her closer to me and kiss her fiercely. I kiss her like there's no tomorrow. A kiss that consumes me, her—*us*. A kiss that expresses everything I can't say, because I don't know how.

I wrap both of my arms around her waist, lifting her as I fuck her at a punishing pace. Sliding my cock in and out as she takes every single inch like the good girl she is.

"So fucking tight," I say through gritted teeth.

I thrust harder, my balls slapping against her soaked pussy. She meets every thrust, moaning next to my ear, driving me fucking wild. Her pussy clenches my cock and my balls tighten at the feel of her orgasm enveloping me. My thrust becomes sloppy, and uneven, as I chase my own climax.

"Damian," she moans my name softly, and I'm a fucking goner. I thrust one; twice; and my vision blurs as her cunt milks every ounce out of me, filling her up.

She slides off of me, and falls back into bed, panting. The sight of her, so satisfied and filled with my cum just does something to me. I bring one of my fingers to her pussy, that's leaking with a mix of our cum and I pick some of it in one swift motion.

I then take that same finger and hover it between her lips and order, "Open."

She obeys and parts them softly, and I coat her lips. Then, I close the gap between us and give her a kiss, picking up the cum with one lick and crashing my tongue with hers, a mix of our warmth and our arousals coating our mouths as we keep kissing, making me instantly hard again.

As we break apart, I lick my lips with a satisfactory groan. "We taste so good together, don't we, Darling?"

She hums in agreement. "Yes, we do."

We go and clean ourselves up, then we both lay on the bed, her head resting on my chest.

My heart races at a rapid, uneven pace as I realize how in love I am with this beautiful; kind; dedicated woman. The words are at the tip of my tongue, yet I can't seem to formulate them.

To say this morning has been insane is an understatement. The caterer will be an hour later than agreed and apparently two of their servers called in sick, so they'll probably be short staffed on top of it.

I can feel the panic sneaking in, but I won't let it get to me. This day is too important, and we've worked so damn hard to get here, I'm not letting anything ruin this.

Looking around to ground myself, I try to focus on the things I can see around me and take a deep breath as I try to redirect my focus far away from my anxiety. The first thing I focus on is my desk. It's a little messy, considering I've been working nonstop.

I take a deep breath.

Looking at my hands next, I focus on the nail color. Sophia convinced me to get them done for the gala and I decided to do this delicate nude pink color. It's a nice color, I guess.

I take another deep breath.

Last thing I focus on is the floor to ceiling window

behind me that overlooks the city buildings and Lake Michigan. It's a nice, sunny day and the lake looks beautiful.

I take one last deep breath.

My breathing has significantly calmed down as a knock on my door takes me out of my trance.

I shake my head, already feeling much better. "Come in."

Isabella pops in her head. "Hey, what are you still doing here? You need to go get ready!"

"But—"

"I don't want to hear it. I'll take care of whatever's left. Leave, *now*," she says before shutting the door.

That's Isabella Walton for you. Very bossy.

I grab my things and walk out of the gallery quickly because she's right, I do need to get ready. The last thing I need is to arrive late at our own gala.

Arriving at my apartment, I text Sophia to let her know I'm home since she's going to come over and style my hair. I take off my shoes as I walk toward my bedroom, then drop them in front of my bedroom door, too exhausted and late to care about making a mess.

Opening the door, I glance at my bed, where a black matte box sits with a note on top of it. I furrow my brows as I get closer, picking up the note.

The perfect dress for my Darling.
- Damian

As I open the box, I carefully lift the tissue paper that's wrapping the delicate fabric. Picking it up carefully, my eyes roam the dress, excitement flooding through me. The strapless layered red dress is made out of mesh fabric, and it flows naturally, giving it airy delicate layers. It's simple and elegant all at once. It's perfect.

ME

Thank you for the dress. It's lovely.

DAMIAN

No need to thank me. After all, I get to be the one to rip it off of you later.

ME

Smooth.

DAMIAN

Always.

A laugh escapes me. He's such a shameless flirt and so unserious half of the time. If people knew the real Damian, they'd be shocked. He's funny, kind, and protective. I've never felt so cared for and safe around someone.

Sophia arrives a few minutes later and styles my hair as I do my makeup. She's quieter than normal, which is so strange. She's my best friend and I love her, but boy can that girl talk.

"Are you okay?" I frown.

"Ye–No. Not really. Fucking work," she sighs, "our editor dropped the stolen painting piece. He said there wasn't any point in pursuing it since it's been so long and it already fizzled out."

"Did you make a lot of progress already?"

She slumps her shoulders. "Not really. That painting disappeared off the face of the earth, and when I tried to contact the lead Europol investigator, he shot me down so quickly."

"Well, this was a big deal. He definitely can't be sharing that information. You know that."

She waves her hand around. "*Blah*, semantics."

I turn around and grab her hand. "Plus, wasn't this job temporary? Didn't you say you wanted to start writing your own book?"

She averts my gaze. "I've been so busy. I haven't had time. Anyway, let's continue because you can't be late."

I hum, unconvinced. She has wanted to be a published author for years now. She's been through a lot, which is why I try not to pressure her. I get it. But I'm going to have to pull a mom act soon, because I hate seeing her with a dead end job. She's meant for so much more. She deserves more than life has given her. Most of the time, we need to create our own happy ending. Fight for it, too. And I get the feeling she's giving up and lying to me, and I simply can't allow that.

She finishes the last touches on my hair as I put on my usual red lipstick, that funny enough, is a perfect match for the dress. I glance at the clock, realizing that Damian is picking me up in about ten minutes, so I quickly get dressed and Sophia helps me with the zipper as I'm putting on my earrings and necklace.

"You look beautiful." She beams.

"You don't look so bad yourself." I wink. "You and Isabella will be arriving together, right? Don't be late. I'm not sure why you guys didn't want to come with us. Damian got a limo, you know, because he's extra." I laugh.

"Nah, I'm fine. I'm going to pick up Isabella right now. I'll see you there," she says, giving me a quick hug before leaving.

Spraying some perfume on my wrist and the corners of my neck, I take one last glance in the mirror. Ever since I officially cut my mother out of my life, I've been rocking my curls nonstop. It's one of the many things I'm grateful to Damian for. He slowly, but surely, has helped me feel more secure. His patience and kindness has little by little rebuilt my broken pieces that I never knew how to pick up by myself.

A knock on my door interrupts my thoughts, and as I walk to open the front door, anxiety suddenly floods through me. This gala is a really big deal. I'm talking there's a red carpet, celebrities are attending, the whole nine yards. I can only hope I did the pieces some justice, because I really am proud of them. I'm just crossing my fingers that whatever mystery painting Damian has been keeping away from me is just as good.

Opening the door, my heart speeds up at the sight of Damian. He looks devastatingly handsome with a black tux that was tailored to hug his perfect broad shoulders and muscled thighs. His addicting masculine scent envelops me as he takes a step closer and kisses me.

He takes a step back, his eyes filling with heat. "You look... wow. There are no words. Perfetto." *Perfect*.

My cheeks heat up because only he can make me blush over something so simple as a compliment.

"You ready?"

I nod as I pick up my clutch and walk out the door, grabbing his hand as we walk to the elevator.

It's a busy Saturday night in the streets of the windy city, so we hit some traffic that hasn't been moving for at least ten minutes.

"We're going to be late," I stress.

"No, we won't. And if we are, it's not like they can start the party without us." He shrugs.

"How are you so relaxed? Oh, right, because you know what the statement piece is and I don't." I roll my eyes.

He grabs my jawline softly and gives me a quick kiss. "I

can think of a few ways to relax you," he says with a sultry voice.

"Not here, are you crazy?" I whisper.

His eyes gleam with mischief. "The partition is up. He won't hear anything. I told him to take the longer route, because there's no way I can last all night looking at you in this fucking dress."

His hand lands on my leg where the high slit is, and starts traveling upward as he raises his eyebrow, silently seeking permission. My core is throbbing already, because with his touch, I'm always on fire. I *need* his touch like I need air to breathe.

I nod with my eyes closed, trying to get my bearings.

His hand arrives at my already damp lacy underwear, and he places his thumb on my clit on top of it, moving it in taunting, slow, soft circles as he lets out a throaty groan.

"Tsk. You're already so wet for me, Darling," he whispers in my ear, nipping the lobe softly. "You want me to fuck the stress out of you?" he drops a kiss on the column of my throat. "Just say the word, baby. And I'll have you coming around my cock in no time," he rasps.

I let out a soft moan, and my body involuntarily moves seeking more pressure, because it's not enough. I need so much more of him, to feel him, to feel his hands all over me. He keeps playing the taunting slow pace, though, knowing how crazy it drives me.

"Use your words, Aria. What do you want?" he asks in a sultry whisper, moving the underwear to the side.

Two of his fingers easily slide inside of me with how wet and ready I am for him. There's not much he needs to do to get me going, because I'll always want him. He's addicting, and I always want to feel him. *All of him.*

"I want you inside of me," I say through a moan.

His fingers are already feeling too good, but not enough. I want his cock. I want to be filled by him.

"Get on all fours, now," he demands gruffly.

I swiftly move, putting myself on all fours as he lifts my dress easily. He drops his head down in between my legs and licks my center in one fell swoop.

"So fucking sweet," he growls.

This man melts my insides with his sultry, demanding voice. It's like he knows exactly what I need to hear.

His knees meet the seat as he quickly unbelts his pants, dropping them halfway down.

"We're almost there, so this is going to be quick. You up for the challenge, Darling?" he asks, swiping his hard, throbbing cock up and down between my folds, coating it with my wetness.

I nod frantically as I push back, wanting nothing more than to feel him inside of me. The need is so desperate, my body feels like an inferno.

He thrusts inside of me in one fell swoop, and the feel of his cock inside of me, filling me up, is too much in the best possible way. An involuntary moan escapes my lips as he starts moving.

"This pretty pink cunt of yours takes me so well, baby," he whispers as he kisses my neck, sliding his cock all the way out, then rapidly sliding it in with such delicious force. "*Fuuuuck,*" he moans.

"*Oh, fuck...*" It's all I manage to say as I place a hand on top of my mouth to stop my moans.

He slaps my hand away as he drops his lips next to my ear.

With a growl, he says, "Don't you dare stop those sweet moans of yours. I want to hear you scream as my cock fills you up. Be a good girl and scream my name."

I nod frantically as I meet each of his punishing thrusts and moan his name.

He's fucking mercilessly with such delicious force that I don't know how much longer I can hold on. There's nothing sweet or delicate about this. He's fucking me with everything he can muster, and I'm enjoying every inch and thrust he gives me. It's rough; animalistic; needy, *dirty*.

I roll my eyes back as his cock starts hitting that sensitive spot inside of me, my orgasm sneaking up on me, and I'm left in a haze and moan as my pussy clenches around him.

He lets out a groan as he brings me closer to him, my back pressed against his chest. As I'm riding my orgasm, Damian's thrust becomes more frantic and sloppy. After a few punishing thrusts, he tenses as I feel his warmth filling me up.

"Fuck," he groans, slipping out of me and kissing me.

As I'm trying to catch my breath, I ask, "How do I look?"

"Freshly fucked." He winks as he takes some napkins from the snack bar and cleans me before adjusting my underwear and dress.

I shake my head with a laugh at his response.

We arrive at the gallery a few minutes later, and walk the red carpet as we get our pictures taken, then quickly head inside because I'm a bundle of nerves and I can't wait to see the end result.

My chest tightens with excitement as I look around. We kept the decorations simple, because the point is for the paintings to stand out and, boy, they fucking do. While the room is warm with soft yellow lighted candles, all paintings have overhead white lights, making them all stand out on their own with their bright, alluring colors.

On the other side of the gallery is the open bar. There are tables scattered all over the place with white and gold linen, as well as a dance floor because we wanted to make sure the guests had a nice time. This is better than I could have imagined, but over my dead body am I doing this again.

All the paintings we've carefully chosen throughout these few months are all standing out on their own, shining brightly and giving the space a sense of comfort and elegance. The only thing I'm missing is the statement piece. That specific painting, we decided was going to be at the end of the gallery by itself, right in the center of a white wall that would help people focus on it.

Damian places his hand on my waist and guides me to the center of the gallery. "I have something to show you."

We're walking to the back of the gallery, to go see the statement piece, I assume. There are people walking and chatting in front of us, so it's hard to see the painting from afar. As we get closer, my heartbeat quickens, an urge of nervousness taking over me and a wave of nausea swirling my body, wanting nothing more than to come out.

"Damian, what the fuck is this?" I whisper, my voice trembling.

I don't know why I ask the question, because I know *exactly* what it is. It's one of *my* paintings.

There's one of my paintings in this gallery.

In this very full, *busy* gallery.

Oh My God, I'm going to kill Damian. Yes. That's it. I can already see the headlines—*Psycho much? Curator Aria Petrov murders billionaire Damian Romano.*

He stands in front of me, grabbing both of my shoulders and squeezing them. "Are you upset?"

I gape at him. "I'm more than upset. I could kill you right now. Is this some sort of sick joke?"

He shakes his head. "No. Aria. You're talented, and I

think it's time for you to realize it. I'm sorry if this was the wrong way to go about it, but if I had to do it again, I would."

"How did you even...?"

"Sophia helped me."

"Sophia is a very dead woman, is what she is," I retort.

He grabs my cheek, caressing it softly. "*Tesoro*, it's okay. This is good. When I told you you were talented, I wasn't kidding. It was the perfect painting to tie the collection together."

My heart stabs my rib painfully, and my hands are sweating profusely. I painted this exact painting thinking about the collection we had so carefully put together. But this is not fucking okay. I'm far from okay.

Why am I so upset? Would it really be that bad for people to see it? It's not like they know who did it. My signature is not even there.

The realization hits me in the smack center of my face.

I'm not upset. I'm embarrassed.

I'm embarrassed because I never thought I was good enough to hang a painting in a gallery, much less a gallery like this one. Because it's like I'm a kid all over again, excited to show my mother my very first painting. Remembering her stabbing words, the way she dismissed something I love like it was... *nothing.*

But this is *not* nothing. I can't let my mother dictate how I live my life anymore. I can't let her take this moment away from me. If I do, then there was no point in cutting her out of my life for good. I need to cut her from the root, starting with those hurtful words. Starting by accepting that I deserve this. Accept for once that I'm talented enough to have my painting hanging at a gallery and let people admire my art. Art was made to share, after all.

Anger floods through me now, but not at the situation or

at Damian. I'm angry with myself, because I've brushed this part of my life as an useless hobby, as something unimportant. But art—*my art*—is more than important. It's a part of *me*. My art is all of me; the good, the bad, and the ugly.

My throat tightens, and the words are hard to put together because I'm hit with so much emotion. "Thank you," I manage to say above a whisper.

He hugs me tightly. "You don't have to thank me. You are good enough. *Tesoro*, you have no idea how good you are. I've wanted nothing but to tell you this since the day we walked out on your mother. You are selfless; kind; dedicated. " His forehead meets mine, our eyes holding each other's gaze. He grabs my cheek and caresses it, softly. "There's a fire in you I never want to see put out by anyone. You deserve this. You deserve the whole fucking world. So let me give it to you."

His voice is hoarse now, his eyes filled with an emotion I can't place. I'm at a loss of words because no one has ever done something like this for me. He brushes his thumb against my damp cheek. "I love you," he whispers hoarsely.

My heart bursts open with a thousand emotions. Surprise; relief; happiness. Because goddammit, I've fallen in love. And I've fallen in love *hard*, with the last person I thought possible.

I close the distance between us with a kiss, tuning out everything happening around us. All I can see is him, standing here, in front of me. A man that's so much more than the coldhearted asshole everyone thinks he is. Because I see a completely different side of Damian. A man who, just like me, had broken pieces he needed help picking up. And God, I'm here to pick them up for him for the rest of my days, until my last breath. Put them together one by one, like he has done with mine.

I break the kiss as I look into his eyes containing so much longing and emotion. I get lost in them for a moment, because that's what he does to me. He envelops me, becoming my weakness. Funny thing is, I've always felt stronger by his side. There's no other place I would rather be than here.

I place my hand on his jawline, brushing it softly with my hand. "Damian, I—"

"Damian Romano?" a male voice behind me interrupts.

"Yes?" Damian answers, looking up to address the man.

As I turn around, the man lifts his FBI badge as he walks toward Damian. "You're under arrest for possession of stolen property," he says as he grabs Damian's arms, putting them behind his back.

"What?" Damian asks, confused.

"You have the right to remain silent. Anything—"

"This has to be a mistake," Damian interrupts.

The agent places the handcuffs, ignoring Damian as he continues, "You say can and will be used against you in a court of law. You—"

I interrupt this time, "Sir, I think—"

He keeps ignoring us as he continues, "Have a right to an attorney. If you cannot afford an attorney, one will be appointed for you. Do you understand the rights I have just read to you?"

Damian's eyes meet mine with uncertainty and confusion as he replies, "Yes."

"Let's go," the agent says, pushing Damian toward the exit.

My eyes fill with tears as I run after them.

Isabella is hot on my heels, trying to get a sense of the situation. "What is happening?"

I'm hyperventilating, breathing becoming harder and

harder with every second that passes. "I-I-I don't know. One second w-we were talking and t-t-then..." I can't finish the sentence, my words caught between sobs and the need to breathe.

Isabella takes her phone out of her purse and starts firing out some texts, to Matteo or his lawyers, I suppose. "It's okay, Ari. Everything will be okay."

Then why do I have the feeling everything will be far from okay?

I haven't slept one bit, just going through the motions these past seventy-two hours. Right after they took Damian, I went into panic resolution mode. The gala had to be canceled, obviously, and Isabella contacted Damian's lawyer as soon as the agent walked out that door with him in hand-cuffs. As soon as everyone was out of the gallery, I went to the station to try to find out more information, but of course, they refused. He also wasn't allowed any visitors except for his lawyer. The first twenty-four hours was all of us—Isabella, Lorenzo, Matteo, and even Sophia—who showed up at some point when everyone else had gone home. I was the only one that refused to go. I stayed there, in my gown, my eyes swollen from all the crying and confusion. Granted, Sophia was there mostly for emotional support and trying to get me to eat or drink anything, which I didn't do. That dread in the pit of my stomach simply didn't allow me to.

Sophia and Isabella pretty much forced me to go home to get some sleep and a shower about a day and a half in. They insisted so much, I caved in. Though, I still didn't get any sleep.

And now, we're here. I've been pacing back and forth outside of the station as Liam—Damian's lawyer—is inside, waiting for him to come out. I'm a blubbering mess. The press has been lurking around trying to find why he got arrested, because the information has been kept under wraps.

Liam has been nothing but vague at providing any further information, so I still don't exactly know why he got arrested. For stolen property, right, but what exactly are they claiming he stole? I'm trying not to spiral right now, because he's walking out of that door at any moment, but I am hanging by a thread. Do I think he did anything? Honestly, I don't know.

You do know. Come on, Aria, it's Damian we're talking about. He wouldn't do anything like this.

I have a feeling of dread I can't pinpoint, but can't seem to shake nonetheless. All I know is... I trust him, and I trust he's a good person. All he has shown me these past months has been nothing but kindness and patience.

And love. So much love.

40

Damian

I don't know how to explain what has transpired these last seventy-two hours of my clusterfuck life. Let's start by the fact that I poured my heart out to Aria, and damn it, I don't regret it for one second. But what transpired seconds after the happiest moment of my life has been a complete shit show.

I got arrested.

I'm in fucking jail.

Why am I in jail? That's the biggest clusterfuck of it all. I'm the prime suspect for the stolen painting that happened in Rome *almost* a year ago. Apparently, they've been looking into me after they got a couple of anonymous tips that I was the mastermind behind the heist.

Listen, I'm a ruthless businessman. I've pulled my fair share of tricks over the years. But stealing is *not one of them*.

The first twenty-four hours were *hell*. All I could see every time I closed my eyes was Aria's face, drained of color. Lost. Confused. It fucking shattered my heart.

The following forty-eight hours was me, in a interrogation room, two FBI agents drilling me into admitting guilt for something *I didn't fucking do.* After much back and forth between the authorities, my lawyer, and me, they got enough grounds to get a warrant approved to search the gallery.

Which leads us to today. Seventy-two painful hours later, I'm getting out on bail. I don't have to present myself in front of a judge until later this month, so it's just a matter of proving my fucking innocence. But none of that matters to me. I know I'm innocent. That will be easy to prove.

All I want to do is see Aria. Hug *her*. Kiss *her*. Let her sweet scent ground me. They didn't allow me to see anyone but my lawyer, so I have no idea what I'm walking into. I just hope she'll hear me out.

Liam sits outside in the waiting room as they hand me my things— keys, phone, wallet. I don't even bother looking at my phone because it doesn't have any charge, which is fucking inconvenient, and there's only one thing in my mind.

Aria. I need to talk to her. *No.* I need to *see* her.

Liam is talking on the phone, but hangs up quickly as he greets me, "Romano."

I nod. "Hawkins. What's the update?"

"How about we go to Vortex, sit down, and talk over bourbon?"

That is the absolute last place I want to be. I can already envision all the elites with their claws out, trying to find out why I got arrested and already plotting how to take advantage of this and take me down for good.

"Get straight to the fucking point, Hawkins. That's the last place I want to be right now."

He sighs. "They found the painting."

My shoulders relax. "Good. Fucking where? So we can put this shit to rest."

He purses his lips. "They found it in the basement of your gallery."

My world is thrown upside down when those words come out of his mouth. He keeps talking, but I completely tune him out. I don't even know where to start grasping what the fuck has happened these last couple of days.

"...prints," he finishes.

I laugh humorlessly, running my fingers through my hair in exasperation. "I'll be honest with you. I didn't hear one single thing you said."

"The painting has your prints all over it."

I put my hands on my face and make a wiping motion, trying to clean away the frustration and murmur, "Oh, for fuck's sake."

"Listen, Romano. I'm your lawyer, and I will defend you until the end of time, but I'm your friend first." His voice drops an octave, whispering ever so slightly, "Did you do it?"

I glare at him in disbelief. "Of course, I didn't do it," I spit. "I'm being set up, man. That's the only reasonable explanation."

He nods in understanding. "I believe you, but we have work to do."

"I need you to make a stop first." If I have to wait one more second without seeing or talking to Aria, I'm going to lose my shit.

"You should know... Aria's here. She's outside. She has been here day in and day out. You have a good woman by your side."

Knowing she's here makes my shoulders instantly relax. She's not just a good woman, she's the fucking best. In a world where I have shut everyone out of my life to be completely alone, she found a way in.

I sprint outside, frantically looking around for her. And

then I spot her, sitting on the sidewalk. *God.* She looks so beautiful. Call me a lovesick fool, but the three days apart were the longest days of my life.

Her eyes gleam with excitement as she stands and runs toward me, throwing her arms around my shoulders, and hugging me tightly. "Oh, Damian. Thank God."

I hug her back and instantly feel at ease. I hide my nose at the crook of her neck, letting the scent I've correlated to peace, calmness, and tranquility envelop me.

"I'm so glad you're okay," she whispers, her voice laced with emotion.

"Hey, hey. I'm okay. I'm here now. It's okay, *Tesoro*." I kiss her softly. God, I missed her soft lips. Her soft hands. All of *her*.

"The gallery is flooded with FBI agents now." She sighs. "Damian—"

"I didn't do it," I blurt out.

I need to make sure she knows. It would break my heart to think she believes I'm capable of something like this. I know people have a lot to say about me, and I've done everything I can to stay on top, but that's not the real me, and I know she knows this. She's the only one that has been able to see me for, well—*me*. Not only that, I would never stoop so low and do something so reckless.

She takes a step back, surprise plastering her face. "I know. I know *you*. You would never do anything like that."

I sigh with relief. "God, these have been the worst three days of my life." I shake my head, closing my eyes in relief. "I'm so fucking glad you're here."

She grabs my face, then waits until I open my eyes to speak. "Of course. I'm here for you. *Always*."

"I need to go with Liam, set up a plan in motion to get ready for the indictment."

"I can go with you."

I shake my head. "No, it's fine. It will probably take a while. But I'll drop by your place later, stay over."

Her eyes gleam as she smiles. "I'd like that."

After meeting with my lawyer and deciding I'm going to plead not guilty and hope for the fucking best as we gather evidence, I arrive home to take a shower and pick some clothes to stay over at Aria's.

As the elevator of my condo opens and I walk in, I notice I'm not alone. There's someone in my living room. I know this because they're... *humming*.

"Who's there?" I yell from the foyer, walking toward the humming noise.

The person is sitting in a chair in front of the window, overlooking the busy city life. "Oh, you're here. Great," says the familiar voice.

My hand trembles with anger when the last person I want to fucking see right now turns around.

Alex Motherfucking Brown.

"What the fuck are you doing here?" I stride toward him. "How the fuck did you get in here?"

He waves his hand dismissively. "Too long to explain," he replies with a maniacal grin.

My knuckles turn white with how hard I'm clenching my fists, trying my best to hold myself back. I could just punch this motherfucker right now. I have so much pent up anger, that throwing a few punches would do the trick to relieve some very annoying stress.

"*Why. Are. You. Here*?" I ask through gritted teeth.

He stands, buttoning his suit. "Rough couple of days?" He tilts his head.

I thin my lips and glare at him, opting for silence.

He sarcastically snaps his fingers, as if he suddenly remembered something. "Oh, that's *right*! I'm the one who tipped the feds." He laughs. "God, I didn't know it was going to take them that long to arrest you. I guess the system really is broken, *huh*?"

A wave of nausea settles at the pit of my stomach as anger keeps vibrating throughout my whole body. It's suddenly too hot here. The place feels so fucking small I feel like I'm going to pass out. Is this what panic feels like?

"Cat got your tongue? It's okay. I'll keep talking. I have *many* things to say." Alex grins as he circles me. "See, Damian, I know you never saw me as a threat. Because I let you see what you wanted to see."

We have similar builds, but I'm about four inches taller than him. That doesn't stop him from trying to stand all tall and *macho* in front of me.

"After all, I'm a nobody. Right? Isn't that what you said?" he snarls.

My ears are ringing, and I'm trying my fucking best to stay composed, to not show weakness. To put up the facade I learned many moons ago. The anxiety is creeping in slowly, but surely, and I'm trying my best to shove it down and fucking drown it.

With a bored expression, I look down on him. He may only be four inches shorter than me, but with one single, determined look I can make it feel like more. That's how you dominate your enemies. But the shift in demeanor doesn't come. He looks... amused. He looks like there's nothing in this world that can bring him down, and that just tells me one thing.

I am utterly fucked.

"I told you once I was going to bring you down to your knees, and that was a fucking promise."

"What do you want?" I say hoarsely.

"You will plead guilty."

I laugh humorlessly. "You're out of your fucking mind if you think I'm doing that."

"*You will plead guilty,*" he repeats. "Otherwise, you will find out the lengths I will go to make sure you do it."

"Is that a threat?"

"Oh, that's a promise," His eyes gleam with mischief. "You wouldn't want anything to happen to Aria, now, would you?"

My heart drops.

No.

He wouldn't dare.

"You're bluffing," I challenge.

"I can promise you I'm not," he replies, his tone unwavering.

"Aria is your friend. What is wrong with you?" I ask in disbelief.

He lets out a condescending laugh. "She *was* my friend, but the *bitch* decided to side with you, and now she's collateral damage. I tried to save her. I told you to fire her and you didn't listen."

The threats. It was this fucking idiot all along?

The fact he called her a bitch doesn't escape me. My hands take a life of their own and I grip him by the collar, closing the distance between us.

Through gritted teeth, I say, "Why are you doing this? You were the one that stole that painting? And now you're blaming it on me? *Why?*"

He laughs in disbelief, but makes no effort to escape my

grip. "After all these years, you still don't get it, do you? I'm the one who stood by your father's side, day in and day out, working at the gallery. He taught me everything I know, and what do you do? You just take over the place after he dies. A place you don't deserve."

I push him, exasperated. "I'm his son!" I yell from the top of my lungs, my voice becoming hoarse. "The place belonged to me. He even acknowledged that by leaving it to me when he died, Alex." I sigh in defeat. "You need to accept that."

"I don't need to accept shit, *brother*."

Time stand stills as my gaze locks on his. "What did you just say?" I whisper.

"You heard me."

I stare at him with a blank expression. It takes me what feels like a lifetime to process the words he just spat out. *Brother*? What does that even fucking mean?

A maniacal laugh escapes me. I'm laughing uncontrollably now. My shoulders shake and my eyes brim with tears.

Oh, I'm losing it. I'm so losing my shit right now.

"Alex, I don't know what you're plotting, but my brother? This is desperate, even for you."

Alex takes a step back, smirking. "And why would I make up something like that?"

"Beats me! But you are not my fucking brother. You're talking like a crazy person right now!" I'm yelling now, running through the motions, trying my best to escape the feeling of dread and realization.

Deafening silence falls between us, and my gaze locks on him. *All of him.*

He's shorter than me, sure, but not by much. His hair is more light brown, whereas mine is black like my mother's. Our eyes though, are the exact same ones. That unmistakably deep green, like the lush canopy of an ancient forest.

The same eyes as my father's.

Fuck. How didn't I see this sooner?

Alex is about two years younger than me if I remember correctly, so it had to have happened right after we moved to the States.

"You and I both know I was more of a son to him than you ever were. So imagine how I felt when he left you something that *belonged to me.*"

I wince at the words. They hit the center of my chest like a dart aimed straight at the bullseye. I know better than anyone that my father didn't care about me. He made sure I knew every fucking day of my life. It fucking wrecked me to see he bonded with Alex over art, something I loved as much as him, maybe even more. How he taught Alex everything he knew—which, at this point, I don't know if I should feel thankful it wasn't me, knowing now how Alex turned out. It still fucking hurts, though. I never understood why I was cast aside. This is fucking why? All because he knocked up God knows who and had a guilty conscience and decided to raise only *one* of his sons. The one that was most similar to him, nonetheless.

I wonder if *Mamma* knows. I wonder if maybe this is why she never got in the middle of it, because she was dealing with her own hurt.

Alex is just like our father. Filled with anger; envy; hatred. That's why my father was never able to take the business to the next level, like he wanted to. Because he refused to show emotion and his human side—if he ever had any— when it was necessary. Even the most ruthless men in the world have a human side and are not afraid to show it. Not showing any, at all, is what makes you fucking weak. It took me long to realize it, but now I fucking know better. And I let my father convince me along the way that I was good for nothing. That I wouldn't make it. That I was weak. When in reality? He was fucking deflecting.

There's no point in dwelling in the past that has been drowning me for so long. What can I do about it now? I've made my life's mission to do everything my father couldn't do. I'm a goddamn billionaire. I made sure to set up my life. To be successful. All to spite him, and it got me nowhere.

Until I met her. Aria is all that matters now. And I need to protect her. If there's any human side to Alex, he'll see it, too. This is between us. There's no reason for her to be involved.

"Alex, don't do this," I plead.

He laughs, striding to the elevator, me hot on his heels. He presses the button as silence blooms in the room. You can cut the tension with a knife.

The ding of the elevator cuts the deafening silence.

As Alex stands inside the elevator and the doors start to close at a painfully slow pace, he says, "*Tick-Tock,* brother. You have a choice to make."

41

Aria

Three weeks have passed since Damian's arrest, and he's been avoiding me like the plague. That day, he was supposed to stay over at my place, but stood me up.

He said he was busy, so I let it go.

I tried to meet with him the day after, and he said he was still extremely busy with meetings and coming up with a game plan for the indictment. I understood and decided to let it go—*again*—trying my best to be understanding.

But now he's blatantly avoiding me. And it stings, especially with what happened at the gala right before everything went to shit. In other instances, I would be the good little patient girl who sits and waits for him to show his face. My new self, though? The exact opposite.

Hence why I'm outside of Vortex after Isabella gave me access to his calendar. I don't care if I seem like a crazy stalker. I'm worried. So fucking worried. I heard from Isabella that the indictment is next month, and he didn't even tell me.

I'm trying not to take this personally. I really am.

From what the calendar showed—which was extremely vague—his meeting should be finishing up right now.

I lean against a building across the street, looking at the club entrance. Once I spot him, I cross the sidewalk and stand in front of him, crossing my arms and raising an eyebrow expectantly.

His gaze snaps up, surprise lacing his features. "What are you doing here?"

His voice is slurry, and he smells like a distillery. I'm not too sure now if the calendar was right. He doesn't drink more than one glass of bourbon during meetings, saying that it clouds the mind.

"You're avoiding me. And you're drunk," I state in a matter-of-fact tone, void of emotion.

He takes his phone out of his pocket, avoiding my gaze. "I'm not drunk." His slur is more pronounced now. "And I told you, I've been busy."

I take the phone out of his hands, which is relatively easy since his movements are slower than normal. "Twenty-four hours a day? You can't take a moment to call me? Text me?" I gulp, trying my best to compose myself. "You stood me up."

He runs his fingers through his hair, still avoiding my gaze. His eyes are glassy, though. His face flushed from the alcohol. His words are cold, and a little sharper now. "I'm trying to get my shit together, Aria. I don't have time for this," he mutters, walking to where his driver is waiting for him.

I follow after him like a pathetic fool, but God, I don't care. He's not getting away with this. I deserve more than this. I don't deserve to be brushed off.

I grab his arm, stopping him. "Damian, talk to me.

What's wrong? Why are you drunk in the middle of the fucking day?"

He snaps, shaking off my grip rudely. "Aria, I will fucking talk to you when I can. Now, I have another meeting to go to."

"With who? Your bottle of bourbon?"

He snarls. "Stop worrying about me, you look pathetic."

His words are like a whiplash; a slap to the face.

A wave of emotion crashes over me, and my eyes well up with tears as I reluctantly take a step back, nodding in silent understanding. A heavy ache tightens around my heart, squeezing it in a vise of conflicting emotions. Just a few weeks back, he told me he loved me and that he believed in me. The words *felt* real. Now, it's like those moments never happened.

I brush away a tear from my cheek. "Pathetic, huh?" I mutter unsteadily.

His face drains of color as he tries to close the distance between us. "Darling, no. I—"

I take a few more steps back, keeping even more distance now. "Save it. I don't want to hear your excuses. I'm not some toy you get to play with when you feel like it, Damian. You don't get to pick up the broken pieces and put them together when you have the time and patience, and crumble them when you don't. I'm fucking human. I deserve more than this. I'm done." I throw his phone at him, which he surprisingly catches.

Guess his senses are coming back.

I storm the other way, walking back home. And the worst part? He doesn't follow.

I'm an emotional wreck. Have been for the majority of the week. The girls have been checking in regularly, but I can't even bother to come up with a reply that doesn't sound pathetic.

What was I thinking, falling in love with him? Since the beginning I've known that he has two different lives.

The ruthless, selfish, arrogant asshole—the mask he's so carefully built and perfected for the world, a job he's exceeded at.

Then, there's the real him—or so I thought—kind; thoughtful; loving; patient. The man I fell in love with. The man that navigated through my heart and took it when I least expected it. But was that even the real him? Or was this another mask that he made me believe in? Am I an idiot? Have I been taken for granted?

God, my head is pounding, surely because I haven't eaten anything.

Someone's knocking on my door now, and as I get comfortable on the couch watching *Friends* reruns, I yell, "Go away!"

"Ari, open up!" Isabella yells from the other side of the door.

"I'm not in the mood, Isa. Go away!" I shout back.

"That's it," Sophia says from the other side of the door as I hear her keys rattling. "We're coming in!" she shouts as she opens the door.

"I knew giving you that key was a mistake," I groan.

"I would have found my way in. Don't underestimate me, Petrov."

I glare at her. "Don't last name me."

Sophia points a finger at me. "Don't give me a reason to."

I love my friends, I do. Truly. They are there for me every

time. But I want to be left alone. Can't a girl wallow in peace?

Isabella sits next to me, giving me a side hug. "How are you holding up, hun?"

"Gee, I don't know, let's see." I sigh. "Damian tells me he loves me, then right before I was going to say it back, an FBI agent walks in and *arrests* him. Then, he gets out, excited to see me and suddenly drops off the face of the earth. In summary, I'm *great*, thank you for asking." I smile sarcastically.

"He's miserable, you know," Isabella whispers.

And what good does that do to me? Why is he miserable? Why is he not talking to me? He just disappeared. *Poof.* No explanation whatsoever. I get he's going through a hard time, but *fuck*, I'm here. Right here. Ready to support him in whatever he needs.

I'm ready to pick up his pieces, just like he did with mine.

42

Damian

Greeting Liam as I walk into his office, I get straight to business. "I'm pleading guilty."

His eyes widen in shock as he demands, "And why would you do that?"

The words hover on the edge of my tongue.

Because I rather rot in jail than hurt the woman I love.

Because I rather stain my name than hers; the woman who unknowingly saved my life by simply existing.

"I just am. The details are not important."

As he massages the bridge of his nose, he tosses his pen onto the desk. "Romano, you've got to let me lend a hand here. Are you guilty or not?"

Clamping down on my tongue, a taste of copper fills my mouth. Expecting Hawkins to comply with my plan without raising questions was a stupid way of thinking. What other options do I have, though? Alex made his intentions clear. It's either I save my reputation and ruin hers, or vice versa.

I obviously choose to ruin a reputation that means nothing to me. There's no amount of wealth or fame that would make me change my mind. This is not Aria's fault, so why should she pay for a feud between me and my fucking brother?

God, this is so fucked.

I still can't believe it. Fuck my father, honestly. All I feel is pure hatred for that man. It's been years since he passed, but every decision I've made for my life has been shaped by the hurt he inflicted on me.

But not anymore. Fuck the money. Fuck the fame I didn't even want in the first place. I'll protect the woman I love. *Every. Damn. Time.* No questions asked.

My steps bring me nearer, and I lean against his desk, my tone icy. "Don't forget you work for me, Hawkins. I have no issue reminding you of that. I'm ready to plead guilty; so let's work on securing a beneficial arrangement."

He shakes his head in defeat. "I'll see what I can do."

⸻

I've never felt so all over the place in my life. The bourbon is who I have to thank for that. After slamming glass after glass, I stopped feeling the burn down my throat after the fourth round, but that didn't deter me from drowning in my sorrows, my mistakes, questioning my life and where the fuck I went wrong. I thought the booze would numb me, but it's doing the opposite—cranking up the emotions instead. Without Aria, I'm fucking miserable. I miss her warm hazel gaze, her touch, the sound of her fucking voice, our bodies colliding, and me getting lost in her. Doesn't matter how much booze I drink, the need keeps multiplying.

The elevator doors at my place open, and I catch the sound of someone walking toward me with quiet steps. I'm sitting in the kitchen, perched on the island, facing away.

I gulp down another glass of bourbon and mutter hoarsely, "Go away."

The steps get closer, and a soft hand fists my hair slightly and I melt at the feel of it instantly, because I'd recognize that touch anywhere. There's only one person in this fucked up world that can make me feel so much with a simple touch.

"Damian," Aria whispers.

I squeeze my eyes shut, clenching my jaw as I bite the inside of my cheek, desperately trying to keep my emotions in check. *God*, I love this woman. There's an overwhelming urge to yell it out, to let her know how damn sorry I am for pushing her away. For calling her pathetic. I'm itching to wrap my arms around her, feel the warmth of her hold, and let myself be enveloped in the comforting scent that's uniquely hers—sweet and addicting—like a familiar, soothing balm to the chaos inside.

"What are you doing here?" I ask, grabbing the bourbon bottle and taking another swig of the golden liquid.

Forget the fucking the glass, I'll be nursing this bottle for the rest of the night. Probably for the rest of my miserable life.

She grabs a seat next to me. "Damian, look at me."

I can't do it. The pain hits hard when I look at her. If I do, I'll lose control. I'll spill everything, and her life will be ruined. I won't let that happen, even if it's my final move, even if she ends up hating me.

I look the other way, feeling the swell of emotions. "Go away, please," I rasp.

"Not until we talk. Not until you tell me why you're pleading guilty."

My eyes fix on her, and I curse myself for the stupid move. There's a hint of worry in her eyes, and she looks as tired as me, if not more. But she's still undeniably beautiful. No makeup, just those golden freckles adding a natural glow to her face.

"Who told you that?"

She looks at me, knowingly. "Isabella. Did you really think you could avoid me forever? I'm here. Let's talk."

Time to play pretend. Wearing the mask I've got down pat.

"There's nothing to discuss. I thought I made that very clear when we last spoke," I snap. "Why are you even here? Are you expecting me to say I'm innocent? Because that's not gonna happen." I down another swig of bourbon.

She gets up and grabs the bottle, slamming it down on the counter. "Can you quit sulking for a second and just tell me what the fuck happened? You said you're not guilty. Are you saying you lied to my face?" Now she's yelling, anger all over her.

Good. This is what I need to break the bond for good and make her hate me.

"And what if I did? I really don't give a fuck what you think of me. Know your place and mind your damn business," I shout back as I get up and grab the bottle.

She jabs a finger into my chest. "You think after all this time I'm going to buy into this? Cut the bullshit, Damian, it's beneath you. I thought we were past this."

"Past what, huh? You really believed I cared about you? Give me a break. Quit being so damn naive; it's beneath *you,* " I retort.

I'm holding on to anything that will drive her away as my heart is fucking clenching so hard I can physically feel it *breaking*. I'm driving away the only woman that has taken down my carefully crafted walls. The only one who has been able to see through the good, the bad, and the ugly. All because I have no other fucking damn option at this point.

"You're lying," she declares, and it seems like she's telling herself that more than me.

Aria is a smart girl. I'm not taking that away from her. But I'm a determined motherfucker.

I gulp, locking my gaze on her. My tone is icy and sharp... one I don't even recognize. "We dated and fucked a few times. I know I said I was going to be there for you, but I'm not a relationship guy, never will be. We just got caught up in the moment. Move on." The lies flow easily, the words tasting like pure vile in my mouth.

She steps back, her head shaking in disbelief, laughing humorlessly. Angry tears fill her eyes, and she squeezes her hands so hard, her knuckles go white. "*Fuck you*," she snarls. "I can't believe I fell in love with a coward who can't face me head on and tell the fucking truth. You're taking the easy way out, and you know what? I'm going to let you. Hope you're happy with your decision." She storms out of the kitchen, her angry steps echoing toward the elevator.

Fell in love with?

My heart drops, body trembling with the knowledge that she fucking loves me too. I've never felt worthy of her love, and while I was falling head over heels for her, I never realized she was falling for me, too. How fucking naive am I?

The elevator doors shut, a dead silence settling in the apartment.

I smash the bourbon bottle against the white kitchen wall, shouting in frustration, "*FUCK!*" The yell that comes out of me is hoarse, raw and fucking brutal.

Tears of anger; sadness, and desperation escape my eyes quickly as I plummet to the floor that has broken glass scattered, mixed with the gold smoky booze. I rest my head against the wall as I let my tears out and I scream from the top of my lungs until my voice gives out.

43

Aria

I'm still boiling with frustration from yesterday's encounter as I bang on the gallery's main door, waiting for Isabella to open up. Couldn't find that stupid key, not that it matters now. I'm officially done. No clue what's next for me. Maybe The Institute will take me back, or maybe not. All I'm sure of is that I'm fucking done with this place, with Damian, all of it. I know deep down he's pushing me away and lying, but I don't have the heart to keep fighting when he clearly gave up.

Isabella comes to the door, swinging it open fast. "Aria, good. You're here."

"I'm just here to grab my things."

Worry shows on Isabella's face. "What happened?"

"Your dumb boss happened, that's what."

"Is that Aria?" a male familiar voice says as he's approaching us.

I recognize him. I think he's Damian's head of security. Lorenzo's best friend too, if I recall correctly. His name is... Matt? I don't know. My brain is still foggy from yesterday's fight.

"Solid detective work, Matteo. I see why Damian pays you the big bucks," Isabella remarks sarcastically.

Matteo. That's right.

He's good-looking in that friendly, guy-next-door way. His blond hair is kind of all over the place, and he always has this friendly, boyish grin on his face. But his eyes? They're icy blue. And they hold... so much. If I look at them for too long, they startle me.

I step into the gallery. "Sorry to interrupt, guys. I won't be here long."

"We actually need to talk to you," he says.

"Matteo," Isabella warns.

He looks directly at Isabella, saying, "Clock's ticking, Sunshine. I can't waste time being indirect." His gaze locks on me now. "What can you tell me about Alex Brown?"

Ugh. I swear he's like a cockroach that refuses to die.

"Not much to tell. We went to school together, and we became close friends quickly. Apparently, he and Damian had some issues in the past? He's been a royal pain in the ass these past few months. They've gotten into a few altercations." I narrow my eyes. "Why?"

He thins his lips, nodding. "If my sources are right, he's the answer to all of our problems. Behind all of this."

I'm all tangled up in confusion now. Is Alex behind this? Somehow, it doesn't shock me. These last few months taught me that he's as sly and shady as they come.

"What sources, exactly?" Isabella questions.

Lorenzo strides in, speaking up for Matteo, "Considering he broke the guy's fingers, a reliable one."

"*Dude!* Not cool," Matteo scolds.

I can't believe it as I watch them. "Are you for real?"

"I never joke about a man's fingers, Red." Enzo winks.

"I'm not signing up to be part of some potential murder

scenario, so you guys need to shut the fuck up right now!" Isabella exclaims.

With a grin, Matteo tells her, "Relax, *Sunshine*, no one's six feet under."

Lorenzo rolls his eyes, looking completely uninterested as he says, "*Yet.*"

I have so many questions right now. I don't even know where to start untangling this whole messed-up situation. I'm clueless about what they're accusing Damian of, and now he's being framed?

"I'm seriously confused. Somebody needs to step back and clue me in on what's happening," I comment.

"You better sit down, Red. This story is long and wild," Matteo chimes in.

Oh, boy.

***

"Are you sure you want to do this?" Sophia questions once I bring her up to speed.

I nod. "I'm more than sure."

Matteo and I had a talk, and he spilled the beans on everything. The email threats, the tailing—Matteo, being a tech genius, traced it all back to Alex. Not exactly directly to him, but to a questionable company he cooked up with more than shady connections. It's a lot worse than any of us anticipated, and Alex orchestrated the whole thing right under our noses. There are so many holes in the story, though.

Like, how did the painting get into our basement in the first place? Or Damian's prints for that matter?

The gallery has a state-of-the-art security system that only the employees that have the app on their phone can access without causing any suspicion. Only me, Isabella, and Damian have that app. Also, the fucking keys. Per the FBI, there was no forced entry into the gallery, hence why it looks even worse for Damian. Whoever did it, walked right in with a key and deactivated the alarm.

"Oh my God," I say as the realization hits me.

"What?" Sophia asks, confused.

"I think Alex stole my keys the day we had lunch to go over the painting I needed. He pretended he didn't know I was working for Damian. We got into an altercation and he..." I get up, walking back and forth, fuming. "The asshole dropped my purse by accident and helped me pick up the things. I couldn't find my keys since then, but I didn't pay much attention. Thought I had lost them."

A hint of guilt floods through me. I'm partly at fault here. I can't believe Alex manipulated me like that. With the fight, acting all offended and worried. Insulting me because he knew I was going to storm away.

I'm fuming with so much rage, it's not even funny. First thing I want to do when we finish talking is go to Alex and kill him. Like, full on stabbing until he's nothing but dead flesh.

He did all of this and for what, exactly? A big tantrum over the fact Damian's father didn't leave him the gallery? Big fucking deal. He's big enough in the industry now that he could have gone to do his own thing. Instead, he made Damian miserable and made him hide everything from me, playing some shining armor hero. I'm so fucking pissed at Damian too, and I was ready to rip him a new one. But Matteo has a way with words, and was able to talk me down and propose a plan.

It's frustrating because I blame myself, too. I should have insisted more and pushed harder when he was clearly pushing me away. I missed the signs, and now we're knee-deep in this shit. Matteo proposed a plan to confront this chaos head-on and put an end to it, and without a second thought, I agreed.

"I swear I'm going to chop off Alex's dick for this," Sophia seethes.

"Nope. Grab a ticket and wait your turn, because I want to *kill him.*"

Of course, I won't. But it's a nice thought, that's for sure.

I take a deep breath as I stand in front of Alex's apartment door. This plan took us about a week to cook up, and it's insane.

Matteo's voice startles me as he speaks in my left ear, "You ready?"

I'm wearing the tiniest Bluetooth known to man in my left ear, so Matteo can hear everything that's about to go down. I hope this insane idea pans out and we can catch Alex red-handed.

"Yup," I whisper as I knock on the door.

My heart beats erratically as I hear steps getting closer to the door. I've never been a good actress, but for Damian? I'll put on the best goddamn show. Oscar-worthy.

Alex opens the door, his features lacing surprise. "What do we have here?"

"Can you let me in? We need to talk."

He smirks as he stands to the side and gestures for me to come in.

Prick. I hope you choke on your own dick and die.

I casually swing my hips as I step in, making an effort to steady my breath.

He lets out a little whistle and says, "You look good."

I'm wearing the tightest sluttiest black dress—sponsored by Sophia's closet. It hugs my body in all the right places. The cleavage is a bit on the wild side, pushing the limits.

I need to tread carefully here. If I seem too eager, he'll know something's definitely up. "Thanks."

He walks to the kitchen. "Want anything to drink? Water? Or how about wine? I know how much you love your wine."

I laugh. "Yeah, wine is fine."

He serves two glasses half way and walks to the living room where I'm taking a seat comfortably. He hands me the glass and sits down next to me.

"Listen, Aria. These past few months, I know I've acted differently, and for that I'm sorry. I just worry about you, you know?"

Matteo chuckles in my ear and murmurs something along the lines of *asshole* and *great acting.*

Hearing Alex's words makes me want to take this cup of wine and smash it against his head, but instead, I say, "I know."

"And you see? I was right. Look at Damian now. Stealing a famous painting? Doing shady business? I told you he was bad news."

I glare at him. "Alex, we've known each other for how many years now? Drop the act. I know what you did."

"I'm not sure what you're talking about." He feigns innocence.

I place the wine on the coffee table before facing him. "I'm not here to bust your balls, Alex. Let's stop pretending like you didn't frame Damian and let me in on the plan."

He smirks knowingly. "That brother of mine sure has a big fucking mouth."

His comment catches me off guard, making me falter. Oh my God. They're *brothers*?

I stare at Alex, and suddenly everything clicks. He's shorter, and he definitely doesn't have those Italian good looks going on for him, but his skin tone is tan. I've seen Alex's mom; she's pale, so that's not where it comes from. His hair's more like light brown, not as dark as Damian's. But what really gives it away is his eyes. They share the same deep green color, but there's a difference. Alex's eyes lack that intense gaze, and they don't stir up the same feelings as the eyes I've grown fond of. Still, they're pretty fucking similar.

His gaze narrows. "You didn't know?"

Think, Aria. Think.

This was such a stupid idea. I mean, seriously, what were we thinking? If all the stuff we've got on our hands turns out to be true, Alex is not just some regular trouble— this guy is *dangerous.*

I've got to tread carefully here. If I'm not super cautious, my life is hanging by a thread. It's not just about some petty danger; it's a real, definite threat. Alex seems to be playing on a whole different level, and I can't afford to make a wrong move.

Matteo's voice in my earpiece warns, "Aria..."

I muster the most honest chuckle I can come up with. "Looks like your brother isn't as chatty as you thought."

Oh, come on, please, whoever's up there, make it happen. I'm begging you, let him take the bait. He fucking deserves it.

With a nonchalant shrug, he comments, "He's not the smartest one around, to be honest."

I let out a quiet sigh of relief, but I keep it in check. I'm already deeply involved in this mess, so I've got to see it through to the end. No turning back now.

Casually crossing my legs, I end up revealing more skin than I planned, but it seems to be doing the trick because Alex is definitely checking me out. Makes me want to crawl out of my skin. To think I considered him a friend for the longest time, and he fucking betrayed me and my trust. Or maybe I was just too trusting and chose to believe a different version of him.

But, at least I get something out of this. I've known him for so long, so there's one thing I know for certain. He thrives on a little ego boost. You give him a compliment and he turns into a chatterbox. He just can't help himself, and, I mean... I was his friend for a while. He has *some* level of trust. He just doesn't fucking respect me. There's a difference, I guess.

I casually say, "So? How'd you do it? I gotta say, whatever you did, it was brilliant."

He casually throws an arm over my shoulders, and I do my best to stay still, look comfortable.

"It was a piece of cake, honestly. We stole that painting from Rome, thinking we could make a quick buck selling it on the black market. But, you see, Damian's made himself a lot of enemies in this business. Let's just say there are a bunch of people eager to see him take a fall, once and for all," he says, giving a nonchalant shrug.

I bite my tongue as I nod, gesturing for him to continue as I try my best to hold back. My anger is reaching a boiling point, and my heart stumbles over itself in frustration. Guilt pricks at the pit of my stomach knowing Damian has been going through something like this all alone.

I nod, impressed. "What about our painting? You stole it too, right? Broke into the gallery?"

He nods, proud of himself. "Yeah."

Idiot.

I already knew the answer, though. Matteo traced everything back and uncovered the deleted surveillance.

"What about the famous painting from Rome? How'd you sneak in the painting, anyway? I was always down in that basement, and it never caught my eye. That was a pretty slick move."

Every time I toss out a compliment, I want to roll my eyes, but I'll do whatever it takes to keep him talking.

He grimaces. "Don't kill me, but when we had lunch and we fought? I already knew you were working for Damian. I intentionally made you drop your purse, helped you pick up your stuff, but hung on to the gallery keys."

Oh, I'm going to jail tonight. I'm killing this motherfucker.

I give a fake nod of approval. "Wow, okay, that's pretty impressive."

"That's some Bond shit, huh?" He gives me a playful wink.

A shiver runs down my spine at the wink, but it's not the good kind. The sense of suffocation takes over, and all I can think of is escaping this damn place.

"Ask him about the prints," Matteo prompts.

I lower my hand onto his thigh, giving it a light stroke. I'm not above using my sexuality to save Damian's ass, even if I want to throw up. I will not be sleeping with him by any means, but some flirting will do. If I'm being completely honest, I don't understand how I'm playing this off so well. It's almost like I'm channeling Sophia. Now, she's a real bad bitch. I'm too mellow; soft; insecure.

Used to be insecure. Not anymore.

With the way Damian worships me and takes care of me, it helped me gain the confidence I need. The confidence that also helped me stand up to my mother. I've grown so much as a person, learning as I go, and I owe most of it to him.

"What's the deal with Damian's prints? How did you make that happen?"

He casually places his hand on my thigh, a bit higher than I'm comfortable with, but I pull through. "On the day of the auction, right after the issue between us and Damian, once you all took off, I doubled back. I grabbed Damian's used glass with a cloth, and tossed it in a bag. Simple stuff. I know a guy who could transfer the prints from the glass onto the corners of the painting."

"Even I'm impressed..." Matteo snickers.

I shut off everything Matteo's saying as we're getting close to the finish line. If I can just figure out what he's planning next, it's game over for him.

Straddling him, I find a comfortable position, purposefully shifting my ass over his cock. The idea of having to scrub my body until it's raw and bleeding to rid myself of his lingering touch is strong, but I'm so close to the finish line, I can almost savor the taste of victory.

He holds onto my hips, his clammy hands making me feel queasy. It's no secret Alex has always had a crush on me. That didn't stop him from screwing around with my best friend, not that I minded anyway. I've truly never seen Alex with any other eyes. Just a friend. And I'm so fucking thankful for that, because I wonder what would my life been like if I had fallen in love with him, been with him?

The thought of it hurts, because that would have meant I would have never met Damian. A life without him is impossible. He's mine, and I am his. We're soulmates. For life.

I twirl his tie around my fingers as I lean in toward his lips, our mouths almost touching.

In a low, husky whisper, I admit, "Honestly, that intelligent mind of yours is a real turn-on. Come on, let me in on the plan. What's next?"

"Well," he starts as his hands slide over my backside, "I made him choose between saving himself or you. My dumb brother fell head over heels for you, making it so much easier. He'll plead guilty, go to jail, and *poof.*" He adds a little explosion sound. "Bye-bye Romano empire."

Yeah, I've heard enough.

Considering this isn't part of the plan, this will probably go south very quickly. Bottom line is that Alex can kill me if he really wants to. He has the means, that's for sure. But for Damian? I'll go to the ends of the earth for him—including risking my life. I quickly slide my hand along my upper thigh, locating the small concealed knife, and press its tip against his neck. I don't give him a chance to react as I swiftly raise my knee and strike his groin.

Thank fuck for those self-defense classes I took when I moved to Chicago.

"What the fuck, Ari!?" he shouts through a pained groan.

"You better listen to me real good. Your moronic plan is done for." I can tell he's still dealing with that groin pain, so I decide to hit him again, harder, just to be safe. I press the tip of the knife a bit more, and a tiny drop of blood appears. "You're lucky I don't fucking kill you right now," I snarl.

Matteo and Lorenzo burst the door open, entering the apartment, quickly striding toward us and forcing me away from Alex.

Matteo whistles. "You went *way* off script, Red."

Alex attempts to rise, but Lorenzo seizes him by the neck and pushes him down to the floor. "If you think I'm going to let you make one single move, you're dead wrong," he snarls.

"I'm going to fucking kill all of you. I have connections. You don't know who you're messing with."

Lorenzo's eyes flash with amusement. "Believe me, you've got no clue who you're messing with," He tightens the grip on Alex's neck, cutting off his air. "I'll kill you. *Don't push me.*"

Lorenzo's whiskey eyes become icy with intensity, making me gulp. There's more to him than I know, and I don't think I want to find out.

Alex grips his hand, struggling to breathe. "P-please."

Matteo strides next to them. "Enzo, man. Let go of him. You're going to kill him."

Lorenzo's gaze snaps to Matteo. "You think I fucking care? I'll end this motherfucker right here and bury him six feet under."

"Yeah? And what do you think it's gonna happen when we go to the FBI with all the evidence and Alex is suddenly nowhere to be found? You really want to take that chance? Let him go. We have everything we need. Damian's safe now," Matteo urges.

The silence in the apartment is deafening, except for Alex's struggle to get out of Lorenzo's grip. His shoulders relax as he lets go of Alex's neck and gets up, brushing his suit like nothing happened.

Matteo points a finger at Alex. "Needless to say, I'm tailing you. If you make one single wrong move or try to flee the country, I will let Enzo get away with anything he wants. And if he fails, I will hunt you until the ends of the earth and kill you myself. And trust me, I won't fail."

Matteo's icy blue eyes become almost gray as he threatens Alex. This is the side of him I knew deep down he had. A scary, menacing one. I'm sure managing a successful cybersecurity business comes with its fair share of horror. If those eyes could talk, it wouldn't be pretty.

He looks over his shoulder and flips his menacing self swiftly, going back to his sunshine personality. "Let's go save your man, Red."

I let out a sigh of relief as my shoulders loose, giving a subtle nod. All I want is to leave this place.

Before going after them, I hunker down to Alex, meeting eye to eye, and I grin. "I hope you rot in hell."

Rising to my feet, my heart beats fast as I eagerly walk out, feeling more alive than ever before.

44

Damian

Days blend into one another. It's just me and my newfound buddy—the booze. It's the only company I've got since I've shut everyone else out. What's the point of talking to anyone? None of them are Aria.

I fucked up, that much is obvious. I should've been honest with her. Over the past year, she's been my rock, helping me transform into a man I can genuinely be proud of. I envisioned a future where I'd stand by her side for the rest of our lives. But now? It's like all those hopes and dreams don't mean a damn thing.

My life's ruined. The woman I love slipped through my fingers. I'm about to plead guilty for something I didn't do for her sake. I don't even care about the money, the fame, or my reputation. I just wish I had one more day with her. If I had known that the last time I kissed her would be the final one, I would have savored it more. I would've expressed everything in my heart, held her close, and gazed at her until every detail was etched in my memory—every feature, freckle, laugh. *Everything.*

My lawyer called me into his office to talk one more time and go over the plan for tomorrow's indictment. Considering my name and status and the fact this is my first crime, I may be looking at serving about eight years, even less if I stay in line. I have a pounding headache from my hangover, but I need to get this taken care of. Last thing I want is anyone barging into my fucking house. I almost fired my concierge for letting people in. Luck was on his side, though, because every name was on the visitor's approved list. I wonder how Alex got his name in there, but again, this man has done more than enough. That was probably nothing for him.

I head into Liam's office and drop into one of the chairs. "Let's get this over with."

Liam presses his lips together, crossing his legs, and fixates his eyes on me.

"What?" I snap.

"There won't be an indictment."

My inner alarms start ringing. Is Alex going off the rails and pinning everything on Aria? I haven't caught anything on the news—well, I haven't exactly been easy to reach. I've cut myself off from the world, so it's a potential scenario. I'm officially entering freak-out territory, so if he doesn't clarify in the next two seconds, I'm going to fucking lose it.

"I can't believe you kept the threats from me. It's not just about the legal side of things; you should've told me as a friend, Romano," he says, shaking his head in disbelief. "What's the matter with you?"

"I don't know what you're talking about," I lie. I've gotten so good at lying lately, it barely feels like one anymore.

The door swings open, and as I glance back, the last person I thought I would see comes in. I frown, as millions of questions rush through my mind.

"You do know what he's talking about. Stop acting stupid," Aria retorts.

I stand up, looking at both of them. Matteo and Enzo walk into the office as if it's a regular day, leaving me utterly confused.

"What's happening here?" I ask, utterly confused.

"Oh, *cugino*, if you think I'm going to miss Red ripping you a new one, you're insane." He snickers.

Matteo nods. "Same here. Let's go, Red. My money's on you."

Aria shifts her gaze in their direction. "If you don't scram in the next second, I'm gonna stab both of you with my knife," she warns with a knowing look.

They both crumble like scared kids away from the office. I've never seen those two so terrified for their lives. It's actually quite refreshing.

She looks over my shoulder. "You too, Hawkins. Take a hike."

"But this is my office," he deadpans.

She folds her arms expectantly, the movement pushing her cleavage together, and I'm doing everything I can to avoid looking.

Liam sighs as he stands. "I guess I'm taking a hike." He walks out of the office and shuts the door.

"What—"

"Sit down," she orders.

Alright then. She's showing a side I haven't seen before. Not that I mind; if anything, I find her even more attractive —if that's even a possibility. To see her so sure of herself, not afraid to speak up. Her confidence makes my heart swell with pride.

"I've been wondering about the cosmic debt you must have accumulated to be stuck with Alex as your brother in this lifetime," she comments while casually leaning against the desk.

"You know?" I whisper.

She nods. "I know everything."

My eyes snap to hers. "How?"

"Wouldn't you love to know?" she retorts.

"Aria, I swear to God—"

She throws her hand up to halt me, saying, "I'm still talking."

I thin my lips, opting to not say anything.

"You should've given us a heads up, Damian. We would've done whatever it took to support you," she continues.

I interject, "You don't understand—"

She interrupts, "Yes, I do—"

"No! You fucking don't. He was going to pin everything on you, Aria. It was either save myself or save you," I shout.

"That wasn't your decision to make! You should have talked to me about it. We would have come out with a plan," she shouts back.

I let out an exasperated breath, getting up from the chair. "You don't fucking get it, do you? Don't worry, I'll spell it out for you. I love you so much it *burns me*. There's nothing in this world that would stop me from protecting you, from saving you. I will gladly sacrifice everything for you, and I'm not going to apologize for it. I will gladly burn a million times over if it means I get to love you for the rest of my days, and that's the fucking truth."

It's like this massive burden finally lifts as I speak my truth. So damn liberating. I'm done with pretending to be someone I'm not. She taught me to love intensely, and loving her is the toughest and most exciting thing I've ever experienced. But the thrill of knowing I get to love such a strong woman makes it all worthwhile. Every bit of it. I know she thinks I'm the one that saved her from herself, but she's dead wrong. She saved *me.* .

She stands from the desk, shouting, "And you don't get that I love you so much, it fucking *hurts*, Damian. *You* need to understand that I, too, would do anything for you. All my life, I've been trying to gather the pieces of my broken life together, not wanting to share them with anyone else because I'm scared to be broken again. I can't handle one more heartbreak! But for you? I'd give my all. Because you sneaked into my life, broke down my walls, and made me believe in *myself*. In *you*. In *us*. And for that and much more, *I love you*."

The confession shocks me. I've never felt loved. All my life, I've been numb to it. Gave up. Never thought it was a possibility. I never thought this all consumable love was possible for me. But she changed my way of thinking; changed me for the better.

I close the distance between us, our lips colliding with an intense, desperate kiss. Gripping the back of her head, I deepen the kiss, our tongues clashing. She responds by wrapping her arms around my shoulders, and I revel in the sweet sound of the whimper that escapes her mouth, engulfing it with my own. We both take a step back and gasp for air against our will.

"You ready to tell me what the hell you did?" I ask.

"Nope. You'll have to beg a whole lot for me to spill."

"Sounds like a plan, *Red*."

"Don't call me that, *Damie*."

God, I missed this woman.

45

Aria

After Damian's and I shouting match that ended with a kiss, I left the office where I made him promise me a thousand times that this time around he was going to show up. He promised just as many times. He had to stay in the office with the guys to figure out the next step and what's going to happen. I decided to go to Sophia's, have an impromptu girl's day and vent.

"I think it's romantic," Sophia says after I explained why he did what he did.

"For once, I agree with Sophia. Very book boyfriend material," Isabella chimes in.

"Okay, but this is real life, guys. This was extremely reckless on his part," I say, glaring at them.

Isabella raises an eyebrow. "And you taking out a knife and placing it against Alex's neck wasn't reckless?"

"Isa," I hissed.

Sophia gapes at me. "You did what!?"

I cross my arms, stiffening my shoulders. They don't get it. Sophia, well, it's Sophia, and has been through enough so she doesn't understand love makes you do idiotic things, and Isabella has revoked love out of her life, so she understands even less.

"I was willing to do anything for him," I confess.

"Yes, and he was willing to do everything for you. How can you be mad at that?" Sophia points out.

Well, when someone puts it like that...

I leave Sophia's apartment a few hours later when I get a text from Damian to go to his condo. The elevator door opens and I'm met with hundreds and hundreds of wildflowers scattered all over the floor and a path of soft yellow candles. Following the trail, I find Damian in the living room sitting down on the floor with blankets, pillows, and a bunch of takeout brown bags.

"What's this?" I ask, my voice laced with surprise.

Damian gets up from the floor and walks toward me and grabs my hand, guiding me to the blanket. "I know these are not New York dumplings, but I researched *a lot* and these are the best places I found. The meeting with the guys didn't take that long. I was just doing all of this..." He waves his hand around the apartment.

I gasp as I take it all in. "Damian—"

He interrupts, "Let me speak first, okay? I have to get this out." He sighs. "I'm so fucking sorry, okay? I was a complete asshole to you and I have no excuse for that. Well, I was trying to protect you and not ruin your life. But it doesn't matter, because I fucked up. I didn't handle the situation well and I hurt you in the process, and I will never forgive myself for that." He brings me in for a hug, kissing the top of my head. "I love you so much, it kills me that I hurt you. I'm so sorry."

I hug him back, then take a step back with a nod. "I know you had good intentions. You were just, well, an asshole about it."

We both laugh at that.

"But I forgive you. I know it came from a good place, even if the end result was fucked."

He lets out a sigh of relief, relaxing his shoulders. "Thank you."

"Okay, shall we eat now? It smells delicious."

He nods and we both sit down and just like that first night in New York, we eat way too many dumplings and rate them. This time around, though? Damian gives them different ratings.

How times have changed.

We lay on the floor, the sheets a mess between us as my head finds his strong, muscled chest.

He runs his fingers through my hair gently while planting a soft kiss on the top of my head. "I missed this."

I lift my head abruptly, meeting his gaze with a glare. "It's your fault we spent so much time apart."

He grimaces. "Please, don't remind me."

I hum. "I'll think about it."

After we ate, we wasted no time on removing all of our clothes to make up for lost time. I'm satiated and exhausted —well, maybe not that exhausted. I can go a couple more rounds.

What can I say? I missed him.

He locks his eyes on me, and I can sense an array of emotions brewing in his gaze. He takes a deep breath and says, "Thank you," in a hushed tone, as if unsure whether to voice his gratitude. "For whatever you did. I don't need to know if you don't want me to, but... thank you."

I try to downplay my role, responding, "It wasn't just me, you know? Matteo came up with the idea. I just went along with it."

"He better have. He was doing a shit job before," he mutters.

I nod knowingly. "I think it's more than that, though. He considers you his friend."

He shrugs. "He isn't half bad."

As we chat, I start sharing Matteo's plan, the details of how we pulled it off, how Alex fell for it hook, line, and sinker.

He huffs an annoyed breath. "I'm going to kill Matteo for putting you in danger."

I gape at him. "We saved your ass and that's what you focus on?"

"Yes. And also, you held a knife to his throat?" He lets out a low whistle. "Who are you and what did you do with my woman?"

I playfully hit his shoulder. "Looks like there's a lot about me you still need to figure out."

He lets out a grunt that makes me laugh.

"Enzo kind of lost it for a moment there, too. He scared the shit out of me," I confess.

He nods in understanding. "Enzo is a complicated man with a complicated life to say the least. But he has always had my back, however that looks."

Knowing Damian isn't alone anymore makes my heart flutter. We both had a rough childhood, but now, he's surrounded by people who genuinely love him and would do anything for him. He deserves all the love because he gives it just as passionately, if not more. He's shown that with everything that went down. Most importantly, he has me too, and I'd sacrifice anything for him, no questions asked.

I entwine my legs around Damian's waist, finding a comfortable spot on his lap, already feeling his erection.

"*Tesoro*," he rasps through a breathy groan.

"What?" I ask, innocently.

He closes the distance with a fierce, passionate kiss, and I eagerly reciprocate. My hands roam over his strong chest and toned arms as my tongue dances with his. His erection grows rapidly, pressing against me. Slowly, I grind against him, seeking that much-needed friction. He firmly grips my ass, syncing the movement with his hips. The sensation of his cock between my slick folds is overwhelming. Too much and simply not enough, all at the same time. His hands firmly clench my hips and lift me up slightly, then he eases me down on his hard, throbbing cock. An involuntary moan escapes me, the sensation of him inside is overpowering. Pure pleasure.

"You feel so good," he murmurs while gently biting my shoulder.

He thrusts at a punishingly slow pace, but I don't mind it. His lips trace along my neck, leaving soft kisses in their wake. He takes one of my sensitive nipples in his mouth, swirling it with his warm, wet tongue and sucking it until I'm a blubbering, moaning mess.

I meet him, thrust after thrust. Both of us lost in each other's bodies, sharing moans and groans. Being with him, like this, in such an intimate way, is pure fucking bliss. Expressing the love we have for each other with our bodies is like reaching Nirvana. The way he worships me with every kiss, every touch, and every sultry word is exhilarating.

My body tenses as my orgasm builds. "Fuck, Damian. I'm coming," I moan.

He holds onto my hips, picking up the pace with punishing, and fast delicious thrusts. It's rougher—less controlled—as if he's really eager to bring me to that point.

"Come for me, Darling. Milk my cock like the good fucking girl you are," he murmurs in my ear.

His words send shivers through my spine, and my walls tighten around him as I reach the sweet moment of release. His thrusts become even more intense and forceful, and he pumps once more before filling me completely.

We're both caught up in the moment, and at our high peaks, he discovers my lips and kisses me with a newfound intensity. "I fucking love you, *Tesoro*."

Damian Romano loving me wasn't something I saw coming. Life, with all its surprises, has led me to this point, and I'm so damn lucky to have the most wonderful man in the world loving me in this space and time.

"I fucking love you, too."

Epilogue

Damian

One year later...

Aria and I get up super early, just as the sun is starting to rise, to do the typical tourist stuff she enjoys whenever she visits New York. I thought it would be a cool surprise to bring her here after she sold her first painting.

That's right. My girl is a full-time artist now.

It's funny how things turned out. The painting I displayed of Aria's last year drove people wild. People contacted the gallery often, every day almost, wanting to see more from this "mysterious artist" who had everyone talk-ing. It really boosted her confidence to take her art seriously. She's been busting her ass for months, painting non-stop day and night. She finally got an incredible offer and sold her first painting. Now, more offers keep rolling in. It's pretty amazing to see her hard work paying off like this.

I'm so damn proud.

But it's not the only reason why I brought her here.

We're on our way to The Met, and I'm so fucking nervous, I want to crawl out of my skin. The red velvet box is practically on fire in my pocket, and my fingers are itching to grab it and scream at the top of my lungs how much I love her.

Walking into the museum, Aria looks around, confused. "Why is this place so empty on a Saturday?"

"I rented the place."

She looks at me, dumbfounded.

"The *whole* place," I continue.

It took some serious connections and effort to pull this off, but I'm so fucking happy I did it. Coming to the Met with Aria holds a special place in my heart, and I couldn't think of a better way to make such an important, life changing memory. As we're walking around the museum, the silence is peaceful, but somehow makes me even more nervous at the same time.

As we admire every painting and every masterpiece, I think about this past year. We've been through so damn much. I reopened the gallery not long after everything went down and the business has been booming ever since. We attended Alex's trial after all the documentation and evidence was "anonymously" submitted to the FBI. Turns out, Alex was running a whole operation with other sleazy motherfuckers from the industry. They all caved in pretty quickly and betrayed him, resulting in a ten-year sentence with no chance of parole.

We tried or hardest to move on from that mess and go on with our lives. If I had to do it all over again, I'd probably be honest with her instead of pushing her away. It was such a stupid mistake. Aria has so much love for me, she'd be on board with anything without a second thought. She's crazy like that, and I love her for it.

We arrive at our favorite collection, the European paintings. We stand in front of *Cypress in Moonlight*. The painting we admired together a little over a year ago as I was admiring the one masterpiece before me—*her*.

"God, I love this painting so much," she murmurs.

I look at her, studying the way her face concentrates on the painting. There's something so peaceful about her admiring art. It's my kryptonite.

She glances up, her eyes fixing on mine. "What?"

I wave my hand around dismissively. "This is a place that's filled with so much art and history, there's so much to admire. But I can't help but to admire you. *Just* you."

I slip the red velvet box out of my pocket, and her gaze drop to the box. Her face turns red as her eyes bulge in surprise.

"Oh my God, Damian." She gasps.

I get down on one knee as I let out a nervous laugh. My voice trembles slightly as I say, "*Tesoro*, this past year has been a rollercoaster, but an amazing one. You've shown me how to love, how to be true to myself, and, most importantly, how to find happiness. I have everything I could ever want. I am so proud of you, and I admire you so much. There's just one missing piece," I express, opening the box to reveal a round diamond. "I want to admire you for the rest of our lives. I want you in my life, forever."

"Yes," Aria replies, nodding as tears swim in her eyes.

I chuckle. "I haven't even asked yet."

She laughs through her tears. "I'm sorry."

"*Tesoro*, will you make me the happiest man alive and marry me?"

"Yes. A thousand times yes," she says, leaping onto me.

We both fall to the floor laughing and she kisses me with so much love and emotion, it makes my heart flutter.

For the first time in my life, I feel complete, happy, and full of love.

THE END.

If you enjoyed reading *Broken Pieces*, consider leaving a review on Amazon. Reviews are like tips for authors, and it helps spread the word to other lovely readers like you!

Would you like to be the first to know what I'm working on, get some amazing book recs, and much more? Then join my newsletter, Yinn's Cove! PS. I always share extra, exclusive teasers over there. ;)

Acknowledgments

The first person I want to thank is you—the reader! Thank you for taking a chance on me. I hope this is just the beginning of our wonderful journey together.

I want to personally thank every person who has shared and talked about my debut. It is thanks to you that I was able to reach the finish line. Because of you, I've been able to overcome imposter syndrome and go through with publishing this story. Damian and Aria have such a special place in my heart, and I can't believe there are thousands of people who were also looking forward to reading about these two characters that have been living in my head for months! Every time someone reads, rates, reviews, and shares, it makes my entire day. It's because of you that I get to do what I love for a living. I will never stop being grateful for that.

Anthony—thank you for being my rock. You have been such an amazing and supportive partner, putting up with my crazy ideas and supporting my dream of becoming an author. Thank you for all the endless nights where you sat with me and let me read you every chapter I came up with.

Thank you for letting me vent and talk about how crazy writing this book was. I'm thankful everyday that I get to be with the most wonderful and supportive man. (And let me go ahead and give you partial credit for the surprise twist that made it into the book, lol.)

Laura—girl, you have been my second rock throughout this journey. You gave me words of encouragement when I needed them most, and you never stopped believing in me—not even for one second. Even when I came to you sobbing, saying this was a crazy idea and that I should quit, you always told me to get my shit together and keep going. Honestly, I'm pretty lucky to have you as my best friend (and know that you're stuck with me for the rest of your life).

ARC/Street Team—To my ARC team and my Street Baddies, you guys are my third rock. The support I've received from you, whether it was by commenting on my posts or hyping the book at random times, has been amazing. Believe it or not, on the days when I was feeling the most defeated, there was always at least one of you giving me words of encouragement by commenting and fan-girling over these characters. You guys have helped me more than you could possibly imagine.

And now, onto the next adventure... Windy City Billionaires Book Two, here we go!

About the Author

Yinn Quirós is an indie romance author who loves writing epic love stories with laugh-out-loud banter, men who yearn like it physically hurts them, and plenty of spice. She loves all things sports (especially F1 and hockey), romance, and music.

When she's not writing, you can find her watching games or races, walking around the windy city with her rescued puppy, or listening to music and curating playlists for all the stories that live rent-free inside her head. You can find Yinn on all socials under **@yinnquirosauthor**.

OTHER BOOKS BY YINN QUIRÓS

WINDY CITY BILLIONAIRES SERIES

BROKEN DEAL

CHICAGO STRIKERS SERIES

FALSE PLAY

www.ingramcontent.com/pod-product-compliance
Lightning Source LLC
Chambersburg PA
CBHW021412010826
48972CB00014B/1311